SCALES of ASH & SMOKE

• EMILY SCHNEIDER •

Scales of Ash & Smoke

For information contact:
Magic Keepers Press, LLC
magickeeperspress.com

Hardcover: 978-1-7374957-1-0
Paperback: 978-1-7374957-0-3
Ebook: 978-1-7374957-2-7

First edition October 2021.

Edited by Andrea Hurst
Copyedit and Proofreading by Lucia Ferrara
Cover Design by Damonza © 2021
Map by Nathan Vanderzee © 2021

For Cody—
who believed in my dreams even when I didn't.

PRONUNCIATION GUIDE

Characters:

Kaida: kye-duh
Tarrin: tare-in
Eklos: eck-los
Lita: lee-ta
Eldrin: el-drin
Martik: mar-tick
Roldan: roll-den
Barden: bar-den
Aela: ay-luh
Meara: meer-uh

Locations:

Elysia: el-lih-see-uh
Zarkuse: zar-koose
Vernista: ver-nih-stuh
Belharnt: bell-harnt
Shegora: sheh-gore-uh
Absult: ab-sult
Myrewell: mire-well
Ilgathor: Il-ga-thor

Others:

Flamaria: fla-mare-ee-uh
Ilusai: ill-oo-sye

ELYSIA
ENDLESS SEA
Shegora
Metta
Zenduro Wastes
Sarphan
Absult
Zarkuse
Royal Palace
Cottage
Belharnt
ILGATHOR MOUNTAINS
BAYWOOD RIVER
BAYWOOD FOREST
Vernista
ENDLESS SEA
Port of Pyrn
Mount Sunder
PYRN
MYREWELL
END OF ELYSIA
Mistwick
N
W
E
S

PART ONE

PROLOGUE

A thousand years ago
Elysia was a world of peace.
Dragons and humans coexisted.
There was no fighting, no hatred, no war.
But there were two dragons, brothers.
One with a heart of frost and death.
The other with a heart of warmth and life.
The former was made of scales black as a nightmare.
The latter a calming midnight blue.
The brother with a disdain for life grew
to despise the human race,
His mind poisoned into believing they
meant the dragon's harm.
Yet the brother with compassion in his
heart did not feel the same.
On one fated day in his hundredth year,
A terrible pain tore through his mind,
Lights flashing over his scales.
When all had ceased,
His scales had become skin,
His wings and tail gone.
He came face to face with his brother,
Who now looked upon him with disgust.
The dragon with a warm heart was a shape-shifter.
And the dragon with a cold, brutal heart
Wanted him dead.

—Legend of The Lone Dragon

CHAPTER ONE
KAIDA

SURVIVE.

The word was a chant winding itself around my bones as I pushed a heavy mop through yet another massive pile of vomit. My stomach twisted at the sloshing that sent a wave of fermented meats and ale up my nostrils, coating my mouth in a bitter tang. The cavernous room of The Den was rank with the sour stench, the air too stifling from the fire that roared in the enormous hearth behind me to dissipate it. Clinking scales and the banging of mugs echoed up to the ceiling, intermingling with the low growls and obnoxious chewing of the beasts occupying the chairs and tables surrounding me.

I sighed through my nose as I tried to ignore them, before scoffing to myself.

There was no ignoring the *dragons*.

Standing upright, they stood anywhere from seven to twenty feet tall, each beast a different color. Some were colored in dark, earthy tones of brown and green, while others were brighter, slightly more pastel. Only males had horns adorning their thick skulls, some straight as a rod, while others curled like a ram's.

Even sitting in their oversized chairs that groaned beneath their weight, they still towered over us humans that served in The

Den. The dragons often loved to toss food and bone scraps at me, throwing their tails beneath my feet, forcing me to crash, dishes and all, to the floor. Although I was fairly certain that their favorite way to torment me was puking their stomachs onto the floor, knowing I would have to clean it up.

A frustrated scream built in my throat as my fingernails dug deeper into the wood handle of the mop, and I choked down the fire that raged in my heart. All I ever wanted was to taste freedom like my mother had before I was born. The thought of freedom lit a fire within me, though it was small, that fueled my goal of surviving.

One more day.

Telling myself that was the only way I could force myself to continue. Survive one more day and perhaps freedom would find me, though I had no true reason to believe it ever would. And yet those thoughts haunted my daydreams, pushing me forward.

I trudged back into the kitchen with the bucket of slop and threw it into the roaring fire that had become affectionately known as the barf bin.

"Kaida," a voice said behind me.

My muscles froze in place. Phantom claws of fear dug into my shoulders, my body expecting it to be my Master before my brain recognized the female voice that spoke. A short, severely thin girl circled me, stopping at the hearth to stir a cauldron of broth.

"Jinna," I breathed, my muscles releasing, leaving my limbs feeling like jelly.

She was the only other slave that worked here. We were not friends; we couldn't be. It had become an unspoken rule among all humans. It was too dangerous. It was one more thing the dragons could use against you. Jinna and I rarely spoke, unless we knew without a doubt that we were alone, and we existed in a strangely comforting place of not being friends but knowing in some way that we still had each other.

"Have you seen Master Eklos today?" Her words were quiet, careful, the distinct mole on her right cheek twitching as she spoke.

"Not yet," I said as I set the vomit bucket back in the corner along with the putrid mop.

A bitter puff of air escaped her mouth as she let out a dark chuckle. She tucked a strand of hair that had fallen loose behind her ear, leaving a black streak of ash behind.

"He is in an extraordinarily bad mood today. I would take care what you say." Jinna's words were not unkind, but a warning.

I released a long, shaky breath, and nodded. It was nothing surprising. His normal demeanor was foul to begin with. I could not recall a time in my life when Master Eklos had acted otherwise.

Jinna's mouth twitched, and I watched as she opened it to speak, but then snapped her lips shut. She turned back to the pot hanging over the fire in front of her.

Jinna always went out of her way to keep herself beneath our Master's notice. He killed her mother several years ago, leaving Jinna as the only person to care for her younger brother, thus ensuring her obedience.

Dusting off my filthy hands on my apron, I stepped over to the large table used for food preparation. Jinna did most of the cooking while I tended to the patrons in the tavern, occasionally helping her when I desperately needed to get away from the dragons and the cinders they blew at my back.

I grabbed a hunk of unidentifiable raw meat and a large knife and began whacking at it, chopping it into bite-size morsels to fit in the stew Jinna was stirring in the hearth. Out of the corner of my eye, I saw her wringing her hands before she uncharacteristically squared her shoulders and turned toward me.

"I am taking my brother and leaving the village," she whispered. "Tonight."

Chills prickled along my skin.

"Leave?" I repeated, my tongue thick in my mouth.

Sweat dripped from Jinna's brow, dampening her chestnut brown hair, and she wiped at it, before patting her hand on her apron. She nodded, her gaze hard, like she had entirely made up her mind.

"H-how can you leave? Do you know what he will do to you if you are caught?" I stammered out. I had heard tales of other slaves trying to escape when I was a child. I had seen firsthand what the consequences were. A shudder racked through my body.

"This is no way to live, Kaida. My brother is beaten daily. I walk as if I am tiptoeing over hot coals, making myself into some semblance of a ghost in an attempt to keep him safe, but it never helps. This may be how the world has always been, but it is not how it should be. Just surviving is not living."

Jinna's words punched through my gut. I knew she was right, but the memory of what Master Eklos did to slaves who tried to escape, of what he did to my mother…

I couldn't help but think she was a fool.

The dragons had full reign over Elysia. There was no place for humans to go. No place outside of the dragon's reach, outside of *his* reach. Eklos would find her, through the sheer might of his extensive influence over Elysia. He would have her hunted down, made an example of, before publicly executing her.

I had seen it before.

All the reasons why she should not run away sat on my lips, but her face remained firm. She had made her decision. Jinna was leaving, no matter what I said. She had signed her own bill of execution.

I nodded without another word, wanting to hug the girl who I had pretended not to know, not to care about, for years. She made a fist with her right hand and brought it to the left side of her chest.

The breath caught in my throat.

That was the symbol of the human rebellion that had been

quelled centuries ago, after the dragons gained control of Elysia. The movement was meant to put an end to the humans' captivity.

Every last human in that movement had been slaughtered.

The only reason that I knew the gesture was because my mother had shown it to me on frigid nights when she hoped to distract me from our nearly frostbitten skin by sharing the old legends of Elysia.

How did *Jinna* know it?

Jinna turned away, going back to stirring the cauldron of stew. My lungs contracted, my heart throbbing at the thought that this would be the last time I would ever lay eyes on her. The room spun around me, and I fought to catch my breath. Air. I needed air.

I dropped the knife onto the table, the metal clanging in the sudden silence, and I nearly ran out of the room in my haste to get out of the sweltering kitchen. I wriggled around the tails and chairs in my path as I made my way to the front counter where the wooden planks that served as menus and various cleaning supplies were stored.

My feet came to a screeching halt as I tried to avoid stepping on the very tip of a blue dragon's tail and caught myself on the back of a chair. Eyes darting to the dragons surrounding me, I held my breath as I waited for one of them to react, to punish me for being clumsy. Air rushed from my mouth in a soundless whoosh when no one turned to me, no one acknowledged my existence. I continued forward, the stretch of the room growing longer with every step I took.

"There has been talk of *them* again," a voice rasped like crunching leaves as I passed by. "The Remnant of the Lone Dragon."

My steps faltered and I glanced over my shoulder.

"Yes," a second dragon hissed, its tongue snaking between jagged teeth. "They were in Zarkuse only a few days ago. Rumor has it they are looking for sympathizers to join their cause."

Ice filled my veins and I struggled to keep my feet moving forward.

"I would assume they will be coming to Vernista next." A sinister smile twisted his brown snout, light glinting off his teeth.

"I have no doubt, not with—"

"KAIDA," a deep male voice bellowed, causing me to jump, my entire body beginning to tremble.

Instincts kicking in, I spun to face him, my head bowed, keeping my eyes on the stones beneath my feet.

"*What* do you think you are doing?" Master Eklos snapped. The color drained from my face and my hands shook, despite this being a daily occurrence.

He was my Master. I was his slave.

Despite the rage that coursed through me that brought air to my lungs and fight to my spirit, my very bones remembered all that he had done to me and ached in his presence. Enormous black scaled feet that absorbed the dim light appeared in front of me. Smoke billowed out, encompassing my neck.

"Is it or is it not your place to listen in on the conversations of these patrons?"

I remained silent, not even bothering to deny the fact that I had been eavesdropping. I learned long ago to keep my mouth shut. Wiping clammy hands against the rough fabric of my pants, I fought down the urge to wipe the sweat that had beaded on my upper lip. Even the smallest movement could set him off.

"*Is it or is it not your place to listen in on the conversations of these patrons?*" he growled, curling his claws into fists.

When I said nothing, a tendril of smoke slithered out of his mouth in the shape of clawed fingers and yanked my chin up, forcing me to meet his gaze. Scales the color of ashes towered over me, eyes red like burning coals piercing through me. Long, curled horns protruded from his head, miniature silver spikes running the length of his arms and the top of his wings.

This was Eklos, my Master since the day I was born.

I had never known a life outside of captivity. According to

tales I had heard, my mother had been a free human before I was born, though I had never heard of such a thing being possible. But Eklos finally found her with a baby in her arms and enslaved us both. My mother had been a rebellious soul, fighting him every chance she could, and in the end was severely punished for it.

I was only ten when Eklos took her away from me, publicly executing her in the village square. It was then that I tried to escape, to flee from his ownership. Eklos hunted me and then kept me imprisoned in Belharnt, an underground dungeon, specifically made for torturing humans, for seven years.

Eklos released me only a week ago from that hellish prison. I had been surprised to find that everything was still the same. Jinna, The Den, my tiny cave-home. It all remained unchanged, and I fell back into the rhythms of being a slave in Elysia with dreaded ease. Now, my only goal in life was to stay alive, if for no other reason than to honor my mother's life.

I squeezed my eyes closed, shutting out the memories that flooded my mind of every hammer crushing my bones, every dark, moldy corner I was shackled to. I let out a shaky breath, returning my attention to my Master.

The other dragons in the room had gone silent, watching our exchange, a deep loathing twisting their snouts into hideous sneers.

Before I could react, a clawed hand slammed into my face, Eklos's immense strength sending me flying sideways, my hip crashing painfully into an oversized table. It collapsed beneath me, sending wood shards burrowing into my skin. I held in a groan as I pushed onto my knees.

I kneeled before Eklos and his snout contorted into an ugly smile.

"Much better," he said. "A slave on her knees before her Master. The proper place for human filth." Sparks flew from his nostrils as he reminded me once again of what I was: a slave. A human cursed to live all my days bound to the vilest creatures in Elysia. This was all I had ever known.

Tears burned in my eyes, but not out of pain or sadness. It was soul-rending fury. It roiled in my blood, growing larger and blazing hotter with every day that passed. My throat burned as I swallowed it down, my entire body trembling with the effort of holding it at bay.

Survive. It was the word I said every time Eklos punished me.

It was the word that I repeated every night when I awoke screaming out of a nightmare of Belharnt, or when I remembered my mother's head rolling off her body and bouncing in a pile of blood on the stones in the village square.

I had to survive. My mother had learned her lesson for disobeying him, countless humans had learned it, and now Jinna likely would as well. But I refused to give Eklos the satisfaction of doing the same to me.

Claws ripped into my scalp, blood seeping down the back of my neck, as he grabbed a fistful of my hair and dragged me upright. He yanked me toward the entrance, and I felt the humid night air meet my skin a second before I hit the dirt road as Eklos threw me out the door. My teeth ached from the impact, and blood filled my mouth as I bit my tongue.

"Go back to your filthy hovel before I send you back to Belharnt," he barked, flames shooting out with each word.

I spit a mouthful of red saliva onto the dirt in front of me. Fire burned through my veins, my rage trying to escape the cage I kept it so tightly bound in. Not for the first time, I could feel something inside me made entirely of fiery anger leap, intending to lash out. But before I could move, smoke shot up through my nose, and everything went dark.

CHAPTER TWO
TARRIN

MY HEART FROZE in my chest as a burst of blue fire soared through the air, aimed at my face. I attempted to dodge the attack, instinct taking over as I threw a scaled hand up in front of my snout to stop it before it made impact. The flames wrapped around my body, the heat unbearable for only a moment before it dissipated into a light smoke that lingered in shafts of midmorning light streaming in from the windows.

I took a step back, twisting my foot to adjust my stance and tucking my wings in tight to protect them. Inhaling the thick summer air, magic flared in my core as I summoned blue flames into my palms. They danced and twirled above my scales before I drew back my arms and launched volley after volley at my attacker.

A green dragon stood across from me, barely half of my twelve-foot height, and ducked beneath the magical flames before slamming his claws into the cold black floor. The dragon jerked his hands in front of him, a wave of water rising with them, before he pushed it, sending it cascading in my direction.

The water crashed over me, lifting my body off balance, and I fell backward, landing awkwardly on my tail. Limbs flailing as I tried to right myself, another wave smothered me, jamming itself up my nostrils. I pulled on my magic, begging it to create flames to evaporate the water, but it simply flickered out in my palms. Coughing and gasping for air, I held up a hand in surrender.

"Enough," I sputtered, spitting water from my mouth.

"Again," the green dragon barked, assuming his fighting stance once more. One clawed foot stepped partly behind the other, one hand across his chest, the other above his head. Water droplets dripped down the sides of his scales.

I shook my head, gasping the humid air in the training room. "That is enough for today," I replied, my voice hoarse from choking on the water.

"Your Highness, you should try again. I am using simple magic to attack you and you cannot even defend yourself. If I did not know better, I would say you are afraid of your own fire."

I couldn't help the wince that twisted my face, the truth hitting too close to home. But my tutor, Alathar, did not know that, and I was not about to share the real reason behind seeking further magic training.

"I have a lot on my mind, Master Alathar," I deflected, turning my snout away. It was not a total lie, but not entirely the truth either. I swiped at the sweat lining the scales above my eyes and glanced at the position of the sun. "Besides, I am late for a meeting with the Queen."

Alathar sighed, smoke leaking from his nostrils, and went to fetch goblets of water for the two of us. "Very well, Your Highness." The ground rumbled quietly beneath his footsteps as he returned to my side.

He handed me a cup and silence descended as we both drank, our dragon teeth clinking softly against the metal. Master Alathar wiped at his snout with the back of a scaled arm and cleared his throat. "Prince Tarrin, I feel the need to tell you that I will be going away for a time."

"Away?" I repeated, unable to fathom my tutor for the last nineteen years leaving.

"Yes, Your Highness. I have family in the south that I have not seen for decades. The King and Queen have granted me leave to go visit them, seeing as your studies are nearly complete."

I swallowed down the rising emotion in my throat. Alathar had been with me since I was a youngling. While we were not close by any means, I had grown to respect and even trust him. Most dragons in Elysia were power-hungry beasts, but not him. He had a genuine desire to better those around him through proper education.

Alathar was the only dragon that I could trust to train me further with magic without asking the very questions that I didn't want to answer.

"I am sad to hear of it, Master Alathar, but I wish you safe travels."

The green dragon smiled fondly at me before raising his arm as if he were going to place it on my shoulder. Instead, he flicked his claws and sent water spraying into my face, and I couldn't help but chuckle as I wiped away the mist from my scales. That was the way we had said goodbye for years. Alathar probably hoped I would have learned to defend against it by now, but I grew fond of the gesture over the years and never bothered to try.

Master Alathar set down his empty goblet and nodded once. "Farewell until next time, Your Highness." He offered a bow and lowered himself to all four legs as he strode out of the room, his tail slithering on the ground behind him. Most dragons preferred to walk upright on two legs, further asserting their dominance by making themselves taller, but not Alathar. He didn't play those typical dragon games or feel the need to make his strength know [illegible] I always liked that about him. For a dragon, he was incred [illegible] humble.

As the door shut, I glanced once more at the sun's [illegible] and grimaced. Any thoughts I had on my tutor leavin [illegible] would have to be dissected later.

My mother was waiting.

The Queen was a strong female, a true and just ruler, and my best friend. And yet, I couldn't help the dread coiling in my gut over this meeting with her.

The scalding sun beat down on my scales as I left the palace proper and wove my way through the gardens. The sweet aroma of flowers filled the air, swirling through my nostrils. What usually calmed the thoughts racing through my mind, and settled the tension twisted tight in my core, had no effect today.

Gravel pebbles crunched beneath me as I peered over the tall rose bushes on either side of the path. My mother's enormous red figure was slouched against a wooden bench near the fountain on the other side of the garden, her gaze fixed on the trickling water in front of her. Inhaling, I sauntered over to her, bracing myself as I slipped into the seat next to her.

This conversation had been building for a while, ever since word of the human girl returning to Vernista had reached the palace walls a week ago. I didn't know anything about her, but it seemed my parents did.

My mother had not breathed a word of her existence to me until that day, even though she claimed to have been close friends with the girl's mother. When my parents had finally come to me, telling me about Aela's daughter, who she was, *what* she was… they had asked me to go find her. Asked, pleaded, begged, commanded, demanded. Every time I said no. Every time they would

ld go find her. It would be easy if she truly was
d her to be. But I refused to bring a human to
the path that my mother had laid before me,
ice of mine on the matter.

ther to speak, watching her clawed hands
ently pulling off petal after petal, thorn

"Your father has always loved the yellow roses," she said, words soft as a whisper. "Planted them himself in these gardens when we came here." She pulled the final two petals off and watched as they fell to the ground.

"I never understood his fascination with them. All I ever saw was a reminder that beautiful things have thorns." She paused, placing her foot over the petals. "And beautiful things often cut the deepest." She squished and twisted her clawed foot into the gravel, disintegrating the yellow fragments into dust before fixing her stern gaze on me.

"Tarrin, you *must* go find her," she pleaded, a slight tremble creeping into her voice. She grabbed my clawed hands in hers and I watched as her red scales flickered in the sunlight, reflecting lights on the ground that danced with the turquoise ones coming from my own body.

"No, Mother."

"*Tarrin—*"

"Mother, we have been going around in circles on this matter for days. I will not track down the human girl and I most definitely will not bring her *here.*"

She sighed, her ruby red shoulders slumping forward. Any other member of the Royal Family would have been reprimanded for such posture, but I had learned to expect such things from my mother. While she was Queen of Elysia, she hated all the protocols and rules that went along with it. I had always admired that she was willing to do what made her happy rather than what was expected.

"Please, Tarrin. Your father and I would not ask this of you unless it was vitally important. She *must* be found and brought here."

The wooden bench groaned beneath me as I shifted my wings to a more comfortable position, unease settling in my stomach. The nearby fountain gurgled and trickled, unable to soothe my nerves.

"We are running out of time. If the Remnant finds her, she will be killed."

I took a deep breath, letting it out slowly as I looked at my scaled hands, studying the cold, smooth texture. "We are dragons. She is human. She does not belong here. Why is this so important to you?"

At first, my mother said nothing, and after a moment, her weight lifted off the bench. Her long tail swished gently back and forth as she walked toward the fountain, scattering the dirt and gravel into small dust clouds behind her. Clasping her claws behind her back, she stared at the ripples in the water.

"I made a promise, Tarrin, to her mother. I have not kept it." She paused, and I noticed her claws were trembling. "But even more than that, it is important to Elysia that she is kept safe. Important for *you.*"

Pebbles crunched as I stepped to her side and peered into the water, turning her words over in my mind.

"There must be another way." *A way that doesn't involve me giving up my last ounce of freedom or bringing a human into the palace, not as a slave but as a guest.* I massaged the space between my eyes, a deep, throbbing ache beginning to form there.

"Our existence in Elysia depends upon you. Upon her," she continued, the ultimatum clanging through me like a death knell. "There is no other way. You need her just as much as she needs you. Even if you cannot see it yet."

What does that mean? Why would I need a human?

"She's a shifter, Tarrin, not just a human. She is just like you. Wouldn't you want someone to save you if circumstances were reversed?" My mother retorted, hearing my inner thoughts.

As shape-shifters, we shared a strange bond that allowed us to communicate within our minds. All shifters had such a bond. Usually, I was able to keep my thoughts closed off, but it grew more difficult as my emotions built up.

A long exhale whistled through my teeth. *Was my mother right?*

"Why doesn't her father find her?"

"Her father is gone."

"Where is he? Dead?" I spat the words, feeling my temper rise.

My mother winced, turning her face away. "I don't know if her father is alive or long dead, nor do I know where he is. He's probably somewhere deep in southern Elysia, if he has managed to survive this long."

My eyebrows furrowed. This was the first time she had mentioned him. Had something happened between them?

"Tarrin, you must go," she repeated, forcing my thoughts back to the girl. My mother turned her snout to look at me, her eyes shining with unshed tears. "Give her a chance. Give Elysia and our race a chance."

I rubbed at the side of my snout. I loved my mother, but how could she be right about this? The girl was *human*. If she were truly a shape-shifter, why would she be willingly living as a slave? Even if she was a shifter, she was more human than dragon at this point. She did not belong here. She did not belong with *me*. She would hate me simply because I was a dragon. I would hate her because she was a human who did not understand our ways.

That was the natural way of life in Elysia. It had been for a thousand years.

A dragon and a human could not be together, let alone fix anything. How could we?

There was too much history, too much hatred between us.

And I would have to sacrifice *everything*. As the Prince of Elysia, most of my choices were already stripped from me, having been decided for me since the day I was born. I had fought hard for nineteen years to maintain some semblance of control over the rest of my life.

Truthfully, I hadn't ever given much thought to a future where I was king, with a wife at my side. My parents were relatively young and healthy for dragons. They would be king and queen for quite some time.

If I brought the girl to the palace, agreeing to my mother's terms, that last shred of freedom, to choose my future wife, would be gone like ashes on the wind. Could I give that up?

My mind emptied out as the resolution echoed like a gong in my mind: *This is what a king does for his kingdom. What he does for his people. Sacrifice.*

A ragged breath blew out from between my lips as I fought to tune out the words, though it was a futile effort.

My mother, Queen of Elysia, had never been wrong before. Not once in my life.

I knew that I needed to trust her; that her reasoning for this, even though I didn't understand it, was valid.

Someday I would be king, and my life would consist of nothing but sacrifice. I might as well get used to it now, starting with this.

Even though a sinking pit opened in my stomach, I knew I would do anything for Elysia; for my family.

I ran a clawed hand over my face, rubbing at the scales on the side of my snout.

For Elysia, I would do it.

For my mother, I would find the girl.

I took another deep breath, inhaling the scent of flowers that did nothing to calm my senses and said, "I will go."

CHAPTER THREE
KAIDA

SWEAT POURED DOWN my face, my heartbeat stuttering in my chest as I sprinted down the cobblestone road, rocks and pebbles skittering out from under my feet. The scalding afternoon sun beat down, causing sweat to slide down my back. Muddy puddles left over from the summer storms splashed and sprayed up as I stomped through them, spattering my legs with grime.

My limbs were numb, and my lungs begged for air, but I couldn't stop. Heart pounding, I willed my feet to move faster, trees streaking past in vibrant blurs in my peripheral vision.

Late. I was so late.

Minutes ago, I had shot awake in bed, frantically looking around the small dirt cave that was my bedroom. The fire in the small hearth in the corner had gone cold hours ago, and the air felt damp and musty. I reached over to the table next to me, the wood nearly falling apart with rot. Grabbing my pocket watch, I squinted in the dim light to make out the time. That was when the panic had started. Tossing back the moth-eaten blanket, I had all but flown out of the cave, hair messy and clothes askew. The sunlight blinded me as I stepped outside, forcing tears from my eyes that streaked down my filthy cheeks. I took off at a sprint toward the center of the village, begging my wobbly legs to hold out a little bit longer.

Last night, Eklos had thrown me out of The Den. Smothering my mind in his toxic smoke, he had numbed all my senses, sending me into an unfeeling sleep.

It was both a punishment and a preventative measure, and unfortunately it was not the first time it had happened. The point was to keep me confined, keep me from trying to escape, keep me in the dark.

It was a reminder.

Eklos was a Smoke Wielder. He called to it, forced it to do his bidding. That was how he was able to control smoke, how he could fill my mind and vision, sending me into darkness.

My stomach twisted. More than anything I wanted to be free, like my mother dreamed of. To go where I pleased, do what I pleased; answer to no one. Be my own master. To finally live in peace and not in fear.

But such a fate, such a place, did not exist in Elysia.

The crimson-steepled building finally appeared in view. The Den was a source of food and gossip for the dragons. Many often came, always of the unsavory sort, to discuss plans and schemes away from prying ears. A shiver crawled over my skin at the memory of the dragons discussing the Remnant yesterday.

According to them, the Remnant of the Lone Dragon was coming. Here, to Vernista. I fought against the sinking feeling in my stomach.

Legend claimed that a thousand years ago, the number of humans in Elysia far outnumbered the dragons. There was a lone dragon that began to stir up animosity amongst the other dragons toward the humans. His mind had been poisoned into believing that dragons were the superior race, and that humans planned to kill them all and take over Elysia.

That dragon, with scales as black as the night sky, was one of the most powerful dragons to have ever lived. He convinced the other dragons to start an uprising against the "lesser" humans.

As one would expect, it did not fare well for the humans, leaving more than half the human race slaughtered. The remainder of the population were taken in chains and forced to live as slaves until their final breaths.

The Lone Dragon died before he could accomplish his mission but left behind the Remnant who were to carry on his stead.

I always thought that it was just legend. Nightmarish stories meant to keep slaves in line.

I slowed my steps and swallowed down the lump in my throat as I neared the front door, the tall red steeples of The Den blocking the sun from my tired eyes. The windows wore bars made of black steel, and the front entrance, a door made of a thick dark wood, loomed high above me.

This was my prison.

Gasping for air, hunched over, with my hands on my knees, I paused. The sand and stone beneath my feet were vibrating slightly from the steps of the dragons inside. I squeezed my eyes shut as my body snapped into a defensive mode, preparing for whatever punishment Eklos deemed worthy today.

I should be used to the ice flooding my veins, the tremors that always overtook my body, the inability to breathe. But I do not think it is possible to get used to the darkness that lives inside these dragons.

I took a deep breath and turned the rusted doorknob, frosty air enveloping my body as I stepped through the door. A dozen heads turned to look at me, but none of them were human. Ruby, turquoise, and emerald eyes connected to giant skulls with long snouts, bore into mine. One by one they snapped their heads away, the silver of their horns flashing in the torchlight, focusing on anything other than me. Even in the dim light, scales glistened, flickering rainbows of light on the brick walls. My eyes slid to the ground and I obediently hung my head and stepped behind the counter. Running my fingers through my sweat drenched hair plastered to my skin, I tied a leather band around it at the base of my neck. My thoughts instantly drifted to Jinna, whether I would find her in the kitchen or dead in the village square. I glanced at the wooden door that led to the kitchen, wishing I could see through it to know for sure what had happened to her.

"You are late," a voice like rumbling thunder boomed, startling me from my thoughts. My breath caught in my throat.

I spun to face my Master but kept my eyes fixed on the ground. It was a sign of disrespect for a human to look a dragon in the eye. Putting my hands behind my back, and letting my head hang even lower, I remained silent, ever the submissive slave.

"No excuses today?" Eklos paused, waiting with expectancy, like a predatory animal ready to pounce.

When I did not respond, he continued, sparks shooting from his nostrils. "What makes you think, *slave,* that you can disobey my orders? Defy me by disregarding my rules?" He towered over me, smoke billowing from his mouth in thick, black tendrils snaking around me.

The desire to meet his unrelenting gaze, to gain the satisfaction of having his pride wounded in front of the patrons of The Den was physically painful. But that was what my mother had done. That was why she was no longer alive. She had been a wild spirit, discontent to sit back and let herself be used and abused, and it had resulted in her death seven years ago.

I pressed my lips together and waited, heart pattering in my chest as sulfurous breath shoved its way into my nose. After a few more moments, Eklos snorted, sending sparks flying out of his nostrils, and I winced as they landed on my skin.

"Get to work," he spat, drawing a sharp claw down my forearm, drawing blood. "And I suggest you think hard on whether I need to remind you of the consequences for disobedient slaves. That was a lesson your mother was never able to learn. Do not be like her." He patted my cheek, right where he hit me yesterday, in a show of dominance. I steadied my hands against my sides to keep from flinching as his scales scraped against my skin, before he turned and stalked away, the mugs rattling on nearby tables.

I was not unused to his threats, for they happened multiple times each day, and I had become numb to all his punishments, except one. The worst was the fire whip: a razor-sharp whip, with spikes of broken glass and blue flames, the hottest imaginable, encasing the entire length. It was not used often but the pain was paralyzing, the burns untreatable. That was what killed my mother, right before they clawed her head from her shoulders.

I forced the thought from my mind, refusing to acknowledge the pang in my stomach that always accompanied my memories of her. I pulled on my tattered work smock and began the daily chores I had become accustomed to. I slipped back into the kitchen to retrieve the vomit pail and mop and came to an immediate halt.

Jinna was not there; her usual perch by the fire abandoned.

A new boy, perhaps fifteen, stood near the wood-burning stove in the corner, stirring an enormous pot of some sort of stew.

Had Jinna escaped? Was she truly able to smuggle her brother away from the village without being caught?

Or was she dead?

My vision blurred and it grew difficult to breathe around the thick lump that had risen in my throat.

A fierce growl in the tavern drew me back to the present and my body moved automatically, grabbing the bucket and a platter piled high with food. I dropped the tray of roasted chickens, turkeys, and other various small birds at a crowded table of dragons and moved toward the back to mop up a questionable pile of slop in the corner.

I finished serving the twelve dragons in the room, their grumbling and growling echoing off the walls. The tables they sat at were three times the size of any human table and scattered around each one were massive wooden chairs with cutouts in the back to account for their wings. The furniture was packed in tight, and it was an effort, even with my small size, to maneuver through it all without disturbing the patrons.

"Watch out, human!" one dragon barked as I shimmied between two chairs, which was then followed by another dragon yelling, "Move, slave!"

I cursed the dragons beneath my breath as I crept back to the counter, struggling to avoid the massive wings that overflowed from chairs into the walkway, and sat on the floor, desperate for a momentary reprieve.

Pulling my legs in close, I wrapped my arms around them and rested my head on my knees, squeezing my eyes against the burning that threatened to spill tears down my face.

It was loud in The Den. The growling of unhappy customers contrasted with the booming deep laughter of others. The sound floated up into the steepled ceiling above and then slammed back down to the ground over and over. Noise pressed in on every side, and I held my face in my hands, as if that would stop the barrage.

I barely registered the smoky scent, like charred bones, that wrapped around my head before claws ripped into my neck. I let out a cry as the beast dragged me eight feet up in the air, bringing me face to snout with a dragon covered in scales the color of dirt.

"Oy, slave. What do you think you are doing on the floor?" The dragon's voice had an unpleasant accent that sounded as if he were speaking through a pinched nose.

He did not give me a chance to answer before my body left the ground and I was thrown toward a sea of eleven other dragons. I landed face down onto the table on top of the huge platter of food that I had delivered only minutes ago. The food exploded beneath me, coating each dragon at the table in a greasy slime. I did not register the pain from animal bones and broken plates jabbing into my skin as every pair of eyes turned their gaze on me. I tried to scramble away, but my wrist barked in protest and I fell back onto the table.

Another set of claws grabbed me by the back of my neck and tossed me onto the floor, my back colliding with several chairs that clattered away on impact. I saw Eklos standing off to the side, a smug smile contorting his snout as he watched the other dragons attack me.

A clawed foot kicked at my stomach, piercing my skin, and I could not hold back the scream that slipped through my lips. Another kick landed on my back and I glanced up in time to see a giant dragon foot poised over my face, ready to smash my skull into pieces. I flinched, bringing my hands up in a feeble attempt to protect myself. I waited for the impact, but a hush fell through the room, the dragons' taunts going silent.

I peeked around my hands and gasped.

Deep green eyes met mine and an eerie tingle pricked across my skin. A turquoise dragon towered above me; his clawed hand wrapped around the brown dragon's foot mere inches from my face. The scales on his forehead bunched together as he narrowed his eyes, studying me.

A suffocating silence filled the room. I felt a heavy pressure squeezing against my brain.

Are you the daughter of Aela?

The words rippled through my mind, unheard by the dragons in the room, and it was all I could do to stifle my gasp. The floor dropped out from under me, and a sharp ache pummeled through my body, eclipsing all other pain from the dragon's attack.

Aela was my mother. I had not heard or spoken my mother's name since she died. It was too painful, carried too much weight.

Stunned, I was unsure whether to be more surprised that this dragon had spoken to me entirely in my mind, or that he knew of my mother.

I am not here to harm you. Are you Aela's daughter?

When I did not answer, he shoved the dirt-colored dragon away, sending him sprawling backward onto his tail, a table splintering in half beneath the weight. I gaped, expecting for all twelve of The Den's patrons to retaliate, but instead each one fell to their knees. I risked a glance up at Eklos and noticed he was frozen, eyes wide and fixed on the turquoise dragon.

"Your Highness," Eklos sputtered, hesitating a moment before bending down and bowing his head.

I struggled to keep my mouth from hitting the floor in shock. I had never seen Eklos submissive before. Dragons were immensely powerful, constantly fighting and battling for dominance. They never bowed to each other, never kneeled, as doing so would make them vulnerable.

Your Highness? What would someone of the Royal Family be doing at The Den? He could not truly be the Prince. The Prince of Elysia would never have stopped an attack on a human.

I started to kneel, knowing I was required to follow their example.

You need not bow to me. A deep male's voice filled my head, and I flinched. I looked at the dragon, mouth gaping, but his face revealed nothing. No emotion and no hint of who he could be or how he had just spoken to me without even breathing a word.

"I have come to collect this girl." The strange dragon's voice reverberated off the walls. Eklos, whether trying to be brave or just stupid, let a defiant mask cover his face. His eyes hardened and he began to stand.

"She is my slave—"

"Silence," the other snapped as he shoved Eklos back to his knee. My Master kept his head down this time, remaining quiet. I would be lying if I said I did not enjoy it, the sight of him on his knees, put in his place like he had always done to me. The dragon gave no further explanation to him and glanced down at me. His expression was hard and distant.

Do not fight. Come with me now. The words ran through my head once again. He reached down and grabbed my arm in his huge, clawed hand, his scales rough, scratching against my skin.

A scream built in my throat and I clamped my lips together to keep from crying for help. There was no point. The dragons would sooner kill me than help me.

The dragon pulled me along, my feet tripping and stumbling beneath me. His aggravation seeped into my mind and he tugged harder as if he were eager to escape the tavern.

Once outside The Den, he released his grip, and I gently rubbed the aching spot where his claws had been. The dragon continued walking down the cobblestone road, leaving me no choice but to follow. There was no way I was staying near The Den, risking that dirt dragon coming out for round two.

Finally, we stopped among a small grove of trees a good distance from Eklos and the rest of the beasts. The dragon turned and fixed his gaze on mine and I instinctively held my breath. I knew it was wrong for me to hold his gaze, but something about the way he studied me froze me in place. Perhaps it was shock or the summer heat causing my eyes to play tricks, but I swear the dragon's eyes softened.

"Who are you?" I asked at last, my mouth dry as cotton.

"I am Prince Tarrin of Elysia."

My mouth popped open as he confirmed my suspicions. "I'm sorry, what?" I asked dumbly. A half smirk bent his snout.

"I am the Prince, the son of King Martik and Queen Lita. You know, the dragons you blame for your abysmal life." His tone was harsh and any kindness I thought I saw in his eyes had disappeared.

"How..." I started to ask how he could possibly know that, but the words dried up on my tongue.

I had never heard much about the Royal Family when I was a child. I always assumed that they were evil, cruel dragons, like all the others since they allowed so many atrocities to happen. Deep down I had always blamed the King and Queen for the life I was forced to live. They could have ended slavery at any point, ending the torture and abuse that I suffered at the hand of Eklos. That countless slaves suffered at the claws of their Masters.

"Never mind, human. Are you the daughter of Aela?" The Prince of Elysia asked once again, interrupting my swirling thoughts.

I crossed my arms, barely letting my temper out of its cage to keep from falling apart at the mention of her name. "Why would a dragon care who I am?"

A knowing smirk spread across his snout.

"Who says I am only a dragon?" he retorted just before his face began to morph. The transformation was like a wavering line gently moving down his body.

The scales on his face flickered back and dissolved before my eyes, and skin, golden from the sun, covered every inch they revealed. Scars marred the right half of his face as if he had been burned and it never truly healed. The same emerald eyes bore into mine as his nose and jawline took shape. Clawed hands became human hands, perfectly clean fingernails popped into place where the claws had been. The transformation continued, his enormous body shrinking down in size, becoming the height of a tall human male, and his wings and tail vanished like they never existed. Clothes rippled into place, as if they had been sitting under his scales the entire time.

An elegant black jacket hung from his muscular frame, each golden button polished and shiny, and leather pants clung to his legs with boots laced to his knees. Dark hair hung in loose waves to his shoulders.

I gaped at the Prince. When I was younger, my mother told me stories of dragons that were able to shape-shift between human and dragon forms. I never imagined there was any truth to them.

I swallowed hard, forcing my mouth to close. The Prince's shoulders loosened a hair, as if he had expected a worse reaction.

"Do you really not know?" he asked. I could see the bewilderment in his eyes.

"Know what?"

"You honestly have no inkling of who you are?"

I tried not to flinch at his exasperated tone.

Prince Tarrin looked at me for a long while. When I did not respond, he shook his head and ran a hand through his hair. The movement was so human like that I found myself momentarily forgetting that he was a dragon. Then he grabbed my wrist, rough calluses brushing against my skin as he pulled me forward and said, "Come with me."

He led me across the road, and through a path of trees that were all different shapes and sizes, and the leaves were bright as jewels in their rainbow of colors. Sapphire, ruby, and emerald leaves shimmered in the sun like crowns upon the trees' trunks. The trunks were of varying sizes and shades of whites, grays, and browns. Birds flitted back and forth from branch to branch, chirping their songs. Pebbles crunched beneath our feet, adding to the music of the woods.

I wanted to pull out of his grip, to get away from the feeling of his skin on mine, especially when I knew a monster lurked just beneath.

Prince Tarrin stopped abruptly, releasing my arm. "I am not going to hurt you." His words were like an ice bath freezing every thought in my mind.

"Then what do you want, Prince? Don't you have enough slaves at your palace?" My eyes widened at the boldness of my own words, but something about him had that small piece of bravery within me awakening. That piece that had laid dormant since my mother had died.

"I was sent by the Queen to retrieve you." He shrugged his shoulders again, and I purposefully ignored yet another human-like gesture.

"Why?"

I could not fathom why the Queen of Elysia would want me at the Royal Palace, let alone why she would even know of my existence.

"The Queen wants Aela's daughter."

I flinched at my mother's name, taking a step back. "My name is Kaida," I snapped, not wanting him to utter her name again.

The Prince looked at me for a long moment, his wide eyes and flared nostrils betraying his annoyance at the way I spoke to him. I feared that he would punish me for disrespecting him so I quickly asked, "Why would the Queen of Elysia want me?"

He sighed. "Kaida, you are *mutator formarum.* A shape-shifter." He paused, watching my face. "Like me."

I could not move. Despite the summer heat, ice poured over my skin, immobilizing every muscle. No. He must have made a mistake. He found the wrong person. I was not a shape-shifter.

Mutator formarum were so incredibly rare, and nearly extinct at that, that they were hardly ever taught about or even spoken of in Elysia. Many dragons thought poorly of them, believing them to be abominations since they were a mixed breed of human and dragon. I had never met one in my seventeen years, and I certainly hadn't known that the Prince of Elysia was one of them.

My thoughts were racing in my head, all jumbled together and running over each other.

"You have the wrong person," I said at last. "I'm not a shape-shifter. You have made a mistake." My palms were slick with sweat and my heart pounded in my chest. I clenched my hands, nails digging into my palms far too hard.

"Kaida," the Prince said, his voice hesitant. "Have you never felt *something* inside you? Something different, something powerful, perhaps? Something that was pushing to get out?"

How could he possibly know that?

The memory of Eklos throwing me into the dirt the previous

night came to mind, and that *thing* I felt inside me, thrashing at the tight leash I kept on it. I always attributed that feeling to my anger and rage. Never once would I have considered that it was a *dragon inside of me.*

I needed to sit down. Sweat slid down my back, and I swayed on my feet. The Prince had to be wrong. I was simply imagining all of this. This was all a vivid dream. I would wake up in a few moments, in my dirty cave of a house, under Eklos's thumb.

This couldn't be real.

"Kaida, it is real. You're a shifter." His words were soft, like he was speaking to an animal readying to bolt. He took a careful step toward me.

Unreasonable tears filled my eyes. "If I'm a shifter, why have I never changed forms before?"

He raked a hand through his hair once more. "Many young shifters are not able to assume their other form until they have learned about their abilities. It has something to do with the shifter magic, which is different from a normal dragon's magic. I would assume that since you have grown up without the knowledge of your abilities… you have not been able to shift before."

Truthfully, it sounded insane to me, and like a convenient excuse that the Prince came up with to convince me to go with him.

But as if his words had been a trigger, I felt a strange warmth in my stomach that quickly grew to a searing heat. The space behind my eyes throbbed and my limbs started to ache. Bile rose in my throat and I fell to my knees, heaving up my empty stomach.

I heard Prince Tarrin's sudden intake of breath before I noticed my hands begin to change. It moved both far too slow and much too quickly. My fingernails extended into silver claws, purple scales flickering in layers across my skin. My arms elongated before my eyes, and I felt a strange sensation near my butt.

I pushed to my feet, watching the scales settle into place, layer after layer, over my body. The pain in my face hit a crescendo and I let out a scream, holding the sides of my head.

As quickly as it began, it stopped. There was no pain, only a gentle heat swirling in my core.

I glanced down at the ground and saw that the earth was crumbling away beneath my feet. My vision instantly grew clearer. I could see every individual grain of dirt lying on the ground, every ant scurrying for the safety of their hill. I could see the ultraviolet rays of the sun and the wispy clouds far above in the atmosphere that a human's eye could never see.

Prince Tarrin was in his turquoise dragon form once again. Grabbing my arm, he brought me to the edge of the river nearby. "Look in the water."

I hesitated for a moment, studying his face, then poked my head out over the water and gasped. I was not looking at a frail human girl. My body was indeed covered in amethyst-colored scales, each one reflecting color off every blade of grass on the ground. Sharp claws poked out from where my fingers used to be, and my long snout curled back into a disbelieving smile, which looked more like a grimace with my dragon teeth. My bright blue eyes were the only part of me that did not change. I raised my hand, opening it and closing it, watching the scales move and contract with each movement.

How is this possible?

Bile rose in my throat once more as I took in my reflection, the purple scales that now covered my enormous body, the membranous, iridescent wings that now protruded from my back. The one thing that I despised with every fiber of my being, the one thing that gave me endless nightmares and haunted my daydreams… I was one of them.

My scales were cool to the touch, but beneath them it felt like a roaring fire. I wanted to scream. I felt disgusting. I felt *wrong*.

My emotions were so strong, it was a struggle to stand beneath their weight. I could not remember ever experiencing these feelings as a human, having learned to shut them down and ignore how I felt. But I could not ignore these.

What did this mean?

If I was a dragon, did that mean I was no longer a slave?

Suddenly my goal of staying alive, making it through another day, was gone. The need to survive as a human had changed. Who was I without it?

"I know this is a lot to process but you need to close your snout before you drool all over yourself." Prince Tarrin could not seem to decide if he was irritated or amused.

I closed my large mouth, a blush creeping over my cheeks, thankfully hidden beneath the scales that covered them. Questions bounced back and forth through my mind as I studied the Prince's face. I looked around again, at the trees, the river, and even glanced toward the red steeples of The Den in the distance.

What now?

As if hearing my thoughts again, he nodded his head in the direction of the road, beckoning me to follow, this time not grabbing my hand.

What other choice did I have? I could not go back, and I could not pretend I was simply a human slave anymore. My only choice was to follow the Prince, as loathe as I was to admit it.

"Where are we going?" I asked as we began walking, two dragons side by side down the endless dirt road.

Prince Tarrin did not respond right away, and we walked in silence a few more moments when, finally, he spoke.

"I am bringing you to the Royal Palace where you will meet the King and Queen," he said, hesitating a second longer before continuing. "You and I are betrothed. Kaida, you are to be my wife."

CHAPTER FOUR
KAIDA

"MARRIED?" I SHRIEKED. Blood rushed to my head and flashing stars streaked across my field of vision. My feet halted, glued to the dirt beneath them. The shock from his declaration pulsed through my veins, and I felt a slight twinge in my muscles before the earth grew larger around me. Trees zoomed toward the sky, appearing much larger than they were a moment ago. I looked down at my feet just as my scales disappeared into my skin, my worn-out boots adorning my feet as if they had never left.

What just happened? Did I imagine all of that?

Examining my hands for any signs of claws, then searching the skin on my arms for a trace of those amethyst scales, I begged my brain to make sense of it all.

I glanced down the road to where the Prince still stalked forward.

What dragon would make a human their betrothed? Never mind the fact that Elysia would *never* agree to a human being their future queen.

I could not marry the Prince. He was a dragon. I would never be able to trust him, let alone love him. If I did marry him, my slavery would transform into captivity of a different sort. I would still be bound, still be stripped of any choice. If I were to marry the Prince, I would never be a free human. An absurd laugh made its way up my throat and I covered my mouth to stifle it.

And from what I had witnessed of the few marriages in my village, both human and dragon, it was enough to make me desire no part in it. There was only betrayal and heartache.

But most importantly, I could not marry him because I was human. I was not a dragon. Clearly evidenced by the fact that I walked on this cobblestone road, adorned with human feet, hands, and clothing. My mind refused to believe that I was a dragon, even though I had seen the scales covering my pale skin and wings spread delicately from my back.

I imagined all of that. Right?

My stomach clenched, my breathing becoming erratic.

"You *are* a dragon," the Prince said, coming to an abrupt stop and shooting a glare my way. "That was not in your head. That really happened."

I squeezed my eyes shut to block out the words before realizing he had heard my inner thoughts yet again. I peeked an eye open and looked at him questioningly.

"How did you kn—"

"Shape-shifters have the ability to project their thoughts onto others of their kind. That is why you could hear me back at The Den," he said matter-of-factly.

"So… you can read my mind?"

"It is not exactly reading your mind per se, but a mental bond between us. You basically screamed your thoughts at me a moment ago," he said, lips twitching as if he were fighting a smile.

Prince Tarrin's eyes followed me as I stomped back and forth over the dirt, kicking up dust moats into the air. I was mumbling under my breath, trying to riddle out how this was possible, when he appeared in front me, back in human form. Our eyes were locked, and I couldn't help but notice a slim ring of gold on the outside of his green eyes.

Despite the scars on half his face, the human in me had to admit that he was quite handsome. If you ignored the whole half dragon thing, that is.

"Prince Tarrin—"

"It's just Tarrin," he cut me off, though his voice was soft. Since when did a dragon not want to be called by their title?

"Believe me, Kaida. I do not want to marry you any more than you want to marry me." The words dug into my stomach like sharp claws, and I tried not to dwell on the ridiculous notion that I somehow cared what he thought about me. He turned to walk away.

"Wait, that's it? I'm just supposed to follow you to the palace and marry you?" I exclaimed.

The sun cast a halo around him as he pivoted back to me, making it impossible to see his expression. He said nothing and nodded his head toward the road, beckoning me to follow. I guess that was my answer.

My mind struggled to keep up. Everything was unfolding so fast, and all that I had ever known was now collapsing to rubble in front of me. I had grown up despising the dragon race, my enslavers, hating the Royal Family for allowing us humans to be enslaved in the first place. I had clung to my humanness my whole life, forcing myself to believe that I was better than them, that I was better than they could ever be. I did not feed off others' fears or parade around relishing the torture I inflicted on those around me. I was not cruel. I was not a monster.

But somehow, I was one of them. Half dragon.

Me, a part of the race that I detested.

The idea was laughable. How could I accept that?

I wanted to shut down, to refuse this new information. Had my mother known? Why would she not have told me?

Though I fought it, my heart knew that all my answers lay with the Prince who was now several paces down the road.

I could not go back. I could never return to that life, not now.

Letting out a sigh, I did the only thing that I could, and took a step toward the Prince.

Just as my legs were about to give out, we crested a hill, and came face to face with a massive stone structure that stood five levels high. The royal coat of arms, twisting flames and vines intertwining over the silhouette of a dragon, was inscribed on two flags, each waving in the steamy breeze on both sides of the manor. My mouth fell open and I heard Tarrin chuckle. He started forward again, seeming eager to be back in his home, and I followed, my eyes hungrily devouring every detail of the palace.

There were enormous gardens stretching down the length of the palace on either side, intoxicating smells and vibrant colors meeting my nose and eyes. Roses, lilies, and tulips intermingled with exotic and extravagant-looking flowers that I had never seen before.

Countless windows speckled the gray stone walls, which darkened by the second as the sun sank lower on the horizon. Tarrin easily pushed open the iron gates that separated the property from outsiders. The entrance doors loomed overhead at the end of a slim gravel path, taller than even the largest dragon I had ever seen, a brass lion's head mounted on each door.

I slowed as Tarrin continued up the stairs, nerves prickling in my stomach. He glanced over his shoulder to look at me and waved impatiently for me to hurry up. I swallowed hard, trying to wipe the scowl from my face, and took the stairs two at a time, my movements awkward and clumsy.

"Welcome to my home, Kaida," he said, as I stopped next to him, panting, his tone implying he wished for me to be anywhere but here.

He swung open the doors and pushed past a milling group of slaves who scurried out of his way as he stomped toward the staircase. My feet automatically slowed and came to a stop as I took in the foyer. The massive staircase was at least twenty feet wide and two stories tall, made of a glistening white marble lined with red velvet from bottom to top. The railings on either side had massive spindles, all made of gold. The cavernous ceiling above held a huge glass chandelier, pieces of it jutting out as if flames had been frozen inside the glass.

There were endless hallways to the right and left, with numerous doors on either side of the staircase. Floor-to-ceiling windows filled the wall above the stairs. The other walls were a rich emerald green with trim and molding also made of gold. Intricate tapestries hung in the bare spaces on the wall where light fixtures were absent.

Rich marble covered the floor beneath my feet, swirls of gray and fire-orange swirling amongst the white. It must have been recently polished due to its luster. Since I was used to dirt floors and bug-infested furniture, it took every ounce of strength I had to not lie down and stroke the floors, or to go run my hands over the drapes of each window.

Every door and archway, every piece of furniture, it was all dragon sized, further dwarfing the humans rushing around in front of me. I glanced over to my right and noticed a door that was only big enough for humans to fit through. Out of it wafted delicious scents of foods both known and unknown to me. My stomach rumbled in response, a feeling that I was all too used to. When was the last time I had eaten?

I was vaguely aware of Tarrin already halfway up the stairs, oblivious to the fact that I stood frozen in the middle of the foyer.

Looking at the pristine state of the house, I glanced down at my tattered clothes. My hair was unwashed and matted in places; my clothes utterly filthy, holes everywhere. My eyes widened at my reflection as I turned toward the window behind me. My cheekbones were sharp, ready to burst from my skin, and pools of darkness rested beneath my eyes. My lips were cracked and crusted with dried blood, and my arms and legs looked ready to snap with a mere tap. As if on cue, my stomach growled once more, fiercer this time. I placed a hand on my stomach and swallowed the dry lump in my throat.

Squashing down the desperate hunger that was growing inside me, I focused on the people milling around. The lobby of the palace buzzed with activity as humans moved about tending to the dragons' every desire. They all wore simple brown garments, indicating their royal slave status, all in better shape than my own clothes. While dirt was smudged in some places, and they had clearly been well worn, they were not tattered or full of holes like the slaves' clothing in my village. I sent up a silent prayer, to a nameless god that had been forgotten long ago, that that was an indication that the royals treated these humans better than I ever was.

"Kaida," Tarrin's voice echoed in the room, snapping me out of my awe-inspired trance. He was at the top of the stairs, back in dragon form, his eyes narrowed at my delay. "Come," he ordered.

The dominance in his voice was strong enough that it spurred my feet forward automatically. I made it to the base of the stairs, about to ascend, when I felt the prickle on the back of my neck that someone was watching me. I glanced to my right and noticed a tall man, with a long face and short greasy hair, standing in the shadows of a corner. His large muscles bulged out of his brown slave uniform. His eyes flashed, holding something that could only be described as violence, and I tore my gaze away and practically ran up the stairs toward Tarrin. I didn't know who that slave was, but my gut told me I didn't want to find out.

When I reached the top, the Prince scowled at me, or at least that was what it seemed his dragon features did, as if having me here was truly a nuisance. We turned a corner, and in a dull flash of blue, he shrunk down into his human form.

I cleared my throat. "Where are you taking me?" I asked. He kept stomping forward, human feet as solid as if they were a dragon's, not bothering to answer or acknowledge my question.

The hallway was well lit with lanterns hanging every few feet. The walls were covered in different paintings, portraits, and tapestries. Some were as small as my hand while others were as large as a dragon. The paintings were a variety of different scenes. Some were of beautiful gardens, others were of the surrounding areas outside my village, and all the rest were portraits of dragons that I assumed were members of the royal lineage.

The floor was a polished gray marble with a thick panel of red velvet stretching down the center, similar to the staircase. I snapped my attention back to Tarrin as we neared the end of the hallway. I cleared my throat again, louder this time, to get his attention. He looked over his shoulder, a muscle working in his jaw, but still he said nothing.

"Where are we going?" I repeated, stronger this time, stopping in the middle of the hallway and crossing my arms. As a slave, I was always told what to do and when to do it, being dragged along day to day against my will. If I were here as the Prince's betrothed and not a slave, I did not want to be subjected to the same thing. The *human* Kaida under Eklos would never have even dared to think such a thought. But the *half-dragon* Kaida under this arrogant Prince… something about his attitude, and his constant evading of my questions, had that rebellious piece of my mind sneaking out.

He halted mid-step and swung around to face me. His stare pierced straight through me, my instincts pushing me to avert my gaze like I was supposed to. Tarrin put his hands in his pockets and offered a shrug and a sly smile.

"We are going to visit my parents," he said, swatting the air to dismiss my question as he resumed walking, his footsteps echoing off the painting-covered walls. Immediate shudders racked through my body. I could not meet the King and Queen. Not now. Not yet.

Too much was happening, too fast. How did they view shape-shifters? Would they welcome me in, because of their son? Or would they kill me on sight because I was some monstrous half breed?

I closed my eyes, begging my own brain to come up with some way to stop this moment from happening.

"I'm filthy," I blurted. It was the only logical reason I could come up with to put this meeting off a while longer. I was dirty, ash and grime covering every inch of my skin, my clothes torn and riddled with holes. I could not remember the last time my hair had been washed. Dirt was caked under my fingernails and dark circles sat stubbornly under my eyes. Physical traits aside, I was not mentally prepared to meet them either. I had only found out who I was, what I was, hours ago and was still struggling to accept it. I had been ripped from my own reality and thrust into a new one, with hardly any explanation. This meeting would get us both nowhere. Surely, Tarrin had to know that.

"You will fit in with all the other slaves then," he quipped.

"The other slaves aren't your *betrothed,*" I muttered.

Tarrin halted and swung to face me. "What was that?"

Ice slid through my veins. "Nothing," I responded, trying to pretend I hadn't said something that would get me punished. He narrowed his eyes.

"You cannot truly believe that meeting them in this state is a good idea." I gestured to my body, scowling.

Tarrin came to a stop in front of a massive door, his hand raised to knock, but froze. After several tense heartbeats that felt like my heart would crack under the pressure, he sighed.

"Wait out here," he said, voice laced with annoyance, without looking at me. The Prince gave the door a sturdy knock that became louder and deeper as he transformed back into his turquoise scales simultaneously. The door stood far over his head and was made of solid gold. It had the royal coat of arms engraved into the center. The massive doorknobs were nearly twice the size of one of my hands.

A slave girl opened the door, keeping her eyes firmly on the ground. Her brown clothes were pristine, not even a wrinkle in sight. She silently pulled the door wider, then closed it a moment later without a sound.

Like blowing out a candle, every cramped and aching muscle relaxed, my eyes burning, and my shoulders slumped under the weight of what had happened today. I closed my eyes, putting my face in my hands. I slid to my knees in the middle of the hallway, and ragged breaths tore through my throat. Hot tears burned my eyes, begging to be released.

I crawled on hands and knees to the nearest wall, resting my back against it. Creeping cold seeped through my clothes, digging into every part of my body, but it was soothing somehow. Pulling my legs in tight, I rested my forehead on my knees, squeezing my eyes shut.

I was human, but also a dragon. My brain rebelled, refusing to inspect that idea further. A familiar numbness spread like spilled water over my mind, like all the times I forced my brain to shut down in Belharnt or The Den to protect myself. My body felt heavy, my muscles unresponsive. I let myself fall into it, needing it like air, and welcomed the sudden lack of feeling.

CHAPTER FIVE
TARRIN

"I CAN'T DO THIS," I snapped. "It was a mistake to bring her here."

The King and Queen of Elysia sat before me, their bodies overflowing on thrones made of gold and silver. Each throne had beautifully carved cutouts on the sides for their wings to comfortably lay behind them. Bright blue and red lights danced on the walls as the light from the torches hit their scales.

"You found her?" My mother sat forward on the edge of her seat, her face lighting up.

"I found Aela's daughter," I declared. "And she had no idea that she was a shifter."

"Her mother did not tell her?" my father asked.

"It would appear not. She was a slave to that dragon Master in Vernista. Eklos."

My mother pursed her lips but said nothing.

"I can't do this," I repeated. "I cannot marry her, and she cannot stay in the palace. Send her away. *Anywhere* but here."

Silence crackled through the room and I could feel my parents' disappointment like a physical blow.

"I could hear her thoughts. Every single one." I took a shaky breath. "She hates me. Us. She blames us all for her life as a slave."

"She will learn it is more complicated than that," the King replied. "It's not as black and white as it seems."

"You didn't see her face, Father. You didn't see the loathing and hopelessness in her eyes. Her sickly body that has not seen any nutrition in years. She has more dirt and grease on her body than skin. She was one step away from death when I found her. And she blames *me* for it."

It got under my skin much more than I cared to admit. It was not *my* fault that Elysia was the way it was. It was not *my* fault that Eklos owned her, mistreated her, and that those dragons would have killed her if I had not stepped in. It was simply the way Elysia was. I was a good male. How dare she blame me for circumstances that were outside of my control.

"Right after I told her she was *mutator formarum*, she shifted, like it had been waiting just beneath the surface all along."

"What was she like?" my mother breathed.

"You are missing the point, Mother!"

"She needs training, Tarrin. To control her shifting and her other… abilities." She scooted back in her seat, nodding to herself.

"We don't even know if she has any other abilities," I retorted. "Send her south to Myrewell or Pyrn where the cruelty toward humans is less severe, or send her off the continent so we never have to see her again."

"*Tarrin,*" my father's voice boomed, the reprimand echoing off the walls. My stomach dropped like an anchor, and I crossed my arms, the human gesture awkward in dragon form.

A swift knock sounded, drawing my parents' attention. Strange. It was evening, well past the time when they usually entertained guests. My father narrowed his eyes as if he were thinking the same thing.

"Answer the door," he commanded the slave girl in the corner. I didn't even know her name, and surprisingly a part of me felt a tinge of regret.

The girl's hands shook as she used her entire body weight to drag open the door, revealing a silver haired woman. It took a moment for me to place her. She was the head slave, in charge of all the others in the palace. I chewed on the inside of my cheek as I fought to remember her name. Berda, was it? I swallowed down the sudden discomfort of wanting to remember a human's name.

"What is it?" my mother asked, adopting her stern, queenly voice.

Berda held up a piece of parchment. "Word from Vernista, Your Majesties. It seems urgent."

My parents looked at each other, silent communication passing between them, before they nodded. Berda strode across the room, head held high, though her eyes were fixed on the floor. It was strange to see a human unafraid in the presence of the King and Queen.

Berda handed the parchment to my mother, waited to be dismissed, then left as quickly as she had arrived.

Silence ticked like a lit fuse on my nerves as they took turns reading.

At last, my father looked up at me, his snout turned down into a grimace. "Tarrin, what did you do?" My mother let out a sigh.

"What are you talking about?"

"What happened in Vernista, Tarrin?" My father's voice was growing more impatient by the second.

Eyes narrowed, I fought to keep smoke from leaking from my nostrils. "I rescued Kaida. Just like you asked."

"And how, exactly, did you accomplish that?" My father's voice transformed into the booming countenance of the King's.

I rubbed the top of my snout. "I followed a faint shifter scent to that tavern in Vernista. The Den." My lips contorted in disgust at the name. It was a foul place if I had ever seen one. "Kaida was quite literally on the floor, about to be crushed into a pile of blood and skin by another dragon. I stopped him."

My father grimaced, though my mother looked thoughtful. "And Eklos?"

My eyes flicked to him, unable to read whatever emotion was twisting his snout. "I told him I was taking Kaida with me. Then we left."

"That's it?" the King demanded.

"Eklos was definitely not fond of the idea, but he didn't try to stop us," I answered, my stomach churning. I nodded at the parchment. "What does it say?"

Without a word, he handed it to me. The words were scrawled in black ink that was clearly still wet when it was rolled up, evident by how the black was smudged in multiple places. The handwriting was unfamiliar, and it took me several tries to make out the words.

Your Majesties,

I have found evidence of the Remnant in Vernista. Be warned: the dragon Eklos has been tearing through the village in a rage, killing at will. I have been unable to uncover any plots he may be planning, but I am certain he is planning to move. Will send word once I know more.

Long Live the King and Queen,

Narron

The scales between my eyes bunched as I read the parchment over and over, trying to make sense of it. Narron was my parents' spy that they hired to make sure they knew what was happening inside Elysia at all times. They felt no need for a guard or dragon soldiers to protect them, deeming themselves quite capable of defending themselves, but instead employed spies that were dispersed all over the continent.

In all my lessons with my tutors, I had never heard of a time when anyone had tried to rise up against the Royal Family. Outside of the slaves, it always seemed like my parents were quite loved by Elysia. Them not having any type of guards never seemed like a problem.

"The Remnant?" I asked. "Like the old tales?"

"Yes," my father replied, his eyes far away. "The Remnant of the Lone Dragon have been underground for centuries. It's surprising that they've surfaced enough to be noticed."

"What does it mean?" I hated that my thoughts instantly went to Kaida. That the urge to protect her flared bright and hot. *What is this? I barely know her. I should not feel protective of her.*

My mother was the one to speak this time. "It means something is coming, Tarrin. Make sure Kaida stays in the palace. Now that she has shifted, her scent will be unmistakable. The Remnant will know what she is if they find her now."

I opened my mouth to speak, but she stood to her feet, her ruby scales casting a red glow across the ceiling. "We will deal with this, Son. Go make sure Kaida is settling in. We will plan to meet her tomorrow night over dinner."

The Queen walked across the length of the throne room, my father pushing to his feet to follow. She was halfway through the door on the other end that led to their chambers when she stopped and looked back at me.

"And Tarrin? Don't give up on the girl quite yet. She might surprise you, dear. Perhaps do not shut the door on this, on her, until you have spent some time with her." With a smile that only she could make look beautiful in dragon form, she winked at me and left the room.

CHAPTER SIX
KAIDA

I LOST TRACK OF time, both an eternity and mere seconds passing in the time Tarrin was gone. When I lifted my head from my knees, letting my eyes drift to meet his, I found him in human form, leaning against the opposite wall, hands stuffed in his pockets. His wavy hair had been tied back at the nape of his neck, but a few stray pieces hung down, floating back and forth over his eyes. His emerald stare shimmered in the lantern light from the wall, and a muscle twitched in his jaw.

Limbs aching from the long trek to the Royal Palace, I stifled a groan as I pulled myself to my feet. "What happened?" I asked. My mind had spun through a hundred different scenarios while he spoke with his parents, all ranging from them being pleasantly surprised that I had arrived to wanting to kill me.

Tarrin cleared his throat and pushed himself off the wall. "The King and Queen want you to stay in the palace."

I blinked. "As a slave?"

His eyebrows furrowed. "No, Kaida, not as a slave."

"But—"

"They want you to stay safe and the only place that can be accomplished is within these walls." He lifted his arms to gesture around him, his voice laced in irritation. The way he avoided my eyes, fidgeting with his hands, made me suspicious. *Is he hiding something from me?*

I opened my mouth to speak but he pivoted on his heel and stalked back down the hallway. It was clear that whatever conversation took place behind those massive gold doors weighed Tarrin down like a ship's anchor. His shoulders were hunched, head lowered, feet shuffling across the floor.

I watched the way he moved, looking for signs of the monster within, but found none. When he was in human form, it was surprisingly easy to forget what he was beneath the skin. I did not want to admit it, but it was easier to set my prejudice aside, seeing him in skin rather than scales.

But the fact remained: he brought me here and I was supposed to marry him, living the rest of my life bound to him in this palace.

I could not fathom marrying a dragon. They were beasts, living nightmares without a shred of goodness or kindness in them.

It was because of that fact that I struggled to believe that the Royal Family did not mean to harm me. For all I knew they were probably going to keep me locked in a cold, dark cell somewhere beneath the palace, with little food or water. Or in a room with too many other slaves all crammed together. They would use me when I was needed and abuse me when I was not. It would be no different than my life with Eklos.

Prince Tarrin was just another captor, another person for me to survive.

I glanced around the hallway and could not keep my mouth from gaping as I beheld thick beams of pure gold lining the ceiling, with intricate carvings and designs all over them. They seemed to tell a story, depicting wars and battles, histories and legends of the dragon race. I was lost in the beauty of the stories they told when I suddenly slammed into something hard and unforgiving.

The Prince.

My cheeks burned as I lurched back and my muscles seized, my bones readying for retaliation.

Tarrin did nothing I would have expected and simply smirked at me. "Distracted by big shiny things, are we?"

My cheeks reddened further, and I forced myself not to glance up at the beams again. I crossed my arms, but my entire body trembled. The smirk was slow to slide from his face as he must have realized I was truly afraid. He rubbed at his neck, looking away, and sighed before gesturing to a door behind him.

"This is your room."

The door was made of thick dark wood with a large carving of a lion sitting on a cliff, overlooking a lake. It was so tall that I had to crane my neck up to see the entirety of it. The doorknob was made of simple brass and was a normal size for a human to open.

"My—what?"

Tarrin blinked and gave me a wry smile. "Were you expecting something else?"

I gave him a wary look. "Yes."

The corners of his mouth twitched up and he opened both doors at once. It was not simply a bedroom, but an entire suite. Huge cavernous ceilings, with gold crown molding, and those beautiful intricate beams that had held my attention in the hall stretched across it. The farthest wall was nearly all windows, from floor to ceiling. Even though daylight had faded, the moon illuminated the night enough that the massive expanse of pastures, farms, and mountains far in the distance could be seen.

The main room was sparsely furnished, with a fireplace on the left, an ugly brown couch positioned in front of it, and walnut tables like book ends on either side. A small round table with an intricate pedestal leg sat on the opposite side of the room with two wooden chairs. Everything was mismatched, but human sized, and looked as though it was all they could scrounge up in such short notice. Although it was immaculately clean, the scent of lemons clinging to the air, it was clear that this room had not been used in quite some time, void of any personal touches. The furnishings were not extravagant by any means, but it was more than I had ever had, more than I could have asked for, and my heart skipped a beat. I swallowed, forcing my gaping mouth to close.

"This is… mine?" I whispered, tiptoeing into the room as if it all would disappear.

To my right was another doorway and my boots clunked on the marble floor as I made my way toward it. A large bed sat directly in front of me, big enough for a ten-foot dragon, with posts of dark wood that stretched up to a wide ivory canopy above. The bedding was a variety of rich purple fabrics with ivory embellishments, and at the head of the bed was a huge pile of pillows. I fought the urge to jump into that pile, wanting to feel all the silks and cottons against my skin rather than the moth-eaten rags I was used to.

"Through that door you will find the bathing room," Tarrin said, pointing at a door to the right of the bed. "And a selection of clothes that were made for you in the armoire," he finished, waving a hand at the oak cabinet standing in the corner.

Tarrin gestured toward the bathing room again, his eyes roving over my body from head to toe. "Feel free to wash up. Everything you need you will find in that room." With that he made his way toward the door. I tried to say something, but all I managed was a small unintelligible squeak as he shut the doors behind him.

I remained rooted to that spot, staring at those doors for a moment longer before removing my boots, a stream of sand falling from each one, and looked down at the thick rug beneath my feet, squishing my toes into it. The strands wiggled between them and cushioned my soles like a pillow beneath my aching feet.

I was only able to enjoy it for a moment before my eyes shifted to the dirt crusting my feet and the black and yellow bruises. I could not remember where the bruises had come from. My eyes hungrily roved around the room. I could not believe that this was *mine.* I was not being forced into a lightless dirt cave, full of freezing mud and belongings that were so rotten they were unusable. I was not being forced to stay in a room with twenty other slaves, all vying for more space. No more rushing to The Den, no more cleaning up dragon vomit, no more trembling while I waited for Eklos to punish me.

These chambers were for me.

An unfamiliar feeling began creeping along my skin, hesitant, as if it might be chased away at any moment. The normal racing heartbeat that I had become accustomed to calmed to a steady beat, and my body loosened, the tight coils of muscles relaxing.

Letting out a sigh of relief, I turned toward the bathing room. The faint patter of my feet as they met the marble floor whispered off the walls. When *was* the last time I had bathed?

In the center of the bathing room, big enough to be considered a pool, stood the bath. It was built directly into the floor, alone and regal. Black marble floors filled the rest of the space, so polished that I could see my own reflection. Even in the dark tiles, I could tell how filthy I was. I put my hands in my hair and felt nothing but matts and grease.

My feet padded softly against the floor as I rushed to the bath and dunked my feet in. The water was warm and soothing, and I groaned. Too long. It had been too long since I had had the luxury of bathing, let alone hot water. If I was ever lucky enough to be able to wash up, it was always without soap, and with bucket after bucket of freezing water, often shared between multiple humans.

A small giggle bubbled up in my throat and a grin spread across my face as I peeled off my clothes and waded down the steps into the water. I walked in until the water reached my neck. Steam rose in smoky tendrils and it parted and ebbed around me. I brought my head under the water, holding my breath, and lingered there for a few seconds before breaking the surface. Taking in big gulps of air, I basked in the glorious foreignness of the calm settling over my body for a few moments before dunking under the water again. When I emerged this time, I began looking around the room.

"Now I just need soap," I muttered to myself.

As if in answer, a basket of various bars and bottles appeared at the edge of the bath and I waded over to it, not even stopping to wonder where they had come from. Scents of lavender, roses, and pine met my nose, along with other luxurious scents I had never encountered before. I picked the bar smelling of lavender and roses and I took my time, savoring the feel of clean soap and warm water. A plush ivory towel appeared at the edge of the bath just as I had determined I was finished. The thought that someone might have been watching me crossed my mind, but I dismissed it in favor of believing it was simply some sort of magic instead.

I wrapped the towel snug around my arms and did not even bother to dry my feet as I padded back into my room, leaving small puddles in my wake. The once open floor to ceiling silver drapes had been closed and the lanterns and candles perched on shelves and tables were lit.

Pulling open the doors to the armoire, I half expected for moths or other creatures to fly out; I let out a loud breath when only a pleasant lavender fragrance met my nose. Inside were a variety of silk and glittering fabrics in stunningly bright colors, each piece so soft and delicate that I could not fathom how much they must have cost. Why would they have given me such luxurious clothes? I was immediately glad that I had not met the King and Queen in my old rags. The thought made my cheeks burn. The only place those belonged was in the fire.

Tucked away behind stunning gowns were several pairs of practical black cotton pants and a few tunics in varying purples, grays, and whites. I skimmed through the bottom drawers and found nightgowns and undergarments, all surprisingly in my size.

Wanting to dive straight into bed, I grabbed a black nightgown and threw it on, paying no attention to how short and revealing it was.

A vanity and chair were nestled in the corner, a hairbrush resting on top. I took a seat in it and dared a glance in the mirror. My face was pale, almost death-kissed, blue eyes shadowed by dark circles. Wet strands of hair hung in my face and in snarled tangles on the top of my head. My collarbone protruded from my skin and I could see the bones of my sternum that the neckline of the nightgown revealed.

This was the first time I had seen my reflection in years. We never owned a mirror when I was younger, and I had never desired to see the results of seven years of torture after Eklos brought me back to Vernista enough to find one. Staring at myself, I thought I could be pretty, someday. When my skin was once again golden from the sun, hair long and silky down my back. When my cheek bones were not as harsh or when the dark pools beneath my eyes disappeared. When my limbs were no longer fragile as glass. When I did not look moments from death.

I hated to admit it, but I found myself comparing my human face to how I had looked in the river's reflection as a dragon. Although I had not felt it at the time, there had been a quiet strength, a hidden confidence, in my dragon form. It shone from the light glinting off my scales, from the fire burning in my eyes, the magic pooling beneath my skin.

But now...I looked ordinary. That strength and power was gone, replaced by a weak frailty made worse by years of malnutrition and torture.

Knowing it was a vain effort, I picked up the hairbrush and attempted to brush out the snarls from my hair. My face contorted into a permanent wince, holding in my groans as the hair pulled and threatened to rip from my scalp. I freed the last of the tangles from my hair just as a brisk knock sounded at the door.

For a moment I was frozen, my muscles turning to ice, holding me immobile. My mind immediately thought of Eklos, that he had come for me, was waiting to take me away again. Another knock, more impatient this time. I flinched. I rose from my chair, each movement of my limbs protesting, and looked around me, desperate for anything I could use as a weapon; anything to protect myself. The room was spotless and decluttered. My only option was the hairbrush. With a grip as strong as steel, I held the hairbrush behind my back as I padded over to the door.

I took a deep breath as I reached for the knob and twisted it, taking a quick step back as it swung open. My breath rushed out of me in a whoosh. Prince Tarrin stood before me in the doorway, fully human, holding a tray of food. His eyes widened as he took in my clean hair, my nightgown, and the hairbrush clutched in the hand now by my side.

"A hairbrush?" he said, his tone bored. "Really? What would you have done? Brush my hair to death?"

The corners of his mouth twitched like he was fighting a smile, and I glared at the ground, my cheeks warm. I could feel his eyes rove over my face and hair, dropping to the low neckline of the nightgown, before finding my gaze again.

He cleared his throat. "I figured you could use some food." He lifted the tray as proof. My body still felt like lead and I could not get my limbs to cooperate. After a few more seconds of standing there staring at each other, my stomach let out a fierce rumbling sound.

My cheeks burned as a vicious smile crept over Tarrin's face. He coughed, masking his laugh as he walked into the room. Setting the tray down on the table in the main room, he looked at me once more and gestured to eat as he sat in one of the chairs beside it. My eyes flicked back and forth between the dishes of food and him, secretly wondering if they were poisoned. The Prince snorted and rolled his eyes.

"Kaida, if I wanted to poison you, I promise, you would already be dead. No need to waste food to do it. You are safe," he said, his voice softer than I thought possible from a dragon. "We are not going to hurt you."

I met his eyes. "How do I know you are telling the truth?"

Tarrin was thoughtful for a moment. "You don't."

I probably should have been alarmed at his response but found myself appreciating his honesty.

"We're both in the same situation, Kaida, so you're going to have to learn to trust me."

Trust a dragon? Yeah, right.

I studied his eyes, looking for any sign of dishonesty but could find none. I marched over to the table, plopped into the other chair, and grabbed the first thing my eyes snagged on, and stuffed a large piece of bread in my mouth.

It was the most heavenly piece of bread I had ever tasted. Notes of cinnamon met my taste buds and the buttery aroma nearly made me groan. I lifted the warming lid off one of the dishes, its golden handle two vines beneath a dragon, and tendrils of steam wafted into my nose. Meat stew. I picked up the lid of another dish on the tray and found roasted chicken with green beans. Actual edible food. These were foods that I had not eaten since I was very young. If we were fortunate enough to be fed at all, slaves usually lived off rotten porridge and the occasional cup of rice.

I began cutting up the chicken like a butcher with fresh meat. The flavors and spices of the chicken were so intense compared to the gruel I was used to, and it exploded on my taste buds. Basil, rosemary, and other spices danced on my tongue as I took bite after bite. It was tender and juicy, each piece nearly dissolving in my mouth.

I took up a spoonful of meat stew, not even bothering to cool it down before popping it into my mouth. Venison was the first thing I tasted, a meat that was unfathomably expensive for humans unless they were willing to risk their lives hunting in the forest, which most of them were not. It was pointless because we could not buy or sell goods and foods in the village, so there was no money to be made, and there were several breeds of animals that prowled the woods that would not hesitate to shred a human into ribbons if they were caught.

Spiced carrots and onions crunched between my teeth, bursting with flavors of honey and maple. I continued to shove as much food as possible into my mouth as if it would suddenly disappear and I would be left hungry again if I didn't.

Out of the corner of my eye I saw the Prince smirk. "When was the last time you ate?"

I stopped midchew. "I don't know." I could not remember the last meal I had. His brow furrowed again as he studied me.

"I will let you eat in peace." The Prince rose from his chair and walked to the door.

"Tarrin," I called after him and he paused, hand on the doorknob. "What really happened when you talked to your parents?"

He turned halfway back to me, his eyes flickering in the candlelight. His hesitation made it obvious that he had kept something important from me.

I set down my forkful of food. "What aren't you telling me?"

The shakiness of his breath as he exhaled had my stomach in knots.

"What do you know of Eklos?"

Just the sound of his name made me want to vomit, every muscle in my body locking up tight. "He is a horrid beast. That's all that needs to be known."

Tarrin blew a strand of hair off his face. "I mean, do you know anything about his future plans? Or…" he hesitated, unable to meet my eyes. "The Remnant?"

The metal fork dropped from my fingers, pinging against the

marble floor. The blood drained from my face and the room spun around me.

"Kaida?"

Tarrin was instantly at my side, gripping my shoulders to keep me upright. Despite the fog my brain had receded into, his light touch sent a spark through me.

"I don't know anything, Your Highness." My voice sounded mumbled, far away. "I heard some dragons from The Den discussing the Remnant, but I know nothing of their plans. Or Eklos's."

Tarrin straightened, releasing me, seeming to remember himself at my use of his title.

"Is he coming for me?" I whispered, tears filling my eyes as I met his.

"No." His voice was firm, leaving no room for argument. "I promised you that you would be safe here, Kaida. You don't need to worry about him."

Picking up the fork I dropped, he brushed it off on his pants before handing it back to me.

"You don't know Eklos," I muttered.

"You don't know *me*," he snapped, before running a hand through his hair. He blew out a frustrated breath. "Get some rest, Kaida. We're dining with my parents for dinner tomorrow." He offered a small smile that looked more like an apology. "Good night." And then he was gone.

My mind was like a whirlpool in the middle of the sea. Why would he ask about the Remnant, especially the day after I heard the tavern dragons talking about it? Had his parents learned something? Did they blame *me* for their presence?

All I knew for certain was that Eklos's reach was enormous. If he wanted me back, there was nothing Tarrin could do to stop him.

CHAPTER SEVEN
KAIDA

SWEAT DRIPPED DOWN the sides of my face and my heart pounded wildly in my chest, shooting knives through every muscle like poison ripping through my veins.

My wrists and ankles were bound with rope, the coarse threads biting into my skin, burning everywhere it touched. The rope was attached to a pole in front of me, holding me firmly in place. My clothes were gone, stripped from my body, and I stood there exposed, frantically looking around for anyone to help me. But I was alone. A putrid-smelling cloth filled my mouth, preventing me from screaming. Thunderous footsteps sounded behind me, shaking the ground and I glanced over my shoulder, my heart stuttering.

Eklos had come for me.

He loomed behind me, smoke billowing from his snout, eyes smoldering like embers. He gave me a vicious smile, smelling my fear, as firelight flashed and flickered in his hands. When the light disappeared, a long blazing whip with thorns of glass rested in his upturned claws. My eyes glazed over as years of torture took over my mind and tears streamed down my cheeks. I couldn't control the sobs that racked through my body.

Eklos stalked toward me, his steps quaking and slow, cracking the whip in the air. I flinched, the rough fibers of rope cutting deeper into my wrists. He let out a barking laugh, and a crack like thunder sounded as light flashed through the air just above my head. A warning. I lunged for the ground, my arms nearly yanked out of their sockets by the rope suspending them. The next snap of the whip would hit home, right between my shoulder blades. Just like it always did. Eklos never missed.

I sent up a silent prayer, begging for death to claim me before the pain could.

"I warned you, *slave,*" Eklos snarled, whip poised to strike. I glanced up in time to see him raise his arm and heard the crack as he sent it piercing through the air toward me, flames licking at my skin.

I jolted up in bed, a scream erupting from my mouth. Soothing darkness instantly smothered my senses, as a cool breeze tickled my sweat drenched skin.

It was just a dream. A nightmare.

Eklos had not found me.

I was in the palace, in my chambers, in a massive bed made for a dragon.

Eklos could not get to me here. Or at least that's what Tarrin promised.

Panting hard, my eyes struggled to adjust to the dim light. The sheets and duvet were soaked with sweat beneath me. I rubbed at my wrists where the rope had burned into my skin, trying to banish the nightmare from my mind.

The first trickles of dawn were just starting to peek through the cracks in the drapes. I crawled on hands and knees across the bed, slipped over the edge, and tiptoed over to the silver-veiled windows, pulling them back. The sun had not yet crested the horizon, leaving the landscape in a dull purple light. Beautiful gardens, lush with every color imaginable, stretched from my windows out for several acres, walking paths meandering in and out throughout the flowers.

Beyond the gardens stretched rich green flatlands, some filled with crops, others with animals. Beyond those, enormous, and very old, trees rose up from the ground, towering hundreds of feet high, easily dwarfing any dragon. The forest covered as far as I could see, kissing the base of the mountains far in the distance.

Minutes passed and my feet rooted in place as the sun peeked its head over the mountains. Rich, golden light burst forth, spreading quickly, encompassing everything in its path, chasing away the shadows of night.

It was the first time, in my entire life, that I was not required to be at The Den at dawn. It was the first time that I could stand here, watching the sun rise and not wish for it to stay firmly beneath the earth so that I did not have to face another day with Eklos. For the first time, there was a slight hope in this sunrise. Today was a new day. Today was different.

According to the Prince, in the palace I was not Kaida the slave, but I still could not accept being Kaida the shape-shifter, the half-dragon.

But I was *something.* Something more than I used to be.

I took a deep breath, inhaling the warm rays of sunlight. It was the first full, easy breath I had ever taken.

A knock sounded at my door, stealing my attention.

An automatic tremor shot through my limbs, locking each of my muscles in place. A second brisk knock rang out just before the door opened a crack and a head poked in.

A human head.

We made eye contact and the clenched fists by my side relaxed. A girl, appearing to be around my age, pushed open the door and walked a few feet into the room. Her simple brown clothing, dirt smudged in several places, confirmed that she was a slave. Soft blonde hair was braided down her back, small wisps of it escaping to frame her face. A tray of food rested in her hands and she offered a hesitant smile.

"Breakfast, miss." Her lilting accent echoed through the room. It was a strange accent; one I had not encountered before. Raising the tray slightly in proof of her words, she walked it over to the table and set it down. I could smell the food from where I stood by the windows. Some sort of quiche sat in the middle of the tray and the scent of smoky bacon drifted over to my nose, making my mouth water.

"I am Meara, miss," she said, grabbing her skirt and giving a small curtsy. "I am here to assist you with anything you need." In other words, she had been assigned to be my slave. I offered a weak smile, fumbling for words. I did not know why the Prince would feel it necessary to give me a slave, especially when he should know that I would not accept one. It was hard enough being a slave to a dragon.

It felt wrong to have her be *my* slave.

For a moment, I wondered if this girl would be questioning her orders to bring me, a human, food. But her face was carefully blank, no confusion or emotion on it.

What message were the royals sending me? I was human, but they had no problem pushing me into the dragon lifestyle. I was struggling to maintain that line in my head between what I knew myself to be, and what they wanted me to be.

"I'm Kaida," I said, at a loss for words.

She curtsied once more and busied herself with stripping the sheets from my bed, tossing them in a basket near the door. Once she finished putting on fresh bedding, Meara opened the wardrobe, pulling out a tunic and loose-fitting pants and laid them out on the bed. Inspecting them from a distance, they were exactly what I would have picked out.

"You didn't have to do that," I said.

"Happy to, miss."

"Are you?" The question slipped out before I could stop it.

Meara paused in her cleaning, keeping her back to me. She didn't respond, which seemed like answer enough.

"How old are you, Meara?"

Turning halfway toward me, she met my gaze. "Sixteen."

I nodded, expecting as much. "How long?" I knew she would know what I was asking: how long had she been a slave in the palace?

"Three years, miss. I was property of the Commander of Zarkuse before."

And just like that, any hesitations I had about Meara disappeared. My eyes filled with tears at the thought of this young girl being a slave to *him.* I had heard horror stories from other humans in Vernista, many that rivaled the cruelty of Eklos.

What horrors had Meara survived?

As if sensing my thoughts, and not wanting to acknowledge them, she sniffed once and walked toward the bathing room. The sounds of trickling water filled the air before she re-emerged, carrying my used towel from yesterday.

"The water will be ready for you by the time you finish your breakfast. You may leave your clothing in the basket and I will collect them for laundering." Meara curtsied once more and made to leave.

"Meara," I called.

She paused, already halfway out the door.

"Thank you." I hoped she could hear all the words I hadn't said in between those two. *I am sorry for all you've gone through. I'm sorry they've made you do this. I am not your enemy. Forgive me.*

Her back stiffened, and the side of her face that I could see revealed nothing. She simply nodded, and left, closing the door behind her.

The sudden feeling of being utterly alone descended like a torrential summer storm. I was the only non-slave human in the palace, with no one to confide in, no one I could fully trust. A deep ache swelled in my stomach over a loss I had never allowed myself to feel. Growing up, I was forced to be alone. I welcomed loneliness because it kept anyone I could potentially care about safe. But did I have to live that way now?

Perhaps the Prince had given me a gift by assigning Meara to me, even if he had done so unknowingly. Could I afford to be friends with her? I swallowed down the unease rising in my throat, knowing it would take a lot of effort to get Meara to open up; be more my friend and less my slave.

If it were even possible.

ꕥ

I had just finished with breakfast, washing up, and dressing when I noticed a piece of paper had been slipped under my door. My bare feet made a soft slapping sound on the marble as I hurried over and picked it up.

I wasn't sure what I was expecting it to be. Perhaps a note from Tarrin, asking me to meet him. Or a note from Meara, apologizing for leaving and wanting to be friends.

I shook my head at myself. I wasn't sure where *that* hopeful thought had come from, but in a life like mine, one couldn't afford such thinking. Knowing where I was, it was probably a summons, the Queen wanting to meet me sooner than our planned dinner. *Would she really have sent a note and not a messenger, though?*

I flipped open the paper and every thought wilted like a dead plant in my mind.

In thick, capital letters it said:

THEY CAN'T PROTECT YOU FROM ME.

There was no signature. Frantically flipping the paper in every direction, I searched for more, needing some explanation. But there was none. Sweat coated my hands, dampening the paper.

I knew this was Eklos. There was no one else who would send me a note like that. My heart pounded, making my eyes throb and head spin. I needed to find Tarrin. Show him the note. He seemed so confident that I was safe here; so confident that they would be able to protect me.

I hated the thought of needing a dragon to keep me safe; of cowering behind one, letting him fight my battles because I was just a weak human.

Except you're not just human. You could learn to defend yourself.

I sighed, shutting down the trail of thought. I wouldn't allow myself to go there.

Shoving the note in my pocket with trembling hands, I yanked on a pair of brand-new boots that put my old ones to shame.

Eklos had haunted me my entire life. I finally escaped him, and yet he still maintained a tight leash of control on me through my fear. Tarrin needed to know that I wasn't safe here. Or anywhere. Eklos would find me.

I knew it in my gut.

I glanced out the window and noticed the Prince's turquoise body in the distance in the center of one of the gardens. I spun on my heel, intending to run all the way out there, to show him Eklos's note.

But instead, I fell to my knees, vomiting onto the marble floor.

CHAPTER EIGHT
TARRIN

I WANDERED THROUGH THE gardens, the sun's rays hammering into my scales as I sniffed flower after flower. This was my place of refuge, the only place in Elysia that offered reprieve, and after last night, I desperately needed it. For hours, pictures and visions intruded my dreams, all playing through the shifter bond I shared with Kaida. I tried to shut out her nightmares but found myself unable to.

I took a seat on the bench near the fountain where only a few days ago I had agreed to my mother's request of tracking down Kaida. Days ago, I never would have believed I would be sitting here, having not only agreed to find her, but *actually* finding her. The shifter I was supposed to marry, now in the palace.

I could see the burning in her eyes when she looked at me. She despised me, wanted nothing more than to leave here, traveling as far away from dragons as she could get.

I wanted to hate her, to look at her with loathing the way she did to me.

But the way her mind was tearing itself apart over this, grappling with the fact that she was a dragon, the thing she hated most in the world… I heard those thoughts. Every single one.

She had no wall, no shield around her mind. Every thought,

every emotion, all the pain and devastation, it was all laid bare through our bond. I tried to block them out, push them away, but they always shoved their way back in, inexplicably strong.

Familiar footsteps echoed at the northern edge of the garden. I had hardly spent more than a day with Kaida and yet I knew the sound of her steps, her scent.

Minutes ago, I felt a sudden flood of panic from her, before her resolve clicked into place to come find me. I wasn't entirely sure what caused the spike in fear down the shifter bond—she somehow managed to keep it hidden—but I assumed it had something to do with her desiring answers about our betrothal while fighting her fear of me.

I had discovered her tells, the small unconscious movements that indicated she was afraid, in a matter of minutes: the way she flinched, her eyes flaring wide almost imperceptibly, how she balled her hands into fists and pressed them into her sides to keep from shaking. It was all subtle, earned from a lifetime of living under Eklos's ownership. But I saw them. After my brief glimpse of what her daily life was like in The Den, I could imagine how difficult it would be for her to overcome that kind of fear.

Yet here she came, her footsteps closer, only seconds away.

Perhaps discovering her dragon form had revealed a boldness that, like her magic, was just beginning to awaken.

Remembering my mother's words to give her a chance, I shifted into human form in an attempt to put Kaida more at ease. With us both now in human form, that bond between us became more muted and muffled. I could still feel her but was unable to pick out the individual feelings or thoughts.

Kaida's feet skidded to a stop as she rounded a rosebush and saw me on the bench. I watched her arrange her face into a blank expression before hesitantly walking toward me. Her hand pressed into the side of her pants, looking like she was checking to make sure whatever she'd put in there remained.

A large fountain sat between us, gray stone lining the outside, and water trickling down in the center from the mouth of a lion statue. Gravel pebbles stretched in a ring around the fountain, with flowers and bushes in another ring around the gravel. Birds flitted back and forth, some stopping to bathe in the fountain, others chirping a happy tune.

When she was halfway to me, she switched direction and stepped up to the fountain, peering into it before perching on the stone edge of it.

I took a deep breath before getting to my feet and approaching. "Beautiful, isn't it?" My voice felt too loud in the peaceful setting of the garden.

Kaida flinched, nearly losing her balance, and I reached out without thinking, gently grabbing her shoulder to keep her from falling into the fountain.

She recoiled, shooting to her feet, and backing away. I remained where I was, my hand still outstretched where it had been on her shoulder. My mouth opened before I mastered my shock, pulling an emotionless mask over my face. My stomach twisted. I would not admit how much it bothered me, her reaction to my touch. I moved my focus to the fields beyond the garden, letting Kaida settle.

Once more, I could sense that flare of fear and panic, though it was duller than before. I narrowed my eyes, trying to read the emotions she was struggling to hide on her face.

"Why are you so afraid right now?" I said, after seconds of tense silence. "I've already told you that I won't hurt you. You have nothing to fear from me."

Kaida's eyes widened, though she refused to look at me. "I'm not afraid." Her wobbling voice gave away the lie, and her throat bobbed as she swallowed. I felt her decide *something* and it frustrated me more than I cared to admit that I couldn't dissect what exactly it was. Her hand patted the sides of her pants again.

"What are you hiding in there?" I asked, nodding to her pocket.

"Nothing," she snapped, turning the full force of those icy blue eyes on me. I refused to find them beautiful, especially when I was trying to find a way out of our betrothal.

"Are you sure about that?" There were noticeable damp spots beneath her palms.

Kaida remained quiet, beginning to wring her hands as she stared into the fountain. I could see the war of words battling behind her eyes. At last, she nodded, and replied, "I'm sure." She smoothed down the fabric of her pocket before leaving it alone, as if she decided to ignore it rather than tell me what was in there.

She turned and started wandering through the flowered paths. I automatically followed, keeping a few steps behind.

"How did you know I was a shape-shifter?" Kaida finally asked, breaking the silence. She stopped to smell a flower before turning halfway toward me.

My eyebrows rose, both at the fact that she was willingly speaking to me, and at the question she chose. Part of me had expected her to start questioning our betrothal, and how to get out of it. Although that was probably more to do with my own hope that she would come up with an excuse to call off the betrothal that I had not thought of yet.

"My mother and father knew your mother many years ago, and knew of your existence, although they were unsure whether or not you would manifest the gifts of *mutator formarum*. They decided to wait until you came of age, to see if your mother would tell you of your identity, but then she was killed." I paused, watching how she would react to talk about her mother. Kaida swallowed hard, continuing to wring her hands, her knuckles a bright red.

I still remembered my mother's reaction when news arrived that Aela had died. Her face had remained expressionless, but through that special shape-shifters bond, I could hear the weeping.

The gut wrenching sobs. It was a sound I would never forget. A sound I never wished to relive.

"After she died, you suddenly disappeared, and no one was able to find you. My mother had nearly given up hope that you were still alive." I dared a glance at her and found her eyes far away.

"When word came that you were back in Vernista... my mother took no chances, insisting that I come find you and bring you here." I paused again, struggling to find the right words. "I fought her... I did not want..." I trailed off, running a hand through my hair, letting out a long breath. "Anyway, I found you. That's all that matters."

I was not sure why I was telling her all of this. She did not need me telling her that she was not wanted, or that I didn't want her here. The hurt flickering in her eyes told me she already knew. I ignored the tang of regret seeping through my body.

Kaida continued on through the garden. "How did you know it was me? The girl you were looking for could have been any number of humans in the village."

I followed her, watching as she kneeled by a rose bush to sniff a freshly bloomed flower. "Ah. Well, shifters have a very specific scent. It is unmistakable. Before younglings come of age and are able to shift, the scent is masked as that magic has not yet been released. While you did not have the full scent, it was still there, *barely*, beneath the surface. Only those who knew to look for it would be able to recognize it. And then there was the whole mental bond thing. Being able to hear your thoughts was a giveaway." I offered a small smile as her cheeks became pink.

Kaida put her face in her hands, her hair falling forward. In the sunlight, I noticed that the simple brown color seemed to come alive, shimmering similarly to her scales.

"I do not understand how this could happen," she started. "I'm human. I always have been. I have never had magic. I never even knew that *mutator formarum* still existed. I thought they were extinct."

"Your mother was—"

"Human. She was human." Kaida's words came out with a bite, leaving no room for argument.

"Then I think it would be safe to assume that your father was a shape-shifter," I said cautiously, feeling her walls rising.

"I don't know who my father is." The words were cold, void of any emotion.

I expected that and shrugged, letting an awkward tension fill the space between us. Running my hand over the stalk of a rose, a sharp thorn bit into the side of my finger and I bit my lip. Human skin was so much more fragile than dragon scales. I watched the blood bubble up before sliding off and hitting the pebbles beneath me. Kaida watched the whole thing with wary eyes.

Feeling the inexplicable need to change the subject, I asked, "How did you sleep last night?"

She threw me an incredulous look. "Fine."

I knew it was a lie. I felt her terror in the middle of the night, had tried my best to shut out the pictures that she unknowingly sent into my mind, felt the calming of her heart and gasping breaths when she finally broke free of the nightmare.

While I was not ashamed of my dragon heritage, I could not help but find Eklos's actions in her nightmare to be despicable. Kaida's fear had been suffocating, smothering all my senses until only that fear remained. Had I grown numb to the way dragons treated humans? In truth, I had never spared them a thought before.

"Why am I here?" she asked, the sudden confidence in her voice making me blink.

"My mother wanted you here, safe." She threw me a skeptical look, as if she were not convinced that she was any safer. "They also wanted you in the palace because we are betrothed. It would ruin things if you were killed." It was an attempt at humor, but Kaida did not smile. Instead, she winced and turned away, her eyes settling on the fields of swaying grass beyond the gardens.

"Why me?" she whispered.

I was not sure if she meant why the Queen wanted her in the palace or why they were betrothed, and since I did not fully understand my mother's reasons, I only answered the latter.

"The race of shifters has dwindled down to its final few. We are amongst a rare breed." I rubbed my neck. "Simply put, we are betrothed because it is necessary to keep the line going." I shrugged. Kaida's eyes widened, her hands trembling at her sides.

I had grown used to the idea over the past week, though I still was not particularly fond of it. This was all new for her, terrifying to her, evidenced by the scent of fear now coating her like a second skin.

Silence filled the air between us, the hummingbirds resuming their flight between flowers, their wings like a soft roar even in my human ears.

"You keep saying I have magic." It wasn't exactly a question, but I could hear the curiosity in her voice.

"Yes. All dragons have it, some more than others."

"Shouldn't I have shown… symptoms?" She struggled to find the right words and I chuckled.

"Magic varies from dragon to dragon, and the type and strength of that magic determines when it manifests. With the increased stress from… Eklos… and the life you were living, it is possible that it stayed dormant longer than normal." I found myself hating the look that crossed her face at the mention of her old Master's name, but I could not bring myself to determine why.

"Magic requires training, however. Once it starts manifesting, it is important to learn to control it or it could destroy you."

Kaida turned to face me, meeting my eyes for the first time since arriving in the garden. "What's yours?"

I smirked, a bright flower suddenly appearing in my hand, with flaming orange petals jutting out almost in spikes, the center swirling in reds and yellows. They looked like little bursts of flames. I never knew how to put the smell into words. If there were a way to combine sugar and smoke into a scent, that would be how the flower smelled.

Kaida's eyes lit up in wonder, the first signs of awe rather than fear.

On a whim, I handed her the flower.

"They are called Flamaria," I explained, as she took it from my hand. "They have many medicinal properties, although the main use for them tends to be as decorations during the Beginnings Festival."

The Beginnings Festival was an annual celebration during the summer that commemorated when the new era of the dragons ruling over the humans began; when they had silenced the humans and took their "rightful" place as rulers of this world. The dragons recognized it as a new era of triumph and supposed victory. Humans were never allowed at the festival. They faced death, or worse, if caught at the celebration.

"So you…" she wiggled her hands in the air, searching for words. "Poof flowers into existence?"

I blinked before a laugh erupted from my mouth, Kaida's cheeks reddening in response.

"I'm a World Weaver. I can manipulate, move, and create physical things; weave the world how I desire."

Truthfully, I had expected more of a reaction from her. Many dragons coveted my ability. Even if I had not been the Prince of Elysia, I would have been a prince in my own right just based upon my magic.

"It is a rare type of magic, strong, but it has its limits. I can only *create* non-living objects. If something already exists, like this flower, I can manipulate it, move it where I desire. Unfortunately, distance effects my ability, so I cannot move an object *anywhere.* But it does come in handy when somebody needs soap and towels." I smirked at her, and her cheeks turned a deeper shade of red.

"It still works in human form then?" Kaida asked, gesturing to the flower.

"With proper training, yes. You could learn to use magic as a human."

"And I suppose *you* are going to train me?" she asked, crossing her arms.

I offered her a half grin and felt an immense satisfaction as she squirmed.

"One thing at a time, Kaida. First, you need to meet my mother and father."

CHAPTER NINE
KAIDA

I COULDN'T DO IT. I couldn't tell Tarrin about Eklos's note.

I fully intended to pull it out of my pocket and hand it to him, let him deal with it, but when I saw him in the garden in human form… I couldn't do it.

Perhaps it was because seeing him in human form made it a little easier to forget he had a beast lurking beneath his skin. Or maybe I just didn't want someone else to fight my battles; my old instincts of taking the full brunt so no one else got hurt kicking in.

Regardless of what the true reasoning was, I didn't show him the note, and now it weighed a thousand pounds in my pocket. I tried to ignore it as I sat in the ridiculously oversized dining room.

Tarrin sat at one end of a long wood table, with me at the other end. The table could have easily fit twenty people. A large spread of food, way too much for the two of us, was neatly laid out across the length of it. Various fruits and cheeses were on a platter closest to me, and roasted meats and vegetables were in the middle.

The Prince and I chewed in silence, avoiding eye contact. His brow furrowed as he bit a large chunk of meat off a chicken bone. Grease coated his full lips and I forced myself to look away.

I nibbled on a piece of cheese as the silence grew uncomfortable. For a moment, I thought maybe I should say something to break the tension that hung between us like a thick cloud. But I was not really interested in getting to know my enemy. My new Master. That's what he was now, and I wanted nothing to do with him. Even if we were both forced into this betrothal, he was still a dragon, and that was something I could not overlook.

I was content to stay silent and let the tension stew in the air, but my mouth had other plans. "Do you like cheese?" The words blurted from my mouth before I could stop them.

His eyes snapped to mine, glaring at first before sitting back in his chair, his face going blank. I thought I saw the corners of his mouth wiggle slightly, but I might have been imagining it.

Prince Tarrin stood up, his chair groaning as it scraped the floor behind him. In four quick strides he arrived at my side. My heart pounded faster with him suddenly so close, and I sat back to look up at him. A chair appeared behind him and he took a seat, only a foot away from me. I could feel the heat emanating off his body, the smell of chicken on his breath. His hair was hanging loose around his face and for a passing moment I had the sudden urge to run my hands through it. Internally scolding myself, I tried to calm my racing heart.

Placing his elbows on the table, he grabbed a chunk of cheese from the platter in front of me and popped it into his mouth, then clasped his hands together beneath his chin and looked at me with a smirk as he chewed.

"I do enjoy cheese." Amusement laced Tarrin's voice. Light flickered in his green eyes, and I forced myself to look away. The Prince cleared his throat.

"Tonight, we will be dining with my mother and father and tomorrow we will begin your training."

My brain stuttered to a stop and searing ice prickled over my skin and into my veins. "Training?"

Tarrin nodded, chewing a piece of bread before speaking. "Magic training. Like I said, you need to learn to control it, or it could become lethal to you."

"What if I don't have magic?"

He looked thoughtful for a moment. "All dragons have magic. It's more of a question of *what* magic and *how much*."

I tore off a large piece of bread, spread some honey butter on it, and shoved it in my mouth to avoid speaking.

I didn't want magic. I didn't want to be a shape-shifter. I wanted nothing to do with Tarrin or the dragons.

Why can't I just be free?

Though it was a useless thought, it made tears fill my eyes. Missing nothing, Tarrin misread my emotion for fear.

"Relax, Kaida. Every youngling goes through magic training. It's nothing to be afraid of." Tarrin tossed the remaining food in his hand back onto the table.

"I have other business that needs attending to," he said, drawing our meal to an abrupt close. "You will find appropriate attire in your bedroom and I will send for Meara to help you dress and make yourself presentable for the King and Queen."

At the mention of Meara, my head snapped up. "I don't need my own slave," I retorted.

Tarrin rolled his eyes. "Nevertheless, she is yours to help with whatever you need and—"

"I do not *want* a slave." I cut him off, immediately wishing I could rake the words back into my mouth. That was the type of tone that would result in punishment. His eyebrows rose and he crossed his arms.

"Well, we do not always get what we want, do we?" Tarrin gave me a knowing look. "She is *yours* whether you like it or not. Show some gratitude for what you have been given."

My mouth dropped open. Show *gratitude* to a dragon? Show gratitude for being given a slave when I was one just yesterday?

When I know what they go through? Show gratitude for making that girl submit to not even a dragon, but a human? Absolutely not. Stupid entitled dragon. I inhaled, about to say as much when he abruptly stood, the chair clattering to the floor behind him.

"Go dress for dinner. I will send for you when it is time," Tarrin growled. He stalked out of the room, the floor quaking under his stomping footsteps as he shifted back into his dragon form.

The muscles in my jaw worked as I stared at the door. My stomach was on fire, the food I just consumed churning violently. How dare he. How dare he suggest that I be grateful to a *dragon.*

How *dare* he suggest that I be accepting of a slave.

Perhaps the thing that bothered me the most was that *he* was accepting of it. He did not appear regretful or repentant, even though half of him was human.

How could I marry someone like that?

As I stomped out of the dining room, and all the way to my bedroom, I decided on the first order that would be addressed at dinner with the King and Queen: I refused to marry their son.

"Good afternoon, miss. His Highness sent for me to assist you in preparing for your dinner," Meara chirped as I opened the door to her smiling face. It was a fake smile, but I appreciated her effort. She trotted over to the armoire and opened the doors. The sound of fabric rustling echoed in the room as she ruffled through the different gowns stuffed inside. After a few heartbeats, Meara pulled out a sapphire blue dress, the bodice tight and fitted with sheer sleeves to the wrists. The skirt was a lightweight material that flitted about in the breeze coming in through the windows, with glittering jewels all over, catching the light and reflecting it onto the walls. She held it up in the air, presenting it to me.

"This will be perfect for this evening." Meara paused, eyebrows furrowing. "Do you like it, miss?"

I struggled to keep my mouth from dropping open in surprise. No one had ever asked for my opinion before, nor had I ever seen such a beautiful piece of clothing in my life. I always wore the same clothes day after day, having to make my own once those wore out. Scraps of cloth roughly sewn together were all that had ever touched my skin.

But this gown... it was like someone had taken the dark blue hues of a sunset, stitched them into a dress that moved like the night breeze, and then placed stars all over it.

The thought of how much it must have cost made my head swim, and the amount of time and labor that a slave must have put into it made my heart ache.

"It's beautiful," I managed, the only words that I could come up with.

A reluctant smile crept across her face, and she carried it over to the bed and laid it flat, undoing the line of buttons down the back of the bodice.

Meara motioned to the chair by the vanity, beckoning me to take a seat. I ambled over and sat down, glancing up in the mirror at her as she stood behind me. She had a simple face, lovely in her own way, and her blonde hair was twisted in a tight bun at the base of her neck. Her skin was fair, indicating that she had not been in the sun for quite some time, and her deep brown eyes were soft as they met mine. A slight smile curved her mouth as she took my hair in one hand, and the brush in the other, and began stroking small sections until they were soft as cotton.

Even when my mother had been alive, she never once brushed my hair. It was pointless, she always said, since my hair was always dirty and matted. I closed my eyes at the sensation, enjoying the calm that was slowly spreading through me. Minutes passed. Hours. I was not sure.

"Are you from Vernista?"

My eyes snapped open, settling on Meara's questioning face

in the mirror. Even the name made my insides coil into twisted knots. Eklos and Vernista went hand in hand in my mind. It was nearly impossible to separate the two, which meant any time the village name was uttered, my body went into survival mode as if Eklos were right behind me.

"Yes," I answered, avoiding the urge to squirm.

Nodding her head, she looked like she wanted to ask more, but held her tongue.

"Why do you ask?"

Meara's fingers stilled in my hair. She avoided meeting my gaze in the mirror. "I didn't recognize you from Zarkuse. When the Prince was gone for only half the day when he left to retrieve you, I put two and two together. Vernista is the only village close enough, aside from Zarkuse." Her fingers began moving again, parting and weaving my hair into sections.

"Do you have any family?" I dared to ask, suddenly wanting more than anything for Meara to be someone I could confide in and befriend. Someone that I didn't have to worry about getting hurt or killed like I had to with Jinna.

The color seeped from her face as she formulated her response.

"I was taken from my parents and younger brother when I was little. The Commander has a knack for separating families." Her mouth twisted in disgust and her hands trembled in my hair. I clenched my own hands tightly in my lap because I understood, probably better than anyone. Eklos was to Vernista what the Commander was to Zarkuse.

"I found my aunt and uncle a few years ago when I was brought here. My brother was with them, fortunately." Meara picked up some pins from the vanity and began pinning pieces of my hair into place.

"And your parents?" I knew I shouldn't pry; it was none of my business. But every slave had a story. And each and every one deserved to be told.

Meara gave a slight shake of her head. "My aunt told me they were caught trying to escape." She paused as her voice grew hoarse before expelling a shaky breath. "They were trying to escape to find me. The Commander broke their bodies into pieces and left them in the town center for the crows."

Nausea swirled in my gut and I closed my eyes, fighting back tears. I had no words left to say. There was no proper response; nothing I could say to help her or take the pain away. I knew from experience with losing my own mother. Silence settled in the air between us. A warm summer breeze drifted in through the open window, the canopy above the bed rising and settling in answer.

Meara finished twisting my hair into loose curls, braiding and pinning the top of my head into a thick crown. She cleared her throat, swallowing down the tears that I saw her fighting to keep at bay, before stepping away to let me look in the mirror.

My jaw dropped as I stared at my reflection. Although still deathly thin, the color had returned to my face and the dark circles beneath my eyes were not quite as pronounced. Meara had painted my cheeks with a slight blush and added a paste to my lips that turned them a rosy pink. The braided crown was soft and elegant, the perfect finishing touch.

"When you're ready, miss."

I looked behind me and saw Meara standing with the dress in her arms. Surprised, I glanced out the window to find the sun setting. I had not realized so much time had passed. I quickly stripped my clothes off, hardly sparing a thought at the fact that I was undressing in front of a stranger. I had lost the embarrassment of being naked long ago.

I stepped into the dress, holding onto her shoulder for balance. The dress should have weighed an absurd amount, but it was as light as could be, gently gliding over my skin. The bodice clung to my body in all the right places, the sleeves just the right length. Meara began clasping the buttons lining my back.

"What should I expect tonight?" I asked her.

"From what I've heard, the King and Queen are quite anxious to meet you," she began. "The Queen in particular. They've had everyone preparing for this meal since you arrived here. You are their guest of honor."

Butterflies sprang to life in my stomach. Guest of honor? But I was human. I fought the urge to run and hide under the duvet.

"How am I to… behave?" I struggled to find the right words.

Meara hummed to herself for a moment while she thought about it. "There is no precedence for this; no human has ever been invited to dinner with the royals." She paused, thoughtful for a moment, then let out a quiet chuckle. "They know who you are and where you came from. I'm sure they already have an idea of what you'll be like. I do not think that anything you say or do would change their mind about all this so just be Kaida. No one, or *nothing,* else."

At a loss for words, I nodded my head, her fingers finishing the last of the buttons.

"There, all finished."

I turned to face her, keeping my back to the mirror, knowing I would lose my nerve and refuse to leave the room if I saw my reflection.

"You look lovely," she said as she stepped to the door and opened it.

I offered her a small smile and made to step out the door right as someone arrived on the other side. We both stopped mid-step and stared at each other.

Tarrin's eyes were wide, brows raised as he looked at me, my face most likely the mirror of his. His thick hair had been tied back, and he wore a formal green jacket and pants that matched his eyes, with different insignias and crests on each shoulder. He stood stick straight, hands clasped behind his back.

My heart pitter-pattered in my chest and I scolded myself

internally, hoping that the Prince's hearing was not as strong in human form. I fought and kicked at the words that kept popping up like weeds in my mind. *He looks handsome.*

Meara cleared her throat delicately. The Prince blinked, schooling his face back to that stoic, emotionless beast I had come to expect from him, and offered me an elbow.

"Shall we?"

After hesitating for a moment, I stepped forward, placing my hand on his arm. Tarrin took a deep breath, and I wished desperately that I knew how to read *his* thoughts for once, as he led me, arm in arm, through the palace to meet his parents.

CHAPTER TEN
KAIDA

I COULDN'T BREATHE.

The Prince and I were steps away from entering the massive doors that led to the dining room. I was mere steps away from meeting his parents, the King and Queen of Elysia.

My breath came in frantic, shallow gasps, and black stars swam in my vision.

"Kaida," Tarrin murmured, most likely feeling my distress. I squeezed his bicep harder, needing an anchor. I refused to note that the significant muscles beneath his jacket flexed at my touch. "Kaida, relax. It's just dinner."

I glanced up at him, but he wouldn't meet my eyes. It seemed like he avoided looking at me the moment we left my bedroom. *Why?*

"Easy for you to say," I said beneath my breath, but of course he heard me.

Finally, his eyes met mine as we paused outside the doors. *Something* flickered in them and I felt a very faint pulse through our shifter bond, but I was too nervous to try to pick apart what any of it could be.

"Kaida, they invited you here. For some unexplainable reason, they *want* you here. There's no reason to be nervous for a dinner."

I blew out a breath, choosing to let his comment roll off me instead of feeling insulted. His rudeness only added fuel to the fire in my gut and added further proof of why I would not marry the Prince of Elysia.

The absurdity of the whole situation hit me like being slapped by Eklos. I was a lowly slave, worth nothing, and yet the King and Queen chose me to marry their son. They chose me to carry on the shifter line and be the next Queen. The idea was so ridiculous that I burst out laughing right as Tarrin opened the doors.

It swung back on its hinges to reveal two magnificent dragons near the far windows. Both towered above their surroundings, the one to the left a sparkling turquoise, the other a burning ruby red. Each had their enormous wings tucked tightly against their back. They wore no crowns or sashes, nothing to indicate their royal status. If I had seen them outside of the palace, I wouldn't have guessed they were the King and Queen.

At the sound of my laughter, both dragons turned around.

Instinct took over and my head bowed, eyes pinning to the floor as they approached. While the temperature of the room was fairly mild, sweat pooled in the small of my back. I found myself wishing Meara had done something else to my hair, the weight suddenly feeling unbearable and too warm. My heart thumped in time with their rumbling footsteps. I held my breath as they came to a stop in front of us.

"Mother, Father, this is Kaida," Tarrin said, giving me a small nudge, but it ended up being more of a push and I was forced to take a step forward to keep my balance. Though I knew better, my eyes snapped to the dragons before me. I met the King's eyes first before squeezing my eyes shut. I looked directly at the King of Elysia. I knew punishment was swiftly coming. I braced myself, but the room remained silent. They stood like statues, and I felt their gazes examining every part of me.

"Welcome, Kaida. We have waited many years to meet you,"

the female dragon suddenly said, before her body started morphing out of the corner of my eyes. Red scales flickered into fair skin, and long brown hair erupted from the top of her head, settling on her shoulders. A formal gown, tight in the bodice and voluminous on the bottom, adorned her, the same color as her scales. A small tiara with sapphires and emeralds was nestled in her hair.

When the shift was complete, Tarrin's mother closed the distance between us and fully embraced me in a hug. My jaw hung open, my brain slowing to the speed of a snail trying to understand why the Queen of Elysia was *hugging* me.

I was literally dumbfounded. I was a slave. A fragile human that had been tortured and abused. Yet here I stood, in the palace with the Royal Family, the Queen holding me in an embrace. By Elysia's standards, they should have hated my very essence. They should have forced me to kiss the floor under their feet and worship them, tend to their every desire. That was what all dragons in Elysia did.

I saw Tarrin aggressively rub the bridge of his nose as if he were irritated by his mother's actions.

The King cleared his throat.

"Let us eat then," he declared, his voice tense. His footsteps rumbled as he went to an enormous chair at the head of the table, with cutouts in the back of it that I assumed were for his wings. Tarrin's mother stayed in her human form and took a seat on the King's right, in a normal sized wooden chair. I couldn't help but wondering, if dragons found themselves so superior, why she chose to stay in human form rather than shifting back.

The Prince took a seat to the left of his father, pointedly ignoring me when I hesitated to follow. The Queen looked at me and smiled. "Come, sit." She gestured at the chair next to Tarrin's. I swallowed the thick lump of anxiety in my throat before walking on tiptoes over to my chair. Food was stacked up in the middle of the table so high that I could barely see over it.

Hunger roared in my stomach, but I couldn't shake my nerves enough to put anything on my plate. Tarrin didn't seem to have any reservations and was eagerly devouring the roasted chicken on his plate. I wondered if he could feel my nerves crackling in the air like lightning.

"Tarrin, do not be rude to our guest. Put some food on her plate. She's far too thin as it is," the Queen snapped. I bit my lip and noticed, with no small satisfaction, that a pink tint rose on Tarrin's cheeks. With an aggravated sigh, the Prince began to roughly scoop vegetables and potatoes onto my plate, ignoring the scattering of peas that fell to the floor.

When he finished, he scowled down at me. Though I knew I would most likely be punished for it, I scowled right back. Tarrin's eyebrows shot up his forehead. A snort sounded from across the table.

The Queen's lips were clamped together as if holding in a laugh. There was a faint flicker of amusement in her eyes as she watched the two of us. The King simply ignored us and continued to stuff food into his snout. Every so often, he would send a small flame from his mouth to heat up his food, and the room started to smell of smoked meat and ash.

"What do you think of the palace, Kaida? Are the accommodations to your liking?" Tarrin's mother asked.

I blinked. "Yes, Your Majesty—"

"Please, call me Lita."

The King choked on his food and launched into a coughing fit. The look both he and Tarrin gave her spoke volumes about their disapproval. She offered a soft smile and a nod, ignoring the males in the room.

"Very well, Your Maj… Lita," I said, drawing the words out. "The palace is beautiful, and my room is more than I could have hoped for."

She seemed pleased with my response and continued to dig

into her food. Although she attempted to be graceful with a fork and knife, she ate quickly, eating large amounts at once, hardly pausing between bites. It appeared like she was trying to act human, but her beast side held too much sway over her actions.

Our meal continued in silence, creating an awkward tension in the air. My body ached with the stress of trying to sit still, and every time I shifted in my chair, it creaked and groaned, setting my nerves on edge.

"How did you know about me?" I blurted.

The King leaned back in his chair and fixed his gaze on me. Though I knew it was a foolish move, I met his eyes, channeling my mother's strength and bravery.

"We have known of your existence since your mother carried you in her womb," he began, the low bass of his voice causing the dishes on the table to rumble quietly. "Aela told us about you but was unsure if you would inherit certain... traits."

I struggled to maintain a stoic face at the mention of my mother's name. "How did you know my mother?"

Tarrin's parents exchanged glances before his mother cleared her throat.

"There is much for you to learn, Kaida, many stories to tell you." She paused, taking a heartbeat to gather and organize her thoughts. "Your mother was a close friend of mine, a long time ago, before you were born. It was before Martik and I came into power, and well before Tarrin was born."

I saw Tarrin glance at me out of the corner of my eye before he sat back in his chair, arms crossed.

"I'm not sure how much she told you when you were a child, Kaida, but she escaped her previous Master before you were born. She never told me how she did it." Lita looked thoughtful for a moment. "After she escaped, we ran into each other in the tunnels beneath the city. I was in human form when we met; she didn't realize I was a shifter."

Tarrin's chair creaked as he shifted and learned forward, as if this story greatly interested him.

"When she discovered what I really was, she was terrified. Aela thought I was going to turn her in. Instead, I took pity on her and the state she was in. Martik and I hid her in my village, kept her safe."

My eyebrows rose as I glanced at the King. I never would have imagined a dragon to offer help to a fugitive slave.

He simply shrugged. "Just because I'm a dragon doesn't mean I'm heartless."

I internally shook my head. *Yes, that's exactly what it means to be a dragon.* Cruel. Heartless. Merciless. Ruthless. The words were all synonymous with dragon.

"Your mother met another shape-shifter in my village, and they fell in love. She left to live with him in Vernista. We didn't hear from them again until one day when Aela came back to us. She was pregnant and the father of the child was gone." Lita swallowed, studying my face to gauge my reaction. It took great effort, but I kept a blank face, unwilling to let them know how much this story was ripping apart my insides.

"Martik and I had been married less than a year and I was six months pregnant with Tarrin. We were next in line for the throne, and my father had grown ill, days away from leaving this world." His mother paused, taking a sip from the pewter mug in front of her.

"She had nowhere else to go, so we took her in again… until Eklos found her." Queen Lita grew quiet, and her shoulders slumped in response to whatever memory she was recalling.

"Your mother went into the village to find supplies one day, after you were born. She was the only slave walking around without a slave crest. And Eklos… Well, he was infuriated by the sight. Before she even had time to react, he captured her, slapping a crest around her arm in the process. The rest…" she trailed off, gesturing to Kaida.

"Why didn't you try to help her? Save her?" Tremors shook my voice.

Tarrin slammed his fork onto the table. "What could they have done? Why should they have risked their lives for your human mother?" he growled. My mouth fell open at the anger in his voice.

Somehow Tarrin's mother managed to utter a fierce growl in response, even in human form. Smoke started billowing from the King's nostrils.

"That is *enough*, Tarrin."

Tarrin glared at his parents, his back stiffening as he crossed his arms.

Silence reigned for several tense heartbeats. Glancing out the windows, I watched as the sun set beneath the horizon, the night dew beginning to form on the leaves and bushes in the garden, sparkling from the mingling light of the setting sun and rising moon.

I placed my palms on the table and looked at the King and Queen. "You know who my father is?"

Lita hesitantly met my eyes, as if she didn't want to have that conversation now. My heart pounded in my ears as I waited for her answer. She opened her mouth to respond, but a voice interrupted her.

"*That* is a story for another time," the King snapped, causing everyone to flinch, fixing a hard look at his wife. Abruptly, he stood, chair scraping back against the floor. Without another word, he stalked out of the room.

The sudden movement combined with his anger had every survival instinct in my body roaring to life. My shoulders hunched to my ears and I slid down in my chair as far as possible without falling off. I could feel my pulse pounding in my neck. Squeezing my eyes shut, I started counting my breaths, trying to calm my body.

A callused finger brushed the back of my hand and I automatically flinched away.

"Kaida, you're fine," Tarrin said at the same moment his mother said, "You are safe."

"Martik meant no offense. I believe your question caught him off guard," Queen Lita hesitated before letting out a loud exhale. "My husband and your father had a complicated relationship." Without elaborating further, she stood, the food on the table instantly disappearing. Tarrin's mother looked at me with a sad, apologetic face.

"I assure you, dear, you are safe here. No harm will come to you while you are inside this palace, with us. With Tarrin." She fixed him with a pointed look.

Without another word, she strode out of the room, simultaneously transforming back into her dragon form. Ruby lights flashed on the walls and ceilings just as she disappeared through the door.

With a long exhale, I pulled myself up, straightening in my chair. *Why would the King have such a strong reaction to the mention of my father? Were they friends at one point? Or perhaps enemies?*

I swallowed down the tears that were building, calling on that empty, numb feeling that had helped me survive this long. I let out a quiet breath of relief as that familiar nothingness spread over me.

"Would you like an escort to your room?" Tarrin's voice was quiet, as if he was afraid to reopen my emotions after I had just shut them down. That shape-shifter bond between us seemed to be both a blessing and a curse.

"Not from you," I replied, completely void of emotion.

As if he had silently called her, Meara appeared in the doorway, her face grim.

"Meara will see you to your room then."

I watched out of the corner of my eye as Tarrin left the room, shifting into his turquoise scales in a dull flash of blue. Meara appeared at my side, gently taking my arm and helping me to my feet.

"Come, miss. Let's get you settled."

She led me through several back hallways through the palace, and to my bedroom, my mind spinning the entire time. Surprisingly, it wasn't replaying Lita's story of my mother, or that they knew who my father was. No, it was stuck on the fact that I never got to tell them I refused to marry their son.

CHAPTER ELEVEN

TARRIN

SHE LOOKED BEAUTIFUL.

I kept denying it to myself, but I couldn't stop picturing Kaida's face, transformed from death to radiance by whatever the slave girl Meara had done. It had been distracting enough that I could barely meet her eyes over dinner, and now it clouded my mind, as I flew over the palace grounds.

I had never found a human attractive before.

I kept scolding myself, wishing I could slap some sense into my brain. I didn't want to find her attractive. I didn't want this sudden desire to see her or to spend time with her. I did not want to marry the girl, dragon or not. And the fact that I could not stop looking at her was only confusing my determination to get out of the betrothal.

I needed to get out of the palace, to clear my mind and put some space between us, so I took off into the sky the moment I left dinner. It didn't matter that the place was enormous. It was still too close to Kaida. Countless stars filled the night sky above me, the earth seeming darker than usual with the new moon.

The cooler, damp air of night, as pleasant as inhaling water, slid over my scales. I had hoped it would soothe the fire in my core and calm these racing thoughts, but I realized I had flown nearly all the way back to Vernista without any relief. Letting out a sigh, I landed in a grove of trees on the outskirts of the village. A small pond sat nearby which I glided to, before crouching down on all fours for a drink. It still did nothing to soothe the flame inside.

What is happening to me?

Out of habit, I reached for that bond that kept me continuously connected to Kaida. Distance affected the strength of it, but it seemed I was still too close to the palace for I could feel her emotions. It was like a ticking clock hidden under a blanket. It was faint, but you could hear it.

Mercifully though, all was quiet. She must have been asleep.

I bent my knees, intending to take off again, when I heard the voices.

"Hurry! The Master is waiting," a voice barked somewhere in the trees behind me.

I heard a low growl before another voice spoke. "We are the Remnant. The *Master* can wait for *us.*"

A chill prickled beneath my scales like being caught in a winter storm in Baywood Forest. *The Remnant? As in… the Remnant of the Lone Dragon?*

Their footsteps grew closer, and I frantically looked around for a place to hide. I couldn't take to the sky without the risk of being seen. It would make it easier to remain hidden in my human body, but then the dragons would be more likely to catch my scent. I caught a glimpse of dark green scales through the trees.

I was out of time. Tucking my wings in tight, I pulled myself up into an enormous tree, eternally grateful that the trees in this area were easily larger than any dragon. I situated myself on a branch that faced away from them, begging the branches to hold my weight and not make a sound. Their voices creeped closer, and I held my breath.

"What's he upset about this time?" one of the dragons asked.

A cackling laugh echoed between the trees. "Someone stole his property. Took his slave away right in front of all the dragon folk.

He's furious, and rightfully so. He said it was one of them *Royals*." The way he spit the word made my stomach drop.

"Does the Master truly think he can stand against them and win?"

"I suppose we're about to find out. I am guessing that's why he called this meeting in the first place. Leave it to the heir of Xalerion to make the Remnant do his dirty work."

The other dragon scoffed. "Why should we risk our necks for his wounded pride? Seems like a poor decision to cross the Royals. We need to keep the bigger picture in my mind. Exterminating the humans has nothing to do with them."

My mind felt like a whirlpool swirling faster and farther down into a pit. I couldn't keep up. *Are they talking about me taking Kaida away from Eklos? Who is Xalerion? Exterminating the humans?*

They walked past the tree I was hiding in and I willed myself to be invisible. If either dragon were to look behind them, they would see me. They continued forward, discussing vague plans that my already confused mind couldn't make sense of. They were just about to disappear between the next set of trees when one of them came to a halt. His snout twitched.

Oh no.

"What is it?" the other dragon snapped, clearly annoyed at being delayed.

The dark green dragon kept sniffing, his head swaying side to side. I knew it was mere seconds until he discovered me. If I didn't move, he would look behind and see me. I curled my claws around the branch I was standing on while reaching up to grab the one above. With a silent exhale, I jumped and pulled myself up before grabbing hold of the trunk, then used my wings to glide around the other side of the tree. I snapped my wings in again just as I heard the dragons' bodies shift.

"Thought I smelled something." I felt the green dragon's eyes searching the trees.

"There's nothing out here but the Remnant. Let's go."

A low growl rumbled in the dragon's mouth, but he turned away. The sounds of their steps slowly faded before I heard a chorus of deep rumbles and growls. The Remnant's meeting place was close by, which meant I needed to leave immediately.

What did all this mean? Was Eklos planning retaliation for me taking Kaida away? Was the Remnant planning a way to rid Elysia of the human population? My questions were endless, rolling over each other and compounding by the minute. I needed to get back to the palace.

A deep, eerie feeling washed over me as I pushed off the branch I was perched on and took to the skies. I pictured Kaida having to defend herself against these dragons and knew she didn't stand a chance. I let out a frustrated breath as I soared through the sky toward home. Training her would be a nightmare and I didn't even know how much time we had before they made their move. *If* they made a move.

CHAPTER TWELVE
KAIDA

I AWOKE THE NEXT morning to Meara's face hovering inches above mine.

"Good morning, miss!" she chirped. Groaning, I rolled over onto my stomach, covering my head with a pillow. A quiet chuckle sounded just before sunlight burst through the room as she flung the curtains wide.

"It's time for breakfast," Meara announced, throwing open the wardrobe and rummaging around inside.

"I'm not hungry." I pressed the pillow down harder onto my face to block an ounce of light from reaching me.

"You have been requested in the garden to have breakfast with the Queen."

My heart slammed to a stop, then stuttered as it began to beat overtime. Nerves danced along my body as I threw the pillow halfway across the room and struggled to escape the mountain of blankets piled on top of me. I heard Meara chuckle before she helped to untangle the heaviest duvet from my legs. I let out a yelp as I fell to the floor. My palms and knees stung, but I did not spare it a second thought as I ran into the bathing room to wash up.

When I scurried back into the room, Meara had a pristine purple tunic and pressed white pants with wide legs laid out for me. Most likely sensing my inner panic, she calmly helped me dress, and I once again appreciated her choice in clothing. It was the perfect outfit for summertime in Elysia: loose, lightweight, and flowing. Finally dressed, I paused long enough to smooth down my hair in the mirror before leaping for the door.

The door swung open, and I barely managed to dig my heels into the floor before walking right into the Queen. Mercifully, she was in her human form, wearing a stunning midnight blue gown. Her brown hair fell in silky waves over her shoulders, the same tiara from dinner the night before nestled in her hair.

"Oh! I'm sorry, Your Majesty!" I scrambled backward, and the Queen raised her eyebrows. Her earlier request echoed in my head.

"Lita, I mean," I amended, and she smiled. "I thought I was to meet you in the garden?"

"I thought I could walk with you. I would like to show you my favorite spot." The smile that lit her face was like seeing the sunshine after days of rain.

She led me to the staircase, my legs wobbling with each step. Warm light drifted in through the windows, bathing the foyer in a bright light, making the emerald-green walls burst with color.

Lita opened the front doors, and the sunlight grew blinding, a wall of summer heat crashing into me, stealing the breath from my lungs. Sweat formed in tiny droplets on my forehead. The Queen glided down the steps, her movements smooth and graceful, my clumsy footsteps loud in comparison as I followed. She led me in what felt like circles, rounding corners, and squeezing through bushes before we came to an iron bench with swirling flowers. Queen Lita took a seat, her gaze reaching out to the fields and mountains in the distance. She patted the seat next to her.

"Come sit with me, Kaida," the Queen summoned.

Perching on the edge of the bench next to her, I folded my hands in my lap, my back straight as a rod. Next to her was a small table piled high with fried eggs, fruits, and smoked meats.

A servant appeared the moment we sat down, his brown uniform perfectly clean, and filled two plates with generous portions and handed it to each of us.

"Thank you, Halvor," Lita said, dismissing him. She sat there for several minutes, picking at her food, her lips pressed in a tight line.

"Kaida, I would like to apologize to you, on behalf of my husband and myself."

I blinked, my eyes widening.

"F-for what?"

"For many things, but to start, I am sorry that we did not protect your mother. That we did not protect you." Tears sprang to life in her eyes, and her throat bobbed as she swallowed.

"I knew that day, when your mother went into the village to get supplies, that she should not have gone. Call it woman's intuition, a premonition, whatever you prefer. I knew I should not have let her go. At the very least, I should have sent Martik with her, especially when I knew she was bringing you along." The Queen folded her hands in her lap, wringing them, as her head dropped.

"Your mother was a wild spirit. Nothing I said would have stopped her..." she trailed off, her voice overcome with emotion.

"I do not have many regrets in my life, Kaida, but this is one of them. Your mother's death, and your enslavement were entirely my fault. I watched from afar how Eklos treated her. How he treated his other slaves. It broke my heart, but still I did nothing." My brow furrowed and Lita opened her mouth as if to continue her rant, burrowing herself deeper into her hole of self-pity, when I interrupted.

"With all due respect, Your Majesty, my mother made her choice. She *chose* to go to the village that day, with me. She *chose* to take that risk, knowing what could happen. She *chose* to try to escape Eklos seven years ago, to leave me, knowing the consequences if she were caught. She *chose* the paths that would end in her death, and my enslavement." My voice grew louder, the nervous shake disappearing with every word. "You condone slavery. You allow it to happen. Why are you feeling guilty now?"

Tears spilled over onto the Queen's cheeks, leaving wet trails down her face before plummeting and landing on her now stilled hands. She remained silent, her lips clamped together, chin trembling trying to keep the emotions locked tight.

"I have always felt that slavery is wrong. How could I agree with it when I am half human myself?" She paused, taking a shuddering breath. "The Lone Dragon was a terrible beast for inciting such loathing amongst dragon kind. I remember the stories my father used to tell me when I was a child. I remember the nightmares that came afterward." She tucked a stray piece of hair behind her ear. "I am not oblivious or ignorant to the terrible things the humans go through."

"And still you have done nothing to help us," I retorted. Empathy did nothing to help a slave. In some ways it only made it worse. And the Queen had remained stagnant, watching from a safe distance for too long.

At the heart of it all, she was a dragon.

I thought of saying as much but was interrupted by the sound of Lita blowing her nose into a handkerchief.

"Back then, I was a in a precarious position," she said in between sniffles. "I am the first female dragon to inherit the throne in Elysia's history. The male dragons did not agree with my ruling when I first came to power. It would have been disastrous to have fanned the flames by creating laws to ban slavery." She dabbed at her eyes.

"You've had nineteen years to do something," I said softly. No matter what she said, I still had a distrust for dragons. Her tears, even if they were genuine, did nothing but stoke my anger. I didn't want her apology, I wanted her to *do* something.

"Kaida, you don't understand—"

"No, Your Majesty, you don't understand. You may be half human, but you've never been a slave. You've done nothing to help us and that tells me all I need to know."

Her mouth opened and closed like a fish. I stared out at the scenery, unable to meet her gaze. The valley in front of me stretched as far as I could see. There were sheep grazing in some areas and stalks of corn stood tall in others. Mountains littered the landscape far in the distance, storm clouds ominously spread over the tops, like a smothering blanket.

I felt the Queen's weight shift on the bench, and she cleared her throat. "I understand why you would be angry with me, which is why I'm trying to make amends. With you marrying Tarrin—"

I couldn't hold back the laugh that bubbled up my throat. "I'm not marrying your son."

Truthfully, I expected more of a reaction from her, but she remained silent, her eyes studying the approaching storm. Part of me wanted her to argue with me, while another part of me just wanted her to hold me. The longing for a mother hit me at odd times, and I swallowed the lump in my throat.

"Kaida," her voice was quiet like the trickle of the fountain. "I know you don't understand right now, but I'm doing this not only for your own good, but for all humans in Elysia. Tarrin has agreed to this, and you will marry my son by summer's end."

I had no words left to say. I knew it was unlikely that they would accept my refusal to marry Tarrin, but my mind hadn't imagined actually going through with a wedding.

The storm clouds had moved closer, far closer than I would have thought possible. Lightning flashed in long streaks through the tops of the mountainous clouds, the heavy rain visible on the horizon.

"Those storms will be heading this way," Lita said, nodding toward it, as if she knew where my thoughts had been. Remembering that shape-shifters could project their thoughts onto others, I turned to her with questioning eyes.

"How does it work? The 'reading my mind' thing?"

The Queen smirked. "I cannot read your mind, Kaida. When you are in an extreme emotional state, your thoughts may present themselves to me. It is sort of like you are yelling at me, only in your mind."

Heat bloomed on my cheeks. "But how does it work?"

"Shape-shifters all share a special bond, different and unique from any other type of dragon. That bond allows us to speak and communicate with each other with our thoughts. It is not known exactly how it came to be, but it can be quite useful. Tarrin can teach you how to block others from hearing your thoughts as you practice shifting."

A snort came out of my nose before I could stop it. I made no effort to hide the skepticism on my face.

"Give him time, dear. This is as much of an adjustment for him as it is for you."

I suppressed another snort.

"With all due respect, Your Majesty, I have to disagree. Your son knew he was a shape-shifter his entire life. He's had years to practice and master his abilities. He was able to grow up peacefully and well taken care of. *I* just learned of this a few days ago. I have been raised to loathe the dragon race and then I find out I am part of it. Not only that, but I supposedly can shift whenever I feel like it and have these supposed magical abilities, neither of which are working. And your *son* has been less than helpful in all of this. *And* I am supposed to marry him too, a beast that I despise. Forgive me, but no. It is not as much of an adjustment for him."

Lita looked away and glanced out at the storm clouds that were nearly upon us now. Thunder rumbled in the distance and lightning spider-webbed through the tops of the clouds.

When she met my eyes again, all sadness and regret from our earlier conversation had disappeared, and she fixed me with a hard look.

"Give him time," she said as she rose from the bench, offering her hand to me. I didn't take it. With a sigh and a nod toward the palace, she said, "Let's head inside, Kaida. The approaching storm promises to be a violent one."

CHAPTER THIRTEEN

KAIDA

"THIS IS A waste of time."

Prince Tarrin rolled his eyes at me for the fifth time.

Not long after my breakfast with the Queen, Meara found me saying that it was time for my first training lesson with the Prince. She brought me to an odd room, with a bare black floor. The room was massive, with a thirty-foot cavernous ceiling, keeping it comfortable for even the tallest dragon. There was nothing else in the room, aside from a short bench that lined the back wall, and a small counter with a wash basin in the corner. The few windows that lined the very top of the walls were covered in fireproof drapes. "Just in case," Meara had said with a wink before shutting me in.

Thankfully, Prince Tarrin had chosen to arrive in his human form. It would have been impossible to make any progress with a giant dragon hovering over me. Although even with him as a human, I still managed to make zero progress shifting.

I didn't shift once. I couldn't even manage turning my fingers into claws.

Tarrin was no help, and only stood there with his arms crossed, not offering any advice or direction, smirking when I asked him what to do.

"Just try again."

"We have been at this for hours," I said, wishing I could stomp my foot in a tantrum like a child. "Is this some kind of punishment? Or a joke? What's the point of this?" I asked, hands on my hips.

He went still, an unknown emotion flashing in his eyes.

When he said nothing, my patience snapped, and I stomped toward the door. If he wasn't going to be helpful, or even talk to me, then I wouldn't participate in this 'training.'

The Prince was instantly at my side, gripping my shoulders, holding me in place. "Kaida, stop."

"Look, I know you don't want to marry me, but I am *not* the one you should be punishing," I scolded, surprised at myself for being so bold.

He winced. "Please, stop. I'm not punishing you." Yanking his hands away from me like my skin had burned him, he ran his hands through his hair. "We'll move on to something else."

"What else is there? I am a *shape-shifter*. I thought learning to shift was the whole point."

"Your magic," Tarrin said simply. I scoffed.

"I don't have any magic."

He rolled his eyes. "A normal dragon's magic will typically manifest as a child. Shape-shifters will not begin manifesting their magical abilities until they have shifted for the first time. But again, that is usually as a child. Since you are a... late bloomer, it might be more challenging to summon it. Especially since you have no idea what your abilities are at this point."

I spit on the ground next to me, showing him what I thought of him and his training.

"Very ladylike," he drawled.

"Maybe next time I will spit on you." The retort left my mouth before I could stop it and my eyes went wide. I had the mental picture of grabbing the words with my hands and scooping them back into my mouth.

The corners of his mouth twitched. "I would like to see you try."

I considered it for a half a second until he took a step back, crossing his arms.

"Try to summon something. Anything," he said, changing the subject.

I glared at the floor.

"You will not think it is a waste of time if you face Eklos again and you are unable to shift or use magic to defend yourself. Or if you do not learn to control it and you end up depleting your reserves and kill yourself."

A shiver tingled over my skin. Did he know about the note Eklos left under my door? I gave him a wary look. "Why would I need to defend myself against Eklos? You said I was safe here."

Tarrin fidgeted with his hands. "You are."

I narrowed my eyes, studying his face. Beads of sweat sat on his temples like condensation.

"What aren't you telling me?" I dared to ask.

He turned away from me, making it impossible to see his reaction. "Nothing, Kaida. You're safe here, as I said. It's just always a good idea to be able to defend yourself." Tarrin spun on his heel to face me, his face carefully blank. I couldn't escape the feeling that he was hiding something from me.

"Plus, if you do not train and build up your endurance, it is quite easy to pull on too much magic, draining yourself too quickly. It should be like a slow burn, a candle wick that slowly gets smaller and smaller, rather than a burst of fire doused by water. If you draw upon your supply all at once, especially without training, it will kill you."

"Great," I said, feeling defeated. I ran my hand over my sweat damp hair, smoothing it down.

"Try closing your eyes," he offered. "Picture the magic as a tiny spark somewhere in your body. A tiny flame that has not been kindled into a fire yet. Find it. Pull on it. Let it fill your body. Release it into something physical."

"Well, that sounds easy," I retorted.

"Try."

Closing my eyes, I took a deep breath and tried to focus.

My lungs expanded as I inhaled, my brows furrowing as I searched within my body. At first, I felt nothing, cold blankness covering every inch and my teeth ground together with each unsuccessful moment that passed.

"Breathe," Tarrin whispered.

Exhaling, I moved my focus from my mind to my torso. My breath caught in my throat when something small finally came into focus. It was only the size of a kernel of corn or a small flower seed. It was a dark orange color, almost invisible amongst the frigid black that surrounded it.

"Good," the Prince said, somehow knowing I had found something. "Now send your energy into it. Make it bigger."

I let out a sigh but held tight to that spark.

Without moving, I pictured myself grabbing it with my hands and pushing on it, then pulling, like the ebb and flow of water. Seconds felt like hours as I waited for something to happen. I was about to give up when the spark suddenly flared and then bloomed, petal-like flames unfolding and growing bigger. It was no longer a burned orange color but was now bright as a flame with blues and purples flickering in and out.

It soared through my body. Every inch where that cold blank feeling had been, was now on fire. It coursed and surged through every vein, every muscle. I opened my eyes just as I thought I was going to be sick from the intensity of it, and fire burst from my hands toward the Prince.

Tarrin turned sideways, easily sidestepping my flames. He gave me a smug smile.

"See? Magic."

I scowled at him even though I felt flutters of excitement running through my veins. I had magic. Me, a human. I fought the urge to giggle.

"Try again. Now that you've filled your body with the energy, try to pool it in your palms this time."

I nodded, closing my eyes. I was somewhat expecting to find that flame extinguished and to have to begin my search all over again. Instead, it sat ready and waiting in my core, pulsing in time with my heartbeat.

"How do I put it in my palms?" I poked at the flame, pushed at it, but it remained unmoving.

"Try this," Tarrin said, his voice suddenly next to my ear. His fingers gently curled around my wrists. Lightning zinged up my arms at the contact. "Breathe in and picture a hole in each of your hands. As you breathe out, it empties, breathe in, and it fills to the brim."

I tried to focus long enough to do as he said, but his fingers were still around my wrists, sending jolts up my arms. As if sensing my distraction, he let go, but stayed close behind me.

"Raw magic is wild," Tarrin whispered in my ear, sending chills over my skin. "Untrained, it will go where it wills, uncontained. That's why you have to train it; learn how to command it and channel it. Once you do that, it will answer to *your* will instead of its own."

Whether it was that revelation or his close proximity that was making my heart go wild, I felt a sudden heat in my palms. I opened my eyes to find white flames dancing in each of them.

"Good," he remarked and stepped away from me. My body immediately ached for him to come back. A glass of water appeared in his hand and he offered it to me.

"Your shifting is actually a form of magic," he explained as I drank. "It's drawn from the same place you just felt that flame come from. Now that you've found it, perhaps shifting will be easier."

I handed the glass back to him. "I won't hold my breath."

A small sound escaped through Tarrin's lips. *Was that a laugh? Did Tarrin just laugh at something I said?*

Before I could examine it further, a servant appeared in the doorway drawing the Prince's attention. He half-ran, half-walked over to Tarrin and whispered something in his ear. Tarrin's face went from amused, to annoyed, and finally landed on disdain. His hands balled into fists.

"I will be there in a moment," he said quietly to the servant who then bowed deeply and scurried off the way he had come.

"What was that about?" I asked, curiosity getting the better of me.

"I think that is enough for today," the Prince said, ignoring my question. "We will continue working tomorrow. Meara will escort you back to your room."

Sure enough, Meara appeared in the doorway as soon as he said her name and offered me a small towel to wipe the sweat from my face. I gave her a grateful smile. Without another word, Tarrin stalked from the room, shifting into dragon form simultaneously.

"How was training, miss?" Meara asked, drawing my attention away from the Prince.

I blew out a breath. "I'm a human who just found out I'm half dragon, and supposedly have magical abilities I never knew existed. How do you think it went?"

Meara chuckled quietly. "It will get better," she replied, surprising me when she patted my arm in reassurance.

I offered a smile. "I hope so."

CHAPTER FOURTEEN
TARRIN

THE EIGHT MEMBERS of the King's Council all sat around a long wooden table in the Great Hall, my father at the head. Instead of vibrant colors, the Council dragons were all made up of muted colors: shades of brown, dark green, and pasty blue. None in the room were shape-shifters, save for myself. Each ranged in noble status and had assumed the role of advisor to my parents. My mother loathed these meetings and, ever since I was a youngling, my father had attended them on her behalf.

I sat to the right of my father, clawed hands clenched into balls, nearly piercing through the armor-like scales that covered my palms.

"Your Majesty, something needs to be done about the rebellion in Absult. The slaves cannot remain unpunished, or it could further encourage an uprising," said Councilman Barden, steaming saliva shooting from his mouth.

The other dragons echoed his assessment, many nodding in approval.

I cleared my throat. "And what exactly happened in Absult?" I had lost track of time in my training session with Kaida, and arrived at the meeting late, missing the explanation.

Councilman Barden's eyes snapped to mine, a sneer prying open his lips. "You would know, Prince, if you had been punctual."

Fire churned in my stomach and I fought to keep the smoke from leaking out of my snout, unwilling to let Barden know how much he had gotten under my skin. I avoided the urge to look at my father. I didn't need him to defend me, even if the dragon's tone was completely unacceptable when speaking to a member of the Royal Family.

"I'm waiting for an answer, Councilman." I refused to let his arrogance get under my scales. I held his gaze, ignoring the shifty looks the other Council members gave to each other. I had never felt that these dragons were trustworthy, and the more years that passed, the more they proved it.

Smoke swirled out of Barden's nostrils. "The slaves in the mines started an uprising a few days ago. A group of men banded together and attacked two of the Masters before setting off explosives in the mines. Now there are two injured dragons, no resources coming out of the mine, and an abundance of worthless slaves who committed an atrocious act."

My stomach did a backflip and, for some reason, the first thing that came to mind was Kaida and what she would think. I shook my head to expel the thought. It did not matter. *I don't care.*

"Did they give an explanation for their actions?" I asked, the hatred in Barden's eyes causing chills to prickle under my scales.

"An explanation does not matter!" Barden's voice boomed, echoing in the room. "They are humans who thought they could defeat us. They must be punished."

"I agree, Your Majesty," Councilman Roldan spoke up, ignoring me and focusing his attention on my father. His brown wings were folded in tight to his back, his claws leaving gouge marks on the wood in front of him. "The human filth needs to be reminded that we are their rulers. They need to be reminded of what happens when they rebel." Roldan's eyes flashed, darkening with the implied threat. Murmurs of agreement from the other Councilmen floated up to the ceiling.

I wished I could cover my ears and escape from the room. I always hated these meetings. The Council were ruthless and cunning. Why my parents had picked these eight dragons to be on the Council, I would never understand, especially when my mother and I were shape-shifters. The dragons around the table held a strong disgust for both humans and shifters alike.

Much to the disdain of the dragons, I had not grown up being instilled with an intense dislike for the human race, though I was not particularly fond of them. Even though I was half human, I found my dragon form far superior in every way. Even so, I couldn't help but think that the Council often took it too far.

My father never shared with me why he put up with these dragons. We used to be close when I was a youngling, but in the last couple of years, my father had grown distant, shutting me out entirely. He acted more like the King of Elysia rather than my father.

"What exactly are you proposing?" King Martik's deep voice rumbled through the Hall, his gaze piercing into Roldan and Barden.

All eight dragons exchanged glances with one another. None spoke. Several heartbeats passed in silence. The dark green dragon at the end of the table shifted and cleared his throat.

"We are suggesting that you send a small company of dragons to deal with the rebellious slaves. Squash their hope before more gather and we end up with an even bigger problem on our claws." He paused and glanced to the other dragons before continuing. "We recommend the fire chamber."

It took all my strength to keep my mouth from dropping to the floor.

"No," I said under my breath, hands trembling in my lap. While I had never seen a fire chamber, I had learned about them from my many tutors, and had seen paintings of them in old books from the initial uprising a thousand years ago.

The fire chamber was an underground room with no windows or doors, made of an unforgiving steel. The dragons would gather the humans in the room, shut them in, and let loose a steady stream of fire. It was one of the most excruciating ways to die: being burned alive.

My stomach churned violently. My thoughts went to Kaida again, picturing her face among those in the chamber. I squeezed my eyes shut, banishing the image from my mind.

"No," I said, louder this time. Every dragon ignored me, their eyes boring into the King. I half expected my father to shut the suggestion down, knowing he wasn't a cruel beast. I needed him to look at me, to see the pleading in my eyes for him to tell them no, but he stubbornly avoided my gaze. I knew that my father valued the Council's opinion far too much. Looking at the hard set of his eyes, and his snout turned down into a scowl, I knew that even if he heard my plea, he wouldn't have listened anyway.

He sat very still in his seat, his wings rising and falling behind him with every breath he took. An eerie silence took control of the room and I struggled to breathe beneath its weight.

In past Council meetings, I sat quietly, ignoring the dragons and whatever punishments they deemed acceptable. It was not until recently that I really started to question the Council's actions and opinions. It was not until I started seeing my mother in human form more often than as a dragon. It was not until I met *her.*

Kaida.

Kaida had gotten under my skin, far deeper than I cared to admit. She drove me mad with that look she often gave me that completely dissected my insides, with the way she had begun to outwardly question me, and question how we do things.

But her intense fervor for life, the way she viewed everything and cared for everyone around her… I had been taught to see humans a certain way through dragon culture, but between her and my own mother, I was starting to question everything I had ever believed.

"Father, don't do this. Punish them if you must, but not like this." A chorus of low growls echoed across the table as the dragons of the Council let their disapproval of my outburst be known. My father still would not meet my gaze.

The energy shifted in the room as he sat forward. My claws dug in like daggers in my clenched fists. A heartbeat passed. Two.

"So be it," the King said, void of emotion.

I closed my eyes, the air instantly sucked from my lungs as the death sentence for countless slaves was set in motion.

CHAPTER FIFTEEN

KAIDA

I WALKED TOWARD THE training room with a lightness that could only be described as walking on a cloud. Even though I had spent hours trying to shift into a beast, and had failed miserably, I had discovered something far greater.

Magic. *My* magic.

It was utterly mine and could not be taken from me. It was a way to defend myself. Something I had never had before. While I was not entirely ready to accept my dragon half, the fact that I was not just a weak human had its appeal.

I approached the training room, boots clunking on the floor. I came to a stop outside the entrance, hand resting on the doorknob, when a muffled thud sounded through the door. A loud grunt echoed followed by another thud.

Cracking it open, I peered in, one eye pressed into the opening.

Prince Tarrin stood across the room, fully human, dressed in black. There was a large burlap-covered bag suspended from the ceiling in front of him. Sweat glistened on his forehead and his hair had fallen from its leather band, leaving sweat-drenched strands sticking to his forehead and neck. The back of his shirt was soaked.

Splotches of red, cracked skin covered his knuckles, blood smeared in thick lines across the back of his hands. I swallowed hard, nerves prickling like needles across my body. This was the first time I had seen Tarrin display any kind of violence and my hands instantly grew clammy. Heart hammering in my chest, my hair stuck to the sweat sliding down my neck. There was a loud roar in my ears, and I struggled to keep black spots from my line of vision. All the conditioned responses I learned from years of slavery took control of my body. While I knew that Tarrin was a dragon, seeing him mostly as a human coupled with the fact that he hadn't been abusive or cruel like every dragon I had ever known, somehow made it easier to forget.

Had I been a fool? Other than telling me I was safe in the palace, the Prince had never given me proof that he would not hurt me. How did I know if his word remained true when he was in an aggressive state of mind?

But part of me, though it felt stupid, wanted to trust him. To trust that he would not lift a finger against me. And a larger part of me wanted to know what was wrong, what was making him pound on that bag like his life depended on it.

I held my breath as I stepped into the room. "Tarrin?" I called.

Prince Tarrin did not respond and kept up his assault on the bag.

Punch. One. One-two. Kick. Repeat.

"Your Highness?" I tried, and he continued punching. Though every instinct that had kept me alive for seventeen years roared inside of me, I crept on my toes toward the Prince. I made it all the way across the room, close enough to touch his shoulder, when he suddenly stiffened and swung around to face me. His body coiled into a defensive position as if I were about to attack him.

Dark circles rimmed his bloodshot eyes, slightly red and swollen.

I studied his face, trying to find that rare gentleness I had glimpsed a few times, but I saw nothing but hatred. "I'm sorry, I didn't mean to interrupt." I took a step backward. The violence flickering in his eyes reminded me of Eklos and made my stomach lurch into my throat.

I turned to leave, needing to be far away from anything remotely resembling Eklos, when a warm hand wrapped around my wrist.

"Wait." Tarrin's voice was hoarse. He didn't release my arm, and it took several more seconds for his eyes, which had turned the color of the bottom of the sea, to lighten. He let out a long, shaky breath.

"I was finished anyway," he rasped, letting his hands fall by his side. He headed toward a counter in the corner of the room with various medical supplies. Washing the blood off his hands in the wash basin, a little too roughly, he dried them and wrapped them with a wad of gauze.

What had happened to make him react so violently? His emotions rippled down his body and in the air between us, but I couldn't pinpoint exactly what they were. Realizing that I had been staring at his sweat-sodden back for far too long, I tiptoed across to the bench near the wall. When I was younger, and Eklos was in a foul mood, I found myself being extra careful to stay silent around him for fear of bringing down his wrath. I couldn't help those instincts from kicking in once more.

Desperate for anything to keep my eyes and hands busy, I bent over and began untying and tying my boots. Out of the corner of my eye I saw him turn in my direction and saunter over. That cold distant look had returned to his face though any trace of that previous fury was gone.

"Let's get to work," Tarrin snapped, walking to the other side of the training room, stopping in the middle of the cold, black floor. He fixed me with a glare and crossed his arms.

"Shift."

I put my hands on my hips. "I can't."

"Shift. Now."

My stomach writhed like a captured animal. Tarrin was normally in a grumpy mood, but this went beyond anything I had seen from him. He knew that I was not able to, that I had no idea how.

Knowing that there were only two options here—stand here glaring at him, or attempt to shift again—I took a deep breath in through my nose and closed my eyes, trying to find that inner flame that fueled my magic. It was easier to find it this time, and it unfurled in a beautiful bright orange flower of flame in my core.

I tried to will the shift into taking place by picturing the change. I imagined amethyst scales flickering over my skin, claws erupting from my fingers. I imagined my face elongating into a snout, hair disappearing from my head as if it had never existed. I imagined my vision suddenly clearer, as it had been that first day by the river when Tarrin had taken me from The Den.

A sudden peace spread through my body as I released a breath. Without even opening my eyes, I knew that I had done it. I had finally shifted. I felt a cry of relief ready to escape from my lips, and I tried to ignore the fact that I felt relief over shifting into a dragon. *I just wanted to prove to myself that I could do it. I'm not actually happy that I turned into a dragon.*

Holding my breath, I opened my eyes and looked down.

My stomach dropped.

I was still completely and utterly human.

ஃ

Silence reigned in my body for several moments before ravaging heat shredded through my body, seizing my muscles, a fiery bile rising in my throat. *How could I fail again? I* felt *the change this time.*

Some primal instinct ripped away my self-control and I came unhinged. A piercing scream erupted from my mouth, my entire body shaking. Balling my hands into fists, I stomped my foot onto the ground out of pure frustration and felt the black floor shake and crack.

As I stomped again, the fire in my core exploded and blue flames burst from my mouth, shooting into the air causing the room to smell of smoke and ash. Flames continued to shoot out of me as if a never-ending vat of oil had been poured into my stomach. For a moment I thought the fire would consume me, burning, ripping, and destroying my body from the inside out, but I remained cool to the touch. I could feel the intense heat of the fire in my throat and mouth, but it did not burn.

Deep, scorching breaths tore through my throat, sparks of fire bursting out.

I noticed Tarrin shift out of the corner of my eye which snapped me out of my daze. I clamped my lips together, shutting off the flames, silencing my screams which had turned into deafening roars. I glanced down and found myself finally covered in amethyst scales, claws piercing through the scales covering my hands.

Yes! Finally! I smiled to myself, the sensation strange with a snout. *I finally proved to both of us that I could shift, and now I won't ever have to prove it again. I can just be human Kaida and never a dragon ever again!*

Because that's really why I was elated. I would never be grateful to have turned into a dragon, but the fact that I now had the option had its merits. I didn't *want* to be half dragon, but the idea that I *could* shift if I absolutely needed to, say to defend myself against another dragon or survive a night in the cold of Baywood Forest, was powerful to me. I had always been under the dragons' control, always subject to whatever torture they deemed worthy that day. But now I had the choice to stop it if I wanted to. I had the option to shift, or the option to stay human. I wasn't forced into one or the other, and the beast inside me didn't have control to take over my body either.

That's why I couldn't wipe the smile from my snout. For the first time in my life, I had a choice. I let out a breath of relief and glanced over at Tarrin on the other side of the room. His usually bright turquoise scales had darkened somehow, as if his mood affected the shade of blue. His eyes were wide, and I could see the whites of them from where I stood. But what really caught my attention was the emotion written all over his face through the lingering smoke drifting between us. On the surface there was shock and perhaps awe, but beneath that mask was absolute terror.

Like a candle being blown out, the wrath swirling in my gut vanished. It went out in a whoosh of air, my stomach cool and empty. Scales flickered away, flashing purple lights on the walls, and in seconds I was back in my frail human body.

The look on Tarrin's face gutted me. I could have easily hurt him without meaning to. I was one step closer to being a wrathful dragon, and the thought made me double over, dry heaving. My cheeks grew hot, eyes filling with tears, and my chin trembled at the effort it took to hold them at bay.

I suddenly did not want my magic. I did not want to hurt anyone.

Any confusion over being half dragon, and having magical abilities, was gone.

I was human. That was all I wanted to be.

My arms hung limply at my sides, and exhaustion swept over me, black spots crowding my vision. I vaguely heard boots clapping on the ground before an arm snaked around my waist and another behind my knees. The room spun as my body went weightless. I blinked and found myself sitting on a bench by the wall, and Prince Tarrin placing a glass of water in my hand, back in human form.

"Drink," he ordered.

I gulped down the entire glass, the burning in my throat smothered and soothed by the cool liquid.

"What just happened?" I whispered, my voice hoarse from screaming, as Tarrin took a seat next to me.

"I believe that's what they call a dragon tantrum," he replied, rubbing at his face.

I snorted. "I don't think I've ever thrown one of those in my life."

"Dragons tend to be more temperamental." Tarrin wouldn't meet my eyes, but I could hear the amusement in his voice. "Emotions are heightened as a dragon. As a new shifter that hasn't entirely gained control of your abilities yet, your emotions often dictate what your dragon half does. If you are angry as a human, in dragon form it turns into a rage so deep and unending that it's hard to stop." He leaned his back against the cold stone wall behind us and leveled me with a stare. "I'm surprised you were able to gain back control and not only stop, but shift back. It took me years to gain that level of control."

Heat swarmed my cheeks, and I planted my gaze on the black floor.

"How'd you do it?" he asked.

I swallowed and shrugged. "I don't know. I saw your face. I realized I could have hurt you and that reminded me too much of Eklos. I didn't want to be like that. So, I stopped."

I risked a glance at the Prince and found his eyes lit up. "I don't think there's a dragon in all of Elysia that could stop their rage tantrum simply because they didn't want to hurt anyone."

I looked him square in the eye. "I don't want to be a beast." For I had realized that there is a difference. Between Tarrin and his mother, it was clear that perhaps not all dragons were terrible. Some were capable of kindness, even if my life as a slave contradicted it. But then there was the beast inside the dragons that turned them into horrid, abusive, terrifying beings who relished in the agony of humans.

That's what I didn't want.

Tarrin's eyes were like a whirlpool of blue, sucking me into their depths as he studied my face. "For a human, you are surprisingly smart."

I scoffed, unsure whether to take that as a compliment or an insult. "For a dragon, you're not entirely stupid," I retorted. A small smile twisted the corners of his lips.

His bloodied knuckles caught my eye and I nodded toward them. "What happened, Tarrin?"

And just like that, the light in his eyes died. The color drained from his face as he dropped his head into his hands, releasing a slow ragged breath.

"There was some sort of rebellion amongst the slaves in Absult." He paused, swallowing back whatever emotion was threatening to spill out. "The slaves have been sentenced to the fire chamber."

A roaring filled my ears, and I clenched my shaking hands into fists.

The fire chamber. A preternatural calm spread over my bones.

All those slaves. Their lives ended, just like that.

My heart ached, and I struggled to breathe.

"I tried to stop it; tried to stop my father from siding with his Council…" the Prince faltered, and tears lined his eyelids. It was the most emotion I had seen from him. "His Council has too much influence over his decisions. He places them so high on a pedestal that he cannot see reason."

Tarrin's head hit the wall with a thump. The mounting tears disappeared as his hands balled into fists. "I am not king, so the weight is not mine to bear. But I cannot help but feeling like I have failed every single one of those people. Perhaps they deserved punishment, but never… never like that."

The irony that the dragon Prince of Elysia felt like he failed the humans was not lost on me. I took a deep breath before saying, "Perhaps if they had not been tormented, denied their own free wills, they would have had the chance to choose a different path.

People without hope choose desperate actions and you blame them as though they did it only to upset you." I tried to keep my voice gentle, surprising myself by not wanting to make him feel worse.

Tarrin blinked, fresh tears filling his eyes, his chin trembling with the effort of holding them in. I had thought, coming into the palace, that the entire Royal Family would loathe humans since they continued to allow the enslavement, torture, and murder of them. But it seemed Prince Tarrin had a conscience. He had sympathy and compassion for human slaves, even if it was deeply buried.

Maybe I had been wrong. Traitorous tears filled my eyes as he looked up and I met his gaze. For a heartbeat, I was hit with the desire to grab his hand. As if he had sensed my intention, he jolted up from the bench and began pacing. Rubbing at his chin, his brows furrowed in thought.

"Tarrin?" I asked, concern flaring in my body.

"Kaida, did you ever hear… Eklos," he stumbled over his name, "talk about the Remnant?"

Any sadness, grief, or concern that was in my brain jumped in a frigid lake and drowned. "The R-Remnant?" I stuttered, trembling as if my whole body had fallen in the freezing waters of my mind.

He nodded before blowing out an exasperated breath and kneeled in front of me. "I need to tell you something. I think they're planning something. And I think this rebellion in Absult is only the start of it."

CHAPTER SIXTEEN
KAIDA

TARRIN WALKED ME back to my chambers, a strange tension swirling in the air between us. He stood much closer to me than he ever had before, our hands brushing against each other multiple times, sending a shock through my system. He refused to tell me whatever it was that he needed to tell me until we were back in my chambers where we couldn't be overheard.

The familiar lion carving on my door came into sight and we both lengthened our strides to get inside faster. Opening the door for me, Tarrin waved me in before swinging inside and shutting the door behind him.

"What is it?" I demanded, hands on my hips. "What do you mean you think the Remnant is planning something?"

Tarrin plopped down his tall frame in an oversized armchair next to the hearth. There was already a small fire blazing away, despite the summer heat outside. Sweat beaded on my forehead.

"I overheard some dragons talking in the forest just outside Vernista." He scratched at his scalp. "They didn't know I was there."

I sat down on the ugly gray couch across from him. "What did they say?"

His green eyes pierced into mine. "They were talking about

how one of the Royals stole their Master's property. They mentioned doing his dirty work. Sounded like they were planning some sort of retaliation."

"You think they were talking about you rescuing me?"

Tarrin snorted. "Who else would they have been talking about, Kaida? There's no other royal family, and I'm the only one to rescue a slave in recent history."

My blood thickened like curdled milk. "If all that is true, does that make Eklos the leader of the Remnant?"

"I can think of no other explanation for what I heard."

I rubbed my hands over my face. This must have been why Eklos left me that note when I first arrived here. He was already planning for the Remnant to retaliate on his behalf. I should have known Eklos would not let the slight stand; I should have shown Tarrin the note immediately. We could have been preparing this whole time. My magic training suddenly felt immensely important.

"What's that?" Tarrin asked, pointing to the white slip of parchment on the table, breaking through my stampeding thoughts. A deep pit opened up in my stomach. It was the note from Eklos. I had meant to burn it, or at least hide it better, but between breakfast with the Queen and training with the Prince, I never got around to it.

"Um," was all I managed to stay before he stomped across the room and snatched it up. I watched as his eyes ran over the seven words I had memorized, sliding back and forth as if he were rereading it over and over.

"What is this?" Tarrin asked, voice morphing into the deep dominance of the Prince.

"It's a note."

His voice was shaking now. "A note from whom?"

When I didn't respond, he marched over to me, grabbed my shoulders, and pulled me to my feet. "Is this from Eklos? How long have you had this?"

I couldn't look him in the eye. "I found it under the door the day I arrived here."

If it were possible for smoke to slither from his nostrils in human form, I had a feeling it would, judging by how his face twisted in anger. Tarrin clamped his lips tightly together, his fingers pressed into my arms. He pushed against me, slowly guiding me toward the wall. "How can I keep you safe if you don't tell me about things like this?" His hands landed against the ivory wallpaper on either side of me, pinning me in place, and he hung his head. "What if he had gotten to you, and I never even knew there was a threat?" Tarrin's voice broke on the last word.

I didn't understand the emotion in the air between us. I knew he didn't like me, but even with our shifter bond muted in human form, I could feel he had a strong need to keep me safe.

Lifting his head, his green eyes met mine. Heat rolled off his body in waves, his face only inches from mine. I watched his pupils widen and he licked his lips, his eyes flicking to my own. My heart pounded in my chest as his hot breath whispered across my cheeks. I couldn't hold back a flinch as he lifted a hand toward my face, but instead of hitting me as my internal conditioning expected, he tucked my hair gently behind my ear. He glanced at my lips again. *Does he want to… kiss me?*

As if the thought broke the spell, Tarrin released my shoulders and stumbled backward. He wouldn't look at me, and somehow that stung worse than him being angry at me for withholding the note from him.

"Tarrin—"

"I need to go," he whispered, flinging himself toward the door as if he couldn't stand to be in my presence for another moment.

Tarrin did not show up for training the next day.

Or the day after that.

On the third day, still the training room remained dark and empty. No sign of the Prince. I had not seen him at meals or anywhere around the palace. Was Tarrin really so angry at me that he would abandon my training with the threat of Eklos looming over us? Surely, if he wanted to protect me so badly, he would have prioritized my training and not left me alone for three days.

Even his mother hadn't called on me. Maybe Lita was angered by my outburst in the garden a few days ago and had decided she no longer wanted me around. Maybe Tarrin had decided I wasn't worth the effort; that the Remnant was too big a threat to protect me from. My mind swirled in all the maybes and what-ifs, sending me into a tailspin of despair. Knowing Eklos and the Remnant were plotting something was ticking on my nerves like a clock counting down. I jumped at every noise, peeked around corners before I walked through the hallways, and had taken to eating entirely in my room. Meara attempted conversation once or twice, but no longer tried after my one-and-two-word replies.

But what scratched and clawed beneath my skin even more than any of that was the rising disappointment at not seeing Tarrin every day. It was stupid. I had no claim to him. Just because we were betrothed didn't mean I had actual feelings for him, right?

We were in this… whatever it was… together. We were both shape-shifters. We were supposed to be married at summer's end, even though neither of us wanted it. We had to navigate our own abilities and being both human and dragon together. And now we had the threat of the Remnant creeping at our backs. More than anyone, he would know how I was feeling.

That was all the disappointment was, or that was what I told myself anyway.

I sauntered out of the training room, making my way back through the palace. Warm summer sunlight pierced through the hallways, heating them to an unbearable level. The farther I walked, the more I found myself annoyed at the fact that Tarrin had been absent for several days.

He had made it seem like my training was of the utmost importance, especially with talk of Eklos retaliating. Why would he leave me alone for three days, abandoning my lessons? I knew the situation with Absult and the fire chamber had affected him, and then Eklos's note just added to his stress, but to disappear for days on end, shutting me out entirely… I blew out a long breath. As much as I didn't want to admit it, we needed each other.

I meandered through the hallways for a while, sticking close to the windows that stretched to the ceiling. Rays of light illuminated the halls, painting rainbows on the floors. My fingers weaved through the fabric of the tapestry closest to me. It was made of a beautiful turquoise thread, interwoven with rows of amethyst and emerald. It held my attention, and the longer I studied it, the more it seemed the lines of color were moving, wavering up and down, intermingling, creating new colors, and then settling back into their original places.

I rubbed my eyes, sure that it was some sort of illusion. Sweat beaded on my neck, hair sticking to my skin. Perhaps I was overheating, my eyes playing tricks on me. I scrunched my sleeves up higher and continued, intending to return to my chambers.

I peeked around the next two corners, starting to feel silly. These hallways were empty. Surely, no one would attack me here. My shoulders loosened a fraction until I rounded the next corner and stopped dead in my tracks. A short distance down the velvet lined hall sat two chairs near a window, Prince Tarrin occupying one of them. One leg crossed over the other, he sat reading a book, brows furrowed in concentration.

Suddenly feeling like I was intruding on a private moment, I slowly stepped backward, meaning to disappear down the way I had come. I made it only two steps when Tarrin's head jerked up, his eyes meeting mine, eyebrows shooting up his forehead.

"Kaida?" My name was a whisper on his lips, his body frozen in the chair.

Shoulders slumping, feeling like a kid who had been caught stealing candy, I winced, taking another step back. "I-I'm sorry, I got lost." I turned to run the other direction.

"Wait," he said, jerking to his feet and dropping the book in the chair.

My tongue felt like it weighed a hundred pounds, unwilling to move, to speak.

"H-how are you?" Tarrin stuttered out awkwardly. A confusing emotion swirled in the air between us through our shifter bond, causing my head to spin. It almost felt like he was happy to see me. But that could not be the case. He had made it clear on multiple occasions that he did not want me here.

"Where have you been?" I said, in a forceful tone that I had never used with him, ignoring his question.

He winced, arms hanging loose at his sides. "I had something important to take care of."

"For three days?"

Tarrin tucked his hands into his pockets and nodded.

"I thought my training was important."

"It was. It is." Tarrin's eyes turned pleading. "Kaida, I wouldn't have left you, putting your magic training on hold, without a good reason."

I bit my tongue to hold the words back that tried to claw their way from my mouth. "What was so important?"

Tarrin just blew out a long breath and shook his head. "Just trust me, Kaida."

My stomach churned, my teeth gritting together, and I took another step back. "Trust you, Your Highness? *Trust you*?" I couldn't believe he would even say those words. Dragons had lied to me, abused me, tortured me, and used me every moment of my life. The Prince may be half human, but his heart was fully dragon, and that meant I could not trust him, no matter what he said.

I knew he could hear everything I was thinking. His eyes, pained and apologetic, told me as much. But I did not care. And I did not want to hear his excuses. I backed farther down the hallway, and he tried to follow. I shook my head, and he froze mid-step.

"I will never trust you." I ignored the way his face fell as if I had wounded him and turned on my heel so he wouldn't see the unreasonable tears filling my eyes. Just when I thought we were taking a step forward, perhaps building some sort of friendship, leave it to a dragon to drag us ten steps back.

CHAPTER SEVENTEEN
TARRIN

THE EXPRESSION ON Kaida's face cut through my stomach like a stab wound. Hours had passed since she found me in the hallway, and I still had not been able to shake it off. I knew I should not have left her alone for the past three days. Her training was vital, especially if the Remnant was planning to strike, and she desperately needed to build her strength. If she didn't master her ability to shift or have a store of magic built up, there was only so much I could do to protect her if they came for her.

But what I did over the last three days was something that my own conscience deemed more important, more valuable. At least at that moment. After I left Kaida in her chambers, I took to the skies, remaining high above the clouds until night fell as I flew toward Absult.

I arrived in the dead of night, and soundlessly snuck into the chamber those slaves were being held in, and one by one flew them to a boat that was bound for Myrewell in the south. It had taken hours, the first lights of dawn just peeking their heads over the horizon when I had dropped the last human onto the ship.

428.

There had been 428 slaves in that room.

They had been terrified when I arrived, many of them losing control of their bowels at the sight of me, expecting me to be their executioner.

None of them ever knew I was the Prince of Elysia. They didn't need to.

All that mattered was that they would live to see another day. A better day.

It took me nearly a day to fly back to the palace, then another day in bed recovering. More than anything, I wanted to tell Kaida what I had done. I wanted to share in the victory of it, the sweet justice that the Council's plans had been ruined. If I was being honest with myself, I wanted her to be proud of me; to not see a cruel beast when she looked at me, but someone she might be happy to be with.

But when she found me, I could not bring myself to tell her. I was not sure why.

There would be backlash. I knew that the dragons would think another human had orchestrated their escape. No one would ever expect a dragon to have helped them. Maybe that was why I couldn't bring myself to tell her. Whatever happened now would be entirely my fault. I might have saved 428 slaves only to cause the deaths of countless more.

My thoughts were like a rampant plague in my mind that I couldn't escape. I wandered for what felt like hours and found myself deep beneath the palace, in a musty, cold hallway. There were endless tunnels running beneath the palace with countless rooms and crevices in which to hide. When I was a youngling, I would hide down there from my tutors, only coming out when my mother would inevitably find me. I never understood how she did it, especially with the maze-like configuration of the tunnels, but she always knew exactly where to find me. I let out a quiet chuckle at the memory.

Embracing the smallness of my human body compared to my

dragon form, I took advantage of the stealth of my quieter feet as I wandered the maze of halls. The chill bit into my skin, my breath clouding in front of me as I wandered farther and found myself in an unfamiliar part of the tunnels. Wet streaks were smeared on the stone walls as if there were running water filtering down from above.

A faint yell followed by a muffled scream sounded in the distance and I froze mid-step. My ears strained as I tried to hear where it was coming from, but the only sound was water dripping in a puddle a few feet away. After a minute of silence, I started to think I had imagined it when an unmistakable dragon roar echoed back and forth amongst the stone walls, much closer than was comfortable.

Spinning on my heel, I begged my feet to stay silent as I half-walked, half-ran back the way I had come. I turned corner after corner before throwing myself against a wall to listen. My pulse pounded in my ears like the hammering of a freshly forged sword, which made it impossible to concentrate. I forced myself to inhale slowly, trying to calm my racing heart.

The sound of pebbles skittering over stone sounded before the rumble of footsteps. Whatever was down in the tunnels was still there and far too close. I took off running, unwilling to risk finding out who the source of it was. The hallways were endless, one leading to two which led to three or four. It was a maze and I had wandered too far into unfamiliar territory. I could still hear the low growls and footsteps nearby and I knew I needed to find a place to hide.

Turning another corner, hoping to find my way back to the stairwell, I encountered a deep crack in one of the walls, a faint light shining through. *That's strange. I don't remember there being any hidden rooms in these tunnels.*

I pressed my ear to the wall, listening for any sounds, but it was silent. Sticking my fingers in the crack, I took turns pushing and pulling to no avail. The wall didn't budge. I peered through the crack, hoping to get a glimpse of the room beyond, but all I could see was the flickering light of a torch hanging on the wall.

Knowing it was useless, I tried to pry it open one more time, bracing my feet apart. As I went to pull, my knee knocked against the wall, simultaneously pushing in a piece of the hidden door. With a faint rumble, the door unlocked and tilted open.

My heart hammered in my chest as I guided it open the rest of the way. I flung myself inside and shut the door just as another growl sounded even closer than before, perhaps only one hallway away. Pressing myself against the door, I prayed that whoever the dragon in the tunnels was, would pass by and ignore whatever fear-filled scent my human body may have left behind as I ran. I tried to count my heartbeats to distract myself, but they pounded too fast.

Who would be wandering these tunnels in the first place? Other than countless rooms filled with heirlooms and other useless junk, there was nothing else down here.

Except the dungeon.

A shiver racked through my body. If that dragon had come from the dungeon, I was enormously thankful I had found a place to hide before they found me. Everything went silent on the other side of the door, but I didn't leave right away, just in case they had caught my scent and were waiting for me to come out.

I glanced around the room for the first time and noticed that it appeared to be an old, abandoned office. An empty bookshelf was built into the wall on the right side of the room, and a small desk stood in the middle. A thick layer of dust coated every surface except the desk, where large papers were strewn about haphazardly.

I carefully shuffled through them and realized that someone must have left them there recently; they looked to be freshly written on, without any sign of dust or yellowing. Ink was smeared in one of the corners. It took a moment, but clarity snapped into place.

They were blueprints of the palace.

They covered the layout of every level, including the catacombs beneath the palace. Every door, every tunnel, every way in and out of this place was drawn on them, including this room.

A creeping feeling inched along my spine.

Why would someone have these? Who has been in this room?

My pulse pounding in my ears, I picked up one of the blueprints and examined it closer, looking for any clues. I was about to move onto the next sheet of paper when I caught a glimpse of the back side, where a small note was scribbled:

Meet. 4 a.m.

Meet *whom?*

Questions rattled around in my brain. The meeting was still hours away, but if someone was hiding out in here, I was certain that I did not want to be here when they returned. I only wanted to get out, back up to the main level of the palace where it was warm and bright.

I slipped out the door, careful to leave everything as I had found it, and breathed a sigh of relief when I finally found the stairwell that led up to the foyer.

Scratching footsteps echoed down the stone hallway from behind me. My heart pounding like an army of horses, I skipped up the steps two by two, not wanting to see whoever stalked the darkness of those passages. I released the breath I had been holding as I arrived in the warm lobby of the palace, back in the light of day.

CHAPTER EIGHTEEN
KAIDA

A LIGHT TAPPING NOISE interrupted my dreams, forcing my heavy eyelids to open. I blinked, trying to adjust to the lingering darkness. Glancing toward the drapes covering the windows in my bedroom, no signs of dawn peeked through the cracks. It was still the middle of the night. Had I dreamed the noise?

I rolled over, curling deeper into the blankets when the tapping noise sounded again. Stifling a groan, I scooted off the bed and grabbed a green silk robe to cover my lacy nightgown and wrapped it around me as I tiptoed through my chambers.

"Who's there?" I murmured through the door.

"It's me," a male voice whispered back.

"I do not believe I know someone by the name of me," I retorted.

"Open the door, Kaida," Tarrin demanded, not responding to my sarcasm.

With a sigh, I pulled it open, and Prince Tarrin stood in the hallway, dressed in black, his hair unbound, gentle waves framing his face. His body was tense, one arm raised above his head to rest on the doorway. My cheeks grew warm as his eyes roved down my body, and he took a step back.

"I need to show you something."

I crossed my arms. "What is it?"

He shook his head. "I found something earlier, and I need to show you." Tarrin gestured for me to follow him.

I debated slamming my door shut and staying in my chambers, but my curiosity got the better of me, burning away the lingering anger I felt toward him for abandoning me the past few days.

Down, down, down he led me, staircase after staircase. Cobwebs littered the hallways, growing in size and intricacy the deeper we went, and the temperature dropped steadily, my breath billowing in front of me. The freezing stone floor bit into my bare feet.

I pulled my robe tighter, wishing that I had worn something more substantial.

"What are we *doing* here?" I whispered, the sound echoing off the stone walls.

"Shh!"

"Tarrin—"

He cut me off with a look. "I've been thinking about that conversation I overheard between those Remnant dragons," Tarrin whispered, then blew out a breath. "I found a room down here yesterday. The doorway was hidden as if someone didn't want it to be found. I managed to get inside, and I found blueprints of the palace along with a note for a meeting that was supposed to take place."

We came to a stop in a narrow hall, just wide enough for us to stand shoulder to shoulder. It was a dead end.

"The more I've thought about it, the more it makes sense. The Remnant is planning something, and they've already found a way into the palace. They've been meeting here." Tarrin gestured to the wall next to us. There was nothing there but rough stone.

"I see nothing," I deadpanned.

He bent over and pressed his fingers into an indent in the wall by his knees and a faint click sounded before the door lifted open.

I studied the door, contemplating his words. "How would they get in here? Isn't this place supposed to be impenetrable?"

"These tunnels are endless, and they're so twisted and long, that perhaps there are areas none of us have explored yet. It's not hard to imagine one or more of these leading to a door somewhere else."

I folded my robe in tighter, the chill penetrating my skin, not entirely from the cold hall. "So, you think the Remnant found a hidden entrance to the Palace, and has been meeting here in secret all this time?" I tried to keep the skepticism from my voice, but by the look on his face, I knew I failed.

"I know how it sounds, Kaida. But I can't think of any other explanation for what I heard and what I've found."

"All right," I said, drawing out the words. "Why bring me here? Why show me?"

Tarrin looked away, a slight pink tint on his cheeks visible even in the dim light of the tunnel. "I can't go to my parents about this until I have proof. I thought that if you were a witness to all of this as well, they would believe *us* more than they'd believe just me." He ran a hand through his hair. "I also needed someone else to see this. To know I'm not crazy or paranoid."

My heart ached at his words. The Prince was normally so confident, so self-assured. It was strange to see him question himself. Oddly enough, I found myself wanting to comfort him.

I opened my mouth to speak. "What—"

Tarrin silenced me with a finger to my lips. It was a small, insignificant touch, but electricity crackled through my body. Footsteps echoed somewhere close by. His eyes widened and I felt his panic surge through our bond before he grabbed my arm and yanked me into the room. It was dark and impossible for my human eyes to see anything.

"Tarrin—"

The Prince grabbed my hand, and I ignored the spark that jumped between us. He yanked at my arm and shoved me down beneath the desk that sat in the middle of the room. There was definitely not enough room for both of us, but Tarrin squeezed himself in behind me. To make us both fit, I ended up with my back to his chest, my legs tucked up against my stomach, and his legs and arms wrapped around me.

I could feel his heart pounding against my back, and though I felt some fear coming from him, I also felt a pulse of something else. The same something that was running through me from our skin touching.

I let out a shaky breath. *Dragon. He's a dragon.* I couldn't let myself forget.

Voices sounded outside the door before it swung open, and we both froze.

"We have to get rid of him, Roldan." A voice rumbled through the gate and Tarrin and I held our breaths.

"I am well aware of this, Barden, but our hands are tied right now."

Their voices sounded oddly familiar, but I couldn't place them.

"Martik is still very much under our control, but that brat of a prince has begun to question too much. Something needs to be done."

There was a sigh from one of them and they went silent as the sounds of ruffling papers drifted through the room. I felt Tarrin tense as the dragons walked around the desk. They only had to look down to find us. Neither of us dared to breathe out of fear that they would smell us.

"Be patient. For now, we must bide our time and wait," Roldan commanded, and brought his enormous hand crashing onto the wood above us.

I flinched and Tarrin's arms tightened around me. I dared a

glance up, his face close, our hot breath mingling. I could feel his pounding heart beneath his muscled torso as he pressed closer to me.

"Let's head back, there's work to be done."

Scuffling footsteps sounded as they retreated from the room. We remained frozen, not making a sound as they grew farther away before disappearing altogether. Tarrin waited until the echoes went silent before he let out a slow, shuddering breath. His eyes met mine and I became acutely aware of his warm body pressed tight against me. Another second passed and he slowly untangled his limbs from mine. I crawled out from under the desk, and as he stood, his eyes drifted down to my robe, which had fallen open. The blue lace nightgown was hiked even higher, revealing my too-thin legs.

I heard Tarrin's breath catch. I met his eyes and, suddenly self-conscious, snapped my robe tight together. His throat bobbed as he swallowed. Unable to stand the heat roaring through my veins, I broke his stare and glanced down the dark hallway.

"Let's get out of here," I whispered as loud as I dared.

For a moment he did not move before he nodded, slowly, stepping farther away from me. Cold seeped into my skin where his warm body had been. Swallowing hard before turning away, Tarrin led me back down the freezing hall, up through staircase after staircase, my sore legs aching and barking in protest with each step.

By the time we made it back to my chambers, the adrenaline had left my body, each of my limbs growing heavier by the second, and I did not bother to speak a word to Tarrin before I slipped inside, shut the door, and stumbled over to the welcoming bed.

My chest tightened as I crawled beneath the blankets, thoughts swirling incessantly in my mind.

The Remnant was planning something.

And it involved the King.

And Prince Tarrin.

And Eklos may or may not be their leader.

Where did that leave me?

All I knew for sure was that I would not be sleeping again tonight.

CHAPTER NINETEEN
TARRIN

I SLUMPED INTO THE lumpy armchair in the corner of my bedroom, rubbing my face with my hands. My fingers remained stiff and slightly frozen from being in the passages under the palace, no matter how much I blew hot air on them. I debated, more than once, shifting into my dragon body that always felt like a furnace, but decided better of it. Emotions in beast form were like being slapped in the face repeatedly. Everything was stronger, had more effect, a little more sting.

Being human was a little easier, duller. Slightly less painful.

My mind reeled at the thought of what happened.

Roldan and Barden were the ones meeting in that hidden room. Members of my father's Council. How many more of them were corrupted? I ticked through their faces in my head, trying to guess which ones might have been involved with their plot. The Council always seemed devious, especially in recent months, goading my father into making hasty decisions that only hurt Elysia, rather than helping it prosper.

In the last Council meeting, I could see the war in my father's eyes. The King was never one to make rash decisions. He always thought carefully about every possible outcome; the consequences of every small decision. But the rebellion in Absult… he had decided in *seconds.* The memory of my father's eyes hardening and his voice ringing in the Great Hall made my eyes burn.

The way Roldan and Barden always spoke to my father, as if he were a lesser dragon they could control rather than their king, always sat wrong with me, but I never would have expected them to stoop to treason.

I blew out a long breath. The two males were involved with the Remnant, which meant they were in cahoots with Eklos, assuming I was correct about him being their leader. How deep did Eklos's reach extend? Was there anyone we could trust?

A small part of me hoped I was being paranoid. That perhaps I had imagined that conversation in the forest, or that I had simply dreamed that hidden room. I didn't want to think that it was possible for the Council to be conspiring against the Royal Family. But Kaida had been there with me, heard everything they said as well. I felt her fear which was as real as mine. I knew I wasn't being paranoid.

What was I supposed to do now?

I couldn't go to my father, who would tell me I was being absurd, denying everything, and I could not tell my mother because she would no doubt side with my father, even if she disagreed with his decisions.

That was the duty of a wife.

The duty of a queen, she always said to me.

And then there was Kaida.

I knew it was a poor decision to show her that room. If I had known that we would have been so close to being caught, I never would have put her life in such danger. I cringed at the thought of what they would have done had they found us. Every reason I could come up with as to why I felt the need to show her what I found didn't seem good enough. Perhaps I wanted someone else to be in on this. To know that I was not making it up, that I was not delusional. If anyone would ever be on my side, I knew, somehow, that she would be.

Or maybe I just wanted to spend more time with her.

It was stupid and reckless, and she was irritating and foolish, with a smart mouth. Timid one moment and explosive the next. But that did not explain, or extinguish, the quickening of my heart when I was around her. Or the way the breath was stolen from my lungs when our eyes met, emotions whispering between us.

It had taken a huge amount of self-control to keep my hands to myself when we were tangled together beneath the desk. The moment my body met hers, a flaming hunger came alive in the small space between us, despite the danger I had put her in. When her robe had fallen open, revealing that short nightgown, my tongue stuck to the roof of my mouth, my heart beating a little bit faster.

For the first time since I had brought Kaida to the palace, clarity snapped into place, and it was almost like I was seeing her for the first time.

The kindness and compassion of a human heart mixed with the ferocity and strength of a dragon. She was not just human or dragon, but a beautiful combination of the two, bringing the best of both halves into one being.

And I realized, much to my astonishment, that I no longer minded the idea of marrying her.

I leaned back in the chair near the fireplace, running a hand over my face. The first peaks of dawn appeared beneath the drapes and I rose from the chair, stumbling over to the balcony doors. Pulling back the curtains, I braced myself for the onslaught of summer heat as I opened the doors and stepped out onto the stone balcony. It was surprisingly mild with the sun just beginning to show its face over the mountains in the distance.

Gripping the iron railing, I inhaled and exhaled.

As the sun crested the horizon, burning light burst forth, bathing the valley in front of me in beautiful rich golden light, chasing away the shadows of the night. As it reached my body, strength coursed through every vein and artery, filling my lungs and soul. The sun was the dragon's source of power. It healed, restored, and strengthened them. During the summer months, when it was the strongest, was when the dragons were the most powerful. I stood there for several minutes, letting the sun soothe my mind and strengthen my body, burning away the worries of the previous night.

When the sun had shifted higher into the sky, no longer keeping me in the center of it, I moved off the balcony, quickly dressing for the day. Pulling on a clean blue tunic and pants, I decided on my first course of action for the day. I needed to talk to Kaida; figure out a plan to stop the Remnant while making sure she was as strong, physically and magically, as possible.

Whatever this was, we were in this together. I was surprised to find I *wanted* her to be in it with me.

The plot against my family, against me. The devilish Councilmen. The Remnant of the Lone Dragon.

Whatever *this* was, we would face it together.

❧

It was a long night.

Not only was I unable to sleep a wink, but Kaida tossed and turned all night too. I could only get a vague sense of how she was feeling, and it inexplicably drove me nuts. Halfway through the night, I ended up shifting into dragon form just so I could hear her thoughts more clearly through our shifter bond.

Surprisingly, I didn't feel much in the way of fear, and even more surprisingly, I felt something more heated… desire, perhaps? I could feel her replaying our bodies squished together beneath the desk in her mind. Instead of disgust like I would have expected from a human, that same type of hunger that had awoken in me when our skin was pressed together, had also trickled into her. I could feel her confusion about it, as if she didn't want to feel such a thing for me.

I didn't blame her. I had never truly proven that she could trust me or let her walls down for me. Especially after putting her in such danger last night. The thought of what would have happened had the dragons found us sent smothering ice over any desire pooled in my stomach.

At the first signs of dawn, I fled my room and went out to the gardens to clear my mind. I weaved my dragon body through path after path and row after row of bushes and flowers, making my way toward my favorite bench on the west side of the palace. It had an expansive view of the Ilgathor Mountains far in the distance that I never grew tired of seeing.

My feet skidded to a stop as I rounded a particularly large Flamaria bush and found my mother, adorned in her bright ruby scales, seated on the bench. She glanced at me, completely unsurprised to see me.

"Tarrin," she said, patting the seat next to her.

"What are you doing out here?" I asked, settling my dragon body onto the bench.

Her snout twitched into a dragon's version of a smirk. "Same reason as you, I suspect."

I couldn't hold back a snort. "I truly doubt that."

My mother gave me a look and hummed softly. She kept her mental barriers locked tight, making it impossible for me to hear what she was thinking. Silence settled between us as we both stared out in the distance, enjoying the sunshine warming the air.

"How is Kaida faring?" she asked, her eyes following a flock of birds flying low over our heads.

"About as well as you'd expect a human finding out they're actually a dragon to fare."

My mother gave a quiet chuckle. "That's fair. Has she made any progress with her shifting?"

I shook my head. "Kaida managed to shift once, but it was

a result of her anger. She was in the middle of a magic outburst when she just shut it off."

My mother's eyes widened. "All that raw magic and she just stopped?"

I nodded. "She told me she didn't know how, just that she didn't want to hurt anyone."

A smile slowly spread across my mother's snout. "She's strong."

"And stubborn."

She let out a deep throaty laugh that I hadn't heard in quite some time. "Kaida's a good match for you then."

It was my turn to laugh. "I don't know about that."

My mother sobered. "Has she come around to the betrothal yet?"

I shrugged. I wasn't sure how to answer. With her words, Kaida seemed to be against marrying me, but after last night, feeling those new and strange emotions from her, I wasn't sure if that's how she still felt. Truth be told, I wasn't entirely sure what I felt either. Kaida wasn't what I thought she'd be, but I also didn't know if I could picture myself with her forever. I blew out a breath.

"Give it time, Son. Preparations for the wedding have begun, and by summer's end I'm sure you two will be head over heels for one another." Her eyes twinkled with something that resembled mischief.

I didn't answer and scratched at the scales on the side of my face. I didn't offer an answer because at the mention of summer's end, my mind snapped back to the Remnant, wondering if they would have made their move yet; if there'd even be a reason to have a wedding by then.

"Tarrin?" my mother asked, concern edging her voice as the scales on her brow bunched together. She could most likely feel the sudden change in my emotions, though I made a conscious effort to seal my exact thoughts away.

I wanted to tell my mother what Kaida and I overheard from

the Council members down in the tunnels. I wanted to tell her about the conversation in the forest outside Vernista. I wanted to tell her about Eklos and the Remnant, and how they were planning something. The problem was I didn't know if she would believe me, take my side, or dismiss my concerns and defend my father and the Council.

"What's wrong, Tarrin?"

I pushed to my feet and paced back and forth in front of her. "I need you to hear me out. Don't make any assumptions or judgements until I've told you everything." I glanced at her and she nodded, her lips pressed tight together.

"I overheard a conversation a few days ago when I flew to the forest outside Vernista. Two dragons were talking about the Remnant, and how their leader was upset that someone took his slave away." I watched my mother's face slacken, and as I continued with how they planned to target the Royal Family, everything Kaida and I heard in the tunnels, and Roldan and Barden's involvement, the color of her scales dimmed, similar to how a human would grow pale from shock. Once I had finished, my mother clenched and unclenched her hands, staring at the gravel beneath her feet.

"I know that you will defend the Council unto death, but I firmly believe they're involved with the Remnant. Eklos is their leader."

"I don't disbelieve you, Tarrin. I should have expected Eklos to retaliate when you took Kaida away from him. That was my fault." My mother stood from the bench and walked to the end of the pathway to stare out at the mountains. "When you were in the tunnels, did you see Roldan's and Barden's faces?"

I opened my mouth to speak but froze. We didn't actually see their faces.

My mother nodded as if she expected it. "Perhaps whomever you heard, used those names to frame the Council."

"You're suggesting the dragons knew Kaida and I were there. That they knew and left us alive."

"Either it truly was them and they didn't know you were there, or it wasn't them and they wanted you both to hear what they had to say. I don't know the truth here, Tarrin."

"The truth is what I've told you. The Council is corrupt. They're working with the Remnant. If we don't plan for their attack, who knows what will happen."

My mother let out a long sigh. "I will handle this, Son. Release it from your mind and be at peace. You just continue Kaida's training, and we'll continue with the wedding preparations." She turned toward me and patted my shoulder. "Don't worry, Tarrin. Everything will be just fine."

CHAPTER TWENTY
KAIDA

"GOOD MORNING, MISS," Meara chirped, popping her head into my bedroom.

I let out a groan and rolled to face her. I hadn't slept at all. After sneaking through dark passageways with the Tarrin, overhearing the Remnant's plans, and the strange way our bodies reacted to each other, I could barely even close my eyes.

The secret conversation between those dragons would have been the normal thing to have been thinking about for hours. But then again, when you are a shape-shifter, half human, half beast, is there such a thing as normal?

Instead, when I closed my eyes, I saw the Prince's hungry eyes, felt the electric charge that had caressed my skin as his body touched mine.

I was being stupid, I told myself repeatedly. Above all else, Tarrin was a dragon at heart. Dragons had always hurt me. Broken me. Why would the Prince be any different?

Meara cleared her throat. "Prince Tarrin is here to see you."

My mouth flopped open as my sleep-addled brain tried to comprehend her words. I remained frozen for a heartbeat before ripping the blankets back and flying across the room to the wardrobe. I grabbed the first pair of pants and tunic my hands landed on and hastily threw them on, not even bothering to comb out my hair before braiding it back, my fingers snagging on tangles.

With a deep breath, I marched over to the door that Meara was now holding open for me. I offered her a small smile and a quiet "thank you" and stepped out of the room. The exhaustion that had kept me anchored to my bed retreated with every step I took. A strange fluttery, breathless feeling danced in my stomach.

Tarrin sat on the couch near the fireplace in my chambers, in human form, a leg crossed over the other, one arm slung across the back. Dark circles lined his eyes, and he looked moments from falling asleep. He clearly hadn't gotten much sleep last night either.

"Morning," I mumbled, unwilling to meet his eyes as I grabbed a glass of orange juice sitting on the table, and settled into the chair across from him.

"How are you feeling?" His voice was soft but not weak.

"I'm fine," I said, brushing off the question. "How are you?"

Tarrin sat forward, placing his arms on his knees. His hands were still wrapped in gauze, old blood, like dark rust, staining the stark white of the bandages. The firelight flickered over his face, casting shadows that made him look older, wearier.

Tarrin wrung his hands, his knees jostling up and down. "About last night..." he began. "I wanted to apologize. I should not have put you in danger like that." He sat back and yanked a pillow to his chest.

"Why did you?" I crossed my arms, waiting. He opened his mouth once and quickly shut it, before he cleared his throat, gripping the pillow a little tighter.

"I didn't know their meeting was planned for last night." He ran a hand through his hair. "There are many passages, both known and hidden, under this palace. That room those dragons were meeting in was a hidden room I stumbled across. The room had been empty when I found it, save for a table strewn with documents and blueprints of the palace."

Tarrin paused to gather his thoughts. "On the back of the one that I picked up was a handwritten note for a meeting in the middle of the night. If I had known what day it was meant for, I never would have brought you."

"Why did you bring me in the first place? I thought you didn't want anything to do with me."

Scrubbing his face with his hands again, he sat forward, elbows on his knees. He kept his eyes on the rug beneath his feet. "I needed someone who would believe me; be on my side."

I blinked, contemplating his words. "How'd you know I would?"

Tarrin let out a breath and gave me a half-smile. "I didn't. I just hoped you would."

I couldn't hold back the small smile that spread on my face. Heat rose on my cheeks. Tarrin's eyes roved over me as if he were trying to solve a puzzle. The fire in the hearth suddenly felt far too warm and I gulped down the cool orange juice in my hand.

He cleared his throat. "Anyway, I tried to tell my mother about it. I hoped she'd take me seriously, but she didn't. She believed that Eklos is most likely planning something, but she refused to believe that those dragons would be involved in it."

"You know who those dragons were then?" I asked. Their voices had sounded familiar to me, but I still couldn't place them.

He gave a single nod. "They are two of the advisors on my father's Council."

My mouth dropped open. "Why would his advisors be plotting against him? Against you?"

Tarrin ran his hands over his face. "I don't know. Perhaps Eklos's influence reaches further than we originally thought. He hasn't exactly hidden his loathing of shape-shifters and humans. But I never would have imagined that he would manage to corrupt the Council. It's only two of them, but who knows how many others are involved. The problem is my father trusts them explicitly. At times he values their opinions over his wife's and son's. It is impossible to convince him of any wrongdoing on their part."

He shifted his gaze to the flickering fire, seconds passing in silence.

"And your mother is on his side?"

"Always," he answered without hesitation. "She said she would handle it. Whatever that meant."

The crackling of the fire filled the room, easing the tense quiet that had settled over us like a cloud. Tarrin looked lost in thought, his brows furrowed, casting his eyes in shadow.

"What do they have against you?" I dared to ask. "Why did they specifically mention you?"

He shrugged. "I wish I knew. Roldan and Barden have always been the most vocal in the Council meetings. They are usually the ones to convince my father to take specific actions. I always side against them, and try to sway the King, which I am sure they don't appreciate. Whatever their end goal is, they cannot accomplish it if I am working against them, putting doubts in my father's head."

"So, what now?"

Tarrin made eye contact with me, my traitorous heart quickening slightly, despite my internal scolding.

"We keep training. We make you stronger. My mother wants us to continue like nothing is wrong. Wedding preparations have begun, and by the end of summer we'll be wed. Assuming the Remnant hasn't killed us all."

I winced at his words. His fear was tangible in the air between us, prickling like needles over my skin, and it grew difficult to swallow. I had never seen a dragon like this before. The way he was about the Absult situation and how he was now. He was *scared.* And perhaps rightfully so.

I had never known a dragon to show compassion. To show kindness. Or true fear. Perhaps it was a shape-shifter trait. When you walk the line between two worlds, maybe you take on the cares and concerns of both of them as well.

I blew out a breath, choosing to ignore his comment about our wedding. That was another battle to fight when he wasn't doused in the scent of fear. "We'll train then. We'll be ready."

Tarrin offered me that half smile again and my heart stuttered a beat. He rose from his chair and walked to me, pulling me to my feet. His arms wrapped around my waist, his nose nestling into my neck. He was… hugging me?

I felt his stomach expand against me as he inhaled deeply, his body trembling from head to toe. Tarrin pulled away just enough for his hand to cup my cheek, sending sparks shooting across every nerve. He held me immobile with his eyes as his thumb gently stroked my cheek.

My eyes flicked to his lips, and I found myself wondering what they would feel like pressed against mine. Tarrin leaned closer, my heart thundering beneath my skin, when a loud crack sounded from the dying fire in the hearth, breaking the spell between us.

He offered me a smirk. "I should go."

I nodded, scolding myself for wanting him to touch me just a little bit longer.

"I believe you, Tarrin," I declared, trying to extend the moment. "I'm on your side. Whatever comes, we'll face it together."

His eyes widened as if he couldn't believe the words had come out of my mouth. Without warning, he leaned forward and planted a kiss on my forehead. His lips were hot like a forge, but soft as a flower petal. I was so unprepared for it that I barely heard him whisper "thank you" before he left my chambers, leaving me to calm my pounding heart alone.

CHAPTER TWENTY-ONE

KAIDA

"I WANT TO COME with."

"No," the Prince said shaking his head, starting to walk away from me.

I wanted to pull my hair out. We had been going back and forth for hours.

"But—"

"I said *no.*" Tarrin whirled toward me, hands braced on his hips. "Do you not understand what would happen if you were caught? There is a reason why humans are not allowed at the festival. You are staying here, *safe*, in your room."

Today was the day of the Beginnings Festival. The celebrations began at dawn, just as the sun appeared over the horizon, and would continue until it had fallen out of sight on the other side of the sky. The climax of the festival would happen when the sun was at its highest, in roughly three hours, when the dragon's fire was supposedly at its strongest.

That was as much as I knew about it since humans were never allowed to attend. If any were foolish enough to try to sneak in, it was free pickings for the dragons. I swallowed hard at the thought.

"But I am not just human anymore. Nobody would ever know." I tried to keep my face neutral. Since a few days ago when

I lost control and shifted, I had not been able to summon my beast form. I was still conflicted on whether I was happy or infuriated by the fact.

"Kaida, you still cannot control when you shift. What would happen if you suddenly turned human in the middle of the festivities, in a sea of dragons? There is a reason why the festival takes place on the Summer Solstice. The power that the dragons can access on this day is unparalleled. I don't think even I could save you, not to mention the political mess that would create for my parents." He rubbed his chin as he debated his next words. "Nobody knows about you yet. About our betrothal."

Some emotion flashed in his eyes, but I could not place my finger on what it was.

"Trust me, it is not even that fun. It is just a bunch of cranky old dragons asserting their dominance and blowing fire into the sky." Crinkles appeared in the corners of his eyes and his lips twitched, fighting a smile.

"If you would *help* me—"

"We've been over this, Kaida." I really hated when he said my name like that. It was like a parent scolding a child. Condescension appeared to be the favorite tactic that Tarrin pulled out of his pocket at every chance. It was ever-present and forever unattractive. I fought the urge to roll my eyes at him.

"You have to learn it for yourself. I cannot force you to shift. Learn your triggers. Learn what puts your body at peace. *You* are in control of your dragon side, not the other way around."

This time I did roll my eyes.

"I mean it," his voice softened. "Stay in your room. Meara will be in and out to supply you with food and anything else you might require, but you must stay here." He paused, studying my face. "Please, above all, *do not leave the palace.*"

He held my stare a moment longer and then turned on his heels and sauntered out.

For several seconds I was frozen where I stood.

Surely, as a shape-shifter he would have *something* he could offer me. Some advice that helped him shift that I could try. But no matter what I said, or how much I pleaded, he would not budge. It wasn't even that I wanted to go to the festival, but more so that I couldn't stand the thought of being stuck in the palace all day without Tarrin. I didn't particularly feel like examining that thought either.

I stuck my tongue out at the closed door.

I saw that.

I could feel Tarrin's amusement in my mind, and groaning loudly, I stomped over to my balcony, swinging the doors open so hard they banged against the stone wall on either side. The balcony faced the road that led to Zarkuse where the festival was to be held. The air shimmered from the scalding summer sun, humidity clinging to every surface, causing sweat to bead on my neck and forehead.

Just as I stepped onto it, gripping the railing until my knuckles turned white, Tarrin strode out of the front doors, his turquoise scales flashing and glittering in the sunlight.

My heart skipped a beat, against my better judgement, as I watched him trudge down the path that led to the heart of the festival.

When he had disappeared around a bend in the road, a sudden panic crept into my bones. I turned back to my room, my breaths coming in quick gasps. Half-running to my bed, I flung myself onto it, burying my head into the pillows as unreasonable tears spilled from my eyes.

Trapped. Trapped in this room. In this palace.

It was utterly ridiculous because I was safe and well cared for. This was not a dirt cave, nor the torture chamber Eklos had kept me in. I was not starving, wondering when my next meal would be. This was not Eklos's domain. Tarrin was not a master. He *wanted* me to be safe.

Despite telling all this to myself over and over, I could not fight the tingling in my limbs or the burning lump rising in my throat causing me to gasp for air. By the time Meara arrived with lunch, I had fallen into a fitful sleep, wrapped so tightly in a ball under the blankets that she had to yank the blanket off me to wake me from the fear-induced sleep.

"Are you all right, miss?" Her lilting accent was a soothing song in my ears. The corners of her lips turned down as her forehead creased in concern.

A sniffle was my only response as I untangled my limbs, stretching my aching bones.

She eyed me skeptically. "I've brought you lunch, miss. It's on the table." She gestured behind her to the main room of my chambers.

I didn't feel like eating, but a painful growl erupted from my stomach, and I let out a sigh, plopping my feet to the floor and walked out of the bedroom. That twisted ball of anxiety still sat in my stomach, but I fought to ignore it as I took a seat at the wooden table. Lifting the cover off the plate, warm tendrils of meat-scented steam wafted into my nose. A large bowl of stew sat in front of me, accompanied by a loaf of bread and some honey butter. I wasted no time slathering the rich butter onto a chunk of bread and shoving it into my mouth.

"What do you know about the Beginnings Festival?" I asked, the food in my mouth muddling my words.

"Not much, miss. I have never been to one."

"First off," I said, pointing my spoon at her, "please stop calling me miss. Either call me Kaida, or nothing at all. Second, you must take me for a fool if you think that I do not know that is a lie. Slaves hear everything. Slaves share everything."

Meara tried to act outraged before her shoulders curved inward, caught in the lie. She let out a small sigh.

"What do you want to know?"

"Everything."

"That could take a while." She glanced quickly at the door, wringing her hands.

"Take a seat, Meara. I could use some company today."

She hesitated a moment longer then blew out a slow breath and padded over to the chair across from me. The chair let out a small creak as Meara's thin body settled into it. She spared a glance at my bread then quickly looked away.

I could have sworn I heard her stomach rumble in response.

Cutting a big piece of bread, I set it on an extra plate and slid it across the table to her.

"Help yourself."

Her mouth fell open, her eyes as round as the saucer in front of her. Her fingers shook as she hesitantly picked up the bread, eyeing it like it would grow teeth and bite her. I watched as she nibbled the corner before chomping off a large chunk. The crackling of the dying fire and Meara's chewing filled my ears. When she had devoured the bread, I offered her what was left of my stew, which she quickly and thoroughly declined.

"I know that the festival celebrates the dragons' defeat of the humans, but I don't know much more than that," I started, hoping it would spur her into conversation. Sitting back in my chair, I crossed my arms and waited.

"The festival is the dragons' celebration of the near extermination of the human race," she began. "It commemorates their rise to power and their dominance over Elysia. It lasts from sunrise to sunset and is basically just a bunch of beasts partying and being imbeciles." She stopped talking to roll her eyes. "There's feasting and drinking and dancing, or whatever the dragon's equivalent to dancing is."

She paused for a moment to take a sip from the cup of water that I offered her.

"At noontime, when the sun is at its peak, the King stands in the center of the crowd and starts the Current. The Current happens when the sun sends its strength and power directly into him, enabling him to use magical abilities that he would not otherwise have. It is a tradition that goes back for a thousand years. The legend behind it is that the release of such power would seep into the earth, strengthening every living thing for the coming year, allowing the lands to prosper.

"The festival is the one day of the year where anything goes when it comes to the dragons and their behavior. While the King and Queen normally enforce, or try to, the already 'loose rules,' if you can even call them that, the Beginnings Festival is the time when there are *no* rules. No consequences, reprimands, or punishments for unsightly behavior. Especially toward humans. If a human is stupid enough to walk into their party… they won't walk out again."

Clenching my fists, I swallowed down the fire that had awoken in my core, burning like the hottest flames.

"That is why Prince Tarrin wanted you to stay in the palace, miss."

My eyes snapped to her, both from her calling me miss again as well as her revealing that she had been eavesdropping on our conversation. I raised an eyebrow.

Meara began wringing her hands. It must have been a nervous habit of hers. "I overheard your conversation just before he left for the festival. I meant no disrespect."

I burst out laughing. I could not tell if it was from the irony of a slave eavesdropping on my own conversation, or if it was a way of releasing the tension that had been escalating in my body.

The girl sitting across from me was dumbfounded, her mouth hanging open.

When I finally caught my breath enough to speak, I said, "I would have done the same thing."

She looked at me as if she didn't believe me but offered a tentative smile. "If you do not mind me asking, why did you want to attend so badly? Especially after your life experiences."

The question caught me off guard. I definitely wasn't about to tell her that I found myself looking forward to spending my days with Prince Tarrin, or that the idea that he would be away for the remainder of the day filled my stomach with a deep, sinking feeling.

"I didn't," I lied. "I just like getting the Prince worked up." I tried to wink, but with the way Meara studied me, I could tell she didn't buy it. It was a lousy lie. While bantering with Tarrin was quite enjoyable, I truly didn't want to add to his stress.

She pushed back from the table and began gathering the empty dishes into a pile. "If that is all you require right now, I must get back to my other duties."

I offered a nod, but the way her brow shadowed her eyes, and her hands were shaking didn't sit right with me. The teacup rattled in the saucer as she lifted it onto the top of the pile.

"Is something wrong, Meara?"

She dropped the porcelain with a loud clatter back onto the table, avoiding my eyes. "I shouldn't say anything. Especially to the Prince's betrothed."

"Meara," I said more firmly. "What is it?"

She continued to wring her hands, glancing at the door as if she were about to make a run for it. I got up and stepped in front of it. "Don't even think about it. Tell me what's wrong."

Meara blew out a shaky breath. "I heard something yesterday, down in the kitchen. One of the other slaves was talking."

I nodded in encouragement when she paused. "Go on."

She took a long breath and then spewed the words from her mouth in a nonstop tidal wave as if she couldn't hold back the pressure anymore. "He overheard dragons talking about Eklos planning something for the festival. He didn't say what it was or who it was meant for."

My stomach sank deep into a pit. Was this the start of Eklos's retaliation? Did he plan to strike the Royal Family during the festival while they were all gathered in one place?

I jerked toward the door, intending to run all the way to Zarkuse to warn Tarrin. A hand wrapped around my wrist, holding me in place.

"You can't leave, miss. The Prince forbade it. We're to stop you from leaving." Her eyes sparkled with apology.

"You expect me to stay here while they walk into the festival with no warning?"

"Prince Tarrin said you weren't to leave under any circumstances. Besides, you're just a human. Who are you to stand against dragons?" It was the most freely Meara had spoken to me, and while it wasn't said with cruel intention, it cut deep into me.

I knew she was aware that I was a shape-shifter, but she still saw me as only human. The old me would probably have rejoiced at the fact. But now that I had discovered my magic, and found a strength I never knew was there, maybe I didn't want to be only human.

"I'm not just a human," I whispered, unable to get my voice to declare it any louder.

Meara's eyes narrowed. "What was that?"

My eyes snapped to hers. "I am half dragon," I said, a little louder this time. I was beginning to discover that being a dragon didn't automatically equate to cruelty. There was a form of strength that came with being a dragon. Sometimes it corrupted, as was the case with most of Elysia, but other times it bloomed like a bright flower, bringing hope and beauty in the world. I saw proof of that in Tarrin and the Queen.

Her mouth pressed into a tight line. "If you're proud of that, then you are no human like me."

The words doused any indignation I had felt like a tub of ice water being tossed over me. My limbs went numb, words drying up on my tongue as I watched her leave my chambers, balancing the tray of porcelain dishes on her hip.

I understood why Meara would be angered by me. I was a slave who was rescued, something which every human dreams of, who then was brought to the Royal Palace as the Prince's newly betrothed. If I were her, I would hate me a little bit too. I thought we were making progress on being friends, but perhaps some wounds went too deep.

I let out a sigh.

An audible click on the other side of the door echoed into my ears.

Meara had locked me in.

CHAPTER TWENTY-TWO

TARRIN

I STRODE BETWEEN THE ramshackle buildings, keeping my wings and tail tucked in tight. Each twist and turn through the streets and alleyways were narrow and unforgiving. When coming from the palace, I had to walk through the slums of Zarkuse to get to the center of the festival where I was expected. The smell emanating from the puddles I carefully navigated around was nauseating and caused me to gag on more than one occasion. I could have flown directly to the center, bypassing all of it, but that meant getting to the celebration sooner, and staying longer.

Unsurprisingly, the streets were empty. Every dragon would already be at the celebration, and every human would, very wisely, not be. I couldn't help the feeling that I was being watched, especially when I gazed at a broken window and the piece of tattered fabric acting as a curtain quickly fell back into place, a small face vanishing behind it. I avoided glancing at any more windows after that.

In all honestly, I wasn't in any danger. The slums were inhabited by humans who posed no threat, and the dragons wouldn't dare to attack a shape-shifter, given our strength and magic. That's why I had never needed an escort. I was my own special form of protection.

Forcing myself to breathe through my mouth to avoid smelling the putrid streets, I continued toward the center. Zarkuse was the closest city to the palace, as well as the largest. It often held the dragons' large celebrations and festivals, much to the disdain of the human slaves that inhabited a majority of it. The city was formed in a circular pattern, the slums creating a ring around the outside, and each ring grew wealthier the closer they were to the center. The Commander of Zarkuse, a ruthless dragon who created and enforced any rules or punishments, felt that if the city ever came under attack, the humans in the slums should be the ones to take the brunt of the attack, thus protecting the more important dragons in the center.

I rolled my eyes at the thought. Not even a month ago, I would not have had a problem with that logic. I would have remained in ignorant bliss and not blinked an eye at it.

But then I met Kaida. Half dragon, fully human heart.

I did not want to admit it, but she had begun to wear down my own stubborn dragon heart, chipping away all the arrogant broken pieces that had never thought twice about human slaves, and started to glue them together, making them whole and somehow compassionate, better.

I could not quite comprehend the effect she had on me.

My shoulders slumped as I walked. In previous years, I had looked forward to the festival. I had always reveled in the food and wine, gotten swept up in the party atmosphere.

But today… I did not even want to come.

For a split second, I wished that Kaida was with me. I knew how much she wanted to come. If she had been able to control her shifting, I might have considered it. *Maybe.*

But the idea of her attending and suddenly becoming human again… the thought of what those dragons would do to her… It put a stabbing feeling in my gut and made my hands sweaty, despite the thick scales covering them. Taking a deep breath, I pressed on into the wealthier parts of Zarkuse, leaving the slums behind.

Before I even neared the city center, the music and raucous shouting and growling slammed into my enhanced hearing. The ground rumbled faintly beneath my feet, the dragons moving and stomping around.

As I arrived in the center ring of the city, Flamaria were strung up between houses and shops, scattered everywhere, painting every surface a bright orange color. As the sun neared its apex, the flowers grew so vibrant they looked like true flames.

Dragons were scattered everywhere, thick in some places, sparse in others. A good number were dancing to the off-kilter music over in the far corner, their movements wild and animal-like, while most others were either eating near the tables piled with food or milling about, carrying on conversations. The best part of the festival was the colors. Every dragon was so vibrantly colored, it was like a piece of living artwork standing in front of me. Even the muted and natural tones seemed brighter amongst the others.

Pushing my way through the crowd, I made my way to the center, where I spotted the King and Queen, my mother's fiery red scales unmistakable.

"Ah, Tarrin, you finally made it," my mother said as I arrived in front of them. Her tone was pleasant. but her eyes were scolding me for my tardiness. I offered a shallow bow to them both, and an unrepentant smile.

My father grunted at me both in acknowledgement and disapproval. I opened my mouth to speak but two dragons approached, both in unfortunate shades of brown.

Barden and Roldan stopped in front of us and bowed deeply. "Your Majesties," they addressed my parents followed by merely a glance at me and a hurried, "Your Highness."

Memories of the hidden room beneath the palace flooded into my mind. These two dragons discussed getting rid of *me.* I bit my tongue to keep from saying something I would regret, and uncharacteristically forgetting my dragon strength, nearly pierced all the way through. My face contorted in a wince and I groaned internally. It took every bit of self-control to keep smoke tendrils from sneaking out of my nostrils.

"That sounds like a great idea, Roldan," my father's voice boomed, snapping my attention back to the dragons conversing in front of me. I spared a glance at my mother and despite her calm demeanor on the outside, alarm flashed in her eyes. Something was wrong. Whatever Roldan had suggested, she did not agree.

"What is a great idea?" I dared to chime in, knowing very well it would give away that I had not been listening.

The Councilmen and my father swung their snouts in my direction, and all three narrowed their eyes. My father absentmindedly rubbed at the back of his neck, his claws clinking against his scales.

"Councilman Roldan suggested that it might be a good idea for you to begin observing the members of the Council when we are not in session. Shadowing them, observing them, learning what they do and how they make their decisions. Someday you will have to confer with them when you are king, so it is best to get well acquainted now. I find myself agreeing with him." The King nodded his approval as he finished speaking.

My heart stuttered. Was this their plan to get rid of me? Create a ruse in which I was constantly by their side making it easier to kill me? *Clever.*

"As fun as that sounds," I said, struggling to master the quiver that wanted to creep into my voice, "I currently have other, more pressing matters to attend to back at the palace."

"Oh, nonsense. That girl can wait. You will start right now. Stay with Roldan and Barden during the Festival. See how a *real* dragon behaves. You may go home once the sun has set." Pure command laced my father's voice, leaving no room for argument. There was no disputing an order from the King.

I had planned to sneak home early even though in past years I had stayed until nearly everyone else had gone home. But now I was stuck.

The sun scorched higher in the sky. There would be no escaping. All four dragons fixed their gaze on me, and I tried not to sway under the weight of it. I met my mother's eyes and silently pleaded with her to do something, but she only stared blankly back at me. Bile rose in my throat, the summer heat becoming unbearable, my scales sticking uncomfortably together. My mouth was bone dry.

Left without a choice, I nodded in submission.

"Excellent," Barden hissed, a little too happily. "After the Current, come find us by the fountain." He pointed behind him to the fountain in the archway between the next ring of houses.

"He will," my father answered for me as he took a step toward the center of the throng. It was time for the Current.

CHAPTER TWENTY-THREE

TARRIN

THICK HUMIDITY WRAPPED around my body like a warm, itchy blanket. It was only made worse by the horde of dragons pressing in on every side. The King stood in the center of the courtyard, the Queen at his side, everyone else scattered in circles around us. The Queen technically should have been the one to perform the Current, being the rightful ruler, but ever since I was a youngling, it had been my father. I had never thought to ask why.

My father planted his large, clawed feet into the ground, nails piercing stone. Lifting his arms to the sky, the sun was directly overhead. Immediately his turquoise scales, twin to my own, began flickering and shuttering in the light.

The sun offered its strength and the King breathed it in, eyes closed, letting it fill his every limb, every scale. Breath after breath, power and flame built up in his body.

I watched as my father grew impossibly taller, added muscle, his body thriving on that direct line of power. Only once a year, during the Current, could a dragon receive and access such power. Laws had been written to keep it so that the King was the only one who could take in the sun's power in such a way. It was too dangerous to make it available to every dragon.

Of course, all dragons had their own well of fire deep in their core that would recharge when it was drained, but this was different.

It was an unending, unrelenting, unstoppable kind of power.

Raw.

The kind that drove even the strongest dragon to near insanity. It was not only flame that they could wield with intensity, but other elements too: water, wind, and ice. It took an enormous amount of willpower and self-control to draw in that energy and redirect it into the earth so that it would continue to prosper for the coming year.

Only disaster awaited a dragon who tried to keep it all for himself. A dragon's body was not made to keep that level of power contained in themselves for a long period of time. It was like having the very embers from the sun burning within, scorching and destroying from the inside out.

My father's sudden movement brought my attention back to the present. On a normal day, I would stand at an equal height with my father. During the Current, the King grew to tower several feet over me, over everyone.

Squinting up, I blinked back the tears that were welling from the bright light. As if taking a cue from some unknown source, my father began speaking in a language older than Elysia. A language that had created the world. He chanted the words over and over, smoke billowing out of his nostrils in thick black wisps.

Raising his arms even higher to the sky, the world itself seemed to dim until daylight had turned into dusk. Every creature, every plant, every stone, *everything* froze.

I held my breath, waiting.

An eerie feeling prickled across my scales just before my father detonated.

Flame and ice and wind exploded from his snout and hands, shooting into the air. A fierce wind circled through the courtyard, so strong that every dragon was forced to its knees. A rumble and pop as I hit the ground were carried away in the wind.

Ice and fire twisted around each other shooting in every direction like spears. They encompassed each other completely, turning into white hot lightning which zigzagged up into the sky, nearly striking the sun that had dimmed considerably from the massive dragon in front of me that had drawn on the entirety of its power.

Fire, ice, and lightning rained down from the sky in large droplets that fell to the earth, seeping into the dirt and stone, illuminating it like spiderwebs beneath the ground. As if in answer, every tree, flower, bush, and animal seemed to awaken, growing taller, more vibrant. This was the Current. This was how the King took the sun's resources and deposited it back into the earth to keep it healthy and flourishing. Every living thing flocked to that power.

Despite seeing my father perform the Current every year, I stood in awe, mouth gaping. Most years I had always been so drunk on wine that I had not paid much attention. Even now I could see those that had indulged a little too much with glazed, unseeing eyes.

My mother stepped forward and took my father's hand. Slowly, so slowly, the King shrunk in size, returning to his original height and physical stature. Daylight returned, though less bright, as if something permanent had been taken from it during the ritual. My father's scales remained vibrant and dazzling, steam rising off them, though his face was laden with exhaustion.

King Martik turned to face his wife, his eyes blazing. My mother met his gaze, entirely unafraid. She was his tether to this world, his reminder of who he was and what he was meant to do. The power from the Current could draw him away, claim him. She was the one living thing that could break through that stupor and wake him up, bring him back.

My father blinked a few times, attempting to smile. It came

out as more of a grimace. The other dragons started to break off, some heading home after the climax of the festival, others returning to their drinking and mingling. I spotted other members of the Council on the other side of the courtyard, talking in hurried whispers. When they noticed my attention, they immediately straightened and walked off.

Without even a parting glance at me, my parents headed back toward the palace. My father's body was drained, and it would take a miserable amount of time to get back home since he was now unable to fly. I wished desperately that I could join them. I could not wait to explain what the Current was to Kaida, how it felt to have the raw elements slam into your body and shoot through your veins. How I would be the one to direct it someday; how she would be my own tether.

I half-smiled at the thought. That smile vanished as I spotted Roldan and Barden waiting for me, each wearing a vicious grin, smoke curling from their nostrils.

Dragons did not believe in gods, since they believed themselves to be deities, but I knew humans did. I prayed to whatever of those gods might be listening as I turned to face them. My throat bobbed as I swallowed, took a breath, and slowly sauntered over to the fountain, to the awaiting dragons that wanted to kill me.

CHAPTER TWENTY-FOUR
KAIDA

I PRACTICALLY HAD TO tie myself to my bedposts to keep from leaving the palace. I was lying on my bed, staring at the ceiling, when the sky dimmed, followed by an intense twister of fire and lightning shooting into the sky. Every bone and vein and piece of me thrummed in response. The sudden need to get to that source of power was overwhelming. If it had not been for the locked door, I would have been out of the palace and long gone, in search of what had caused it.

The power sang to that inner fire within me, my mind roaring at the demand, the *need* to go, my bones aching at the restraint it took to stay. Without even thinking about it, I shifted into beast form, then fell to my knees from the deluge of raw energy that swept through me. The feeling had been strong when I was in human form, but it was *nothing* compared to this. My entire body trembled, amethyst scales clinking softly together. If I knew how to use the wings on my back, I probably would have flown right off the balcony.

When the strange dusk turned back to daylight, my entire body was buzzing. Was that the Current? The words Meara had spoken about it seemed to fit what had just occurred. She had never mentioned what it would feel like, gave no warning that it would be so intense. Perhaps normal humans could not feel that energy. Maybe she had never experienced it like I did.

Like a candle being blown out, I exhaled, and my scales flickered away, skin sliding back over my limbs. I scrubbed my face with my calloused hands. Sitting on the fluffy rug on the floor, I gazed out the window. While the sunlight had returned, it seemed darker, not as bright as before. All traces of that elemental storm had disappeared, only the slight smell of burning grass lingering in the air, blowing in on a breeze through the balcony doors.

It seemed like only minutes had passed as I sat there watching the sun creep lower and lower over the horizon when the chiming of the clock on the fireplace mantle began. *Hours* had passed and it was now only two hours until sunset.

I jumped to my feet, feeling suddenly brave, and decided that it was safe enough to leave the palace by now. Surely once the absence of that magnificent magic set in, the other dragons would get bored and head home.

I pulled on my boots and went to find a hairpin that might unlock the door. It took a couple of tries, and the internal begging for my hands to quit shaking, and I was out of my chambers, bounding down the stairs for the main entrance. The palace was a ghost town. Not a dragon or human in sight. *How strange.*

Deep in the back of my mind, hardly even noticeable, a small alarm started to ring, warning me against leaving. It grew louder with every step toward those wooden doors, screaming by the time I put my hand on the handle. I knew I should stay; knew I should heed that warning. But I took a deep breath, swallowed, and the ringing in my head stopped. The sudden silence was deafening.

Needing to get out, to breathe in fresh air, I gripped the handle so hard my knuckles threatened to split and swung the heavy door with all my might.

Humidity slammed into my body, shoved itself down my throat, into my lungs.

My attention went to a glowing dome of light in the distance, in the direction that Tarrin had gone. The magic fire in me that went dormant in human form peeked an eye open, willing me forward to that energy. Before I could consciously decide, my feet were moving forward of their own accord, stomping down the steps and down the rough stone path that the Prince had walked hours earlier.

✥

I reached the outer ring of Zarkuse, my body thrumming with every step forward. The power that was generated during that magic storm was thick in the air, growing stronger the closer I grew to the festival. It was a song in my blood, drawing my feet toward it.

The sign for the city was so dilapidated it was unreadable, and many of the houses were in the same condition. The slums. Every window was broken, scraps of fabric hanging in place of drapes, flapping in the summer breeze. Doors hung crooked on their hinges and several roofs had gaping holes in them. Foundations were crumbling and some houses were slanted so violently it was a wonder that they were still standing at all.

Thoughts of my dirt cave home flooded back into my mind. I was not sure if living amongst darkness and dirt was any better than these ramshackle buildings. Perhaps they were equally terrible.

A fire simmered in my stomach that the humans had to live in conditions like these. The dragons had stolen everything from them. After meeting the Royal Family, I had been quite confused. I had expected for them to be terrible beasts with no remorse, no conscience. But I had been wrong. Thus far, they had been truly decent beings. Even though Prince Tarrin had been ignorant and uncaring for much of what had been happening, he had proven that he had a heart, one that was capable of warmth and compassion.

And yet they all allowed this to continue.

And I was supposed to be a part of it.

I shook my head, trying to expel the thoughts that had flooded in, unwanted.

I made it through the two outer rings of the slums when the houses began to improve. The farther into the city I went, the more lavish and expensive everything looked. While there had been crumbling shacks and tiny cottages in the slums, these houses were huge. Ornately carved doors and large windows, with beautiful stone siding were fixed upon each dwelling. I was surprised to find the streets completely empty. I expected the humans to be hidden in their homes, but I didn't expect it to be so easy to walk through the streets without a dragon spotting me.

As I entered the second to last ring from the center, I could see the courtyard in the distance through the archways. I took one more step forward and halted. I could not shake the feeling that I was being watched. The hair on the back of my neck stood on end. Warning bells pealed in the back of my mind again, louder than they had ever been. Sweat sprung up on my hands as I spun in place, looking at every house, every window. No faces, human or dragon, greeted me.

There were several alleyways shrouded in shadow on either side of me. A dark creeping feeling emanated from each of them. Silence rippled in the air, my breath escaping in loud, quick gasps. I debated running back the way I came, but I knew whatever was hidden in the shadows would catch me before I made it to the next ring. The courtyard did not promise safety either. If there were still dragons there from the festival, I was as good as dead there too.

What had I done? I was a fool. Ice ran through my veins, freezing my muscles. *Maybe if I make it to Tarrin, he can protect me.* I eyed the distance to the courtyard. It was two archways away, which meant I had to cut through two rings without getting caught. The odds weren't good.

I filled my lungs, readying my muscles to sprint as fast as possible when heavy steps thudded behind me, the ground quivering beneath the weight. I closed my eyes as dread set in.

Tarrin was right. I should not have left the palace. That magic pull from the Current had been like a drug, fogging my mind, clouding my judgement.

I was going to die.

I willed a fierce calm into my bones as I turned to face the dragon, pushing my fists into my sides to hide their shaking. I would not give him the satisfaction of seeing me afraid.

A dragon, dark as ashes, stood before me, like a demon emerging from the shadows.

Eklos.

My heart stuttered and then pounded like a beating drum as fear latched its talons into every part of me. His red eyes blazed bright, flashing as he studied me from head to toe, a predator analyzing its prey. He took in my face, no longer gaunt but filled out, the pristine clothes, not a smudge of dirt on me. I had gained considerable weight since Tarrin had rescued me from The Den, and I no longer looked like a slave struggling to survive. I did not even look like one of the slaves in the palace. If there were a human equivalent to dragon royalty, I assumed that is what I looked like.

Eklos realized it too, and thick, suffocating smoke began billowing from his snout as he bared his teeth in a snarl. I took an automatic step back.

"Hello, *slave,*" he hissed in greeting.

Years of panic-driven submission took over my body and my eyes pinned themselves to the ground. Shoulders curling inward, my body slipped back into that fearful slave girl unwillingly.

A large-winged shadow passed by overhead followed by another. I didn't dare glance up to see the dragons flying home for the night as the fading sunset turned to darkness. Eklos had picked his spot well. There were no dragons around, most of them likely still at the festival. We were in a shadowed alleyway, so even if someone flew overhead, they still wouldn't see us. There would be no one coming to save me, not that a dragon would waste time rescuing a human.

"What? Not happy to see me?" Eklos crooned. Taking another step toward me, he bared his teeth in a snarl.

"Not particularly," I said, boldness flaring for a moment and then dissipating to embers as Eklos unleashed a growl.

"Have you had fun playing princess, girl?" In an exhale, smoke spread through the air between us, twisting around my body, coating it in ash. Without looking down, I knew that my clothes, my skin, my face, everything was filthy, the fabric ruined.

A gentle breeze blew through the street, sending my hair blowing in every direction. As I lifted a hand to tuck it behind my ears, my fingers were covered in soot, a familiar sight that set my nerves on edge.

I had tasted freedom. I had experienced something so wonderful that I never could have imagined; that I was not sure I deserved. But freedom had come to me, nevertheless. And now the threat of it being stripped from me, leaving me bare, poor, naked, a slave again… I struggled to keep the tears from spilling down my cheeks.

Eklos noticed the silver lining my eyes and a triumphant, wicked smile pulled at his lips as he mistook it for fear. He took another step toward me, and I took a step back. His smile began to falter as he took another step and I moved farther from him.

"Enough, slave!" he bellowed, windows rattling in the nearby houses. "It is time you learned what happens to worms like you who think they are worthy of freedom," Eklos spat the words, his face twisted into a hideous grimace. "A wretched slave like you, useless, pathetic, worthless…" He halted, his entire body trembling. "You think you can just *stop* being a slave?" His voice kept rising with every question, every accusation.

My old Master spewed black smoke from his mouth, whipping it through the air toward me, encircling my neck like a collar. Grabbing onto the smoke leash with his massive, clawed hands, he tugged me forward. I scratched and ripped at the collar, but it only grew tighter with every attempt. Blood oozed where my nails cut my skin.

"You are going to learn the consequences of trying to leave my household. You are going to learn what should have happened the first time when you tried to escape. This should have been done long ago. Mercy will not find you. *You are mine,"* he hissed, yanking me closer, within touching distance.

I tried to summon my voice but the only sound that came out was a choked squeak as the collar grew tighter, suffocating. Black spots danced in my vision, my lungs spasming from the lack of air.

Eklos tugged on the smoke leash one last time and closed the distance between us. I fell forward to the ground, my knees barking in pain as they hit stone. On my knees before him, the fire that had grown cold inside me rekindled as I realized that this was what he wanted. For me to bow to him one last time before he ended me.

I knew this was it. I was going to die.

Nobody was around to save me. I debated screaming but the aching in my air-starved lungs kept me silent. This was my fault. I had left the palace when I had been warned not to. Meara had said that Eklos was planning something for the festival. I thought that meant an attack on Tarrin or his parents. I never thought I would be the one caught in his trap.

A dark calm spread through me, acceptance of the death that was waiting for me to breathe my last breath. A furious boldness filled my veins and I snapped my tear-lined eyes up to his, that otherworldly calm seeming to radiate out from me. His eyes widened as he sensed it, and I took advantage of the pause in his attack.

"I am not a slave, and you are *not* my Master." I ground the words out, letting a growl seep through, that fire now boiling in my core, threatening to erupt. I knew that those words would set him over the edge, perhaps prompting him to end it quickly rather than making it slow and painful. A merciful death rather than a punishment.

Eklos froze for a moment, the words sinking in.

Then white hot, blazing wrath exploded around me.

CHAPTER TWENTY-FIVE
TARRIN

"ENOUGH, SLAVE!" I heard a deep voice growl in the distance.

Barden and Roldan stood next to me, refilling their cups with wine, oblivious to the sudden outburst. They had had so much to drink at this point that it was a wonder they were still conscious. The Councilmen's wings kept unfolding and banging against each other, followed by mumbled curses and empty threats. If this time alone with them was supposed to be when they got rid of me, they were not doing a very good job of it. In fact, they had hardly spoken to me or even acknowledged me.

"Did you hear that?" I asked to neither of them in particular.

Roldan's eyes narrowed, but they roved back and forth like they couldn't focus. "Flabber… quiet… you…" His words were jumbled nonsense and I fought back a laugh. I wondered if I could use their drug-addled brains to my advantage and pry some information out of them.

"Are you involved with the Remnant?" It was a direct question that I half expected to startle them, but they continued staring at nothing, as if I hadn't even spoken. "Are you trying to kill me?" I tried.

Barden let out an absurd giggle that jiggled his dragon belly.

"Kill the Prince, kill the Prince. That is what he wants." He sang it as if it were a dark nursery rhyme. "Kill the girl, kill them all. That is what he wants."

"Shh," Roldan half-heartedly scolded his fellow Councilman. "That's a sssssecret."

Barden giggled again.

That's what *who* wants? Eklos?

I glanced around to see if anyone else had heard this odd exchange. There were still a few dragons left at the festival, mostly drunkards who were writhing their bodies around the courtyard, or sitting in a heap on the ground with an enormous goblet of wine in their claws. But most of the partygoers had already left, which felt strange. I couldn't remember a time when so many had left so early.

I couldn't escape the feeling that they knew something I didn't. I scratched at the scales on my cheek, wondering if I could sneak away without the Councilmen noticing. They seemed more and more out of it the more seconds that passed. I sniffed once, catching a strange, sweet scent that I hadn't smelled for quite some time.

I glanced at their glasses, my eyebrows furrowing as I noticed a slight film coating the inside of the glass. I sniffed in their direction. I recognized the scent from one of my tutor's lessons on toxic flowers and herbs. It took me a second to place it and my mouth fell open when I got it. A non-lethal poison had been put in their drinks. It was the kind of drug that would confuse the mind, prevent them from thinking clearly.

My mind spun and I closed my eyes, sorting through the day's events, trying to put it together. Who had done it? Who had managed to be discreet enough to slip poison in their drinks? I remembered my mother's promise to take care of things. Could she have been the one to poison the dragons? I couldn't imagine her resorting to such a thing, but much like a mother bear, a mother dragon would do anything to protect her youngling.

Another growl rippled through the air, interrupting my swirling thoughts. The wind shifted, blowing the warm summer breeze into my face. A familiar lavender and cedar scent caressed my nose, circling my head.

My heart stuttered a beat.

Kaida.

The wind carried her scent. It was intertwined with the unmistakable tang of fear. My breath came in quick, shallow gasps as I tried to get air into my lungs, fire rising in my throat, and settling in my mouth. Why was Kaida in Zarkuse? I had *warned* her not to come. Begged her to stay in the palace.

The breeze sailed over my scales, her scent surrounding me again. I had to find her. *Now.* I only considered Roldan and Barden for a split second before grabbing two large bottles of wine and brought both down upon their heads. They collapsed to the stones beneath them in a pathetic heap of brown scales. I shook my head. They hadn't even seen me coming. I left them behind, heading in the direction the scent had come from.

Two rings away, I could barely make out smoke wafting through the air, faintly visible through the archways. The sun had set, and darkness descended like thick fog over the city. The wind grew stronger, battering and smothering, as if beckoning me. It seemed to whisper, "hurry."

Snapping my wings out behind me, I used the momentum from their movement to propel my feet faster. The ground shook beneath my steps, stone crumbling from walls and archways as I hurtled past, wings scraping against them. In the shadows of an alleyway, I came to an abrupt stop, the sight chilling the fire in my gut, turning it to mere ashes.

A dragon, dark as smoke and ash, stood farther down the street, red eyes ablaze. Memories of saving Kaida in The Den flooded my mind when I saw him. I could never forget the red eyes of her former Master, Eklos. Kaida was on her knees before him, hands at her side, hair blowing in every direction, covered in ash and dirt. He kept a collar of smoke leashed around her neck. It was only by my magnified dragon hearing that I heard the words she spoke.

"I am not a slave, and you are *not* my Master."

The dragon froze.

I understood the implications of what Kaida said at the same moment Eklos did. She was defying his ownership, letting him know that she was no longer his, and she would never be his again.

Scorching white flame erupted from Eklos's mouth, shooting in every direction. It arched and swirled around her, submerging her under a sea of white fire. I gasped, wanting to lunge after her, but my legs gave out and I fell to my knees on the cobblestone street. I could do nothing but watch as Kaida, my betrothed, burned alive where she stood.

CHAPTER TWENTY-SIX
KAIDA

THE FLAMES SMOTHERED me, hissing and roaring, twisting around like a cyclone. I tried to breathe, but there was only suffocating heat. Somehow, the flame wasn't burning me. It coated every part of my body but didn't seem to penetrate my skin.

A burst of air speared through the flames, causing it to expand like a balloon, creating a cocoon of wind and fire around me. It wasn't coming from me and I glanced around to find the source. I found Tarrin in the shadows of an alley, on his knees. He reached for me, as if he were trying to get to me, tears glistening on his scales. It couldn't have been him. He didn't have the ability to control wind.

Eklos was dumbfounded. His giant mouth hung wide open, disbelief contorting his face which quickly turned to outrage, and he sent wave after wave of wrath-filled flames at me. The fire completely engulfed my body but did not touch me, stopping an inch short of my skin.

Eklos bounded toward me, stones crumbling under his feet, leaving a trail of embers in his footprints. "*I OWN YOU!*" he roared, white flame exploding from his mouth again, the shape of a sword with a fire-laced blade, aimed straight for my heart. It was a shot meant to kill.

This was it. I turned my head slightly, fixing my gaze on Tarrin. Pain was etched all over his face, and he was crawling and clawing, try to get to me, but it seemed Eklos had created a barrier of smoke around us.

If I was being honest with myself, I didn't mind that Tarrin's face was the last thing I saw before I died.

The sword of fire shot straight for my chest and tears slipped down my cheeks. I closed my eyes only to snap them open again when something landed with an earthshaking crunch, directly in front of me and the fire blade aimed at my heart.

My muscles melted into puddles as a cry of grief escaped my mouth.

For it was the Queen that had landed in front of me.

It was Tarrin's mother who now fell onto her knees, a shaft of white flames protruding from her chest. It was his mother who had taken my death blow.

Wrath swirled in my core like a fiery abyss as I watched the Queen crumple to the ground, her red scales growing dimmer with each of her slowing heartbeats. The beast within me snarled and thrashed to be unleashed. Though I knew it meant losing control, for once, I was more than happy to oblige.

I let go and felt my skin harden into scales, my limbs lengthening as I grew to match Eklos's size. The anger and rage I had felt as a human morphed into something enormous, something deadlier, that I couldn't even put into words.

Blue flames filled my palms as I looked at Eklos. His jaw hung wide open, and I spread my snout in a wicked smile. He hadn't known I was a shape-shifter; he hadn't known I would be able to fight back. I swirled my claws in a circular motion, growing the flames, making them hotter.

"Impossible," he growled.

My smile turned feline as I bared the sharp dagger-like teeth in my mouth. "You know, Eklos, you really should take care who you keep as a slave." I took another step closer. "You never know which one you might be torturing and coaxing into a monster just like you."

With a combination of my human side screaming, and my beast side roaring, I sent a volley of blue fire directly at Eklos's head. He threw an arm up to block the brunt of the attack, before he sent a stream of white flame into my chest. He let out a snarl when the flames bounced harmlessly off me once more.

He blocked attack after attack but slowly retreated backward, not realizing that I was backing him into a corner. Letting the beast take over completely, my claws contracted, then snapped outward, a whip made entirely of lightning sitting in my palms.

Lightning? Do I have more than one form of magic?

The thought was swept to the side as I stepped forward, the ground trembling beneath my footsteps, and cracked the whip in the air, just above Eklos's head. It perfectly mimicked the dream I had after coming to the palace, and all the times in Belharnt when he had taken the whip to me. It was the mirror image to the whipping he had given my mother before he beheaded her. I snapped it again, wishing he could feel every ounce of pain he had ever caused me as it coiled around his ankles. I gave a mighty yank and sent him sprawling onto the stones.

I raised my hands to attack again, as did Eklos, and our flames collided between us. It was a mid-air painting of white and blue explosions before we were both sent flying backward from the force of the collision. The rough cobblestones scratched and marred my amethyst scales, but thankfully that was the worst of my injuries.

The Queen stirred, drawing both of our attention, her hoarse voice calling out to Tarrin. He stumbled to her side, his wings drooping behind him as he kneeled next to her. Eklos's eyes went wide, and I took advantage of his distraction and raised my hands, palms filling with a combination of blue flame and flickering lightning,

Eklos's eyes snapped to mine and a smile spread beneath his red eyes before his fire blinked out like a snuffed torch. Darkness descended over the alley, and the sudden lack of heat from the fire chilled my bones beneath my scales. Even with my dragon sight, it was impossible to see as if the darkness was made of smoke.

I raised a bundle of flames into the air, trying to illuminate where Eklos was. The light only revealed scorched stone and blood.

Eklos was gone.

CHAPTER TWENTY-SEVEN
TARRIN

BLOOD SEEPED OUT of the wound in my mother's chest, dark and thick. Her scales had dimmed to a pale red, her breathing wet and labored. I cradled her head in my lap, tears sliding down my scales and onto her forehead.

"Why would you do that, Mother?" I whispered, pushing gently on the wound, trying to staunch the bleeding. Through our shifter bond, she sent a picture into my mind, explaining. The wind. That was her magical gift. She was a Wind Wielder. She had made the shield around Kaida, protecting her from Eklos's fire. She had shifted the wind, blowing her scent directly in my direction so that I would come to save her.

I didn't understand. By the time Eklos attacked, mother should have been long gone, back at the palace with my father. The only way I could make sense of it was that somehow, my mother knew that this was going to happen, that Kaida would come to Zarkuse and Eklos would attack her. She either never left the city or came back once she got my father home. That was the only explanation that put her close enough to stop Eklos's attack.

The picture of her landing in front of Kaida just as the fire spear pierced her heart replayed over and over in my mind. It clawed at my insides, ripping them apart like an animal with raw meat. I stifled a sob, trying to be strong for her.

A sudden darkness fell over the street and I glanced up to find Eklos had disappeared, and Kaida was limping over to us.

"Remnant… here… Eklos…" My mother tried to talk, but blood was thick on her tongue, her voice hardly intelligible.

"He's gone. You're safe," I reassured her. Kaida settled her body awkwardly on the ground next to me, her turquoise eyes bright as a wildfire from her magic. My mother coughed, sending a spurt of blood between my fingers, and Kaida placed her hands over mine in an attempt to help.

"Look at you, Kaida," mother whispered, her voice cracking. "I never imagined Aela's daughter would turn into such a strong, beautiful dragon. She would be so proud of you." My mother struggled to get the words out, red liquid seeping out the sides of her mouth as she tried to smile. Fresh tears flowed down Kaida's scaled cheeks. "You must… stay with Tarrin." Kaida nodded fervently, choking on a sob.

Her eyes turned to me. "Keep… Kaida… safe. Need… her." My mother tried to say more but was overtaken with a spasming cough.

"Hold on, Mother. I will get you to the palace. You'll be all right." I felt like a child, recalling all the times when I would get injured and my mother would rock me, telling me I would be just fine. Tears spilled onto my cheeks as she weakly lifted a hand to my face.

"P-proud of… you, Son. Stay…" she started but did not get to finish. A mighty exhale left her mouth, hitting me in the face.

My mother's hand fell to the ground as her eyes shut.

A scream built in my throat. I tried to shake her shoulders, begging the life to come back into her body. But her chest remained still, her heartbeat silent.

The Queen. My mother.

She was gone.

ঌ

Tears slid down my cheeks as I let my dragon body dissolve, falling to my knees in the foyer of the palace. With the help of Kaida, we had carried my mother all the way back from Zarkuse, not stopping until we both hit the marble floor inside, instantly shifting. Kaida mirrored my pose, both of us bent over the Queen's pale, lifeless body.

My mother is dead.

The words continued to repeat in my head until Berda, the head slave, spotted us and began issuing quiet orders to the others to help. I almost wished for the humans to scream, to voice the emotions that swirled on the inside of me. But they all stayed reverently silent.

A few came to help Kaida, and I vaguely noted that her human form was covered in cuts and bruises, dried blood smeared across her temple and crusted in a ring around her neck. Meara and another slave helped her to her feet, leading her in the direction of the infirmary. Part of me felt like I needed to go with her, especially since she was just attacked. I needed to make sure she was safe. But when nine slaves brought in a long, thick slab of wood and carefully moved the Queen's body onto it, thoughts emptied from my head. They hoisted the wood onto their shoulders.

I didn't know where they took her.

I couldn't watch them take her away.

My mother, my most trusted confidant, my best friend. Dead.

Not just dead. *Murdered.*

I wanted to feel angry, wanted to feel anything but that suffocating nothingness, but my body wouldn't move, my mind wouldn't move. My limbs ached and my heart throbbed.

Somehow, my leaden feet managed to make it back to my chambers. The room was quiet, a heavy silence pulsing in my head.

I did not want to think, did not want to feel the grief that sat on the threshold, waiting to pounce. I settled back into the couch, gazing at the fire in the hearth, and watched the flames dance and crackle around each other as my mind faded into nothing.

CHAPTER TWENTY-EIGHT

KAIDA

SUNLIGHT STREAMED THROUGH the windows, the air sweltering and thick. I was tucked beneath several layers of blankets, wrapped in a soft cocoon. Sweat drenched my body, soaking the sheets beneath me, and I struggled to wiggle my limbs out from beneath the covers. My mouth and throat were parched, making it painful to swallow.

My arms escaped from the tangle of bedding enough for me to sit up when the bedroom door swung open. Prince Tarrin stood in the doorway, frozen, one hand on the knob, a tray of food in the other.

"You're awake," he said, his eyes widening in surprise, dark circles rimming them. He padded over to my bedside table, keeping eye contact with me the entire time, as if he were scared to look away. Setting the tray down, he filled a glass of water to the brim and handed it to me, sitting on the edge of the bed. "I thought you might be a little hungry."

"Thank you," I whispered as I tilted my head back, gulping down the water in a matter of seconds, liquid splashing down my chin. Without a word he refilled it and handed it back. Three glasses later, my thirst finally quenched, I felt life returning to my body.

"How are you feeling?" he asked.

Tarrin handed me a piece of bread slathered in honey butter which I obediently stuffed into my mouth.

"Like I was attacked by a dragon," I said without thinking. A smirk lit up his face, but it darkened a moment later.

"What were you doing in the city?"

"I…" I hesitated. I knew it would sound stupid. He would laugh at me, scold me for being such a child.

Swallowing the last of the bread, I cleared my throat. "I felt something." I paused, glancing at his face. It betrayed nothing. "Something was calling to me. It was like a twin song to my flames. I could not keep my feet from moving toward it, whatever was beckoning me."

Tarrin stilled beside me, lines creasing his forehead.

"I knew the moment I entered Zarkuse that I should turn back. I could *feel* somebody watching me, waiting. But my feet kept moving forward." I shrugged, somewhat ashamed to meet his eyes.

"The Current is a very strong release into the earth. It is not unusual for dragons to be drawn to it, although I have never heard of one being controlled by it." He paused, rubbing at his chin. "Do you remember what happened?"

I nodded, unable to meet his eyes. "I thought I was going to die. I never expected to be rescued. Your mother…" My voice broke on the last word, my stomach dropping like an anchor. Tears lined my eyes and I blinked furiously, begging them to go away.

His mother had saved me. She had stepped in front of me, taking the blow that should have been mine. Why would she do that?

When the Queen's breathing had halted, her heartbeat fading to nothing, Tarrin began to scream, entirely in his mind. Much of it was garbled and unintelligible, but his grief was unmistakable. He kneeled there next to her, still as a board, just staring at her face; the peaceful look, death's pale color already leeching through her body. I hoped I never heard such a grief-stricken sound again in my life.

Looking at him now, the circles under his eyes, the red rimming them… I did not know how to help him. I felt a desperate need to fix this, to make him better. To make it all better. But I didn't know how.

Death was a strange thing. It always came when you least expected it, uninvited and unwanted. It ripped the world out from beneath your feet, taking everything and returning nothing. Some lived their lives in fear of it, hiding amongst the shadows to escape death's piercing glare, while others longed for it, yearned for it to find them.

It was a natural part of life, to experience death.

But not like this.

This was murder.

There was nothing natural or painless about it.

And I knew I should be sad, in anguish like Tarrin, but I simply felt nothing.

Too much death, too much sorrow.

My heart had blocked it out, saving it from shattering into a million pieces.

For a moment I wondered if he blamed me for her death. If I had not gone to Zarkuse, Eklos would not have attacked me, and his mother would still be alive.

"Are you all right?" I asked, knowing it was a stupid question.

He exhaled slowly before opening his mouth to speak. "I smelled you from the center of the city," he began. "My mother had the ability to control air, and she caused the winds to shift, blowing your scent in my direction. I could smell your fear. I raced after it, after you. I came as fast as I could…" Pausing, he ran his hand through his unbound hair.

"My mother should have been back at the palace. I have no

idea how, but she must have known that Eklos planned to attack you. I could think of no other reason why she would be back in the city."

I blew out a breath. "Is that possible? Do dragons have such gifts?"

Tarrin shrugged, leaving it at that.

"What happened after she saved me?" When I allowed my beast form to take over, I retreated to a small part of my mind, and could only remember bits and pieces of fighting Eklos.

I looked up to meet his eyes and found him fully focused on me, nothing but honesty on his face. "You shifted. Eklos seemed surprised. I don't think he knew that you are a shifter." He ran a hand through his hair again. "You used magic I have never seen you use before, with the control of a well-trained dragon. You attacked him, and he fought back, but took off when he saw me helping my mother."

"I… don't really remember any of that," I admitted. Suddenly restless, I ripped the blankets back and swung my legs over the side of the bed. Warm air kissed my sweaty bare legs sending a sudden shiver through me. A second too late, I noticed that I was wearing that short nightgown once again, most of my legs exposed. I glanced up at Tarrin, finding his gaze upon my body. He looked away and heat bloomed across my cheeks.

I started to wring my hands out of habit, fingers shaking. Yanking the fabric as low as it would go, I deemed it useless and tossed the blanket back over my legs, eliciting a static shock on my skin. *That reminds me…*

"Is it possible that I have more than one type of magic?" I asked, having a vague memory of summoning lightning in my palms.

Tarrin looked thoughtful for a moment. "Most dragons only have varying degrees of fire magic. The exceptions, such as my mother and myself, are few and far between." He paused, studying me. "I saw the lightning you held in your hands. Dragons can't normally do that." He rubbed his chin. "Perhaps we should explore your magic further, see what else might be beneath those scales."

My cheeks flushed with heat, and I grabbed the other piece of bread on the tray, using a knife to spread a thick layer of butter across it. "Does that make me weird?" I asked around a mouthful of bread.

Tarrin smirked. "You're a shape-shifter that can move between human and dragon bodies, and you think having another form of magic makes you weird?"

I snorted, fighting a smile. "Fair enough."

Tarrin moved to a chair across the room and gestured for me to eat. Roasted chicken and spiced vegetables overflowed on the plate he had brought, and my mouth watered at the smell.

"How is your father?" I asked, swallowing a spoonful of carrots.

His eyes darkened. "He has not spoken to me."

"Why—"

"My mother was his one tether to sanity. With her gone, he is not fully himself." The words were sad, empty.

"What can I do?" I felt the need to make this right. I found myself wanting to help.

I *wanted* to help a dragon.

I struggled to accept the thought as Tarrin shook his head.

"There is nothing you can do. The King puts his duty to Elysia over his duty as a father. He will make sure all the affairs are in order before he ever checks to make sure I am all right." The words were harsh, bitter.

"And to answer your question," he continued. "No, I do not blame you for this. My mother made her decision to step in. I must believe that she knew what she was doing. That it was for a reason."

Once again, he had heard exactly what I was thinking.

Although it put me more at ease to know he did not resent me for his mother's death, I still wanted to fix it. I could see tears lining his eyes, feel the emotions pushing against his mind, like water against a dam. It wanted to be released.

I set my food tray down and crossed the room to his chair, kneeling in front of him.

"I'm sorry," I said, grabbing his hand.

He looked up, eyes wide, electricity crackling between our skin. He swallowed, intertwining his fingers with mine. A shiver slid over me as his thumb stroked the back of my hand.

"Thank you." His voice was gruff as if it took all his willpower to hold the emotions at bay.

I studied his face, really allowing myself to see it for the first time. He had scarring on half of his face and I had never thought to ask what they were from. "How did you get those burns on your face?" I blurted, breaking the moment we were having, in typical Kaida fashion. His eyes snapped to mine, startled. He sat there unmoving for a heartbeat longer, then jumped to his feet and stomped over to the door.

"Tarrin, what—"

"It's none of your business," he snapped without glancing back, and shut the door behind him, a little too hard, leaving me on the floor confused.

CHAPTER TWENTY-NINE

TARRIN

KAIDA COULD SEE them. My burns.

Touching the rough skin on the left half of my face, I winced at the memory of how I had gotten them. Fire magic is a dangerous thing. It is not a toy and needs to be respected. That was a lesson I had learned many years ago.

Running my hand through my hair, I slumped onto the couch in the main entry of my chambers, lying down on my stomach. My legs were longer than the furniture, forcing me to prop them up on the end. I knew I should not have left like that. But I was not ready to share that part of me yet. I could barely deal with the memory of it myself. It took me years to not fear my fire magic afterward.

Her gentle face, both careful and curious, filled my mind as I closed my eyes. It had been an honest question, nothing malicious or hurtful, but it had caught me completely off guard.

Because she was not supposed to be able to see the burns. Nobody was.

In fact, no one even knew about the incident that had caused them. Not even my parents. The injury was non-existent in my dragon form. As for when I was human… an incredibly old dragon once showed me how to cast an illusion, an *ilusai,* forcing others to see something that was not there. I always thought it was a vain trick, that only people who cared too much about their appearance would use it.

But I had never wanted to see the burns again. I followed the ritual exactly as the old dragon had taught me. It was an ancient spell, Old Magic, long forgotten by most. The illusion was different than shape-shifting or normal dragon magic. It required no thought or focus to keep up. Once it was cast, it stayed put until you ended it. It was not draining on your energy nor did it cause any harm.

I had been wary to use it, not knowing if the dragon had simply lied to me, a naïve youngling. But when I had looked in the mirror and saw a sudden clearness rippling across my cheek, I knew it was real. Not a soul had ever seen my true face from that day onward.

Until Kaida.

How could she see through the *ilusai*? *I* could not even see through it. The only time I remembered there were remnants of an old injury on my face was when I ran my fingers over it, for even an illusion could not fill the grooves and scars from the blistering.

Those first weeks afterward had been agonizing. I had bit my tongue and cheek to keep from screaming in pain, the blisters filling with puss, ready to burst. I did not put any salve or ointment on them for fear of word getting to my parents that I had needed it. I did not want anyone asking the wrong questions.

Perhaps if I had treated it properly, it would not have scarred so badly, and healed correctly.

I shoved my face into a pillow and exhaled slowly, trying to calm the swirling thoughts in my head. I had just started to doze off when a swift knock sounded at the door. I jumped up to a sitting position, momentarily dazed. My first thought was perhaps Kaida had decided to come find me, but then I recalled her tired, pale face, and dark circles under her blue eyes. I shook my head as I stood.

Despite that, a part of me secretly hoped that it was her on the other side of that door. I started walking over as another knock sounded. I took a deep breath, bracing myself and swung open the door.

It was not Kaida.

"Your Highness." A slave in a pristine brown uniform was standing in the doorway. Offering a quick bow, the man kept his eyes on the floor as he spoke.

"The King is requesting your presence in the Great Hall. Immediately."

❧

The King sat at the end of the dimly lit room upon his throne. All the curtains had been drawn and only scattered torches were lit. No one else was present. His turquoise scales flashed a dark blue when the light hit them.

As I drew closer, I noticed wet streaks on my father's face, scales glistening, his normal turquoise eyes, darker, brimmed with red.

My father had been crying. I could not recall ever seeing my father cry.

I bent down on one knee before him, and swiftly rose.

"My wife is dead," he whispered at last, leaning forward and covering his snout with his hands. I hesitated, unsure of what to do.

"What happened, Son?"

I drew in a deep breath. "Kaida was attacked at the Festival."

Fire flared in the King's eyes as he looked at me, his claws piercing into his palms.

"And what was a human doing at the Beginnings Festival?" His words were quiet but laced with violence.

"I didn't bring her, Father. She claims that the power from the Current compelled her to come. She was unable to control herself.

She made it all the way into Zarkuse before she was able to stop, and by then Eklos had found her."

His body went ramrod straight. "Eklos?"

"Yes, he cornered her and attacked, planning to kill her. I had just arrived when Mother stepped in front of Kaida, taking the brunt of his attack."

Scales bunched around my father's eyes, and he turned his head away.

"She saved Kaida?" he asked sadly, voice only a whisper.

I nodded, confused by how quickly his anger had dissipated. My father heaved a sigh, tears sliding down his scales.

"Your mother made a promise to Aela, when Kaida was born, that she would do whatever it took to protect her." He swiped at his eyes, the gesture half-hearted as more tears fell. "She must have seen this as fulfilling her promise."

His words were not harsh, but resigned understanding.

Mother always kept her word.

My heart felt like it was being ripped into pieces as I watched my father break down in front of me.

"Why would Eklos attack her? What purpose did it serve? She is just a slave girl," my father asked, voice cracking.

I cleared my throat, forcing the tears down as I swallowed.

"I have a theory, Father." I paused, taking a deep breath. These were words I would not be able to take back, and there was a good chance that my father would not believe me.

"I believe that the Council has been conspiring with Eklos," I declared. "And I have reason to believe that Eklos and the members of the Council are working with the Remnant of the Lone Dragon."

⁂

I spent the better part of two hours telling my father everything that had happened.

Everything from the conversation in the forest, finding that secret room, overhearing Roldan and Barden in the middle of the night, and their plans against my own life. I didn't have any solid proof of Eklos being involved with the Remnant, other than what Kaida and I had inferred from the conversation I heard in the forest, but everything was too planned out. Especially when one considered the two Council dragons trying to keep me busy and distracted while Eklos went after Kaida.

Either they were all working together, or they all just happened to want to kill us at the same time. I didn't believe in coincidences enough for that to be plausible though. I assumed that Eklos, along with the Remnant, planned to kill all the slaves, either one by one or in mass. Kaida had wronged Eklos, in his eyes, so it made sense for him to start with her.

No matter how much I thought about it, I couldn't understand his motive. As Elysia was, Eklos had all the free labor he could ever want. If he accomplished his mission of getting rid of the humans, he'd be left without anyone to do his dirty work. Did he expect the dragons to pick up where the slaves left off? I had a hard time believing anyone would agree to that.

My father's claws gouged deeper and deeper into the stone arms of his throne. "You're telling me that my own Council, the males that are my closest and most trusted advisors have been manipulating me, plotting with Eklos, had a hand in my wife's death, whether intentional or not, committing high treason in the process, and now are plotting against my son's life, along with his betrothed?" he asked incredulously, eyes wary.

"Yes." I lifted my chin, unwilling to back down. "They have been feeding you lies, causing you to think differently, act differently. They have been manipulating the way you think, the types of consequences you come up with, the decisions you make." I chose my words carefully as I thought through each one. The moment I said the wrong thing, the conversation would be over, and my father would shut the door that was hanging precariously open.

"You are asking me to choose between my son and the dragons I have grown up with, grown to trust and admire." It was not a question. His face remained void of any emotion. The tears had dried from his scales and the redness in his eyes was gone.

I froze in place, my feet aching and my back throbbing. Darkness crept deeper into the room as the scattered torches along the wall ran out of oil, beginning to flicker out. I glanced to the curtain-covered windows and thought about using my magic to let some light in, but one look at my father and I dropped the idea.

"No." The word rumbled through the room, echoing back and forth between the walls. My heart skipped a beat, then raced faster, my breaths becoming shorter, shallower.

"What?"

"I said no. I do not believe that the Council would do something like this. They would never betray my trust in such a way." The King looked away, toward the flickering torches, unable to make eye contact with me. "Eklos will be held accountable for murdering the Queen, if what you say is true, but my Council will remain untouched."

Against my will, tears sprang to life in my eyes. I curled my claws into fists, nails piercing through scales. I spent hours explaining and yet my father still chose them. Where anger should have been roiling in my stomach, it was simply empty, and a numb hollow feeling seeped its way into my bones like a winter morning. The King of Elysia sat before me, not my father. From the vague, unrecognizing look he gave me, it looked as though the King had died right along with his wife.

CHAPTER THIRTY
KAIDA

WHAT HAD I said wrong?

I rubbed my hands over my face, Tarrin's startled reaction replaying over and over in my mind as I sat on the outer edge of the pool-like bath, water lapping into me. I still felt the sudden absence of the Prince like the stillness after a strike of lightning.

It was an innocent question. I thought things between us were improving. That maybe our hatred for each other was subsiding enough for us to be friends—or whatever we were trying to be. But Tarrin refused to let me in, to share his story. I did not expect him to tell me everything but asking about a scar on his face seemed harmless enough.

I watched the steam rising in wispy tendrils for several minutes, the water rippling against my skin, easing the aches in my limbs.

I suddenly sat up straight.

A slight tugging sensation danced in my stomach. It didn't resemble the feeling I had when the power of the Current had beckoned to me. This was different; it had a strange sense of urgency.

Rushing through the water, I grabbed the towel on the edge of the bath and dried off, running into my bedroom in search of clothes. I grabbed the first set I saw, a white cotton shirt with wooden buttons and black pants, and slipped them on.

Another tug pulled at my stomach. It felt like an invisible rope looping around my waist, pulling me out the door. A shiver crawled over my body, and I clenched my fists as I trudged through the hallways of the palace. They were surprisingly cool, thanks to the stone walls, compared to the thick summer heat outside. As I rounded a corner, a sudden stillness hit me. I came to a stop at the end of a hallway. A simple wooden door loomed high over my head.

Come in. Tarrin's voice echoed in my head.

Reaching for the brass handle, I swung open the door. Air lurched to a stop in my throat, a tremble settling into my hands as I realized where I was.

Prince Tarrin's chambers.

The main room was simple, not at all the lavish, extravagant rooms of some of the other places I had been in the palace. A soft gray couch sat in the middle of the room, a large table to the right meant for dining, and several bookcases stacked full of books, sat on the left. The couch faced the fireplace, a crackling fire already blazing away, despite the summer heat.

Tarrin was slumped on the couch, his back to me, staring at the fire.

My boots scuffed against the marble floor as I made my way over to him and sat down, plopping my hands in my lap. His shoulders were curled inward, his eyes distant and unfeeling, his cheeks wet from tears.

"Tarrin," I said gently, trying to draw him out of that haze.

The fog around his mind seemed to recoil from the sound, a spark of life flaring in his eyes for a moment before dying again. I grabbed his chin between my fingers, forcing him to look at me. I searched his eyes, waiting for a response. He just kept staring blankly back at me.

"What happened?"

Tarrin slumped back into the cushions, returning his gaze to the fire, and simply sat there, staring. He grabbed my hand, holding it tightly.

"My father chose the Council over me."

My stomach sank. "How?" I replied, my brow furrowing.

"My father's mind has been manipulated by the Council for too long. I should have known that my words would fall on deaf ears." A silent tear streaked down his cheek and I ran my thumb across his face to wipe it away without thinking. Leaning into my touch, he closed his eyes.

Tarrin went through phases of quiet weeping, tears dampening his shirt, and I watched as his mind spiraled down into that numbness once more. Somehow, he would work himself out of it and tears would begin anew just as the damp spots on his shirt dried.

The fire drifted to embers, turning to ashes, the sunlight fading into night.

Meara tried to bring us food at one point, but I waved her away.

Hours passed and the Prince did not move. Still, I stayed.

It was something that I wished had been given to me when my mother died. Someone to stay with me, help me get through the night.

When darkness settled, whole and complete, I stifled a yawn, and pulled him to his feet, guiding him to his bedroom. I helped him slip his shoes off and waited for him to finish undressing for bed. When he stood there, unmoving, I let out a loud sigh.

"You need to remove your clothes, Tarrin."

Will you help me?

The hesitant words floated across my mind, and I groaned internally.

This was not how I imagined undressing him for the first time. Not that I had ever imagined it. My cheeks burned.

"Um, all right." I unbuttoned his shirt, fingers shaking, and it took multiple attempts on several of the buttons to free the shirt from his body. Next time, I would just pull it up over his head I told myself. I bit my cheek. There would be no next time. This was a onetime thing.

I shook my head at myself as I slipped the shirt from his shoulders, unfastening his pants before I could think too much, letting them fall to the floor. He stood before me in nothing but his undershorts. Tarrin's chest was sun-kissed, covered in muscles. With his skin exposed, his night air and blue cypress scent filled my nose, and it took quite a bit of effort to keep my hands from sliding over the planes of his chest. I glanced up at him, cheeks blazing and red, and found him watching me.

The look on his face was not the same as the blank one from before. It was still a vague, slightly lost look, but there was contemplation there. Curiousness. Needing to put some space between us, I gathered up his clothes in my arms and walked them across the room to the basket meant for dirty linens. I took a deep breath as I turned to face him.

"It's time to get in bed," I muttered to him, hoping he would snap out of the haze.

Before I could second-guess myself, I took three long strides toward him, grabbed hold of his hand, and brought him over to the large bed. Yanking back the blankets, I pushed on his chest to make him sit on the bed, trying to ignore the pounding that had started in my veins from the skin-to-skin contact. Some small part of him must have known what was going on because he laid down on the bed, pulling the blanket over his body.

He still would not release my hand.

"Will you stay with me?" Though he whispered the words, there was a desperation there.

I chewed on my lip. I should not even be in his chambers.

Dragons and humans had very different views on morality.

Because of the risk of slavery, humans were more careful when it came to physical relationships. The thought of bringing another life into the world, only to subject it to a terrible, abuse-filled existence was enough of a deterrent for us.

Dragons, however, did not carry that same burden, especially since they felt the need to make sure the dragon population was higher than that of the humans.

Letting out a resigned sigh, I climbed onto the bed next to him, making sure to stay on top of the covers and a respectable distance away, and curled into a ball. His fingers tightened around mine for a split second, as if thanking me for staying.

I was just comforting him, I told myself. He didn't want to be alone. That was all. This was purely platonic. Cheeks still flaming, I tried to calm the roaring in my core as I willed my body to relax, one limb, one muscle at a time. Somehow, sleep mercifully stretched over me. The last thing my eyes saw before drifting into unconsciousness was Tarrin peeking an eye open to look at me, his thumb gently stroking our intertwined hands.

CHAPTER THIRTY-ONE
KAIDA

No.

I jolted awake to the sun streaming in through the windows, my body curled against the Prince's, his arm draped over my stomach.

No, I repeated to myself. At some point in the night, I must have crawled under the blanket, looking for warmth. I scrubbed my face with my hand. I laid there for a few heartbeats, unsure whether I should get up and move away from him, or if I should stay. My body begged me to stay as it savored and enjoyed every place our bodies touched.

I waited, holding my breath, and felt him begin to stir. Tarrin propped himself up on an elbow to look over my shoulder and see my face. He gently moved my hair, tucking it behind my ear, and let his arm fall back over my stomach.

"Good morning," he murmured, his voice deep and husky from sleep. "You stayed."

Surprised at his words, I turned over. I froze at the closeness between our faces, at the look in his eyes.

"Of course, I stayed," I answered. "I was not about to leave you alone when…" I couldn't finish the sentence. He knew what I had meant to say.

I swallowed, the distance between our faces growing smaller. Barely a hand's-breadth between us. My breathing hitched, and it was an effort to keep still and not wriggle away out of nervousness. I glanced only once at his lips, as he licked them, and quickly looked away, anywhere but there. I noticed his eyes flick to my lips too, for a brief second, before pinning them back on my eyes.

"Thank you for staying," he said, his gaze fierce, unrelenting. A couple of heartbeats passed, both of us unmoving, the tension mounting in the air between us. Before I could understand what was happening, he planted a kiss on my forehead. It caught me so off guard that my cheeks turned fiery, redness creeping over them. Tarrin chuckled and pulled away, rolling over and plopping his feet onto the floor. A sudden cold shocked my body in all the places he had been touching.

He walked into the bathing room, his bare feet padding on the marble floor, and I took that as my cue. I ripped the blankets off me, shivering at the sudden cold and walked out of his bedroom and into the main room of his suite. A fire was already crackling away, and I settled down next to it, savoring the warmth. I knew I should leave, go back to my own room, let him be, but I couldn't bring myself to. Especially when I noticed a large spread of food on the table. It was way more food than one person needed. My stomach grumbled at the sight of it.

I glanced back through the bedroom. The laundry bin was gone. A servant must have come to collect it and no doubt would have seen us in bed together. My cheeks burned as I glanced away from the food, and Tarrin walked in, wearing a soft gray shirt and black pants. Noticing my blush, he glanced at the table before giving me a wry smile.

"Hungry?" he asked, taking a seat at the table. Grabbing two plates, he loaded each up with an assortment of fruits, followed by bacon, sausages, and fried eggs. He set one next to him and gestured for me to join him.

I searched his face for any sign of yesterday's fog, that blank expression or the grief that had threatened to consume him. But there was nothing. He either had grown numb to it or he had learned to hide it very well.

I joined him, the chair groaning softly as I sat down. All I could think was that I should not have been there. Nausea filled my stomach at the thought of the other humans thinking we spent the night together. I couldn't help but feel like I was betraying them by being with the Prince, though I knew it was absurd since we were betrothed. The humans would understand, wouldn't they? I kept my head down, avoiding looking him in the eye. I had just popped a strawberry in my mouth when he spoke.

"Did you know you are wearing my clothes?"

I choked, nearly swallowing the strawberry whole. "Excuse me?"

He flashed me a knowing smile, glancing down at my attire. Sure enough, the white button shirt and pants I had hurriedly thrown on yesterday were nearly identical to what he was wearing. My cheeks burned and I ducked my head, hands clutching the fabric of the shirt.

"That's all right, you can keep them. After last night, I would want something to remember me by too." Tarrin winked at me, his smile widening.

I knew he was just taunting me, but I couldn't help wanting to defend myself. "Nothing happened."

"Oh, *I* know that, and *you* know that. But nobody else does." His mouth bent into a feline smile.

I bit into a pineapple slice, shoulders slumping farther.

"Don't worry, Kaida. Once news spreads about my mother, anything they think happened between us will be old news. Besides, it wasn't so bad, was it?"

No. Truthfully, it was the best night of sleep I've ever had.

Tarrin smirked at me, hearing my thoughts through our bond. *Likewise.*

My ears were on fire, and I stuffed a grape in my mouth before I could say something I might regret. The air between us had grown thick and hot, his body somehow singing to mine, beckoning me closer. Tarrin leaned toward me as if he felt it too.

"What will you do now?" I blurted, dousing us both with a bucket of cold reality.

The amusement faded from his eyes. "I'm not sure." He shrugged his shoulders and shoved the last piece of bacon into his mouth. "If my father won't believe me, there's not much I can do. We could try to stop the Remnant ourselves, but without the might of the King behind us, I'm afraid we don't pose much of a threat."

Tarrin propped his elbow up onto the table, resting his chin on his fist. His brows shadowed his eyes, stress creasing his forehead. Seeing his smile earlier, the carefree way he had looked at me, joked with me… I wanted to bring that back. Chase the sorrow from his eyes. Out of instinct, I grabbed his other hand that was resting on the table. A comforting gesture, meant to soothe and let him know that I was there with him. He met my stare and held it, much longer than was comfortable, and I started to squirm. I tried to pry my hand away, but he was holding on, his thumb stroking small circles again.

When I looked up, he had leaned closer, his eyes fixed on my mouth. I froze.

"Thank you," he whispered, his breath tickling my lips. "For staying last night."

I swallowed hard, both nerves and heat bubbling in my core. I licked my lips out of habit. Knowing I should pull away, but not really wanting to, I held still as he leaned closer, his hand leaving mine, gently pushing my hair behind my ear, then cupping my cheek. A blush crept over my face.

I had never kissed anyone before. Being a slave, there was not much in the way of opportunities to meet a boy, nor had it ever really been on my mind. Survival was all I had ever been focused on.

Tarrin pulled me toward him, both of our chairs squeaking under the shifting weight. He held me there, meeting my eyes, a question flickering in his. I felt my fear melt a little from the fact that he would ask my permission, rather than forcing a kiss on me. It was yet another thing Tarrin had done that proved he wasn't a cruel monster. My cheeks were on fire from his unrelenting gaze, heart thundering in my chest, and I barely managed a nod before his lips found mine.

The world exploded around me.

Heat and light and flame seemed to swirl around us, dancing and twisting above us.

His lips were warm and soft, confident in every movement. The kiss was light, hesitant at first, but when he realized I was not pulling away, it escalated. His hands found my neck, drawing my face tighter to his and quickly moved to my hair, his fingers knotting in it. My own hands rested on his legs, soon finding his neck as he pulled me onto his lap, never breaking contact.

The kiss was heated, full of passion and desperation, his hands digging into my waist, as if he couldn't hold me tight enough. His hands roved up and down my back, over my legs, mine grabbing fistfuls of his hair. A small sound escaped from my mouth and he jerked back, searching my eyes. A sheepish smile curved my lips and he relaxed.

Slowly, he leaned forward again, touching his lips gently to mine.

A sweet, fluttering filled my stomach.

What was this? I had never felt anything like it.

From somewhere far away, I heard a voice that I had not heard in seven years.

My mother's voice.

This is what happiness feels like, sweet girl.

Tears welled in my eyes and spilled down my cheeks.

Tarrin pulled back, looking concerned at first, before tucking my hair behind each ear, then kissed each tear away. That feeling began to grow, slowly, like a pool of warm water lapping at my ankles, and then rising, covering every inch of skin. I knew he could not have heard my mother's words, but somehow, I felt he understood.

He wrapped me in his arms, cradling my head into his neck. I marveled at how wonderful such a feeling could be and felt remorse at the loss of never having experienced it before.

Tarrin drew soothing circles on my back. I didn't know how long we stayed like that. It could have been hours or only a few minutes. I didn't care. All I knew was that I wanted to feel this every day for the rest of my life.

And maybe the idea of marrying Tarrin didn't bother me as much as it used to. I blinked at the thought. But did that mean I was turning my back on the humans? Could I be both dragon and human without betraying one or the other? Did I deserve to have all of this?

My mother's words filled my mind once more, bringing fresh tears to my eyes.

Be happy, sweet girl. Be happy.

PART TWO

CHAPTER THIRTY-TWO

ELDRIN

I SAT AT A table in a crowded inn, waiting, the midnight-blue scales of my body barely flickering in the torchlight. I could feel it in the air, some sort of shift. Something was stirring on the continent, a change that was affecting both dragons and humans alike. The other dragons huddled together, whispering, unease settling in the air between them. Even the humans were more on edge than usual.

No one bothered to tell me what the cause of so much concern was; most choosing to ignore my presence. So, I simply sat at the small table, dented and covered in chips and dings, and watched. Waited.

Night had fallen hours ago but the brutal summer heat lingered, sticking to every surface, every scale. Even the lanterns on each table were heavy with it, as if they could not get enough oxygen to breathe. The smell of food wafted out from the kitchens, setting my stomach growling, but tonight I was not here to indulge.

I had been walking on the docks near the sea when the atmosphere moved. A tingling started from the ground and ricocheted through my body, a heavy feeling, like dropping a ship anchor into the sea, sinking into my stomach once it had disappeared. Quickly deciding to move farther inland, I stopped at the inn, hoping to glean information on what it might have been.

Slaves hurried past, back and forth, tending to the other dragons, sweat slick on their foreheads, the salty scent tickling my nostrils. I took a sip of the ale in front of me, glancing over the rim at the human girl making her way down the aisle.

"Excuse me," I said to the girl, keeping my voice low. The girl's eyes widened, a mole on her right cheek twitching as she took in my size and the color of my scales. In the dim lantern light, my scales appeared black instead of their deep shade of blue. Although the other dragons in the tavern were large, I towered above them. Twenty-foot dragons tended to be a rare sight, especially in Myrewell.

"Yes, Master Eldrin, how may I serve you?"

I barely managed to stop the cringe from crossing my face. I despised being called Master. I owned no slaves or land and traveled wherever I wished. In many villages, they knew me as the rogue dragon for I was always alone and didn't abide by traditional dragon customs. If it were not for the tab I had opened at the inn when I arrived a few weeks ago, they would not even have known my name.

I met the slave's questioning gaze and she immediately looked to the floor, and I held back a sigh. "I'd like another ale, if you would." Picking up the large mug in front of me, I downed the rest of its contents before handing it over to the girl. She dipped her chin in acknowledgment and hurried off the way she came.

A large party of dragons near me rose from their chairs and stumbled toward the doors on the other side of the room, casting curious glances my way. They murmured amongst each other, but it was all slurred and unintelligible thanks to their heavy indulging during their meal.

The room quieted in their absence, and the slave girl appeared in front of me with a mug of ale and a large bowl of stew. I opened my mouth to object as she set it on the table, but she simply said, "It's on the house." She pivoted on her heel to return to the kitchen.

"Wait," I blurted, far louder than I had intended, and the girl froze. A couple of dragons looked in our direction but most continued eating and chatting amongst themselves.

"Do you know why the dragons have been all worked up tonight?"

The girl swallowed hard; her lips pressed into a tight line. "Have you not heard the news, Master Eldrin?" she asked.

"What news, girl?"

Her throat bobbed as she swallowed, and she glanced anxiously toward the door to the kitchen. The other slaves were still bustling in and out, delivering food and clearing plates. Turning back to me, she let out a silent breath.

"The Queen of Elysia is dead."

The world spun and rocked beneath me; an earthquake rumbling through my mind though the inn remained still.

"Dead?" The word came out as a strangled whisper. The girl nodded, her face grave.

"Rumors are circulating that it was one of the Remnant." She paused. "The funeral is in two days, near Vernista."

My mind slammed to a stop, focus narrowing in on a single word. *Vernista.*

Vernista was a dangerous place for me. I had met a beautiful girl there nearly two decades ago and we lived together in the village for a time. Aela had been full of life, her humanness experiencing the world in ways that I never could. But it was also where Eklos lived. My wicked cousin who had been hunting me for years.

When Eklos discovered my presence in Vernista, I knew that I had to leave. Both for Aela's sake and my own. I knew that my cousin would discover our relationship and use it against me. I couldn't bear the thought, so I had moved south, as far from the village as I could get, to Myrewell. It was one of the most painful decisions I had ever made in my thousand years of existence. I often thought about Aela, about what had happened to her, if she was still a slave or if she had escaped like we had always talked about.

A sharp pang pierced my stomach at the memory of her face, the way she used to smile at me. I swallowed, pushing her face from my mind, and cleared my throat.

"Thank you for the report," I answered. The girl bobbed her head once again and hurried off toward the other tables where dragons demanded service.

The noise level returned to a deafening roar as another large gathering of dragons entered the inn, already well inebriated. I decided it was well past time to leave. I rose mostly unnoticed from my seat, and moved between the tables and chairs, far more gracefully than a dragon of my size should have been able to and slipped out the door before the other party had even sat down at their table.

I made it only a few steps outside when I stopped, breathing in the fresh sea air, tasting of salt and wind. The cobblestone street was empty and only scattered lights could be seen in nearby houses. The moon shone bright, illuminating every street and alley, leaving little need for a lantern as I started the long trek down to the docks for the second time that day.

Myrewell had been my home for seventeen years. While I never stayed in one place for very long, never had any permanent residence, I had grown to love the land, the culture. While the humans were still enslaved, it never seemed to be quite as hostile or as violent as what I had witnessed in the north. It was more of a home to me than Vernista or Shegora, the village I grew up in, had ever been.

As I walked down a hill, my dragon feet shuffling on the loose stones, claws digging lightly into the sand that had blown in from the beaches, the sea came into view. The southern coast of Myrewell stretched out before me. The end of Elysia.

There was supposedly another continent somewhere out there, hundreds, perhaps thousands, of miles to the south. Many dragons thought that the world just ended once you got far enough from Elysia. Some were filled with an insatiable curiosity and decided to sail away to find out. Any who decided to go on that journey never came back. At least that's what the locals always told me when I had asked.

I planned, one day, when I was ready to leave this world, to find a boat to take me south. Find out for myself what lies beyond Elysia. My thoughts came to a halt as I reached the line of docks, the boat I planned to visit sitting at the very end.

A sudden darkness enveloped my body, covering me from head to toe, as I strode toward that boat. Midnight scales that reflected the pale moon were snuffed out, leaving an endless cloud of dark smoke, devouring any light. It was only for a heartbeat, and when the darkness receded, my human body remained, clad all in black, my long silver hair whipping in the briny breeze. My amethyst eyes glowed in the moonlight, and my leather boots made a solid clunking noise on the wooden dock.

Reaching the edge of the boat, I let out a low whistle and waited. A moment later a higher-pitched whistle, mimicking a bird call, sounded from inside. I leaped off the dock and swung myself gracefully over the boat's edge, landing on the deck. I strode toward the cabin, again noticing the strange silence that had fallen over Myrewell. The docks, the beach, and every surrounding boat were all quiet, unmoving. It was as if the Queen's death had reached every edge of Elysia, a hush falling over every living and non-living thing.

Slipping inside the door, I winced at the groan of the rusty hinges. The cabin was small, barely enough room for two men to live comfortably. Two beds, one on top of the other, were shoved into the far corner, the bottom with linens askew. A tiny wood-burning stove sat across from the beds, a pot simmering away on top. It was stifling with only a small port window to allow in fresh air. Sweat began to pool on the back of my neck, my long hair sticking to it.

On the floor stoking the fire with a stick of iron, sat a middle-aged man with short graying hair, his clothes worn and old. His blue eyes widened in surprise at the sight of me, his tall frame making the space feel even smaller.

"Eldrin," the man said, a groan escaping his lips as he unfolded his legs and stood. He crossed the short distance between us, grasping my hand in his and my shoulder with his other hand.

"It is good to see you again, Noam." Memories flooded back into my mind at the mention of my old friend's name. Noam had been my closest friend since leaving Vernista. When I had needed to escape, I flew to a port near the southern tip of the Ilgathor Mountains and had found a younger Noam docked in a humble little boat, scrubbing the deck. He had been so proud of that vessel, so eager to go out to sea, to see a world in which he was his own master. I knew in an instant that we would be like brothers; that Noam would help me get as far from Vernista, from Eklos, as possible.

Without even thinking, I had dived for that boat, landing on the stern, fully dragon. Noam had fallen flat on his face out of fear, not for himself but for his beloved boat. I had let out a quiet chuckle and morphed into a man, Noam's sea-blue eyes widening in shock, and perhaps awe.

It had not taken much to convince the man to sail south. Noam had agreed, wholeheartedly, and within a couple hours, we had gathered enough food and supplies from a nearby village and began our voyage down the coast of Elysia. We docked in Pyrn for a few short weeks before continuing. It had taken two months to sail from the Ilgathor Mountains all the way to Myrewell, the place I now called home.

"What brings Eldrin the Great back to my humble little boat?" Noam asked, his eyes crinkling at the corners. Noam came up with the nickname back in the early days of our friendship and I had never bothered to correct him or stop him from saying it. I smiled at my old friend, before settling on the floor across from him.

I cleared my throat. "Queen Lita is dead."

Noam's mouth fell open, his brow furrowing. "That's what the strange stillness has been today," he murmured to himself. Even as a human without dragon senses, he was remarkably perceptive, always sensing things that most could not. It was one of the qualities I liked most about him.

"I need to get to Vernista."

Noam's eyes widened. "Why would you go back to that place?"

One night deep into our journey south, there had been a fierce storm at sea. It was so violent that our only option was to hunker down inside the cabin, wait it out, and pray that the boat stayed afloat. It was during that storm, moments away from possible death, that I had told Noam everything. About Aela, about the race of shape-shifting dragons that most humans believed to have gone extinct. I told him that Aela was my greatest love, that I had never felt such love for a person in my thousand years of existence. I also told my friend about Eklos. That he was my cousin, but not a shape-shifter, and that he was hunting me, and desperately wanted to kill me.

Noam had been surprisingly calm as he listened to the entire story, but that could have been due to the bottle of wine we had been passing back and forth throughout the storm. In all honesty, I had not even been sure that the man would remember any of it in the morning.

When the wind had finally died down and dawn broke over the water, Noam went out on the deck and watched the sun rise.

When he returned, he acted like his old self, like our conversation had never happened. He never brought it up and we had never spoken of it since.

"The Queen's funeral is in two days. I should be there."

"Two *days*? Eldrin, it would take two months by boat. Even if I had a faster ship, it couldn't be done." Noam ran a hand through his gray-brown hair, letting out an exasperated sigh.

"I do not intend to sail there, old friend. I have only come to say goodbye."

Noam's hands fell to his sides. "You intend to fly," he said flatly. It was not a question. It was the first time he had spoken of my dragon abilities.

I crossed the short distance between us, placing both hands on my friend's shoulders. For a moment, I could not think of any words to speak. We had embarked on many adventures, saving each other's lives multiple times. It was unfathomable to think that I might not ever see this man again. Although emotions were dulled in my human form, tears fought to the surface of my eyes, and I swallowed hard.

"Thank you, Noam, for your friendship these many years."

Silver lined Noam's eyes and he blinked furiously to keep the tears from falling. "Will you be returning to Myrewell?"

"Perhaps one day." I hoped that Noam was unable to see the lie in my eyes. I wished I could say for certain that I would return, that I could repay my friend for all he had done for me.

But the knowledge that I was going back to Vernista, to the village where Eklos lived… I knew returning was unlikely.

I folded him in an embrace, Noam's tears falling like steaming embers onto my shirt. When we stepped away, we each put a fisted hand over our hearts, and without another word, I turned and walked out the door.

I made it out of the boat, down the dock, and only a few steps onto the sandy shore before the tears burst from my eyes, cascading down my cheeks.

It was not simply saying goodbye to my closest friend, but to my home, my life. Every ounce of normalcy that I had gained back, fought for over the last seventeen years, it was all about to disappear. Although I never stayed in one place long, Myrewell had become my home, a place of safety and surety. The moment I crossed the border, it would all be gone.

And if Eklos found me again, I was not so sure I would escape this time. It was enough of a miracle that I had managed to stay hidden this long. Going back would only be tempting fate, and fate was never something to play with.

Sand filled my boots as I continued walking down the beach, the moon high in the sky, illuminating the gentle waves lapping at the shore. I breathed in the salty air, the soft breeze whipping my hair behind me. The shoreline ended at a large cliff and I stopped within the shadows. Glancing back at the town, I drank in every detail of the city, begging my mind to remember this place. My home.

Before I could change my mind, darkness smothered me, snaking and wrapping around my limbs, back, and head. Everywhere the dark cloud touched, my skin changed to scales, wings erupting from my back, my face elongating into a snout. I sighed through my nostrils, smoke curling out of them as my inner fire was once again ignited.

I looked toward the north. I knew that if I flew for two days straight, while I might make it in time, I would be drained. No strength left to fight or defend myself if I came face-to-face with Eklos. Noam thought I intended to fly all the way to Vernista. That was only partly true. I did plan to fly, for a day or so, to the border of Myrewell. What Noam did not know was that I possessed a special gift. A rare magical ability to move from one place to another, instantly. My well of magic took a large hit whenever I used it, but it regenerated fast enough to not dissuade me from utilizing it.

I planned to "jump" from the border of Myrewell to the outskirts of Vernista on the second day, arriving in time for the Queen's funeral.

I took a step out from underneath the cliff overhang, my dark scales consuming more light than they reflected. Taking a deep breath, I unfurled the wings I hadn't used in weeks, groaning quietly as they stretched out to their full length. The twenty-foot wingspan, wrought with strong boning and thick muscles, had taken hundreds of years to perfect.

I spared one last look at the town and inhaled deeply, before turning toward the sea and pushed off the sandy ground, jumping higher than any human or beast should be able to, wings tucked in tight. When I had cleared the top of the cliff, I snapped out my wings, immediately catching an updraft as I soared higher into the sky. My midnight-blue scales blended in with the night sky, making me almost invisible to anyone below.

Switching directions to head north, I passed over Noam's boat and found my friend sitting on the cabin roof looking up into the night sky. The man was waving as if he had been waiting for me to pass by. Even with the impossible distance, our eyes met, and Noam clapped his fist over his heart. I mimicked the gesture and fought back tears as I continued northward, knowing this was most likely our final farewell.

CHAPTER THIRTY-THREE
TARRIN

I RAN A HAND through my hair, walking through the palace halls, unable to quiet my restless heart after that kiss. It had been like an earthquake, shaking the ground beneath my feet, brimming with fire and crackling electricity. It sparked and flared with every clash of our lips, every touch of our hands.

And she did not pull away.

Kaida had been so difficult to read the past few weeks. Some days she looked at me in a way that sent fire bubbling through my stomach, but then other days she would hardly look or speak to me, as if she couldn't stand to be around me. But she had stayed last night. She took care of me, helped me into bed, and stayed all night.

I told myself upon waking that morning that our bodies nestled together beneath the covers had been purely platonic. I knew she had fallen asleep on top of the blankets and assumed that she did not want to cross any boundaries.

A slight trembling woke me in the middle of the night. Kaida had been shivering so violently, despite the heat still lingering from the summer day, that it was causing the entire bed to shake. I could not bear the sight of her curled-up body, freezing. I wondered for a moment if that was what her normal life had been under

Eklos's ownership. She had not shared much about her life back then, and I could never bring myself to ask.

I had gently pulled the blankets out from under her, and moved shoulder to shoulder, offering what warmth I could as the sheets settled over us. I was not sure when we had ended up curled together, our legs tangled, my arm draped over her stomach.

The overwhelming desire to kiss her had almost taken control as we laid there together, faces inches apart. I settled for a kiss on her forehead, praying she would not recoil from my touch. When she blushed instead, hope kindled inside me. Maybe she was not entirely repulsed by me after all.

I walked down the stairs, into the foyer, and found the palace buzzing. Slaves were scrambling around, back and forth, carrying platters of food in and out of the kitchens and enormous bouquets of flowers from the gardens. Shuffling feet and the squeaks of shoes on marble filled the air, and hurried whispers followed by the occasional shouting of orders ricocheted off the walls. The entire manor seemed to be in a state of controlled chaos to prepare for the Queen's funeral.

My mother's funeral.

Time slowed down and my chest tightened. *This should not be happening. We should not be preparing for her funeral, preparing to celebrate her life. She should still be here.*

It was a difficult task to kill a dragon, but it was close to impossible to kill a shape-shifter. They were stronger than most, their scales thicker and more resilient than a normal dragon's, with the addition of a shifter's magical abilities. They were as close to immortal as you could get.

Yet, here we were.

Dragon funerals were always strange. They were so infrequent that everyone always seemed to forget what to do. No one could remember the correct rituals or procedures. The slaves would oversee preparations, but human funerals were very different from those of a dragon—or so I had been told. Since dragons and humans were unable to work together, dragon funerals tended to be a hodgepodge of different traditions.

In all honesty, I was not even sure what to expect. It was to be held in the gardens, in my mother's favorite place, but whatever my role was to be, I had no idea.

Part of me had been wondering what all of this meant for me. The Queen had inherited the throne, making the King merely her consort. My father had only been working with the Council all these years on her behalf. He could not rule without her. I did not know if that meant my family would forfeit their control of Elysia or if I, being the sole heir, would now become king.

The thought sent a shiver crawling down my spine.

I was not ready.

Not yet.

"Prince Tarrin," a tired voice said from behind me. Turning, I found it was Berda, the old woman in charge of the slaves in the palace.

"The King is requesting your presence in his chambers." She curtsied once and marched away, barking at another servant who struggled to see over a giant vase of flowers.

What did my father want now? He had made his opinion, his position, very clear the last we spoke. Heaving a big sigh, I made my way down a long corridor to a massive golden door. It was the most elaborately carved piece in the entire palace.

In a brief flash of blue, I shifted into my scaled body and raised a clawed hand to knock. The door opened before I even made contact.

"Come in, Son." My father stood there, eyes bloodshot, holding the door open. His voice was strangely clear in a way I hadn't heard in months.

"What is it, Father?" I asked as he took a seat at a nearby table.

His chambers were dark, every curtain drawn. Even the fire in the hearth had reduced to embers.

"There is something you should know," he began, scratching the back of his neck, his scales making a subtle *plink* sound.

I crossed my arms, waiting.

"When you were two, your mother transferred her right to rule to me. For the last seventeen years, she has been queen only by marriage to me, rather than from inheriting the throne." My father paused, letting the words sink in.

My jaw went slack. "Can she do that?" I asked, incredulous.

"Technically, yes. Because she was a female who inherited the throne rather than a male, it allowed for a loophole in the law," he said matter-of-factly. "If it were not for that decision, you would be crowned king after her funeral."

The floor dropped out from beneath my feet. "Why would she do that?"

The King hesitated, silence pulsing like a heartbeat in the room.

"Your mother was not only a Wind Wielder, Tarrin. She had a second gift. One that has prompted every decision she has made since before you were born."

My mind churned. Dragons having *two* magical abilities were so rare, I had never met one before Kaida. Why would she have kept this from me?

"Your mother had the rare gift of Foresight. She was able to see events in the future; things that had not yet come to pass."

Suddenly it all made sense.

Why she was so insistent on me finding Kaida, bringing her to the palace. How she had known that Kaida would be attacked and had known that she would be the one to save her.

Why she had transferred her right to rule to my father.

The biggest realization hit me like a slap in the face, chilling my blood to ice.

My mother, the Queen of Elysia, had known she was going to die for a human.

⁂

"Why wouldn't she tell me?" I demanded, pacing the length of the marble floors.

"She wanted to, Son. But that gift is particular. The future is already decided on. There is no changing future outcomes. The only thing her gift truly granted her was the opportunity to change her own decisions to best adjust to what the future had in store.

"The future deemed she would die before you were ready to be king. She transferred her title to me, so you wouldn't have to bear that burden too early. She knew Kaida had to live through Belharnt before we could rescue her, despite her promise to her mother. Once Kaida was back in Vernista, we were able to rescue her. Every decision had a purpose."

The room spun and I sat down in the middle of the floor in an awkward heap of dragon limbs, drawing my wings around me. My father's words both made sense and didn't. And one part in particular stuck out to me.

"Why did Kaida have to live through Belharnt?" My voice was low.

My father let out a sigh. "To become who we are meant to be, we must go through trials. That is how we grow. Though it is unfortunate that Kaida had to endure such horrific years in that dungeon, it resulted in a strong human, and an even stronger dragon."

"That seems like a lousy excuse that enabled cowardice," I snapped. I refused to believe that someone as kindhearted and compassionate as Kaida *had* to live through Belharnt in order to turn out that way. My parents were cowards.

"Tarrin, I know it's hard to understand—"

"No," I cut him off. "It's not. It's quite easy to understand that you both put her at risk needlessly. She could have died there. She *should have* died there!"

My father let out a low growl. "Tarrin, you must trust your mother's decisions. She didn't make them foolishly. She did what she thought was best knowing the outcome of the future."

"My mother is dead, and she knew that would happen, and never told me about it. That seems like a poor decision to me." I jumped to my feet, fire filling up my core. I needed to get out of there.

"Son, wait."

I shook my head. "I don't want to hear anything you have to say, especially when you've brushed me aside all these months." My father's eyes softened, his mouth opening to explain, but I held up a hand. "You've always put duty ahead of family, the Council over your own son's word. I always just let it go, trusting that the King and Queen of Elysia knew better than I did." Smoke leaked from my nostrils in a steady stream. "But know this: if you, or anyone else, come against Kaida and try to hurt her in any way, I will do whatever it takes to protect her. That's a promise."

CHAPTER THIRTY-FOUR
KAIDA

AFTER SPENDING THE morning practically floating through the gardens due to this newfound happiness, I came in the front doors and witnessed the bedlam for only a second before Berda spotted me, scowled, and shooed me up the stairs to prepare for the funeral. I made it through the maze of slaves in the hallway and to my chambers where I barely had a moment to breathe before Meara appeared, ushering me into the steaming bathing room. In a whirlwind of steam, soap, and fabric, I ended up in the soft chair in front of the vanity, Meara hastily combing through the tangles in my long hair.

There had been a strange tension between us ever since she locked me in my chambers during the Beginnings Festival. I didn't fault her for it, knowing she had been ordered to keep me in the palace, but it saddened me that any progress we had made toward a possible friendship had already died a swift death.

"Will you be attending the funeral?" I asked, breaking the uncomfortable silence that had settled between us. Her hands stilled in my hair, the brush coming to a stop. She met my gaze in the mirror. Her face was young, eyes bright but wary, blonde hair wrapped into a braid on top of her head. The plain mud-brown dress that she usually wore was gone and had been replaced with a simple black dress with long flowing sleeves that cuffed around her wrists, and a skirt that flowed to her ankles. It was just short enough to reveal her clunky and worn black boots.

"I will be present, miss, should you require anything during the ceremony or celebration afterwards," she said matter-of-factly, with no trace of emotion in the words. I studied her face in the mirror, watching for any betrayal of her true thoughts on the matter, but her face remained neutral.

She finished brushing through my hair and began weaving it back, piece by piece, into an elaborate braid that ended at the middle of my back. Quickly wetting her thumb and forefinger, she swiped down at several pieces near my hairline, and curled them quickly, effectively framing the features of my face. She grabbed a small jar of powder and caked it all over my face, following up with a thick line of kohl over each eyelid. A stick of ruby red paste found its way over my lips.

"Where did you learn to do this?" I asked.

"My mother taught me many years ago." Meara offered a small smile that was more of a grimace and stepped away toward the armoire and pulled out a black dress. It hung to the floor, neckline the deepest I had ever worn, the light material and loose sleeves, similar to that of Meara's dress, perfect for the summer heat. As she brought it over to where I sat, the light streaming through the windows caught the fabric of the dress and it let off a subtle glow, a light metallic shimmer.

"This dress is a gift from the Prince. He has requested that you wear it today."

I blinked, swallowing hard. "It's beautiful."

I quickly threw off the robe I had been wearing and Meara helped me step into the gown. The fabric was extravagantly soft, caressing my skin like silk, and hugging every non-existent curve perfectly.

Meara slipped some very expensive-looking silk slippers over my feet that shimmered like the dress, and when I looked at her questioningly, she simply said, "Another gift." When she stood, she hurried over to the armoire and opened the right door, revealing a full-length mirror. My mouth dropped open.

The dress was magnificent, catching the light at the perfect moments, enhancing the features that had once been diminished from years of malnutrition and manual labor.

The biggest difference was to my face. Meara had managed to cover those stubborn black circles under my eyes, lining my eyelids with kohl, making my blue eyes stand out against my pale skin. Once again, I had the thought that if there were a human equivalent to royalty, this was what it would look like. The closer I studied my face, the more I realized I closely resembled my mother. A pit of longing cracked open in my core, and I put a hand against my stomach as if I could put it back together.

A soft knock sounded at the door.

Without a word, Meara left the bedroom and returned a heartbeat later, with Prince Tarrin in tow. Dressed in all black, with a coat adorned with various royal emblems, and his hair tied back at the nape of his neck, my heart skipped a beat.

Meara stepped out of the way to reveal me, before bowing her head at the prince, and leaving my chambers. Tarrin froze, his lips parting as his eyes roved over my face, my hair, followed it down the braid that now draped over my shoulder. When he reached the end, his gaze drifted to my body, utterly mesmerized by the shimmering fabric that revealed both too much and not enough. A slight flicker of emotion flashed over his eyes when he stopped at the slippers adorning my feet. Snapping his eyes to mine, he smiled.

"You look stunning," he said, his voice rough.

Heat bloomed on my face and I planted my eyes on the floor. Despite all the powder on my face, I was sure he could see the redness in my cheeks. The Prince crossed the distance between us, a small box in his hands.

"For you." Handing me the box, he continued, "My mother wanted you to have this."

With shaking hands, I took it from him, our fingers brushing, sending a shock through my body. I glanced up at his emerald eyes that were watching me so intently, as if trying to memorize every feature, every piece of me. When I pulled open the lid, I gasped and nearly dropped it. Tarrin's hands reached out to steady mine, holding them gently.

Inside the box sat an exquisite necklace. It was made of a black silver that emanated a slight warmth where it should have been cold as a rock. Lining it were tiny amethyst stones that seemed to glow. Tarrin lifted the box from my hands, freeing the necklace from the fasteners, and gestured for me to turn around. I was facing the mirror once more and could see every movement he made, every inch his body moved toward mine.

The necklace tied every part of my ensemble together. It was the piece I did not realize was missing. The chain sat just below my collarbone, and a thin piece of metal continued, dangling down in between the fabric of the plunging neckline. At the end of the necklace, in the middle of my chest, sat a large amethyst stone, delicately cut to reveal all the facets, and reflected the light in a dazzling way. A soft purple glow lit up my face and my eyes found Tarrin's, unable to stop the heat spreading over my cheeks.

He took a step forward, his body touching mine, the scent of crisp night air and blue cypress enveloping my senses. His hands dropped from the back of my neck and found themselves sitting on my waist, the heat from them searing through the thin fabric of the dress. Warm tendrils of his breath tickled my ear. My feet might as well have been puddles on the floor for as much as I was able to move.

He closed his eyes as he took a deep breath, taking in my

scent. Bending his neck, he nudged my ear with his nose, then kissed it gently. Once. Twice. My breathing hitched, a fire lighting in my core, and he chuckled.

"You look beautiful, Kaida."

"Thank you," I whispered, and he planted a kiss on my temple before offering a hand to me. Instead of placing my hand on his arm and guiding me as an escort to the gardens, he interlaced our fingers, a gesture that was anything but formal. Looking down at me, he held my stare, and then raised our linked hands, kissing mine. That faint fluttery feeling filled my stomach again and the corners of his mouth twitched just as someone cleared their throat from the doorway.

"Your Highness, it is time," Berda announced with hands on her hips, silver hair so tightly wrapped behind her head that it seemed the skin on her face was being stretched. Those tiny glasses sat precariously on her nose, and the scowl she gave me was almost enough for me to smack them right off her face.

A soft snort escaped Tarrin's nose, and he guided me out of my chambers and into the hallway. "I would strongly suggest not smacking Berda," the Prince whispered in my ear, sending a shiver through me.

I scowled back at him. "I do not care for this mind reading thing."

Tarrin laughed. He put his free hand up in the air in a gesture of innocence. "It is not exactly mind reading when it is written all over your face." The corners of his eyes crinkled in amusement.

We reached the top of the staircase and all the slaves that had been bustling about fled the foyer. In a matter of seconds, the room had emptied, and Tarrin led me down the front steps as I fought to keep my dress behind me and not under my feet.

The Queen's funeral was being held in the gardens since it was her favorite place on the palace grounds. Beds of flowers had been moved and rearranged to create enough seating for the visitors, including the servants in the very back. An aisle big enough for a dragon-sized casket was left between each side of chairs. As we drew closer, I could see blankets of purple wisteria that were draped across the backs of every seat, wrapped delicately around the sides and legs, creating an elegant feel more akin to a wedding than a funeral. The gentle scent of the flowers wrapped itself around the senses, creating a sense of peace.

"Wisteria were her favorite flowers," Tarrin explained, a wistful smile on his face.

"They're beautiful."

He held my gaze for a moment and let go of my hand. Before I could blink, in a brief flash of light, he shifted into his dragon form, and held out his enormous arm to me. Willing my trembling to stop, I wrapped my arm through his and rested my hand on his clawed, scaly hand. What a sight we must have been. Dragon and human, arm in arm.

I noticed several large pairs of confused eyes glancing at us, some with disdain and others with curiosity. Part of me wondered if the King and Queen had ever announced our betrothal to Elysia. I knew preparations for the wedding were underway, but Tarrin and I had never discussed any royal political matters. I could not help but wonder what kind of implications us getting married would have on not only the monarchy, but all of Elysia.

Not just a dragon and a human together, but two shape-shifters.

He led me down the long aisle toward the front row of chairs. His father, turquoise and bright, sat in the first chair on the left. I glanced behind me and found Meara standing in the back, watching my every movement.

As we reached the front row, King Martik stood and embraced his son. It was strange to see dragons hugging. He glanced down at me, eyes landing on my dress, my necklace, and for a moment his eyes narrowed. Without a word he turned back to his son, gestured for him to sit next to him, and Tarrin guided me over to the chair next to his. I could hear the murmured whispers of the other dragons sitting behind us, but I forced myself to tune them out.

As soon as we sat down, the small orchestra of instruments began playing a melancholy tune. Every dragon and human in attendance went silent.

"Please rise in honor of the Queen," a pale green dragon announced from the archway looming a few feet in front of us. As one, everyone rose to their feet and turned to face the procession. The casket that the Queen now laid in was so large it took six large dragons to carry it down the aisle, two on each side, and one at the front and back. They slowly marched down the path, moving together in sync as if they had practiced for hours.

But it was not the dragons carrying the casket that caught and held my attention, or even the tears and whispers of the dragons they passed on their journey forward.

It was the midnight-blue dragon who sat in the back row in the right section of chairs, whose eyes were dead locked on mine. He towered over everyone else, unmoving, attention unwavering from my face. Out of habit I wrung my hands. As if Tarrin were aware of every movement I made, he grabbed hold of one of my hands, carefully keeping his claws from ripping into my skin. His hand dwarfed my own. The midnight dragon's eyes widened in surprise as he looked from my face to the Prince's, to our hands between us.

"You may now be seated." The dragon overseeing the ceremony spoke again, and I snapped back to reality. The Queen's casket now stood on a series of short pedestals, and all other attendees were seated. Tarrin looked at me questioningly and gently tugged my hand for me to sit. I glanced one last time at the dragon in the back and found his eyes still on mine. Heat slid over my cheeks and I plopped into my seat. I faced forward just as the pale green dragon spoke again.

"Let us begin."

CHAPTER THIRTY-FIVE

KAIDA

THE SUN BEGAN its descent toward the horizon, flooding the Great Hall in a warm golden light. Vibrant colors danced over the walls and ceiling as the light hit the scales of the gathered dragons. Long wooden tables lined the entire length of the eastern wall, stacked and piled with different platters and assortments of food. Everything from fruit, to cheese, to roasted meats and vegetables, filling the air with a multitude of smells, sending a pang of hunger shooting through my stomach.

Purple wisteria hung from the ceilings, wrapping around the thick marble columns that ran the length of the room. Large, ornate vases were scattered about, overflowing with a mix of wisteria and some other purple flower I didn't know the name for.

Most of the dragons at the celebration were congregated around the table smothered in barrels of ale, beast-sized mugs of it in their hands, to drown the sorrow from losing their queen. Or perhaps just because dragons were a miserable sort.

A small orchestra in the corner began playing an upbeat tune and Tarrin shifted, in a flash of light, into a young man. He offered me his arm, gesturing to the empty wooden floor.

"Would you like to dance with me?" A warm smile creased the corners of his eyes, and my stomach sank.

"I don't know how."

A half smile bent his lips. "Then allow this to be another one of your training lessons."

I rolled my eyes. "Right, because you are such a good teacher," I taunted back.

Tarrin chuckled, taking my arm, and led me onto the empty floor, abandoning my untouched plate of food on the table next to us. He swirled me around in a circle and pulled me in close, chest to chest, one hand on my waist, the other holding my hand.

Electricity crackled in all the places our bodies touched. He moved us back and forth across the floor, keeping perfectly in time with every change in tempo, graciously ignoring every time I stepped on his toes. Not once did Tarrin's eyes leave my own. That hesitant fluttering returned, filling my stomach.

The musicians in the corner ended their song in a beautiful blend of harmony and started into the next piece. The instruments and their players captured my attention, their fingers moving masterfully over the strings, notes flying and swirling through the air.

I opened my mouth to comment on the music when I saw the dragon over the Prince's shoulder. Midnight blue scales, like when dusk meets the night sky, glistened in the dimming daylight, even from the shadowed corner he stood in. His enormous body leaned against one of the marble columns, arms crossed in an unusual human-like gesture. My brows furrowed as that strange feeling, that strange draw, settled into me.

I glanced up at Tarrin and found him watching me.

What is it?

I wanted to tell him that something felt off about the dragon watching us from the corner, but it was his mother's funeral. I didn't want to ruin this day or taint his memory by adding unnecessary conflict.

He pushed my chin up, forcing me to meet his eyes. "Kaida,

what's wrong?" he asked, tucking a loose strand of hair behind my ear. I let out a sigh.

"There's a dragon over in the corner. There is something… different… off. I don't know what it is." I swallowed hard. "He keeps watching me. *Us*."

"I think everyone is watching us." Tarrin smirked but looked over his shoulder and his body stiffened. Taking my hand, he did the absolute last thing I wanted him to do and led me toward him, simultaneously shifting back into dragon form.

The dragon straightened, setting his mug of ale down as we approached. We stopped a few feet away, Tarrin positioning himself between us. The strange dragon dipped his head in a bow.

"This is a celebration of the Queen's life. If you are here to cause trouble, I suggest you leave now," Tarrin said stiffly, his voice flooding with royal dominance.

"I am only here to pay my respects to an old friend, Your Highness."

His eyes widened before his brows sank toward his eyes. "You were a friend of the Queen?"

"A very long time ago, Your Highness. Before you were born."

I could see Tarrin's mind turning and spinning. "Who are you?"

"I am not certain if Queen Lita would have shared my story."

Tarrin winced at his mother's name. "Who are you?" he demanded again.

Silence hung heavy between us all for several moments, his eyes moving back and forth between us before he answered.

"You may call me Eldrin," he paused, glancing at me over Tarrin's shoulder. "Eldrin the Great." His eyes crinkled as if it were a joke.

Tarrin looked unamused but I could not help the soft snort that came out of me, and Eldrin fixed his attention back on me.

"And who is this lovely lady behind you?"

Tarrin hesitated. “This is Kaida, my betrothed,” he declared, pulling me into his side, though I barely reached his waist when he was in dragon form. Heat bloomed over my face. This was the first time he had officially announced it to anyone.

Tarrin and I had not discussed the whole betrothal situation much since the first day he brought me to the palace. While there definitely seemed to be *something* there between us, I was not sure if it equated to marriage. But hearing him say it out loud, proudly, acceptingly, I could not help a quick look at his face.

You did not think you were getting away from me that easily, did you? The corners of his eyes crinkled, even as his focus remained on Eldrin.

A girl can dream.

A playful nudge pushed against my consciousness and I instinctively nudged back. A light chuckle floated from his mind to mine and my blood heated at the sound of it. The memory of that kiss in his chambers floated back to me.

“It is an honor to meet you, milady.” Eldrin’s voice interrupted my thoughts like dunking me into a pool of freezing water. I found it odd that he would address a human in such a formal manner.

Tarrin’s eyes still smoldered from the heated exchange between our minds, and he glanced in the direction of the door, then back to the dragon.

“Thank you for coming to pay your respects to the Queen. Enjoy the rest of the celebration,” he said, his voice cold, turning toward me and gesturing in the direction of the doors. I managed all of two steps before I froze, Tarrin slamming to a stop behind me. The smell was unmistakable, even in my human body.

What is it?

The hair on my arms rose. Blood rushed into my ears, the noise in the room engulfed by a roaring sound, and I grew dizzy, my legs weakening beneath me.

“Eklos,” I whispered. Tarrin’s eyes widened, and he shoved

me behind him as he took a step forward, peering over the heads of every dragon assembled. They all continued their talking and indulging, not sensing the danger wafting through the room.

My hands began to shake as the memory of the last encounter with Eklos resurfaced in my mind. The sheer terror that had taken over my body as that whip of smoke had wrapped around my neck, choking the air from my lungs. The Queen standing in front of me as she accepted the death that should have been mine.

The Great Hall felt like it was closing in over my head and I struggled to breathe.

Tarrin bent down and muttered into my ear, "He would not be stupid enough to attack you here, inside the palace of all places." We scanned every corner, every shadow, but found nothing. The scent was slowly dissipating. My heart pounded beneath my skin.

I glanced back over Tarrin's shoulder, wondering if the strange dragon Eldrin had anything to do with Eklos being there.

But Eldrin was gone.

CHAPTER THIRTY-SIX

KAIDA

THE SMOKE AND sulfur scent of Eklos filled my nose, choking me as Tarrin and I burst through the front doors. Through our bond, I could feel Tarrin's need to avenge his mother's death twisting with the need to protect me. Tarrin wanted Eklos to pay for taking the queen's life while ensuring that he wouldn't be able to do the same to anyone else that he cared about. While feeling that kind of violence from my betrothed should have terrified me, I found it strangely reassuring.

Because Tarrin was right. Eklos had to pay. For what he had done to the Queen, but also for what he had done to the humans of Elysia. It became a chant that sang through my blood. *Kill Eklos.*

"Stay here," Tarrin commanded me as he ran down the front steps, his turquoise scales flashing in the sunlight as he shifted mid-stride. Most humans would hear the dominance in his voice and cower, listening to whatever he said, and I knew I should heed his warning. But my feet followed him down the stairs of their own accord.

I couldn't let him face Eklos alone. We were better together than we were apart.

I trudged through row after row of flowers after Tarrin, watching his nose twitch, his head moving as he sniffed out the dragon.

He caught sight of me out of the corner of his eye and spun to me. "Kaida, I told you to stay—"

Smoke erupted in a dense cloud, flowers, bushes, and the wood lining the beds exploding, shooting everywhere like daggers. Thick tendrils of smoke formed into whips, snaking out to smother my mouth, and wrapped around my waist as it yanked me in the opposite direction.

"Kaida!" Tarrin screamed.

Cold, unforgiving scales hit my back. I glanced up and found Eklos above me, having used his smoke to draw me to him. His scaled hand covered my entire face as he held me tight against him.

"I told you, *girl.* I do not care if you are the future queen. *Nobody* escapes my house." He spit on the ground next to me and I flinched. I opened my mouth and bit one of his clawed fingers. It was more an annoyance, and didn't hurt him at all, but it surprised him enough that he dropped me to the ground.

"You'll pay for that, girl," Eklos snarled.

Twisting his smoke into a leash, he lashed out at Tarrin, shackling his wrists. With a mighty pull, Eklos yanked the prince into the air, sending him flying several feet away, landing and sliding across the earth with a deep thud. His head made a cracking noise as it collided with the ground. Shackles of smoke erupted from the ground, winding themselves around each of his limbs.

Before I could move to help him, a shaft of smoke, covered in phantom thorns, struck my side, digging deep and ripping open the skin. I couldn't hold back my scream. Choked sobs erupted from my mouth as I fought to get air into my lungs. Blood seeped through my fingers as I put my hands on the wound.

The ground thundered as Eklos took step after step toward me. Dark smoke billowed out of his snout, his eyes glowing like heated coals. I shook my head, trying to clear the black dots from my vision. Tears streamed down my cheeks.

"Kaida!" Tarrin screamed again, yanking at his restraints.

Eklos's snout spread into a grin of delight. "Your stupid mother tried to escape and look what happened to her. Her screaming was a beautiful sonata in my ears, her pleading for me to spare you, a lovely melody."

My muscles fell into a preternatural calm at the mention of my mother. The memory of her head falling into a pool of blood flashed behind my eyelids. The thought of her screaming, being tortured, and enduring pain, that I knew all too well, was too much to bear. Flame ripped through my core, licking my veins, setting my insides on fire. Gritting my teeth, I pushed to my feet, blood leaking from the gaping hole in my dress. I clenched my hands into fists.

"Well, well," he crooned. "At least you have more fight in you than that pathetic excuse for a woman you called your mother," Eklos laughed, the sound like a fork scraping against porcelain. "It did not take much to break her. Pity."

I swallowed, my nails piercing into my palms. Smoke swirled around Eklos as he took a step closer to me. Then another.

"I think it will be much more enjoyable to kill you. Aela died far too quickly."

Time stopped.

The world tilted dangerously.

The beast inside me erupted, a blinding purple light flashing through the air as I shifted into dragon from. A combination of fire and lightning exploded from my snout and hands, sending Eklos careening back into a patch of roses.

My chest heaved in gasping breaths, and white flames encased my hands, flowing like a current in and out and circling around my fingers.

Eklos was sprawled on a bed of thorns and splintered wood, gaping at me. He pushed himself to his feet and took a step back. I mimicked his movements, flames growing higher and hotter in my palms. Alarm flashed in his eyes for only a moment before it disappeared, an arrogant smile replacing it.

"You know, girl, fire cannot exist without air." The moment the words left his mouth, black sulfurous smoke exploded from his mouth, his hands, bathing me in a cloud of toxic fog. It shoved its way into my mouth and nose, my flames going out as I choked and coughed, desperately trying to fill my lungs. Eklos took a step closer, pushing harder, releasing more. He laughed as I dropped to my knees, clawing at the smoke that evaporated and reappeared.

"Kaida!" Tarrin screamed my name, and I could hear the terror in his voice. Eklos had the smoke shackles around him too tight. There was nothing the Prince could do but watch as my old Master sucked the oxygen from my lungs.

And then it stopped. His smoke wavered in the air for a moment as I gasped in precious air, before Eklos sucked it all back into his nostrils.

"You," Eklos spat. It was only one word, but it rumbled the earth.

I glanced up through blurry tears and found the midnight-blue dragon standing on the other side of the garden.

"Hello, cousin," Eldrin answered cheerfully, despite the oncoming death that awaited us all.

Cousin?

"You are a very difficult dragon to hunt down, Eldrin."

"There are always plenty of shadows to hide in." A smirk twisted Eldrin's snout.

Eklos narrowed his eyes, moving two more steps forward. "And where, pray tell, have you been hiding all these years?"

"Now, what would be the fun in telling you? Why should I reveal my secrets? The only answer you need is, wherever is farthest away from you."

Eklos's restraint snapped, and I could do nothing but watch as he whipped a leash of smoke toward his cousin. It was met with a tendril of flame from Eldrin's hand, and the two parried back and forth, each trying to gain the upper hand. When they broke apart, Eklos paused, glancing down at me and then at Eldrin, then back at me.

And then Eklos started to laugh.

"I wondered why you two shared a scent," he drawled. "I thought perhaps you had met before, but seeing her face at the party when she encountered you, I knew that couldn't be true."

Eldrin lowered his hands a fraction, eyes narrowing. "What are you talking about?"

Eklos laughed again, more of a hiss this time. "You mean to tell me that you have no clue who this wretched girl is? You don't see any resemblance between her and the human you abandoned in Vernista?"

Eldrin's face crumpled, but I shoved it from my mind as I pushed to my feet, holding in a scream as my wings stretched behind me. Tarrin and I had to strike while Eldrin had Eklos distracted. It was the only way we could win. I looked over at Tarrin, still on the ground, but it seemed the shackles had dissolved around his wrists. I sent a mental picture through our bond of us attacking Eklos in tandem.

Tarrin met my eyes and gave an imperceptible nod. I slinked my way towards him, my movements slow and clumsy.

Eldrin did not respond, which seemed to only goad Eklos on.

"Well, this is surely a tale that will be told all over Elysia," he announced, proudly, gesturing at the sky. "Eklos, son of Xalerion, finally ending Eldrin the abomination, and his precious daughter too."

I just reached Tarrin's side when I registered Eklos's words and froze, eyes wide. *Daughter? He thinks Eldrin is my father?*

Eldrin did not react at first, the scales on his forehead bunching as his brow furrowed. "I don't have a daughter."

"And here I thought Aela was just some harlot who had gotten herself pregnant out of wedlock," Eklos continued, ignoring Eldrin's words. "Little did I know that my *cousin* was the one who put her in that state. Tell me, did you think Aela would be safe if you left Vernista? That I would not notice your scent all over her?"

My mouth went dry, tongue sticking uncomfortably to the roof of my mouth. Eklos took another step toward Eldrin.

No. He has to be wrong. There's no way this enormous dragon is my father. Eklos is just trying to bait me.

But Eldrin's eyes… they were the same color as my scales.

There had been some strange pull between us that did not make sense before. But if he was my father, why would my mother never tell me? Why hadn't the Queen?

Think about it later. As long as you defeat Eklos, you'll have time to figure out the truth later.

"But there was Aela one day, all those years ago, a baby girl in her arms, alone at the market, covered in *your* scent. So, I took her as my slave, knowing one day you would come back for her, and I would be waiting." He smiled, baring his sharp teeth. "Pity she had to die before you came for her. I guess your daughter will have to do."

Eldrin fell to his knees, and Eklos turned toward me, wicked pleasure flashing in his eyes. We needed to attack, but I couldn't get my body to move.

"How does it feel, girl, to have such a vile beast as a father?" he said, pointing to Eldrin.

I let out a breath, channeling my mother's bravery. I couldn't think about his claim. There was no way I could trust what he said, and if I considered it for even a moment, the wrath that had been simmering in my veins would go quiet, allowing Eklos to escape. I couldn't let it happen.

I glanced at Tarrin before saying to Eklos, "You have spoken nothing but lies my entire life. Why would I believe you now?"

White flame erupted from my hands at the same moment

Tarrin raised his arms, lifting the surrounded wooden flower beds from the ground. As one, wood and flame slammed into Eklos. When the dust and ash cleared, he was sprawled on the ground, not a scratch on him, his body in a cocoon of dense smoke. My claws clenched into fists, cutting into my palms.

Eklos released his smoke, and everything went quiet, as if all sound had been sucked out of the air.

And then I felt it.

In an instant I could feel all the water around me, every drop in the thick humidity, every dewdrop seeping into the soil. It seemed to call to me, beckoning me to use it, weave it.

Fire, lightning, *and* water?

Was it even possible for a dragon to possess *three* types of magic?

A growl erupted from my old Master, sending a chill up my spine. An idea sprang to life in my mind as I beheld the stone fountain a hundred feet behind him. The water within it seemed to sing, a song meant only for me, a desperate plea to free it from its cage.

Holding my clawed hands in front of me, they instantly began to fill with liquid. I clenched my fists, turning them and pulling, as if I were tugging on a heavy rope. The resistance was great at first but then the stone let out a thundering crack that echoed for miles. The water came to me, its frantic song louder with each passing moment. I pulled twice more, and the base of the fountain fractured in half and exploded forward, the pond of water within bursting forth in a foaming wave. It headed straight for us, barreling down every bush and flower, drowning everything in its path.

Groaning internally, I started to move my hands in a circle, trying to gain back the control that I was quickly losing under the weight of the water. Reaching deep down into the beast within me, I drew on its strength, its power.

The wave reached us, cresting high over our heads. Throwing

my hands out, it came to a halt in midair, my teeth clenching with the force of it.

Eklos was still on the ground, the first trace of fear flickering in his eyes.

The water's song grew deafening, a misting roar in my ears as I willed it to obey me, as I weaved it to fit my need, an eternity passing in the span of several seconds.

Almost like a spirit had broken, the song went silent, the push of the wave dissipating. I called to the water, silently telling it what I needed. A pulse rippled through my arms in answer. Taking a deep breath, I dropped my hands.

Like a broken dam, the wave descended, crashing down upon Eklos. He tried to scream but was quickly silenced by the gurgling water shoving its way down his throat.

The water surged and pressed against him, unrelenting, wave after wave collapsing on him, doubling back, and covering him again. Unbidden, it spread like a wildfire, webbing over the ground like cracked ice, frothing and hungry.

What should have hit Tarrin and me next, merely skirted around and past us, as if we were surrounded by a wall of air. By the time the water reached all the way to Eldrin, it had seeped into the ground, only a trickle at his feet.

Lights danced in my line of vision and I grew dizzy, swaying on my feet. My magic was almost out. Drawing on the last bit of strength left in my body, I took a step forward and stood above the dragon of smoke.

I lashed out with fire, coaxing the flames into a whip in each hand and wrapped them around his neck. He roared and cursed, pure hatred shining in his eyes.

"I should kill you. For what you did to my mother, for what you did to me," I growled, his screams turning to pain filled groans as I spoke.

"You deserve to die." The words left my mouth, void of

emotion, black and white spots dancing in my vision. My breaths grew short and frantic, and I gripped the fire whips tighter, willing them to burn hotter. Eklos roared like the beast that he was.

"Kaida." Tarrin's voice spoke in my ear. "You're using too much magic too quickly. If you don't release it, it will kill you."

I snarled in frustration. "I can't let go. He has to die."

Tarrin's emerald eyes flickered, his gaze unrelenting. "Not if you're the price."

His words cracked my resolve and ice filled my bones, the well of fire in my core drying up entirely. I opened my mouth to speak again but my vision went black, cool air blanketing my hands as the flames winked out.

I swayed on my feet and Tarrin managed to catch me before I collapsed, holding me upright with an arm around my waist, struggling beneath the weight of my dragon body. The moist night air made our scales stick together uncomfortably but I was too tired to pull away.

I blinked, trying to clear my eyes, but I could only see darkness.

I had the sudden sensation of falling, before Tarrin called my name.

And then I knew no more.

CHAPTER THIRTY-SEVEN
TARRIN

EKLOS ESCAPED.

Again.

I ran a hand through my hair, letting out a ragged breath as I waited in the main room of Kaida's chambers. After she fainted from magic overuse, my only thought was to get her to safety, as far from her former Master as possible.

The palace was on alert now after the attack, and although we hadn't had a King's Guard to patrol the grounds in years, I figured Eldrin, being a twenty-foot dragon and all, made a pretty good guard in the meantime. Plus, if he truly was Kaida's father, that made for a decent incentive to keep the palace safe from Eklos.

Kaida's father. I shook my head at the thought. I still didn't know what to think. Had Eklos been lying? Was it simply a baiting maneuver to get everyone to let their guard down? Or was there a glimmer of truth in it? Could it be possible that out of every dragon in Elysia, Eldrin not only showed up at my mother's funeral, but was Eklos's cousin *and* Kaida's father?

It seemed like an exceptionally large coincidence to me.

I blew out a breath and stood from the couch, my body aching from crashing into the ground during Eklos's attack. I spent the better part of the last two days in Kaida's chambers in case she woke up. I wanted to be there for her the moment she emerged from her restorative sleep. It also seemed like a good idea to be here to make sure she was safe. Eklos was in the palace during the Queen's funeral. That was far too close for my liking.

But now I was restless. I needed to move. I rang a small bell and a moment later Meara appeared in the doorway.

"Yes, Your Highness?"

"Will you stay with Kaida until I return?" I asked her, needing to go let off some steam and reduce the anxiety that was coiled tight as a snake in my stomach.

"Of course, Your Highness. I'll alert you immediately if she wakes."

I nodded my appreciation to her and left Kaida's chambers, making my way down the staircase and into the foyer. It was empty save for myself and one other human. A man with long silver hair that reached to the middle of his back walked toward me. He towered over me, easily reaching seven feet tall. He was dressed all in black, with a long coat that nearly brushed the floor, made of some sort of fabric that shimmered like scales. Leather boots laced to his knees, his muscles evident even through the layers of clothing.

Ever since I met Kaida, I had found myself actually looking at the slaves in the palace, remembering their faces. For the first time in my life, I cared what their names were. But this man wasn't familiar. "Who are you?"

He gave me a close-lipped smile. "Don't recognize me?" he said, waving at his eyes that were a light shade of amethyst.

"Eldrin?" I sputtered out. "You're a shape-shifter?

"Last time I checked," he replied with a chuckle.

Suddenly Eklos's hatred for him made much more sense. If he held such a hatred for my mother and me for being shifters, I can only imagine how much deeper his hatred went for someone in his own family.

"How is she?" Eldrin asked, breaking me out of my thoughts.

"She's still sleeping. She's never used that much magic all at once. It could take days for her body to replenish enough to wake up."

"Has no one trained her?" It was an honest question, but I felt my hackles rise in defense.

"I have been. But she's been here less than a month. There's only so much that can be accomplished in such a short time. Besides, there have been other pressing matters that we've been dealing with."

"Like what?"

I eyed Eldrin skeptically. "You realize I don't know you. For all I know, you're working *with* Eklos and not actually who he claims you to be." I wasn't about to reveal everything we had discovered to someone I didn't trust.

Eldrin laughed. "Believe me, Your Highness, I am not working with Eklos. He would stop at nothing to see me dead. You have nothing to fear from me." *Hear my inner thoughts, Prince. I am not a danger to you or to Kaida.*

I raised an eyebrow as his words filtered down the shape-shifter bond that allowed us to silently communicate. It was a strange feeling having that bond with someone other than my mother or Kaida. Shape-shifters were so rare in Elysia, that before I met Kaida, the only ones I knew about were myself and my mother. Were there more out there than we knew about? Perhaps they were all in hiding, avoiding dragons like Eklos who would hunt them for sport.

With a long exhale, I nodded in the direction of the training room, beckoning him to follow. We walked through the halls in silence, and I felt Eldrin studying the artwork on the walls. Without looking back, I opened the door and walked into the dark room, using my magic to open the curtains near the ceiling.

"Ah, a World Weaver. That's an impressive ability." Eldrin eyed me with a new fascination. "I haven't met one of you in an age."

I simply shrugged, heading to the counter in the back corner and wrapping my hands in a thick, cushiony fabric. I could feel the shifter studying my every move, watching as I made my way over to the bag suspended from the ceiling that had been my outlet for frustration for years.

"Just how old are you?" I asked as I threw my fist into the bag, my inner dragon rejoicing at the chance to do something physical. I always found that my dragon form would get restless the longer I stayed human. It probably had to do with the basic instincts of the dragons that I was forced to ignore in this form. I threw another punch, the vibration of the bag ricocheting up my arm.

"One thousand and seventy-four years."

A startled laugh burst out of me. "That's old."

Eldrin matched my laugh. "And I feel every day of it."

In Elysia, dragons were often considered younglings up through the first couple hundred years of their life. At that point, their dragon body fully matured, and their magic was the strongest it would ever be. Though dragons had unnaturally long lives, not many made it past the thousand-year mark. It made my nineteen years feel very young.

I shook my head and silence filled the space between us as I pummeled the hanging bag, feeling that tight ball in my core slowly unfurling. Usually when I was upset, I took to the skies. Something about flying was soothing. But sometimes, it wasn't enough, and I had to let my emotions out physically in the training room.

"So, are you really her father?" I asked after a few more minutes. Eldrin had taken a seat on the bench against the far wall. His eyes were on the floor.

"I imagine I must be. The timeline matches up from when her mother and I were together. And she looks just like Aela."

"And you never knew about Kaida?"

Eldrin shook his head. "If I had known, I never would have left her."

Imagining Kaida growing up with her shape-shifter father instead of as a slave to Eklos, knowing her life could have been so much better, made my insides crawl. I spun on my heel, planting a kick on the bag that sent it careening off the chain that had suspended it. My chest heaved from the exertion.

"How could you not have known?" I whispered, staring at the bag on the ground like it could tell me the answers to all my problems.

"Your Highness," Eldrin said, appearing next to me. His voice was gentle like coaxing an angry child. I supposed I was, compared to him. "I promise, had I known that Aela bore Kaida, I would *never* have left them alone."

My breath shook as I exhaled. "It makes no difference now anyway." I sauntered over to the giant stuffed sack and hoisted it onto my shoulder before hooking it back to the ceiling. "We're to be married at the end of the summer."

I looked over my shoulder to see his reaction, though I wasn't sure what reaction I was expecting. Part of me thought he'd be angry that his daughter was marrying the Prince of Elysia, while the other part of me thought maybe he'd steal her away just so that I couldn't have her. Dragons tended to be territorial like that. I couldn't imagine what he was feeling after finding out he had a daughter and had missed the first seventeen years of her life.

Eldrin studied my face for several seconds before his teeth flashed in a smile. "Good."

"Good?" I asked, incredulous.

He nodded. "I've seen the way you look at her. I know what love looks like on a person. If Lita thought you'd be a good match, then I trust her judgement."

My mouth gaped like a fish. "Love? I don't love Kaida." My cheeks grew warm, and the room became swelteringly hot. I half-ran over to the wash basin to pour a glass of water before gulping it down.

Eldrin watched my reaction then barked out a laugh. "Your Highness, you forget how old I am. It's even written in the way you say her name." He gave me a goading smile.

I ran a hand through my hair. He had to be wrong. I couldn't love her. Just because I liked spending time with her and didn't mind our betrothal so much anymore…that didn't mean I was in love with her.

Did it?

CHAPTER THIRTY-EIGHT
KAIDA

I WOKE TO A dark room, in bed, underneath layers upon layers of heavy blankets. The curtains were closed, and only a small candle burned near the door. A quiet hissing noise sounded from just outside the doorway and it took several moments for my brain to comprehend that it was two voices whispering. For the first time, I found myself wishing that I was in my dragon body to be able to hear better.

I shimmied out from under the covers, every muscle and limb screaming in protest, and I bit my lip to keep from crying out. Glancing down, I saw that my clothes had been removed, replaced by a comfortable nightgown. Bumps rose on my skin as the cooler air kissed against my body. I winced at the pain that shot down my arms as I grabbed a scratchy wool blanket and wrapped it around myself. As softly as I could, I padded over to the door, slightly ajar. Two men, shrouded in shadow, stood in the center of the room, bodies tense, ready to fight.

"No. She needs *rest,*" a male voice hissed, the room too dark to make out his face. His voice sounded vaguely familiar, but my mind was still a bit foggy.

"She has been sleeping for four days. I think she has had plenty of rest," a second male voice retorted.

"She completely depleted her magic. It could have destroyed her. We're both lucky that she blacked out when she did."

Blacked out? Snippets of memory started coming in short spurts. Eklos standing over me. Tarrin on the ground. White fire. A fountain. A wave of water. A dizzying headache crashed over me as the memories came faster and faster, but remained incomplete, like missing pieces to a puzzle.

"Well, if she does not eat something soon, she may never wake up."

The two men glared at each other amongst the shadows.

Deciding to leave the grumpy males to themselves, I took a step back, intending to crawl back into the warm welcoming bed. My foot caught in the blanket around my feet, and letting out a yelp, I tumbled backward onto the floor, smacking my sore body onto the cold marble.

I barely managed a breath before they shoved open the door and crowded in the doorway, concern written on their faces, eyes darting around the room looking for danger.

The male on the left was Prince Tarrin.

The one on the right was unfamiliar, towering nearly a foot above the Prince, with broad shoulders that made his flowy white shirt look too small. Half of his pin straight silver hair had been tied back behind head.

The only familiar features were his amethyst eyes.

A small gasp escaped my lips as recognition flooded through me.

Eldrin.

My supposed father.

A *shape-shifter.*

The full memory of what happened in the gardens came back to me. Eyes wide, half covered in the wool blanket, I remained frozen on the floor, stunned by the recollection of the magic I had used.

Tarrin rushed to my side, effortlessly picking me up and carrying me back to the bed. He set me down on the edge like I was made of glass, pulling back the covers for me to slip beneath.

The sudden need to relieve myself was almost overwhelming.

"Actually..." My cheeks heated as I glanced toward the bathing room.

"Oh!" Tarrin said, his own face growing red as he stepped out of the way.

Eldrin watched from the doorway, the corners of his mouth twitching as if he were fighting a smile. Hopping down from the bed on wobbly legs, it took every ounce of self-control to not sprint into the adjoining room.

"I will send for Meara to bring you some food," he called after me, walking from the room, grabbing Eldrin's arm, and pulling him out, rather roughly, to give me some privacy.

I quickly saw to my needs as the silence of their absence descended upon the room.

Eldrin was still here. He didn't leave while I was unconscious. Did Eklos's claim have merit? Was he really my father? I couldn't imagine him staying if he wasn't. My mother had never said much about my father, nor would she voluntarily give up any information when I asked. After years and years of begging for answers, I simply stopped asking.

Part of me didn't want to believe it. We really looked nothing alike. Glancing in the mirror on the vanity, I saw a younger version of my mother staring back. No harsh jaw line or sharp nose, no long silver hair.

I blew out a breath. Eldrin was a shape-shifter, which helped to explain my own abilities. And now he was *here.* Not just in Elysia, but here in the palace. With Tarrin. In my chambers.

I didn't know if it was intuition or the pieces of a puzzle finally fitting into place, but I somehow knew in my gut that Eklos wasn't lying.

I heard a small knock from outside in the main entry. Meara's voice drifted through my door as she brought in food. My stomach made a fierce growling sound, and I threw my greasy, unwashed hair into a knot on the top of my head. Wriggling into a fresh linen shirt and pants, I headed out of the bedroom.

I stopped dead in my tracks as I beheld who stood in the room.

It was not only the two male shape-shifters.

King Martik, turquoise scales dull in the dim hall light, stood in the doorway, eyes fixed on Eldrin. The King could have been made of stone as he stood there, unmoving. The memory of Martik becoming angry and leaving the room after our first meeting, when I had asked about my father, surfaced in my mind. What had happened between them? No one spoke as a tense hollow filled the room. He opened his mouth to speak but closed it again.

Eldrin cleared his throat, taking a step forward. "Martik." He managed to get out, neck craning to meet his eyes. Although Eldrin was quite tall in human form, it was nothing compared to the height of the dragon King.

A darkness that was not quite smoke engulfed him for a split second and then dissipated, leaving a midnight-blue dragon in its wake. He took another step forward, amethyst eyes flickering with some long-forgotten emotion. The King only stared at him and then stumbled forward as he closed the distance between them and embraced him. When they pulled away, both dragons had silver lining their eyes.

Tarrin cleared his throat. "Do you two know each other?" He gestured for me to join him at the table piled with food.

Eldrin chuckled and the King rubbed the back of his neck.

"Lita and Eldrin grew up in Shegora, a small village at the northern tip of Elysia. When I met Lita and began courting her, Eldrin often joined us." Although the words were friendly, I could see a slight tension, a hint of hostility in Martik's eyes.

Tarrin glanced at me, having noticed it too.

"I am deeply sorry for your loss," Eldrin rasped, bowing deeply.

The King studied him for a moment, a cold mask settling over his face, disguising any of the warmth he had expressed toward Eldrin a moment ago. Martik only nodded before turning toward Tarrin and me.

"I have received word that Master Eklos has fully recovered," he announced.

"What happened?" I asked.

Tarrin and my father exchanged glances and I crossed my arms. I didn't like that they felt the need to hide anything from me. I didn't need them deciding what was best for me to know. I wanted the truth. All of it.

I was about to open my mouth to say as much when Tarrin spoke. "After you collapsed in the garden, Eklos managed to take off into the air, catching an updraft, and stayed aloft long enough to get back to Vernista. The only injury I saw was a collar of blood dripping around his neck." He paused, studying my face for some reaction. "I wanted to go after him—"

"But we wanted to get you to safety," Eldrin cut in. "Kaida, you tapped so deeply into your magic, and so quickly, that you were on the verge of destroying yourself. Magic needs to be worked into a steady flow over time. You ripped into that magic well and used so much at once that it almost consumed you. The priority was to get you to a safe place, to let your magic and strength refill. We can deal with Eklos another day."

My brain felt foggy, and I struggled to process the torrent of information.

"And where is he now?" Tarrin asked his father.

"My scouts have reported that he is still in Vernista, in The Den, instilling fear in dragons and humans alike, as usual."

"So, not much different from any other day," I muttered under my breath, although every ear heard me.

"The Council has been strangely silent ever since the festival. The Remnant, too, now that I think about it." Tarrin rubbed at his temple. "Any word on them or Eklos's plans?"

"Nothing specific, but my spies have heard talk from the other dragons that frequent The Den. It seems that Eklos is attempting to stir up animosity amongst the dragon race once more." Martik paused, the sudden silence thick and uncomfortable. "The Remnant of the Lone Dragon are in Vernista, in much larger numbers than originally anticipated. Eklos is using them to put together a hoard of dragons with a hatred for the humans equal to his own."

A weight dropped in my stomach. My mind drifted back to that day in The Den when I overheard those dragons discussing the Remnant coming. I never imagined it would be so soon.

"A hoard of dragons?" I said, voice hesitant, my hands clenched into fists, knuckles bone white.

"Yes, girl," the King said impatiently. "A hoard. An army of dragons, carefully hidden and guarded."

I winced at his tone and then schooled my face into neutrality. "For what purpose?"

"Eklos was bred with a pure and untainted hatred for the human race, instilled in him from his very first heartbeat." Eldrin cut in before the annoyance distorting Martik's face could manifest into words he could not take back. "It would not be unreasonable to assume that he plans to unleash the dragons upon the humans."

Everyone went silent as the words sank in.

"Or perhaps the purpose is to get to you," King Martik growled, turning his attention on me, and I slumped farther into my chair.

Eldrin looked back and forth between all of us, his brow furrowed. "An army for one girl?"

"He thinks I escaped," I said, keeping my head down, eyes fixed on the untouched plate of food that Tarrin had set in front of me. "I was enslaved to him my entire life." I swallowed the lump that had formed in my throat.

"Tarrin showed up at The Den several weeks ago, announced that he was collecting me and took me with him. Eklos could do nothing as he watched me walk out that door, his pride shredding into ribbons." I finally looked up and met Eldrin's gaze. "My old Master does not take kindly to humans that try to leave his service." The unspoken words flashed in my eyes and I knew he could see them. *That's what happened to my mother.*

"Yes, yes, we all know this. But that does not explain why he would need such a large number of dragons simply to retrieve you," King Martik said.

"Perhaps it is not only Kaida that he is after," Tarrin said, looking at my father. Eldrin remained silent.

Martik stood abruptly. "I must go. I will do what I can to draw information from the Council." He turned his snout to wink at Tarrin. "The perks of making them think I'm a docile fool. They tell me things they wouldn't want anyone else to know." Without another word, he left the room, his stomping footsteps shaking the ground.

Tarrin and I exchanged glances at the implications of what he said. Tarrin had said his father had been acting different, pushing him away. Could he have been faking the entire time? Based on the look on his face, his thoughts mirrored mine.

Eldrin cleared his throat, bringing my attention back to him.

"Why is Eklos after you?" I asked.

He grimaced. "My cousin and I have a complicated past. He despises my very existence because of what I am. He was raised in a family that believed shifters were monsters that needed exterminating. Eklos could not even stand the thought of having a *mutator formarum* in his own family. I have evaded him for nearly a thousand years, and it has driven him mad, only fueling his hatred for me."

"Why does he hate our kind so much?" I asked. I realized as the words left my mouth that it was the first time that I had referred to it as *our* kind. It did not bother me as much as it once did.

"I think that is a story for another time, Kaida. You need to eat and rest. You have not quite regained your strength yet," Eldrin said, evading my question. It was such a fatherly thing to say that it caught me off guard. Before I could respond, Tarrin stood, gesturing to the door.

"There is a guest room four doors down to the left. You may stay there as long as you have need of it."

Eldrin nodded in thanks as he stood. "Oh, by the way." He paused in the doorway. "Congratulations, Kaida." A knowing smile spread over his mouth as he glanced between Tarrin and me. "An arranged marriage can be very difficult, but it becomes much easier when it's to someone you already love."

CHAPTER THIRTY-NINE

KAIDA

L*OVE. LOVELOVELOVELOVELOVE.*

The words had repeated in my head going back and forth like a boomerang ever since Eldrin left my chambers. He insinuated that Tarrin and I loved each other. That wasn't true. It couldn't be.

Could it?

"Kaida, would you please eat?" Tarrin asked again for the third time, snapping me out of my spinning thoughts. His muscular human body sat in the chair next to me. He hadn't seemed bothered in the slightest by Eldrin's words. What had they spoke about those days while I was asleep?

"I'm really not hungry right now."

He rolled his eyes, not buying the excuse for one second. "You haven't had any food in four days. If you think I believe you when you say you are not hungry, you must take me for a fool."

Slumping back into my chair, I crossed my arms.

"Will you eat *with* me then?" Without waiting for a response, he grabbed a plate and started stacking various foods on it. Links of spicy sausage, tiny jam-filled tarts, and an obscene amount of buttered bread with runny eggs on top threatened to overflow off his plate. He stabbed a fork into one of the sausages, popped it in his mouth, and then fixed his attention on me as he chewed.

"Do you ever stop eating?" I blurted.

He snorted, nudging my knee with his, and nodded at my plate. "Kaida, *eat.*"

"Is that an order, Your Highness?" I could not help the sassy bite that coated my words.

"If it will get you to eat, then yes, that is an order."

I took the raspberry tart he offered to me with a sigh, jamming the entire piece in my mouth. Crumbs littered my shirt and lap. It was both sweet and a touch sour with a light flaky texture. Before I had fully finished chewing, I popped another one in my mouth.

Tarrin pushed his plate of food toward me as a ravenous hunger awoke inside my stomach, and before I could think, four small sausages and half a piece of bread were stuffed inside my mouth at once.

A loud snort broke my focus, and I looked at the Prince, my cheeks and mouth bulging with food. The corners of his eyes crinkled, his mouth curving into a half smile.

Prick.

He laughed out loud, a deep belly-shaking laugh, and warmth flooded my face. Still chuckling, he nudged my knee with his own, but this time left it there. Electricity crackled up my leg.

A prick I may be, but it got you to eat, didn't it? A wicked gleam flickered across his eyes.

Swallowing hard, I wiped at the crumbs coating my lips, reaching for the glass of fresh orange juice on the table. Lips puckering from the tartness of the juice, I shivered slightly as I swallowed it, and Tarrin let out another laugh, this time leaning closer.

We both froze, and I thought he might kiss me again, before he tugged me to my feet.

"Come on, I want to show you something."

I grabbed another piece of buttered bread, stuffing it into my mouth before he guided me, hand in hand, out into the hallway, around the corner, and up several flights of stairs. At last we reached the top, a large wooden door looming in front of us. Tarrin pushed it open, leading us out into fresh air, and a gasp escaped my lips.

We were on an enormous balcony on the highest turret of the palace. It wrapped around the entire top of the tower, providing a view in every direction. Everything could be seen from there. The Ilgathor Mountains far in the distance, the farmlands and plains that stretched for miles, the gardens surrounding the palace that looked so small and dainty from this height.

Dusk descended, the sun now set beyond the horizon, casting a blue and purple glow that mixed with reds and golds, the first stars beginning to wink into existence in the darkest places.

Leaning on the balcony rail, I took in every view, every scene, like a piece of art in my mind before the darkness of night swallowed everything in sight. Tarrin came up beside me, hands on the railing, so close I could feel the heat emanating from his body.

"Do you remember the first day we met?" A strange emotion, partially muddled from being in human form, rippled off him.

"How could I forget?"

"Do you remember what I said?" His brows furrowed, as if he were contemplating whether he wanted to have this conversation.

"You said a lot of things that day," I quipped.

"I meant do you remember what I said about not wanting any of this either?" The words were tentative.

A pang shot through my stomach, an ache filling the wounded spots as I recalled that conversation. That day I had not cared that he did not want to marry me. At that point, I had felt the same way. But for weeks everything had been changing between us. I no longer saw disgust in his eyes when he looked at me. I saw… something else. I never knew what the emotion was that had taken its place.

My own hatred for him, for the Royal Family, had waned as

well. I found myself looking forward to my time with him. I was not sure if that meant I was changing into a cold-hearted dragon, but when I was with him, I found I did not mind it so much. My father's words came to mind again.

My chest tightened painfully at the turn I suspected this conversation would take and I turned away from him, not wanting him to see the tears that had sprang to life in my eyes.

"Let me finish," he said, putting a hand on my shoulder and spinning me to face him. "What I meant was that I did not want it *this* way. I did not want it to be forced, a requirement. I did not want the only reason we were betrothed to be to sustain the shape-shifter race." He paused, running his hand through his hair as he exhaled, looking out over the plains. More stars appeared as dusk faded further and further into night.

"Your fear of me, the hatred on your face, did not make me feel any better about the whole situation. But the moment I saw you, felt your thoughts and emotions, I knew. Your soul was like a song that had been singing to mine for years but I had never been able to decipher the melody. It was like a soothing lullaby for the darkness that threatened my own soul.

"At first, I had only come by my parents' bidding, they wanted you safe and at the palace. But when I saw you lying on the ground, dragons surrounding you, ready to kill you, something in me shifted, whether I wanted it to or not. I thought that perhaps you would be happy to escape that cesspit of a place, that you would see me as your rescuer, a prince saving his princess. It was not until later that I realized, while you may have wanted to escape, you did not want to be saved."

His words were a truth that settled deep in my soul. I had not realized that by refusing him, shutting him out, that I had hurt him. But he was right. I had wanted to save myself, my family. But I had been unable to. Fear and shame had been my ever-present companion because of it.

"What do you want now?" I asked as he brought his forehead against mine.

"I want *you,* Kaida. And I want you to want me, and not because you are required to."

His words dropped like a weight and I suddenly felt very heavy beneath it. I swallowed hard and turned to gaze at the sky, night's descent complete, and watched as star after star awoke.

Exhausted beneath the wave of emotions swirling between us, I swayed, leaning against the railing. I had tried to keep a careful lock on my true emotions, never letting them escape. They would poke their head out once in a while, letting Tarrin feel bits and pieces, but never everything all at once. I could feel them pushing against the lock now, begging to be freed, shared.

A truth for a truth, a voice seemed to whisper in my head.

"I was only ten when my mother died. No one had been around to teach me about love or marriage. Amongst the humans, the only evidence I ever saw of marriage were broken and shattered people who were bound to those who only desired to hurt them. There was no love, no warmth. Only a cold brokenness that no amount of fire could thaw. And I never saw anything even close to love from the dragons, who do not love anyone more than they do themselves. All I saw from dragon bonds were a constant need for dominance and power. I never desired relationships that would one day mimic those that I had seen. When you showed up, the one thing I feared and hated most in this world, telling me we were betrothed…" I trailed off, the words tumbling out as if they had been freed from their dam, unbound and unstoppable.

Tarrin was quiet, thoughtful. I could feel my heart beating in my chest as I waited for the rejection that was surely about to come. Finally, he turned to me, a soft, kind look in his eyes. Reaching out, he wrapped his hands around my waist and pulled me closer, our chests touching. A slight breeze blew through the air around us, my hair flying around my face.

Tarrin smoothed it down, pushing it to the side and behind my ear, his calloused fingertips grazing my cheek.

"And what do you want now, Kaida?"

I looked up at his face, finding a strange sort of hope shining in his eyes.

"I want to be free," I whispered, barely audible as the breeze swept the sound into nothing. "Free from slavery, from hatred and punishments. Free to make my own decisions, go where I please. Free to be my own master. To finally live in peace and not in fear."

He cupped my face in both his hands, silver lining his eyes. "What if my love is your freedom?" He stared at me a moment longer as his words settled into me. Then Tarrin's lips found mine, their steady warmth spreading through my body. The world seemed to stop, to re-center on the two of us, and began to spin again, faster and faster until the floor felt moments away from collapsing beneath me.

His hands moved into my hair, quickly tangling as our breathing quickened. My hands went up around his neck and he grabbed me around the waist again, tugging me closer, crushing me to him as if I could not get close enough.

The Prince used his magic to create a chaise that appeared behind him, and he moved us toward it, never breaking contact. He laid us down upon the chair, continuing to kiss me, slower now, more intentional, hands roving up and down, from my hair, down my back, to my legs. Hours passed, or maybe minutes. Time trickled to a stop and sped up all at the same time.

I was not sure how long we laid there kissing, or at what point we had fallen asleep, but when I woke, we were still on the chaise, legs intertwined, my head on his chest. His arms were strong and warm around me, holding me close, his breathing deep and slow. I glanced up at the sky, the first signs of dawn peeking over the horizon. The stars began to wink out as a faint blue light, turning quickly to purple, then pink, then orange, flooded across the sky.

It reached farther and farther, like a bucket of paint had been thrown over it, the colors seeping outward.

Dew drops sat on every surface, thanks to the balmy summer night, moistening the ground, the chair, and our clothes. I shifted, trying to peel Tarrin's shirt from my face, and he inhaled deeply, stretching his limbs. He glanced at me out of the corner of his eye, a slight smirk twisting his lips as his arms tightened around me.

"Good morning." His voice was husky from sleep and my heart beat a little faster. The memory of our heated kissing from the night before flashed through my mind and my cheeks burned.

A bird suddenly swooped low above our heads and I let out a startled shriek, burrowing further into Tarrin's shoulder. His whole body shook as he barked out a laugh, my face burning hotter. He untangled his limbs from mine and stood up, extending his hand to help me.

Pulling me to my feet, he wrapped one arm around my waist and cupped my cheek with the other. He nudged my nose with his, resting his forehead against mine.

"Did you sleep well?" The corners of his mouth twitched as if he were fighting a smile.

I scowled at his taunting tone. "I would have slept better if it were not for your snoring," I retorted, nudging his shoulder. A small chuckle escaped his lips, and he planted a kiss on my nose.

"Oh, I will not bring up *yours* then." He winked at me and I scowled again.

"I do *not* snore." Indignation filled my bones, and I took a step back, crossing my arms. Tarrin's laugh shook his entire body.

The sun crested the horizon, bathing the valley below us in a warm golden light. The heat was already stifling, the humidity thick. There had not been much of a reprieve from it overnight and it seemed it would only get worse as the sun rose higher throughout the day.

The light hit Tarrin's face, causing his turquoise eyes to glow.

His burns were illuminated, revealing every ripple, every blister that had struggled to heal, and I stepped forward to put my hand on his cheek, my own calloused fingers running over his scars. He froze, eyes wide, as if remembering that I could see his true face. A heartbeat passed and he leaned into my touch, closing his eyes. His breaths were shallow, shuddering.

"What happened?" I whispered, our faces so close that our breath mingled.

His eyes snapped open. He held my stare before releasing his hold on me and pacing the length of the balcony.

"You can trust me, Tarrin," I reassured him.

He shook his head. "You don't understand. No one knows about them. Nobody can see them but you."

The blood drained from my face. "What do you mean?"

He blew out a harsh breath before settling on the edge of the chaise, dropping his head into his hands. "I thought I could handle fire without any training," he began. "I thought I could manipulate it, force it to do what I wanted, just by sheer will. I was wrong." Tarrin ran a hand through his hair. "I was away with my parents on a trip when I was younger. I snuck out of our tent in the middle of the night. My mother refused to teach me about fire magic, saying I was too young, so I took it upon myself to learn.

"Fire has to be respected. It is not a toy to be played with. I had been trying to create rings of fire around a large tree trunk, when I lost control and the flames hit my face. I managed to regain control enough to put out the fire, but not before the real damage was done." Tarrin waved a hand over his face.

"After the accident, I did not want my parents to know what I had done. I cast an *ilusai* over my face. No one should be able to see them. *I* can't even see them."

I reached up to touch them again. Despite the ripples and discolored skin, I could not imagine him without them. To me, they only added to his charm.

"I think you're handsome," I blurted, and I covered my mouth in surprise. A huge grin broke the sadness on his face and my heart swelled.

Tarrin pulled me down into his lap and kissed me. Forehead to forehead, breathing each other's scent, he said, "And I think you're beautiful." My face ached from the grin that spread across it.

"Come on," he said, breaking away at last, taking hold of my hand. "We will eat a small breakfast and then head to the training room. You have got quite a bit of catching up to do." Winking at me, he kissed the back of my hand.

Tarrin led me down, down, down through the various flights of stairs, through door after door, into his own chambers, where a breakfast of eggs and fruit had been laid out on the table. It was meager compared to what I had become accustomed to.

"We're training today?" I asked as I popped a grape into my mouth.

"Yes."

"What kind of training?"

"Your magic has developed beyond the point of being able to just get by. Most dragons do not have the depth of magic that you do—or the abilities. If you do not learn to control it, to channel it properly, it will destroy you. Like it almost did with Eklos in the garden." He said it all matter-of-factly, around a mouth full of eggs.

"Charming." I scowled at him and he sketched a bow, fork in hand.

He threw the last of his fruit into his mouth and stood from the table, gathering up a bag of supplies as I finished my breakfast. We left his chambers and descended a set of stairs and rounded a bend, still two levels above the training room, when Tarrin shifted, his turquoise scales flashing in the torch light.

"Your turn," he crooned as he disappeared around the next corner.

While shifting had become easier, it still was not a mastered art. Sometimes I was able to will it instantly, while other times it seemed to laugh at me as I stayed stuck in my human body.

I took a deep breath, drawing on the internal flame in my core, calling on it to spread, to shift my limbs from human to beast. Thankfully, the heat expanded, and in a matter of seconds my footsteps thundered down the hall, amethyst reflections bouncing up and down on the walls.

I reached the training room, Tarrin already there, leaning against the wall next to the door, examining his claws.

"What took so long?"

I rolled my eyes at him, and shoved through the doors, simultaneously smacking my thick tail into him. He stumbled backward; his face morphed in outrage as I let out a haughty laugh. When he had regained his composure, he pushed through the doors, stalking toward me.

"Tell me, Kaida, what makes you think you can bash your tail into the Prince of Elysia?"

"Well, seeing as we are betrothed, that makes me some sort of princess, yes? And being a princess, I can do whatever I please." The words left my mouth before I had time to think. My own eyes widened at the sass.

Tarrin stared at me, dumbfounded. "You seem more comfortable with yourself in dragon form. More comfortable with me. Why is that?" I could feel the confusion emanating from him, much stronger now than as a human. Before, it was more like a feeling that coursed between us. Now it was like our souls were connected, and there was no longer a barrier blocking the messages.

Raising my hands to braid my hair, forgetting I did not have hair as a dragon, I bit back, "I don't particularly care for either of your forms. However, this way is slightly less objectionable to look at. At least as a dragon you sparkle."

Whether it be from the freedom I felt after last night's confession or the fact that I was better able to defend myself as a dragon, sarcasm coated every word that came out of my mouth. Tarrin was frozen as he held my gaze. The tie between us went silent, no feeling or emotion coming down it.

A heartbeat passed.

Then another.

Out of nowhere, he nearly collapsed to the floor.

And he was *howling* with laughter.

He managed to sit on the bench behind him, doubled over, gasping for breath as wave after wave of laughter burst out of him.

I stood there, mouth gaping.

"Sparkle," he gasped between breaths which only caused him to howl more.

"It wasn't *that* funny."

He straightened, trying to compose himself. "Right. If I ever question your feelings for me, Kaida, I will always just remember that you love the way I sparkle." He chuckled to himself, winking at me as he stood and walked to the cold, black training floor.

Rolling my eyes at his back, I followed, taking up my place on the opposite end.

"What now?"

The torrent of amusement slowly faded as he took me in, eyes roving from my enormous feet to my head.

He took up a defensive position, curling one arm in front of him and the other above his head. "All right, Kaida. Call on your flames."

CHAPTER FORTY
ELDRIN

I HID IN THE shadows of a marble pillar in the Great Hall as the King met with his Council. I knew the moment that Martik left Kaida's chambers that something was not right with him.

The King sat at the head of the table; the members of his Council seated on each side. The Great Hall had been cleared out after the Queen's funeral celebration, leaving only the throne at one end, and this ten-foot table set up for meetings near the row of floor-to-ceiling windows on the western side of the room. The hot summer sun was streaming in, illuminating each dragon at the table, casting a muted rainbow of colors onto the walls.

From what I had gathered thus far, King Martik had requested this meeting because of the fiasco with Eklos in the garden.

Seeing Martik again in Kaida's room… it had caused so many memories to surface. All the times when we had pulled pranks on Lita. Our midnight talks walking through the gardens, mostly with Martik venting, trying to figure out how he would ever handle being king.

There were times when we hadn't gotten along, mostly when I felt some sort of claim to Lita, even though she was bound to Martik. She would get so annoyed by it. I could picture the face she would make as she rolled her eyes and called us insufferable pricks, saying we were marking our territory like animals.

I chuckled silently to myself as the memory came and went.

"Your Majesty?" Roldan asked, his tone bordering on contempt.

"Hmm?" The King straightened, shaking his head lightly, his distant expression snapping back into focus.

"Here we all are, discussing that abomination of a girl that you have staying in your very home, who has defied Master Eklos, and is causing quite the commotion. And yet you sit there staring off into space."

Martik's mouth popped open, the scales above his eyes bunching together.

I could not believe that they would speak to the King with such derision and arrogance. What had been happening for them to think that was acceptable?

Prince Tarrin told me, in our time waiting for Kaida to wake up over the past few days, about the Council and how they appeared to be brainwashing the King and plotting against the Royal Family. I had once met a few of the dragons that the Prince mentioned by name. This supposed conspiracy did not come as much of a surprise. Those dragons had been full of greed and an insatiable hunger for power nearly two decades ago. Before I left Vernista back then, I debated telling Martik about my suspicions over them, warning him to be wary of them when they came to power, but I kept my mouth quiet. Instead, I warned Lita, who merely laughed it off, keeping the concern in her eyes carefully concealed.

Martik remained still, clearly debating something in his mind. I knew all his mannerisms, the movements in his face and twitches of his fingers, and something was not right. Then it hit me.

The King *knew* what the Council was doing. He was playing dumb. I watched as King Martik slouched farther in his chair, allowing his eyes to gloss over, acting the part of the brainwashed king.

The other Council members relaxed, one even sighing audibly in relief.

He cleared his throat loudly and said, "Apologies, Councilman Roldan. Do continue."

Roldan lifted his head, absolute smugness distorting his scaly face. He thought he had won. I saw Martik clench his hands into fists beneath the table, claws piercing through his scales. I could tell it took an enormous amount of strength for the King to sit there and take that.

"As I was *saying*, Eklos has been an important part of building the dragon community, ensuring that their dominance is well known and unquestioned, while also controlling the slave population, particularly in Vernista. He's had unparalleled success, and no one has dared to challenge him. That is, until that stupid girl escaped from his ownership, sending the whole town into a frenzy. Humans and dragons alike have begun to question his authority, whether or not he is capable of maintaining the leadership position he has gained."

"She has caused a lot of trouble, that girl," Barden chimed in.

"I do believe," King Martik began, "that my son was the one to retrieve her. It was not technically an escape."

"Oh, do not be foolish!" Barden spat. "She could have died, and Eklos still would have considered it an escape. He would have come after her even in death!"

I had to bite my tongue to keep from laughing at that ridiculous thought.

"Oh, do be quiet Barden. Enough of your nonsense," Roldan scolded, and the other dragon shrunk down into his chair.

"Anyway, back to the real reason we are all gathered here." Councilman Roldan paused for dramatic effect. "Eklos has asked for our assistance, and our support."

The Great Hall went silent as death, as if the very air itself was holding its breath.

"Our support for what?" Martik asked.

"For years he has been recruiting dragons. The fiercest, most devious and wicked, most terrifying ones he could find, all with one thing in common: their hatred for the humans. He has kept them hidden, very few know about them. Now the Remnant have added to his numbers."

"And for what purpose has he been doing this?"

"Eklos believes that the human population needs to be dealt with. Exterminated. He has always believed that the Lone Dragon should have finished what he started a thousand years ago. He has made it his personal mission to complete that quest."

I shuddered. The Lone Dragon inhabited many of my memories, making them nightmares I did not want to relive.

"And where does the girl fit into this?" Martik replied, the scales on his forehead bunching.

"Ah, yes. It is very convenient timing. The perfect reason for Master Eklos to display his hoard and his power. He will begin his hunt with the one human he loathes more than any other."

"But she is a shape-shifter. Half dragon."

Several of the Council scoffed, showing their obvious distaste for the race.

"Yes," Roldan hissed, his long tongue snaking out in disgust as if he had eaten something rancid. "Shifters are an abominable species. Unnatural. There are so few remaining in Elysia that Eklos plans to use his army against them too, to finally rid the world of their poison."

My stomach writhed and burned, and it took every bit of self-control to keep from flying from behind the pillar and burning Roldan to a crisp.

"You do realize my son is a shape-shifter." The King's voice dropped an octave.

Roldan waved a clawed hand in the air. "Oh, I'm sure Eklos will spare your son." Everything about the Councilman, from his body language, to the shake of his voice, indicated he was lying. I knew there was no way Eklos would spare Tarrin.

Kaida, the Prince, and I would be the first ones he targeted.

I watched Martik blow out a breath, somehow mastering the outrage in his eyes enough to change the subject. "And what kind of support is Eklos requesting?"

"To start, he has asked for every able-bodied dragon that we can spare to join his cause."

I could see Martik's throat bob as he swallowed, knowing he was fighting to hold his tongue.

"What else?"

The other dragons paused, their snouts pulling back into wicked grins, their sharp teeth flashing in the sunlight.

"He has made one other request. More of an order really."

Giving orders to the King? Who did Eklos think he was, army of dragons or not?

Martik raised an eyebrow, most likely the only response he was able to control.

"Master Eklos has ordered that you give up the girl. Immediately."

CHAPTER FORTY-ONE

KAIDA

I HATED MAGIC.

It was scorching and frigid. Dark and light. Heavy. Controlling. Selfish.

But mostly I hated *my* magic.

It took and took and took and gave hardly anything in return.

It took strength. It took warmth. It took spirit. It took passion. All of it.

I poured them into the well of power within me, driving it, surrendering their life force.

And yet only a few drops of magic would rise to the surface.

No river of water or streams of flame. No currents of lightning. Only small fires burning in my palms, droplets of water pooling beneath my feet, and tiny sparks in my hands.

Training had not gone well, to say the least. Tarrin pushed and pushed but nothing happened. He tried everything from being nice, to flirting, to being a downright prick, hoping *something* would draw the magic out of me.

Nothing worked.

By the end of the training session, we were both so exhausted and sweaty that he began throwing small balls of fire at me, with his own meager supply of fire magic, telling me to defend myself. Create a shield.

I darted and skirted around and between each volley of magic, tugging and pulling at the pit inside my core that I had felt with Eklos in the garden. It had been bottomless, raging, and ready to erupt.

But now it was quiet. Dormant.

Perhaps I had used every drop and there was nothing left. Tarrin said that I should have rested enough for it to replenish, but each time I tried to stop his flames, or create a shield out of water, my magic would flicker in front of me, leaving me more exhausted with each attempt.

Sweat dripped down both of our faces, scales glistening as it ran the length of our bodies. He threw a final ball of fire and it hurtled at me, entirely unstoppable and ended up slamming into my chest, burning quickly through my scales and charring the skin beneath.

I dropped to my knees, screaming in agony as the pain shot through every nerve, shifting back to human as I hit the ground. With absolute horror on his face, Tarrin shifted in a flash, sprinting across the room, slamming to his knees in front of me.

"Kaida, I'm so sorry. Are you all right? Kaida..." He continued repeating the same question over and over, apology after apology, but my brain wasn't comprehending them. The flames had burned right through my sweat drenched shirt, scorching the skin beneath. A large, angry welt covered my chest, pus-filled blisters already rising from it.

The pain was relentless and unyielding. Black spots flashed in my field of vision as each shock of pain reverberated through my body. This was no ordinary burn, but one of magic. Much hotter, stronger than any ordinary flame.

I swayed side to side, groaning and screaming through my teeth, Tarrin holding my face, before I blacked out.

When I awoke, I was lying on the ugly brown couch in the main room of my chambers, alone, a thin towel full of ice gently placed on my chest.

I tried to sit up and bit my tongue to keep from crying out as the cloth scraped and pulled at the blisters. Freezing in place, begging the throbbing to subside, tears welled in my eyes. Every breath was painful.

I was about to yell for help, praying someone would be nearby to hear me, when the door latch clicked and the quiet creaking of it opening and closing echoed in the silent room.

"Kaida?" Tarrin's voice was quiet, hesitant as he peeked over the back of the couch. He breathed a sigh of relief when our eyes met, and he rushed around to kneel in front of me.

"I brought a special salve. It should help with the pain."

The pain was so astronomical that I could only nod as tears slipped down the sides of my face, falling into my hair pooled beneath me.

"I'm so sorry, Kaida. I thought…" He did not finish his thought as he carefully removed the towel of ice, pausing at my sudden intake of breath through my teeth, and looked at what he had done to my chest. His eyes widened for a split second before a practiced calm replaced it. It must have been bad.

The tin of salve clinked as he removed the lid, sticking his fingers into the goopy substance.

"Hold still." His words were gentle, far kinder than any he had ever spoken before, a rare tenderness that few ever saw. I barely had time to brace for the agony that roared through my body as his fingers met my skin.

I could not hold in the scream that ripped its way out of my mouth. Invisible restraints held my limbs in place to keep me from thrashing, but the screams still tore their way through my teeth. The pressure on my chest grew and grew with each pass of his fingers, the pain like tiny daggers being driven into my skin repeatedly. And then set on fire.

Tarrin worked quickly with steady hands, his face a mastered calm. The moment he finished and removed his hand, a soothing coolness spread over the burn, numbing each blister, quieting the relentless throbbing. I closed my eyes as relief flooded through my limbs, more tears escaping beneath my eye lids.

"Better?" he asked, a small encouraging smile tilting his lips.

I managed a nod, throat too raw from screaming to answer.

He knelt on the floor next to my head, setting his forehead against mine, running his fingers soothingly through the tangled mess that my hair had become.

"I'm so sorry, Kaida."

Not trusting my voice, I grabbed his hand and held it, his fingers interlacing with mine. Tarrin's lips found mine, gentle and soft. The pain on my chest had faded to a dull ache and the relief was enough that I attempted to sit up. Putting a hand behind my neck, Tarrin helped me slowly lean forward, spinning me so my back was against the couch. There was concern in his eyes as he took in the burn, carefully watching my face for any sign of the pain returning.

A brisk knock sounded at the door, and we both froze, neither one wanting to move. The knock sounded again, more hurried this time, urgent.

With a sigh, he rose and crossed the room. A sharp ache suddenly ripped through the burn, a gasp escaping through my lips just as he opened the door and Meara's voice drifted through.

"Your Highness, I am sorry for the intrusion. I heard about Miss Kaida's injury and came to offer my services." Her words were rushed, her voice trembling. Unusual for her. Tarrin did not seem to think anything of it as he opened the door wider, ushering her in. The throbbing ache had returned, my skin growing hotter by the second as Meara came into view and dropped to her knees to inspect the wound. Her eyes widened.

"I think it would be wise to bring you to the infirmary, miss."

"I just came from there. They gave me a salve to put on it," Tarrin said, annoyed.

"Oh. I, um. Yes, but I think they will be able to d-do more once they see the severity of the burn." A stutter choked her words, and she wrung her hands. She was nervous. The realization hit just as another spasm rocked through my chest, my mind forgetting her strange behavior altogether.

Tarrin would not have recognized the differences in her speech or body language, he probably would have taken them to be nerves from being around the Prince. He hesitated for several moments, his eyes relentless on my face, on the burn.

"All right. If you think they will be able to help, then go ahead." I could see the reluctance on his face, hear it in his voice.

As if his words were a cue, a large man with arms bulging in his grungy brown slave attire, appeared at the door, pushing a wooden chair with a large wheel on each side. He kept his long face carefully blank as he approached.

"It is a long walk to the infirmary," Meara explained after seeing the confusion on my face.

The man came toward me as if he were going to carry me away, and I was hit with a strange sense of familiarity. I had seen this man before. But where?

"I will help her," Tarrin said, that princely dominance filling his voice, as he stepped forward to block the strange man from helping me. I let out a silent breath of relief.

Biting down on my tongue to keep from groaning, I looped my arms around his neck as he lifted me in his arms and carried me over to the wheeled chair. His shirt sleeves were rolled up, causing my bare back and torso to rub against his arms. Despite the pain on my chest, my blood heated and sang in every place our skin touched. I kept my head down as pink stained my cheeks.

I could think of a thousand other things I would rather be doing right now.

Tarrin's words whispered into my mind, and I met his stare, finding amusement and desire lingering there. He winked at me which only furthered my blush, resulting in a quiet chuckle from him. Tarrin set me into the chair, placing a light kiss on my forehead before stepping back.

The tension between us was palpable as I let him feel an unfiltered version of my thoughts through our bond. *Perhaps we could discuss some of those other things when I return.*

A feline smile curved his lips in response. *I look forward to it.*

In the blink of an eye, the strange man was behind the chair, wheeling me from my chambers, Meara in the lead. I made to turn back to say something else, but the man slammed the door closed, Tarrin vanishing behind it. I faced forward once more, my stomach sinking.

Something didn't feel right. Why was this man so familiar?

I glanced up at Meara and noticed sweat beading on her neck, her hair sticking to it in clumps. They continued down the east wing of the palace, going straight where they should have turned right to head in the direction of the infirmary. I looked up at the man and a wicked grin spread across his face. That's when I remembered. The first day I came to the palace there was a man hiding in the shadows that kept watching me. This was the same person.

My unease grew and grew until we came to a deserted staircase, down which the man plunked the chair, step after step, my teeth rattling with each impact, internally groaning as each stair sent a jolt through my chest.

When we finally reached the bottom, there stood a door, weathered and worn, but sturdy enough. It was clearly old and had not been used in many years. Terror cleaved through my body as Meara opened the door, gesturing for the man to hurry.

"I fulfilled my end of the deal," she bit out, the most anger I had heard from her normally quiet voice. "Make sure he knows it." The man nodded once and continued to push the chair out the door. I tried to stop him, to ask what he was doing, but a rough brown sack was shoved over my head the moment we made it outside. The chair banged and jostled over the rough rocks on the road, my hands holding the arms with a death grip.

He? Who was *he*? Why would Meara help this terrible man? I always expected dragons to betray me, but never a human.

A scream built in my throat, and I readied to release it, ready to beg for someone, anyone, to come to my rescue as the fear coiled around my stomach held me immobile. I opened my mouth just as the man gripped a fistful of my hair in his hand and tugged. Hard. Tears filled my eyes. I tried to cry out again and he pulled harder.

I made to scream for the third time when I felt the prick of a knife at my throat.

"Make a sound and you die."

CHAPTER FORTY-TWO
KAIDA

THICK, SUFFOCATING HEAT smothered my face, sweat clinging to every pore, a slab of cold rough stone laid beneath me, and iron shackles bound my wrists and ankles. The familiar scent of burning coals filled my nose as my sluggish mind slithered back to consciousness. A sharp spasm of pain shot through my chest as I tried to move, the memory of Tarrin's fire burning me flashing through my mind. My mouth was bone dry, making it impossible to swallow. I had a vague recollection of a man with a beard stealing me away from the palace, and the last thing I remembered was his knife at my throat.

Peeking my eyes open, I glanced around the room. Darkness clung to every corner, a large hearth to my right, the glow of simmering coals burning down to ashes the only light source. Despite the dimness, I knew this room. It was the ghost that haunted my waking moments, the cause of every nightmare that had me bolting upright in the dead of night, screams dying on my tongue.

I dared a look to my left and saw what I dreaded most. That table full of tools. Hammers, knives, both sharp and dull, needles of various sizes, shearing tools, an auger, and an axe with a dull rusted edge, all arranged in a neat line. I squeezed my eyes closed in hope that I was hallucinating, but I knew this room. The damp, mustiness of being underground. The tang of iron, blood, and ash. The despair that dug in like claws into skin. I opened my eyes again.

"Belharnt," I whispered, barely able to use my voice.

Gasping breaths tore through my body like a savage beast trying to escape. Tears welled in my eyes as the room grew smaller and smaller, pressing in on every side. It was difficult to breathe, the temperature rising by the second. Each breath was agony as it stretched and contracted my chest, the burn spasming in response. Yanking on the restraints, I begged for them to open, to release me, but they remained cold and unyielding.

My head swam from the lack of oxygen when I heard a series of locks click and unlatch. Slamming my eyes shut, I begged the gods that humans had forsaken long ago, pleading for this to not be real, to wake up in the palace, nestled under the blankets in my massive bed.

Familiar footsteps shook the floor as the door opened and the dragon of ash and smoke crossed the threshold. I swallowed back the tears that slid down my cheeks, as fear cleaved and slashed its way down my throat and into my stomach. Merciless dread was like a poison filling my veins.

This was my hellish nightmare turned reality.

I felt his presence standing next to me before he ever uttered a word. For several moments, the dragon towered over me, those hate-filled eyes devouring my face. I could feel his command in the air, to open my eyes, and I fought it with every ounce of strength I had left. He clucked his tongue in disappointment, turning away toward the fireplace. He threw a large bucket of coals on the dying embers, a cloud of ash erupting and spreading like a dust storm through the room, coating my sweat slick skin.

"So disappointing, Kaida. Really," Eklos tutted. "All that effort in the palace gardens to kill me, and yet *you* pass out, I get away, and then I capture you with hardly any effort required." He clucked his tongue again. "The Prince is far too trusting of his slaves." My eyes popped open at his words, a small spark igniting in my stomach. "I expected more, oh mighty shape-shifter." A devilish grin twisted his snout as he mocked me.

"Not feeling so brave and powerful now, are we?" he continued when I kept silent. Laughing, he walked around the stone table I was shackled to, stopping next to the tools, the metal clinking as he ran his claws along each one.

I pulled once more at my wrists, but they wouldn't budge.

"Do not bother trying to escape, human. Those restraints are meant for filth like you." He paused, bringing his snout close to my nose, and I recoiled at the stench of carrion on his breath.

"I am sure you have already noticed your lack of strength, the weakness in your bones. The sudden coldness of that unquenchable fire within you," Eklos drawled. "Those restraints are made of iron." He paused again, watching my face. "Iron… laced with bluestone." That grin returned, his sharp teeth glinting in the dim fire light.

"B-bluestone?" I stuttered out, my teeth chattering despite the heat. *Fever?*

"They serve two purposes," he continued, ignoring me. He picked up one of the knives, examining it. "The iron, of course, suppresses your ability to access any magic. That dull feeling encompassing your body? Yes, that is the iron, draining every ounce of it."

That utter exhaustion and weakness I felt when I awoke now made sense. It was like an entire lake had been dumped on my inner fire, extinguishing everything, down to the last ember. My core was cold, empty. I tried to draw on water, but that too had been sucked dry, not even a drop to call on.

"But even better than the iron shackles is what lies beneath the surface." His eyes shone with a furious hatred as he turned the full brunt of his gaze on my face.

"Bluestone. A rare substance, only one source of it in all of Elysia. While it's harmless to both humans and dragons separately, it is absolutely toxic to shape-shifters."

I closed my eyes, swallowing the rising bile in my throat.

"It not only prevents you from shifting into your dragon form, but it stifles the very life force inside you that allows you to shift. Eventually you will be unable to change forms, permanently, and in the end, it will drain your life completely, leaving you an empty carcass on that table of stone."

Despair. It jammed its claws into my skin, sinking deeper and deeper, until my entire being was numb, swimming in it. It was a burning cold that seeped into every pore, every shred of skin, shoving its way into my lungs. Down, down, down, it dragged me, my breaths becoming shorter, more desperate, as it pulled me under, drowning me in its murky waters. I tried to break through the surface, to keep my head above the water, but the current was too strong.

This was it. This was where I was going to die. There was no way I would be able to survive Belharnt a second time. All the training I had endured, all the endless hours I had put in, all of it was for nothing. I could not break out, could not escape. I could not summon any magic or defend myself.

I was merely a damaged body with a broken soul chained to a stone table.

Tarrin's face flashed through my mind. Did he even know I had been taken? I had no idea if I had been missing for hours or days. There was no sense of time in this room. Hours, days, weeks, years—they were all the same. It was all just passing moments in the dark.

Tarrin was smart enough to guess that Eklos was behind my disappearance, but this room was deep underground. I had been blindfolded both coming and leaving here the last time, and even *I* was not sure where I was. Tarrin would never be able to find me down here.

Eklos was many things, but he was not stupid. He would stay underground until I was dead, only resurfacing in Vernista when he was ready to gloat, and my body was cold and disposed of.

The idea of dying here, alone, in the dark… it gripped every muscle and bone in my body, I began thrashing around on the table. The shackles cut into my skin, leaving bloody wounds that would not heal so long as the bluestone was in contact with them. I bit my tongue to keep from screaming in pain, tasting the coppery tang of blood. Eklos remained still, watching me, a sly smile twisting his snout.

When I regained control over my body, my breaths were ragged blades slicing through my throat, my wrists and ankles raw and bloodied. I could feel where the blistered areas of the burn on my chest had ripped open. I fought to slow my breathing as the cracking and popping of the hearth set my nerves on edge.

"Are you quite finished, slave?" Eklos's voice echoed, piercing the silence, and I flinched.

I turned my head to look at him, the cold stone biting into my ear. "Tarrin will find me," I spit, blood and saliva flying from my lips. I knew it was a lie, but I had to say something to keep him from grabbing the tools he now stood by. A whimper escaped me, my chin wobbling at the effort it took to keep the tears in.

Eklos's laugh was like thunder in the middle of the night. Dark, eerie, with a promise of violence. He leaned forward to tighten the shackles on my wrists and ankles before setting his snout next to my ear. The carrion on his breath made my head spin. "That's exactly what I'm counting on."

Ice poured into my blood as my exhausted brain riddled through his words. This was all a trap. Eklos wanted to draw Tarrin here, and most likely my father as well. *No no no! Tarrin please stay away!* I knew the distance was too great for him to hear me through our bond, but it didn't stop my internal screaming for him to stay far away from Belharnt.

"Now, let us see if you are stronger than your mother was." The sneer that contorted Eklos's face was like that of a demon. Bile rose in my throat at the thought of Tarrin finding pieces of me, shattered, torn, and broken. Tears burned my eyes, but I swallowed them back, refusing to let Eklos see how his words affected me.

His smile widened further. Grabbing a large iron hammer, the metal groaning beneath his grip, my old Master stalked toward me.

"Let's begin."

CHAPTER FORTY-THREE

ELDRIN

"WHERE IS SHE?" Prince Tarrin bellowed at Meara as she backed herself into a corner. Tears flowed down her cheeks; her eyes wide in terror. Her hands hung limp at her sides, defeated.

Guilt.

That was the look on her face.

Tarrin had found me in the foyer when I had returned from my scouting mission, flying around the palace and the surrounding grounds, informing me that Kaida was missing.

Without a doubt, I knew that Eklos was behind it.

And Eklos had the advantage. He knew the area, had a large following, not to mention his secret army of dragons. He could have a hideout anywhere in Vernista or beyond. She could be underground or in the mountains. The options were endless, and our time was running out.

I knew Eklos would not hesitate to kill her. The thought sent an ache ripping through my stomach. The Prince told me everything he knew in short concise words, which admittedly was not much, and we found Meara burrowed in the wine cellar soon after.

We brought her to the Prince's chambers to question her, and

I could see the effort the Prince was exerting in being patient, and that his fear for Kaida's safety was eroding it away by the second.

"Where is she, Meara? Where did you take her?" A frantic tone worked its way into his voice, his hands shaking. When she continued to stare at him, saying nothing, he let out a low growl and started pacing back and forth.

"Your Highness," I said. Tarrin ignored me.

"Who took her?"

No answer.

"How did you get her out of the palace unnoticed?"

She stared at the ground, saying nothing.

"Where is Kaida?" The Prince's voice broke when he said her name, his hands clenching into fists. He stood a foot away from the girl, glaring down at her, arms crossed. Even in his human body he towered above her.

She only shook her head in response.

"Your Highness," I snapped, tearing his attention away from the girl. "You need to calm down or we won't find her."

Tarrin glared at me, chest heaving. The desperation to find her was rolling off him in waves, filling the room. He paced the room, running his hands through his hair. Taking a deep breath, he let it out and turned again toward the slave girl.

"My apologies, Meara." The words were sincere, but I could still see the anger flickering in them. She barely nodded in response, keeping her eyes on the ground.

"Please, if you know where she is…" the Prince trailed off, his eyes pleading.

"Eklos will kill her," I spoke up. "If we do not find her, and soon, it will be too late."

Meara's face contorted at the mention of Eklos's name. Her shoulders curved inwards, ducking her head down further, almost in a defensive position.

"Eklos threatened you, didn't he?" The threat must have been very great for her to betray Kaida, and the Royal Family.

Tears began to fall like a dam had been broken and she fell to her knees, her face in her hands. Quiet sobs racked through her body.

"What did he tell you?" I prodded.

Sniffling, she wiped at her face, dabbing it with the end of her dirty apron.

"He… he said he would murder my entire family, track down even my most distant relatives. And then he would come back for me. He said it would be long and painful, that I would beg for him to end it, but I would not find death's mercy." Meara's voice broke on the last word, another sob shaking her body. "I knew Eklos's reputation. I knew he would do as he said."

"What happened? How did you get her out? Where was she taken?" I asked, keeping my voice quiet.

Meara curled up into a ball against the wall, her arms wrapping around her knees. Her eyes were wide as she shook her head.

"Meara, I can offer you protection. You and your family. They will stay here in the palace, under guard. Eklos will not be able to reach them. Just please tell us where Kaida is," Tarrin said in a soothing tone.

"I don't know where she is," she admitted.

"But—"

"I don't know where she is," she repeated, firmly. "Nor did I take her out of the palace. The man that came to escort her in the wheeled chair, he was one of Eklos's slaves. I'm sure Eklos threatened him into doing his dirty work like he did to me. Eklos somehow infiltrated the palace, setting up some of his slaves as royal servants. I was supposed help him kidnap her and get him safely out again without attracting attention. It was unfortunately good timing that she was injured, and I was able to use the excuse of the infirmary to get her out." The words tumbled out in a rush as if she had been holding them in for far too long, the pressure finally releasing.

"I am truly sorry, Your Highness. I had to protect my family."

"Who was the man? Do you know where to find him?" he said, ignoring her apology.

"No."

"And you have no clue where he took her?"

"No…" she hesitated. "But there was one time she was sleeping in her room, screaming in bed, must have been having a nightmare. I slipped in to retrieve her soiled laundry when she started talking in her sleep. It was all jumbled and did not make much sense, so I did not think much of it. She had mentioned something about a dark room, underground, and kept telling somebody to get away from her. It was none of my business, so I did my best to forget about it. Perhaps he took her to the place in her dream." She shrugged, her face sad and empty, as if she had given up everything and knew that only death awaited.

"Did she ever mention anything to you like that, Prince?" I asked Tarrin. A haunted look twisted his face. He scrubbed at his face with his hands. He met my stare and my stomach dropped. Whatever he realized was not good.

The Prince turned to Meara. "Go. Send for your family. They will stay in the Maswhil room at the east end of the palace. I will arrange for someone to be stationed outside at all hours."

Meara got to her feet, her knees visibly shaking, and nodded. She gathered her skirt and scurried toward to the door.

"Meara," the Prince called, and she froze. "I understand why you did what you did. But that does not excuse it. If you ever betray the Royal Family again, including those close to them, you will answer for treason."

Meara's eyes filled with tears as she nodded her head, shutting the door, the click of the latch echoing. As if his self-restraint had been popped like a balloon, Prince Tarrin collapsed to his knees, slumping against the back of the gray couch. With the absence of the girl, tears spilled down his cheeks.

For the first time since Tarrin told me Kaida had been kidnapped, I allowed myself to examine how I was feeling. Though I had just met her days before, I knew she was something special. Not just because she was the daughter I never knew I had, but because of her strength. Her magic. Her kindness.

Elysia needed more dragons like her. More shifters. I couldn't allow Eklos to kill her. We had to find her. She was too precious. Too important. I sat down on the floor next to Tarrin, trying to think of everything I knew about my cousin. Admittedly, it wasn't much. I didn't know any of his hideouts or retreats, I didn't know where his followers met, nor did I even know where to begin looking. Trying to narrow down where he might be keeping Kaida was like trying to search for a flower seed thrown in a bed of thorny roses.

I inhaled through my nose and fiddled with my fingers in my lap. "What did you figure out? I saw the look on your face."

The Prince sniffed. "Belharnt. He had to have taken her to Belharnt."

I hadn't heard of such a place, but based on his reaction, I knew it couldn't be good.

"What do we do now?" Prince Tarrin whispered, tears plinking onto his pants.

Just as I was about to answer, the door swung open, banging against the wall as it made contact. Both of us flinched, jumping to our feet, and swung toward the turquoise dragon standing in the doorway.

"I know how to find her," a deep voice declared.

It was King Martik.

CHAPTER FORTY-FOUR

KAIDA

IN MY DREAM I was sprawled on my back in the soft grass, watching the clouds slowly drift by, in a field just outside the palace boundary. Wind blew over my face, and the sound of swaying grass whispered a soft lullaby in my ears. The day was unseasonably warm, even for a dream, and I rolled up the sleeves of my burgundy dress, allowing the sun to seep into my too-pale skin. Clouds drifted through the sky and I found myself trying to see shapes in the wisps and giant puffy ones like when I was a child. I was vaguely aware of someone lying next to me, his dark brown hair rustling in the breeze, eyes closed, a content smile on his lips.

Our hands were intertwined, his strong and steady.

"Don't you wish it could be like this all the time?" Tarrin breathed, like he was afraid of bursting the cocoon of happiness we had made.

"Hmm?" I managed, unable to make my mouth move. A dark storm cloud appeared in the distance, capturing my attention.

"This. Us. Here. Carefree, no worries. No politics. No conspiracies or murders. No dragons versus humans. Just us."

A picture filled my mind of the life he described, and I felt a sudden loss for a life that I knew could never be.

"Yes," I whispered, a single tear sliding down the side of my face.

Tarrin glanced at me out of the corner of his eye and rolled onto his side, head propped up with this hand. With the lightest touch, he wiped away the wet streak from my face, lightning crackling through my veins.

"That sounds like a fairy tale," I said at last, returning my gaze to the sky and the heavy gray cloud that had grown impossibly closer in only a few minutes.

"Hmm?" he hummed.

"A world like that. It sounds like a fairy tale." I paused, considering. "Fairy tales don't exist."

Stories my mother would tell me when I was young surfaced in my mind. The cold, damp cave we lived in loomed in front of me, us bundled beneath a blanket as she whispered into the darkness. Tales of stolen princesses rescued by heroic princes, of a world of darkness suddenly made bright, goodness always triumphant. But it was not long after she told me those stories that she was killed, and I learned that such tales were fables. It was foolish to hope for a better world. There was no such thing.

"Perhaps we need to make our own fairy tale." Tarrin's voice broke through the reverie, bringing me back to the present. I glanced at his face and could not help the smile that curved my lips. His eyes were so full of hope, as if he truly believed we could shape the world how we wanted.

I wanted so badly to share that dream, to believe it. To believe him.

"We could run away, leave Elysia. Be whoever we want. Make a new life. Together." The excitement flashing in his eyes brought a sharp pang to my chest.

"Tarrin..." I started, unsure of what to say next. Lightning forked through the clouds only miles away now, the sun disappearing in their wake.

He swallowed, his eyes flicking to my lips, and my heartbeat quickened. He cupped my cheek in his palm, wiping away another tear that had escaped. He leaned closer, his hand sliding down to my neck, gently pulling me toward him. The storm cloud was directly overhead now. Any second the deluge would drop on top of us, but Tarrin did not seem to notice. Lightning hit the ground a few feet away and I screamed, but still Tarrin did not move, his eyes closed, moving closer to my face.

"Kaida." My name was like honey on his lips, a sweet love song that only we knew. My pulse pounded beneath my skin and I could feel the electricity from the storm in my veins. His lips mere inches from mine, I closed my eyes, though something didn't feel right.

A heartbeat passed. Then another.

Nothing happened. A raindrop hit my cheek.

Opening my eyes, a scream ripped its way up my throat and my heart threatened to shatter as I beheld Tarrin positioned above me, a dagger gripped firmly in his hand, poised over my heart. His eyes were dark, cold, centuries of hatred flashing in them. Lightning speared through the sky behind his head, erupting from the cloud, heading straight for us.

Before a scream could fully enter my mouth, he plunged the knife, hard, into my chest as the lightning collided with it.

Agony tore through my body as my heart struggled to beat, as blood slowed, and spots appeared in my vision. My blood boiled beneath my skin. I tried to grab the knife, to pull it out and roll away, but my limbs were frozen, paralyzed.

Then I was falling. Through the ground, through embers and ash, layers of earth and rock until the heat was unbearable, the darkness crushing. I slammed onto stone, a scream cleaving its way from my throat just before impact. Darkness took me but it was short lived as another dagger was shoved into my chest.

I tried to move but my arms and legs were shackled in cold iron.

Reality snapped into place and my eyes popped open.

I was in Belharnt.

It was not Tarrin above me, but Eklos. Not a knife in my chest, but his claw, slicing open the burn, still raw, blistered, and unhealed.

Another scream tried to work its way out, but my throat was so raw that it came out as a hoarse whisper. The sob that racked through my body only worsened the pain.

"Welcome back, slave," he spit the words like venom. "Did you have a nice nap?" Eklos picked another spot on my chest and ripped his claw across the skin, tearing it like paper. I bit my tongue to keep from crying out, and I tried to clench my fists, but my entire left hand had been shattered.

A piercing throb brought the memory rushing back.

Eklos had slammed the hammer down upon my hand repeatedly, without relenting, until it was just a mangled mess of skin and shards of bone. He made it so that it would never heal properly and would be unusable for the rest of whatever life I had left.

I blacked out once more before he finally removed his claws and stomped away, his massive dragon body shaking the ground as he took a seat near the hearth, wicked pleasure distorting his face.

My heart sputtered a painful beat as I recalled Tarrin's face above mine in my dream, the absolute loathing in his eyes, twin to the one I always found in Eklos's.

It wasn't him. He would never hurt me.

I repeated the words to myself as I attempted to calm my ragged breathing.

"Why are you doing this?" I rasped.

In the past I always stayed quiet, never questioned my Master or his punishments. But I was here, and I was going to die. I would spend my last days in the suffocating darkness, in endless pain, and the afterlife would find me. Knowing the end was coming allowed a strange sort of boldness, a reckless bravery to stretch through my aching body, loosening my tongue.

"Why. Are. You. Doing. This?" I ground out through clenched teeth when he didn't answer. The force of the words sent a sharp spasm of pain arching through the burn, but I swallowed it down, waiting for it to pass.

"Because your kind of filth should never have been allowed in the first place," Eklos spit. "I am continuing the legacy my father left behind. Finishing what he failed to end." His red eyes narrowed, flickering in the dim light from the hearth.

My forehead creased. His father? What was he talking about?

Eklos let out an exasperated sigh, getting to his feet. "You humans really are dull." Towering over me, smoke flowed out of his nostrils, solidifying into a whip of smoke. With hardly a thought, he willed it to stroke my face, leaving streaks of ash behind. I tried to swallow but my throat was parched and raw. I replayed his words in my head, and my stomach sank like a heavy weight.

"Let me tell you a story, Kaida."

Smoke shoved its way into my nose, spreading through my sinuses, encasing my brain. Pictures and moments frozen in time appeared in front of me as if I were reliving memories that were not mine.

The first scene was of a dragon, black as a starless night, standing over me as I laid on the ground, his cold eyes unrelenting. Before I could blink, it shifted to the dragon holding a whip, sending it across the air, colliding with my back. The pain was, mercifully, absent but I knew the agony that came from it. When it changed again, I was in a field, fire and smoke curling from my hands and nostrils, doing what I willed. The scene shifted again to houses burning, humans on fire bursting through the doors, screaming. Other dragons were cutting down the humans left and right as if they were harvesting wildflowers and not taking a life.

Faster and faster the images came, death and pain and hatred pulsing through every picture, the dragon of nightmares visible in each one. Bile rising in my throat, I tried to close my eyes to shut out the horrors of what I had seen, the screams of the dying still lingering in my ears. The moment my eyes were shut, a scaly hand collided with my cheek, the sudden sting bringing tears to my eyes.

"Watch." Eklos's tone was enough to make me pry open my eyes.

This time the scene was different. I was in a room with a large wooden desk, the dragon of night standing behind it, peering out a window, his back to me. He no longer towered over me but matched my height. Ornate paintings hung on the walls, perfectly spaced and not a trace of dust on them, a priceless rug beneath my feet. I stood ramrod straight, barely breathing, hands clasped behind my back.

"You summoned me, Father?" The words came out of my mouth, but the voice was not my own.

"Yes." The dragon's deep voice rumbled as he turned to me, his red eyes glowing. "I have arranged for you to go to Sarphan in the north. There have been rumors of humans trying to rebel against their dragon Masters. You will lead a company of dragons and deal with this nuisance. We do not need the other human filth hearing word of this and thinking they have a chance."

Nausea roiled in my gut as the words sank in.

"As you will it, father." The words tasted like vomit in my mouth. Glancing down to the floor as I turned to leave, I noticed my clawed feet, dark like smoke, but not quite black.

I was Eklos. These were his memories.

I made it to the door, scaled hand on the doorknob when his father spoke again.

"One more thing, Eklos." I turned halfway toward the dragon of night, and I could feel the wariness emanating from my old Master's body.

It was almost fear. I had never known Eklos to be afraid, let alone to show it.

"You will not fail this time. If you lose even one dragon to the enemy, your own life will be forfeit."

Repulsion rippled into the room, and my body was frozen in place, unable to move.

I turned back toward Eklos's father and stepped forward. His back was to me, so he did not seem to notice as I came to a halt, my clawed hands in fists. I took in a deep breath, and his father looked over his shoulder at the sound.

Then the room exploded in smoke.

My arms were extended above my head, balls of smoke curling and spinning in my hands. As if it came from every scale on my body, smoke shot through the room in every direction, consuming everything in its path.

Eklos's father threw a shield of fire around himself, but it was quickly overtaken by the force from the smoke, the sudden absence of oxygen. Summoning more and more magic, I felt my insides twist. I continued walking forward until I reached the desk separating us.

Without another thought, without hesitation, I released a barrage of smoke onto Eklos's father. It shoved and ripped its way into his mouth, up his nose, cutting and whipping at his scales. He tried to scream but the smoke crushed his windpipe, silencing any noise.

His father collapsed to the ground, but still I continued. The hatred that boiled inside my stomach would not relent and the smoke kept coming, ash raining down in the room.

And then it stopped. The well of magic went dry.

I fell to my knees, a thud echoing in the room from the impact. I crawled around the desk to peer at Eklos's father.

Thanks to the poison in the smoke, he was now a scale-covered carcass that had completely decomposed, not a trace of the malevolent dragon that used to inhabit it. A scream worked its way up my throat when I found myself back on the stone table, the cold biting into my back.

Eklos retracted his smoke and stood several feet back from me. Deep loathing twisted his face, but also some emotion that pinched the corners of his eyes.

I tried to put the pieces together, the old dragon lore of Elysia replaying in my mind. The dragon in his memory was black as the darkest night, in charge of sending out scores of dragons with the intention of ending the human race.

There was only one dragon in the history of Elysia like that…

A sneer spread over Eklos's face as the answer clicked in my mind.

"Yes, Kaida." His words reverberated off the walls, chilling my bones. "I am the Lone Dragon's son."

CHAPTER FORTY-FIVE
TARRIN

I SLUMPED INTO AN old armchair.

"If you know how to find her then what are we still doing here?" I asked my father. We needed to find her before Eklos killed her. We could formulate a plan on the way. Every second we sat in my chambers was one more second we gave to Eklos.

Not for the first time, I wished, to no avail, that proximity was not a factor in the mind-to-mind communication with Kaida. I knew she was far away from the palace because I could not hear or talk to her. I missed her presence by my side. I had become so used to her smile, her inner wildfire. They were addictive and I found myself desperately needing another hit.

My father dropped his enormous body onto the couch. "You don't just charge into a battle before getting all the information, Son. We need to make a plan and fully know what we're up against. Eklos is not a dragon to mess with and being a fool will cost you."

Eldrin plopped into the chair next to me. "How do you know where she is?"

My father scratched at the scales on his snout. "I've been informed by the Council themselves that they've partnered with Eklos who has demanded that the Royal Family support his cause. He has asked for every dragon to join his army, and that we would not interfere with his plans."

A frustrated scream built in my throat. "We are not giving him anything."

"Based on the reports I have received, Eklos and the Remnant now outnumber any reserves we might have. Unfortunately, it would be quite simple for him to overrun the palace and take control of it, not to mention Elysia," my father said without a trace of worry, ignoring me entirely.

"I have seen what Eklos is capable of," Eldrin chimed in. "He is relentless, merciless. He will not hesitate to kill all of us in order to get what he wants."

I sat forward, putting my face in my hands. When had this gotten so complicated? How did dragons even get it in their head in the first place that we were superior? After seeing the life and kindness in Kaida, someone who is the perfect combination of the two races, I could never understand where the kind of hatred that Eklos harbored had come from.

"Eklos has made it his life's mission to finish what the Lone Dragon started a thousand years ago. He plans to exterminate the remaining human population." My father paused, looking warily at Eldrin and me. "Including shape-shifters," he amended. "He plans to use his hoard of dragons, including the dragons we supposedly supply him with, to accomplish his plan."

"And where does capturing Kaida fit into this?" Eldrin asked, eyebrows furrowing.

"That is the last demand from the Council. We are to give her over to him immediately."

"*What?*" I shot to my feet, white hot wrath burning in my gut. "*You* let them take her?" I bellowed.

"Tarrin, sit down." Martik's voice was firm, on the edge of scolding.

"I cannot believe you would let those *monsters* in this palace and let them take Kaida. They are going to *kill* her!"

"*Sit. Down,*" the dominant voice of the King of Elysia, not my father, boomed, shaking the walls to the point where I fell back into my chair.

"I did not *let* them take her. I told the Council no. I told them that she was my son's betrothed, and I would not just hand her over." A regretful silence echoed as his words died off. Like a scolded child, I avoided eye contact with my father, my cheeks burning.

"Eklos must have decided to take things into his own hands," Eldrin murmured.

My father nodded his head in agreement. "I am not sure how he managed to sneak his spies into my palace, or how the Council has worked with him without my knowledge for so long, but it happened, and I do not intend to let it stand. We need to move forward and make a plan."

"And quickly," Eldrin interjected. "She's already been gone for nearly a day. We do not know how long Eklos will keep her alive."

My gut twisted at the revolting thought. "How do we find her? That dungeon could literally be anywhere."

"What is this place?" Eldrin asked, his forehead creasing in confusion. Though Belharnt wasn't a place that was widely known about, it still surprised me that Eklos's cousin wouldn't be aware of it.

"Belharnt is a dungeon deep beneath the ground just east of the Ilgathor Mountains. Eklos built it with the sole purpose of torturing its captives until the point of death. No human has ever walked out of there alive."

Bile burned the back of my throat at the thought of Kaida in such a place.

"Except…" my father's voice seemed far too loud in the fragile quiet that had descended on the room. "Well, Kaida did make it out of that room once before.

"What are you talking about?" Eldrin's eyes narrowed.

"She has been to Belharnt before. Eklos kept her there for seven years. She was only released a few months ago. That's when Lita," he stumbled over her name, "sent Tarrin after her."

"Seven *years*?" Eldrin said, incredulous. "How does one survive that long in a place like that?"

My father did not answer, only stared into the dying flames in the fireplace. Kaida's father looked to me and I shrugged.

"She's never shared much of her past with me. If you had seen how she looked when I took her from that gods-forsaken pit they call The Den, you wouldn't have pressed her for more information either."

I found myself wishing that she had told me more about her life. She wasn't alone anymore; she didn't need to carry that burden by herself.

"Why did he let her go the first time?" Eldrin asked.

"No one knows. One day she disappeared from Vernista, was gone for seven years, and then suddenly surfaced again, working in The Den."

I ran a hand through my hair, exasperated. "What would be the purpose? Torturing her for years and then letting her go? It goes against everything Eklos stands for."

"I would imagine," my father began, casting a wary look at Eldrin, "that the purpose was to draw you out of hiding."

"I didn't even know Kaida existed," Eldrin breathed.

"He must have figured that out when you did not come for her. Perhaps he let her go in hopes that you would one day find her."

"Why does Eklos want you so badly?" I asked Eldrin, pinning him with a cold glare. Everything kept coming back to Eldrin, and it was time he explained why.

Once again avoiding my question, Eldrin asked, "Why does Eklos despise Kaida? Why has he gone to such great lengths to capture her?"

A sick sort of amusement twisted my father's face. "Shall we count all the reasons?" His voice was thick with sarcasm. He ticked them off with his claws. "First, she is a human. That is reason enough to Eklos. Second, she is Aela's daughter, and Aela disobeyed him at every opportunity. And now we know that the last reason is to draw you out of hiding, so he can kill you."

For a moment no one said anything, an eerie silence creeping through the room.

"I would assume that Eklos knew you would refuse to give her over," Eldrin said at last. "It was part of his plan to have the Council tell you where she would be. He wants all of us, and Kaida, in one place so he can be rid of us. This is a trap."

My father let out a resigned sigh, nodding his head. "I came to the same conclusion."

I gripped the arm rests of my chair with a death grip, nails digging into the fabric. Answers were being given but only enough to bring up more questions.

"*Why* does Eklos want *you*?" I repeated, enunciating every word.

For a moment, neither my father nor Eldrin moved. It felt as though time had frozen as I watched Eldrin put his face in his hands.

"A thousand years ago, there were two brothers, both dragons. One's heart was cold like a winter's night, the other like a summer's sun. Xalerion, the former. Bakari, the latter. Xalerion, older by a year, was black as the night, as if his scales absorbed every bit of life and sucked the soul out of it. He had an abnormal amount of strength for a dragon and could wield the night in his palm.

"Bakari, a dragon of darkest blue, had compassion in his heart, and a love for life that his brother did not. When he grew into his middle years, he started experiencing strange symptoms. His magic was not developing like it should have, and frequent flashes of light would flicker over his scales, but then disappear.

"One day, the two brothers were out patrolling one of the forests at the northern edge of the Ilgathor Mountains when Bakari fell to his knees, gripping his head. A blinding flash of light rippled through the forest and Xalerion turned back to find, not a dragon, but a human male kneeling on the ground where his brother had been. Bakari was a shape-shifter, one of the first of his race."

Bone-crushing silence descended in the room.

"At that point in history, the dragons and humans had cohabitated peacefully, for the most part. There were not human slaves or dragon Masters. It was just the two races existing together in the same world.

"Sometime during Xalerion's childhood, one of the elders in the village noticed his abnormal strength, his cold heart, and general disdain for everything in life. The elder took advantage of the hatred already beneath the surface and began to nurture it, poisoning Xalerion's mind against humans. He started to believe that the human race was worthless, that they only wanted to overthrow the dragons and kill them all.

"For years, Xalerion's loathing of the humans grew, nearly too strong to contain. He grew to despise his brother for being both dragon and human." Eldrin paused, catching his breath, some emotion that I couldn't name flickering in his eyes.

"When Bakari met Faryn, everything began to spin out of control. Faryn was a human, and they fell in love. She soon became pregnant with a son, and when Xalerion discovered it, it drove him into madness. He killed Bakari and went after Faryn. He intended to kill her, but she survived his attack. When she finally gave birth, she was nearly dead from blood loss but managed to smuggle her son to safety. Faryn died soon after, and the boy was raised in a village up near Shegora, where he found two other shifters that helped to keep him safe.

"Xalerion received word that the baby had survived. Controlled by rage, he stirred up an uprising in which every human was to be killed, in hopes that he would find Bakari's son and kill him before he had a chance to manifest shifter abilities."

Silence fell once again as Eldrin let out a long breath.

"Xalerion was the Lone Dragon," I said. The pieces were slowly fitting together in my mind. Eldrin nodded. "And where do you and Eklos fit into this story?" I asked.

Eldrin stared at the floor. "Xalerion did not succeed in finding Bakari's son. Instead, the Lone Dragon was murdered by his own son, who now has his own mission to rid the world of humans and shape-shifters alike."

My father looked as if he might be sick, the scales on his face glistening with sweat.

Eldrin inhaled deeply then let it out like a soft breeze caressing stalks of wheat. Swallowing, he looked me, then the King, in the eye.

"Eklos is the son of Xalerion."

Shock snapped through the room like lightning.

"And I am the son of Bakari."

CHAPTER FORTY-SIX
KAIDA

"YOU KILLED YOUR own father," I rasped.

Eklos snorted as if I should have expected nothing else. "Xalerion was *weak*," he snapped, flames coming out of his nostrils.

"And you're not?" The words were out of my mouth before I could stop them.

The retort cost me. Eklos's hand slammed down on my face, claws gouging into my cheek from my hairline to my chin, leaving four deep scratches imbedded in my skin. My eyes stung with tears as the pain rushed along my nerves. Blood trickled down my face, thick and burning, a coppery tang filling my mouth. I blinked furiously against the tears, but it was no use as they spilled over, mixing with the blood as it dripped onto the stone table beneath me.

Turning my head to spit out the blood that was filling my mouth, I dared to look at him. He was back near the hearth, with his back facing me. I took advantage of it and squirmed on the table, trying in vain to slip my thin arms through the shackles. But the more I struggled, the tighter they seemed to grow.

"I would not bother with that," he said, his voice calm. "The bluestone will only work quicker, draining your life faster."

The edges of my vision went dark, my pulse pounding in my ears, as I released a guttural roar. Though I was in human form, the sound was all beast. I gritted my teeth, limbs shaking. If I had been able to draw on my magic, that dungeon would have been obliterated by the force struggling to awaken within me. This could not be where I died, alone, broken, and bleeding, with only a hateful Master to spit on me.

Eklos knew I was defeated. Yet he continued to play this game. We both knew I was going to die. Why continue to draw it out?

For the second time in my life, I wished for the ability to be in dragon form. I was taller, braver, *stronger*. I would be able to overpower him and end this. My jaw ached as I clenched my teeth even tighter, wordlessly cursing the bluestone keeping my limbs chained to the stone beneath me.

"If you want me dead, then why don't you just kill me?"

Quicker than a strike of lightning, Eklos grabbed a rusty dagger and held it tight against my neck. One swallow, one bob of my throat, and it would slice into my skin.

"Would you like that? Because I am more than happy to oblige," he crooned.

I fought the urge to spit in his face. "Just seems like a waste of time, keeping me here. You could have ended all of this seven years ago." I paused, my heart pounding. "Tell me, what are you trying to accomplish? What are you trying to prove? That I am weak? That I am breakable? That you can take everything from me, everyone I love? Well congratulations. You have accomplished all of it. So, what is it? What is the point?" My voice rose higher and louder with every word, every phrase. The pressure he was keeping on my neck lightened and his face twisted in disbelief at my brash words.

Eklos held my stare, and I willed every bit of hatred I could muster into it.

"I wouldn't expect a human to understand," he responded in the softest voice I had ever heard him use.

"Of course not," I bit out as he turned his back to me. Before I could even blink Eklos was in my face again.

"You humans will never understand!" he roared in my face as his sulfurous smoke slithered over my skin. "Every single one of you is a monster without a heart. Every single one of you must pay for the crimes of the past."

"What crimes of the past? You can't blame all humans for the mistakes of one!" I retorted.

Eklos retreated over to the fire, his tail sweeping through the air. He kept his back to me, so I was unable to see his expression. "You're all the same. I've seen it for a thousand years. One of you gets the thought that you can overpower us, and the thought runs rampant through the rest of the humans like a plague."

The wound on my chest spasmed and throbbed, forcing me to grit my teeth together until it passed. "What are you talking about?" I asked when the pain finally eased.

Eklos scoffed. "I'm talking about you murdering dragons in cold blood!"

The blood drained from my face and my body began to shiver. "I've never killed anyone."

"Not you, you stupid girl." He pounded his clawed fists into the wall above the hearth, causing pebbles to skitter down from the ceiling. "During a slave rebellion, back before my father died. My mother was in the company of dragons sent to quell it. She never came back."

"And you blame all of humankind because you believe a human killed your mother in self-defense hundreds of years ago?"

"It wasn't self-defense. It was murder."

It was my turn to scoff. "Is that why you're doing all of this? Ridding Elysia of humans because one killed your mother when she was trying to slaughter all of them?"

Eklos swung to face me, and I was astonished to see tears lining his red eyes. "You will never understand, slave." His voice sounded broken, as if I had forced him into a version of himself he hated.

"I understand more than you think," I replied honestly. "But that doesn't justify every crime *you've* committed in the name of revenge."

Eklos pounded his fist down next to my head, only inches from squashing my face. "I'm done with you. Tomorrow you will die, whether they come for you or not," Eklos snapped, his voice rumbling with controlled fury. He turned and stalked toward the door.

"Nobody is coming for me," I retorted, wishing that saying it made it so.

He continued walking in silence until he reached the threshold and turned back.

"On the contrary, slave, I have laid the perfect trap. Your fool of a prince and that abomination of a father should be on their way here right now." His words were smug, a wicked gleam in his eyes as he walked out of the room, slamming the metal door behind him.

I winced as the sound echoed through the room, wishing in vain that I could cover my ears. Every sound, even the tiniest bit of light was too much, burning my eyes, pushing uncomfortably against my eardrums, as if my body had become accustomed to the bitter silence waiting in the dark.

Darkness wrapped around me like a blanket, but this time it was a soothing sort, not evil or devouring. Did Eklos finally reveal his motive after all these years? I thought perhaps I would feel better once I knew what lit the fire behind my old Master's actions. But instead, I just felt sad.

He was hurting, just like the rest of us. Hurt people only hurt more people. Eklos was the greatest example of that. Someone took away something precious to him, and in turn he wanted as many people as possible to feel the same pain he experienced.

It never healed; only festered. Growing and growing into an unrecognizable beast that was nearly unstoppable.

It was then and there, shackled to that stone table, the first signs of fever ripping through my body that I made a resolution to myself.

For the rest of my days, however many there might be left, I would not be like Eklos. Not just because he was a cruel dragon, but because I would not let the pain of the past, and the hatred that has always accompanied it, decide my future. I would choose to step above it, to be better.

Tarrin told me I should believe in a better world.

Perhaps choosing not to hate was the first step.

CHAPTER FORTY-SEVEN

TARRIN

THE BRISK NIGHT air painted ice on my wings as we soared toward the Ilgathor Mountains that held Belharnt. We left the palace nearly four hours ago, when the sun was just dipping below the horizon. Preferring the speed of wings over horses, Eldrin and I shifted to our dragon forms and took to the skies, flying west. As we reached the forest, frost peppered the mossy ground, wrapping gently around roots, clinging to the tree trunks. The sun had set long ago, the moon shining bright overhead, like a torch guiding the way.

My father and Eldrin had argued back and forth for precious hours before settling on a plan to rescue Kaida. They dug through maps of Elysia, comparing them to the hints that the Council had given my father, before discussing strategy, trying to envision every possible move that Eklos might make. My father decided to stay behind at the palace to keep the Council from sniffing around and trying to put a stop to our plans.

We had to be ready. Eklos was a thousand years old for a reason. He was devious, smart, conniving. We all agreed that this was most likely a trap to get us in one place. Unsure of what Eklos might have in store for us once we arrived, we decided the best course of action was to get inside, grab Kaida, and leave as quickly as possible. As the mountains grew closer, I couldn't help but think how foolish our plan might be.

The most important thing was getting Kaida out of there, alive and unharmed.

If it wasn't already too late.

Perhaps Eklos would expect us to come up with a fancy plan, having some sort of retaliation ready in response. Maybe having a very basic, unimaginative plan would prove to be the wisest option. It's what Eklos would least expect.

We crossed hundreds of miles, turning due north when the mountains grew close, a sudden headwind slowing our progress. When the forest that my father had mentioned finally came into view, we were so exhausted from fighting the wind that we landed at the eastern edge and continued on foot. The temperature plummeted, chilling my warm body, even through my shield of scales. At one point I had to warm my mouth with fire just to keep my teeth from chattering together.

Eldrin did not seem much better off, stomping forward, head down against the fierce wind, arms crossed trying to keep the cold from penetrating beneath his scales. Words were sparse between us as we focused on the mission ahead of us. Each of us had very different reasons for rescuing Kaida. I could not help but wonder if Eldrin was truly doing this for her, or for the chance to rid Elysia of his cousin.

"Prince?" Eldrin's soft voice cut through the silence.

"Yes?"

"If our plan fails, I want you to get Kaida out of there and fly as far and as fast as you can. Don't look back. Don't worry about me."

My eyebrows crawled up my forehead. "I don't think Kaida would like that very much."

Eldrin offered a sad smile. "I'm old, Your Highness. I've lived enough life to know that my daughter and her betrothed deserve a chance to do the same. Let me take care of my cousin if it comes to that."

I blew out a breath. While I appreciated his willingness to take the brunt of Eklos's wrath so that Kaida and I could escape, something about it didn't sit right with me. I couldn't seem to find the right words to respond to him, so I simply nodded.

Eldrin smiled, his body instantly relaxing as we came across the mangled tree that indicated we were close to Belharnt, and I let out a nervous breath that clouded the air in front of me. Up until now, we had stayed on the outskirts of the forest, keeping to the path illuminated by the light from the moon and stars.

But now it was time to enter the woods.

We each took a deep breath as we stepped beneath the canopy of trees. All light disappeared. My heart raced like a galloping horse in my chest, and I fought the urge to run back into the moonlight. Sticks cracked beneath the weight of our bodies as we climbed our way over roots, squeezing between trees. Eldrin paused several paces into the woods, and a loud snap echoed, shattering the eerie silence that had followed us in. My head swung in the direction of the sound and I slammed my eyes shut as light flared. Squinting in the sudden brightness, I peeked over at the source of it.

Eldrin had ripped up a shallow root and tied a strange-looking leaf over the end of it. The leaf was almost perfectly round except for two long pieces that jutted out of either side, making it easy to tie the leaf onto the root. I had never seen a plant quite like that. I looked questioningly at Eldrin.

"Enderleaf," he explained. "A special breed of plants. It was created specifically for the purpose of burning. The flames will never die so long as there is oxygen, the leaf itself never burns away."

I had never heard of Enderleaf, but his words were undeniable as I looked at the leaf, very much on fire, but not shriveling or burning up. With a light now illuminating the woods in front of us, that sinking feeling in my stomach receded.

The smell of chilled dirt tickled my nostrils and the temperature continued to drop by the minute. Time seemed to stop altogether, and I lost track of whether minutes had passed or hours. Every so often, a pair of glowing eyes would peer out of the darkness, and I couldn't help but wonder what other sorts of creatures inhabited these woods. When a strange growling noise came from one of the bushes to my right, I decided I didn't want to know. Picking up the pace, we both agreed in unspoken words to hurry.

Through the dense cover of trees above, the sky was beginning to lighten, the first signs of dawn approaching. We had been in the forest far too long. I could no longer feel my clawed toes digging into the frozen ground, and I found himself wishing for the stifling heat of home.

Eldrin came to an abrupt stop, swinging to the left to study a thick wall of vegetation. Roots groaned beneath his feet as he crept over to it, and the faint clink of claws hitting metal sounded as he swept the greenery aside.

Hidden beneath heavy vines, thick with leaves and bushes nearly the size of us, was a large wooden door with iron bars over top. It was built into the mountain itself. I hadn't realized that we had drifted so far into the woods as to be at the mountain itself. To any passersby who did not know what to look for, this door would remain completely unnoticed.

Eldrin and I stood frozen, breath pooling in front of us in the cold, damp air. I could hear my heart pounding in my ears. Eldrin turned to look at me. His words came out as a whisper.

"Belharnt."

CHAPTER FORTY-EIGHT
KAIDA

MY HEAD POUNDED as I fought to stay conscious. The pain from my shattered hand and chest went numb long ago, but it did not stop the fear of infection and blood loss from spreading through me, infecting me with a different kind of poison. The stone table beneath me was cold and sticky, dried blood caked in many places.

An empty pit grew wider and deeper in my stomach where my magic used to dwell, once roiling and hot, now cold and barren. The iron was successfully keeping my magic suppressed, the bluestone weakening my body more and more with each second that passed. I could feel the brittleness settling into my bones, the tap of a hammer all it would take to splinter them into shards. Exhaustion was a never-ending spiral, constantly taking me down, further and further, until I was not sure if I would wake up again.

I clung to the hope that Tarrin was coming for me, though I knew deep down that he would never find me here. Even if he did, it would be a miracle if we made it out alive. Any chance of me walking out of here died the moment Eklos chained me with bluestone.

Sleep fell heavy on my eyes again, my mind slipping into unconsciousness when a light *thunk* sounded on the other side of the metal door, followed by hurried whispers.

My heart stuttered.

As I watched, the door began to glow, turning orange, then red as it grew hotter. A loud bang echoed from the other side, and I flinched as it filled the space, hammering against my ears. The door bent inward, large claws appearing through the crack, gripping the metal, and tearing it backward as if it were a piece of paper.

A midnight-blue dragon stood in the doorway, chest heaving, a turquoise dragon standing behind him. Tears sprang to life in my eyes and a choked sob escaped my lips. They had found me.

The minute Tarrin laid eyes on me, he raced toward me, clumsily running into the scattered tables and chairs littering the room.

He bent on his knees beside the stone table, his clawed hand resting against the side of my face, my forehead. His scales were freezing cold.

"You're burning up," he whispered. *Fever.* The word rippled in the air between us, and I could feel his concern running into me like a current. Looking over my body to check for any injuries, he winced when he saw the burn on my chest, still unhealed, and clawed open in several places. It was too dark for me to see it, but I knew his dragon eyes could see the infection that had set in. A shiver racked my body, and I bit my lip to hold in a scream.

Tarrin found my destroyed hand next, and his sudden intake of breath told me enough.

"Kaida, I'm so sorry." The remorse in his voice nearly broke my heart into two as he planted an awkward dragon kiss on my forehead. His lips were like a scalding fire and I squirmed.

"We are getting you out of here." He reached for the shackles at my wrists, careful to avoid touching my hand, when he suddenly let out a cry and fell backward onto the ground.

Eldrin was at my side in a heartbeat, worry written all over his face.

"What's wrong?"

Tarrin struggled to get to his feet, clutching his hands to his stomach.

"The shackles… something is wrong with them." He held his palms out to show me.

Even in the dim light from the hearth, I could see the blackened scales covering his hands.

"B-b-bluestone." I said through chattering teeth, the cold stone beneath me growing colder, biting into my skin.

Tarrin's brow furrowed while Eldrin's eyes widened in alarm. The ruined metal door slammed behind them and both shifters swung around, my tears flowing anew.

"That's right, cousin," Eklos sneered. "Bluestone." The look he gave Eldrin was death incarnate.

Tarrin and Eldrin both moved in front of the table, placing themselves defensively between me and Eklos.

"Let her go," the Prince commanded. Eklos chortled.

"Now why would I do that?" he growled.

"Cousin, this is between you and me. Let her go," Eldrin said.

Glaring at the two males, Eklos moved around the edge of the room, stopping near the hearth, sending fresh flame into it. The sudden light in the room blinded me and my eyes watered and burned as they struggled to adjust.

"I have three shape-shifters in my dungeon. Three beasts that should never have been allowed to exist, and you expect me to let two of them go?" Eklos hummed in disapproval, clucking his tongue. "No, I don't think so."

He circled the room, like a beast circling his prey.

"What is bluestone?" Tarrin dared to ask, a slight tremble to his voice.

"Ah, yes," Eklos crooned. "Eldrin, care to explain?"

Eldrin's eyes darted from his cousin to the Prince. "Bluestone is like poison for shifters. It draws out the power that allows them to shift between forms," Eldrin explained. "It will weaken her to the point of death."

The color drained from Tarrin's scales as he moved to my side, brushing aside the sweat-drenched hair caked to my forehead.

"I will give you whatever you desire. Name it and it is yours. Just let her go." Every ounce of command Tarrin could muster filled his words.

Eklos huffed out a laugh.

"You no longer have that kind of power, *Prince,"* he spit.

Tarrin's eyebrows furrowed, and Eklos's face lit up, ripe with power.

"Your family no longer has any control over Elysia," he drawled.

The heartbeat of the room accelerated, making it hard to breathe. The ache in my head worsened, spots dancing in my vision as I fought to stay conscious.

"What are you talking about?"

"Oh, do not worry, little prince. Your father is fine. He was simply presented with a bargain he could not refuse." Victory shone in Eklos's eyes and the look Tarrin gave him was of an imminent death.

"What did you do to him?" Tarrin growled through clenched teeth, his claws digging into the scales on his palms.

"Shortly after you left the Royal Palace, the Council found your father. He pretended everything was normal, but they knew better since they were the ones to lay my trap. Without his precious son there, he was left unprotected. King Martik is now in the dungeons beneath the palace, awaiting your return."

"You cannot do that to the King!" Tarrin shouted, his voice far too loud, causing me to wince.

"Ah. Well, you see, Martik is no longer King of Elysia, so I believe I can."

Tarrin took a step back. "What?"

"Your father was given a choice. Sign over all of Elysia to me." He paused, offering his version of a wicked smile as he gestured to himself, "or his son would die the moment he arrived in Belharnt."

Smoke leaked from Tarrin's nostrils and I could see fire in his mouth each time he took a breath.

"As predicted, he did not hesitate to sign this decree," he produced a scroll out of nowhere, Martik's signature in red ink scrawled across the bottom, "stating that going forward, I would be acting as Regent, and King Martik of Elysia would be no more. In exchange for your safety, of course." The look Eklos leveled at Tarrin assured no one that he was safe. "The King played right into my hands."

Black spots expanded across my line of vision.

"I thought *you* would be smarter than this, cousin. But you walked right into my trap." He took a step forward, addressing Eldrin. "Did you really think that the members of the Council just let it *slip* that I was keeping Kaida at Belharnt? That they would just casually leave around maps that would lead you straight here?"

Eklos waited, letting them piece it together.

"The Council has been under my influence for quite some time. Every move they have made, every idea they have planted in the King's mind, every plot and scheme against your life... it was all me." Eklos huffed out a short laugh, pleased with himself.

"It was all part of the plan." He turned to Tarrin. "I had to get you to question your father, to drive a wedge between the two of you. I have no issue with the King, he is fully dragon after all. But his wife and his son, well, they needed to be dealt with without the King getting in the way." Eklos paused to smile. "Of course, there never was an actual threat against your life. At least, not from those imbecilic dragons. I just needed you to think there was, to become protective of Kaida; to be a good little prince and come to her rescue when the time came.

"But you see, Eldrin," Eklos said, turning back to my father.

"This was always about *you*. Granted, I did want control of Elysia, ridding the palace of those infernal shifters, and having the King's reserve of dragons at my fingertips, but it always came back to you. That day when I found Aela in Vernista, your scent was all over her, and that pathetic baby in her arms mysteriously smelled like both of you. I should have thanked my lucky stars for bringing me the perfect present, the one thing that would allow me to get my hands on you.

"But after seven years, when you did not come to Kaida's rescue, I began to question whether or not you even knew of her existence. So, I released the girl, keeping her in my employ should you ever resurface. But then I thought of another way to draw you out, dealing with two problems at once. Precious Queen Lita," he drawled.

Both shifters stepped forward, circling Eklos.

The bluestone in the shackles flared, sucking more of my strength. My head throbbed even worse, my vision going black. The only part of my body that seemed to still be functioning was my hearing.

"Tarrin, I can't see," I whispered at where I remembered him standing. A sudden heat appeared next to me, a scaled hand resting on my arm, careful to stay away from my broken hand.

"Ah, yes. The bluestone has almost completed its work," Eklos said, returning his attention to me. "The senses go out one by one, and soon there will be nothing left of her. Just an empty body on a stone table. It will not be long now, and she will be walking in the afterlife, one less worthless shifter in Elysia." I could hear the wicked smile twisting his face.

"Anyway," Eklos continued, voice cheerful. "I planned out the death of the Queen, hoping that if nothing else would draw you out, *that* would." His words were nonchalant. Taking the life of another was a common everyday occurrence for him.

"And to my surprised delight, it actually worked. You showed up at her funeral like a fool, only to discover you had a daughter." He barked out a haughty laugh. "The stars aligned in my favor and both of my plans came together seamlessly, the two people I despise most in this world finally within my grasp.

"Then it was just a matter of waiting for the perfect moment to capture Kaida, drawing you away from the protection of the palace. It was all too easy, really. Being the old, wise dragon, you claim to be, I thought for certain you would see it coming. I guess even the wisest can fail." A sinister smile was painted on his lips, his red eyes glowing.

A bitter stillness fell on the room.

My body grew weaker, and I wondered how much longer until I drifted off into the afterlife, if I would feel it coming or just slip away into nothingness.

Tarrin leaned down next to my face and gently kissed my clammy forehead. "Hold on, Kaida. I'm going to get you out of here." His words were confident, but his voice was unsure. I knew he had no idea how to get those shackles off my wrists.

Or how to defeat Eklos.

Or how to get out of the blasted dungeon.

It was all too much, causing my head to spin faster, lights flashing behind my closed eyelids.

Wait.

Lights?

I froze, my body going rigid, not even daring to let out a breath. My eyes were still closed, but instead of darkness, there were lights blinking in and out. Reds, blues, greens, purples, the most beautiful colors I had ever seen, all swirling together behind my eyes.

A solitary, quiet ember ignited deep inside me, the sudden warmth enough to make me flinch. My eyes snapped open.

I bit my lip to keep from letting out a gasp, unwilling to let anyone know that something had changed. My vision returned, but now I was seeing through my enhanced dragon eyes.

"Let her go, Eklos. You said it yourself, this is about me. Take me and let them both go." In the back of my mind, I heard my father's words permeating the cavernous room, but I could not pay any attention to their conversation. The ember that had begun to burn in my gut was now a full-on flame, warmth cascading into my frozen limbs.

It didn't make any sense. The bluestone was supposed to be killing me, whisking away every ounce of magic and fire, suppressing my shifting abilities. But somehow the fire had returned. It swelled and burned hotter as each heartbeat grew stronger. It moved first into my chest, and I held in a scream as the flames licked through my burn, prickling and tearing through every inch of it, searing away the infection that had begun to spread. It slithered down my left arm, to my shattered hand, and my breathing hitched, back arching off the table. Sweat beaded on my forehead, my teeth nearly biting through my tongue to keep silent as licks of fire stretched and rearranged the bones that had been broken, mending the skin that had been torn.

I let out a shaky breath.

Tarrin glanced down at me in concern. "What is it?"

"Fire... burning... magic... back."

A skeptical look crossed his face but then his eyes widened.

"Kaida, you're steaming."

I glanced down and saw tendrils of thick steam rising off my body. Every exposed part of me was glistening with sweat and all traces of the fever had disappeared. Strength seeped into all the places that weakness had claimed for itself.

His gaze found the shackles at my wrists and his face went slack. "The shackles. They're on fire."

Letting out a gasp, I shifted on the table to look down at

my wrists. Blue fire encased the iron, causing it to glow a bright orange. It was not burning me, nor could I feel the heat from it.

I pulled at the shackles, prepared for some sort of pain, but the fire did not touch my skin. It danced over it and around it but floated above the skin.

I pulled harder against the shackle, my hand trying to squeeze between the manacles. Taking a deep breath, I tugged one last time and gasped when my hand came free, the iron dissolving into dust.

Tarrin stared at my free hand for what seemed like an eternity. "How is that possible?"

With one of my hands unbound from the iron, I could feel the magic returning in full force, pouring into the empty pit, surging through my veins once again.

"Try the other one," the Prince whispered in my ear.

The other hand was the one that Eklos shattered. Although the fire had mended it, the thought of trying to rip it free danced on my nerves.

Swallowing, I slowly started to pull at my left hand, bracing for pain. It was only a heartbeat later, when Tarrin gasped, that I realized that the iron had already dissolved away, not causing even a twinge of pain, and both of my hands were now free.

At the sound of Tarrin's gasp, Eklos looked at me before a mountain-shaking roar erupted from his snout. "No!" He dove for me, but Eldrin crashed into him, both careening across the room before they slammed into a table of tools.

Like pouring oil on a fire, magic and flame erupted inside of me, strengthening every bone, every tendon, every muscle. It sang to me a song of power and vengeance.

With hardly a thought, I whipped a tendril of white flame at the shackles around my ankles, the iron liquifying, bleeding onto the stone table.

"Hurry," Tarrin whispered as he helped me off the table. "We have to get out of here."

Fire boiled inside my stomach, building and swelling, until I thought it would burst.

Eklos.

The name was bitter on my tongue, like rancid wine.

Too long had he made me suffer.

Too long had he hurt my family. Hurt *me.*

Too long had he stolen from me, broken me, shattered me.

But it all ended here.

I looked at Eklos as he slowly got to his feet, his wide eyes meeting mine.

Magic whispered in my blood, the beast in me urging me forward.

Kill him. Kill him.

I took a step toward him, simultaneously shifting into beast form.

"Impossible," Eklos whispered, taking a step back.

A devilish smile curved my lips as I beheld the fear in his eyes, for he knew what I had become. What he had made me into.

I was rage.

I was flame.

I was wrath.

With a scream that could have shattered the Ilgathor Mountains, I unleashed myself on Belharnt.

CHAPTER FORTY-NINE

KAIDA

THE ROOM ERUPTED in blinding light as bursts of white flame speared in Eklos's direction.

Tarrin and Eldrin fell to the floor, the ground shaking under the sudden impact, their huge bodies bumping into tables and knocking them over, sending tools spilling onto the floor, as they tried to escape the volley of fire that continued to vault around the room. My mind barely registered their presence as the inner beast took control, Kaida, the human slave, retreating into a dark, empty corner of my mind.

Debris from the walls and ceiling rained down at a constant rate as each barrage of flame slammed into them. The ground continued to shake, even after the dragons had stopped moving, but I paid it no mind as I took a step closer to Eklos. He was cowering on the ground, beneath a shield of smoke, his wings folded in tight against his back. Razor whips of white fire shot out from my hands, skirting around his trembling body, aiming directly for his wings.

The whips lanced into each wing, ripping and burning through muscle and tendon. A furious roar, filled with agony, echoed in the cavernous dungeon. My magic fed off his pain, his anger, growing stronger, burning deeper. He thrashed against the fire, but the whips only coiled tighter, like a snake around its prey. The harder they squeezed, the more violent Eklos became, throwing himself onto the ground, rolling, trying to escape the reach of my fire.

My inner beast was smiling, delighting in his pain. For a moment, I looked back at Tarrin and Eldrin who were scrambling to their feet, to tell them to leave.

That was a mistake.

Eklos took advantage of my divided attention and threw a spear of smoke straight for my chest. It bounced harmlessly off my scales, his magic weaker from the injuries he had sustained. He lunged in the air, slamming into me, knocking the air from my lungs.

With the momentum and force behind his jump, we both crashed into the ground, sending tables and furniture flying backward, toppling over. Before I even caught my breath, Eklos was on top of me, his clawed hands around my throat, squeezing. Coughing and gasping, I tried desperately to get air in my lungs, but the more I fought, the harder he pushed.

Stars flashed before my eyes, and I knew I was moments from passing out. I clawed at his hands, digging in, tearing beneath his scales, but still he pressed on, unrelenting.

A thunderous growl sounded and suddenly the weight of Eklos's body was gone. Precious air streamed into my lungs as I rolled to my side, coughing. Disoriented, I laid on the ground for endless seconds before my vision righted itself and my mind was able to focus.

Another loud crash sounded, and I swung my head around.

Tarrin had yanked Eklos off me, both of them flying across the room. Watching the Prince move, the way he went on the offensive and then rebounded in that familiar defensive position, brought back memories of our training days when I had first arrived at the palace.

It was so much different fighting as a dragon than as a human.

We had sparred in both forms, when I could manage it, but the approaches were quite different. In human form it was important to protect your weak spots, primarily fighting with fists or swords. But as a dragon, there was a shield of scales on your body, and sharp claws, and teeth. It was more of an onslaught of biting and scratching, using your weight against them, crushing them beneath your own weight, and using fire against your opponent.

I never thought the moment would come when I would have to use any of that training. I always thought it was a waste of time since I was protected within the palace walls. I had nightmares that Eklos would take me back, but I never truly imagined I would be here, fighting for my life alongside the Prince and my father.

My father.

Eldrin had been so silent since I escaped from the shackles that I had almost forgotten he was there. Scrambling to my feet, I turned around toward the last place he had been standing.

He was gone.

How would he have left the room without anyone noticing?

Another crash sounded from behind me, and I swung around, wincing as Eklos slammed Tarrin's head into the wall. A scream escaped my mouth before I could stop it, and I launched myself into the air, using my wings as an added boost of speed, and I collided headfirst with Eklos, sending us both careening into the wall. My head hit first, and I laid there, dazed, for several precious heartbeats.

By the time my vision came back into focus, Eklos was back on his feet, a large gash on the side of his head, bleeding steadily.

I whipped my tail out from underneath me, smacking it into the back of his legs, knocking him off balance. His arms flailed out to try to right himself, but I sent my tail into his chest, and he fell onto the floor once more. Tendrils of white flame speared from my hands, wrapping around each of his wrists and ankles like shackles.

Standing above Eklos's prone figure, the inner beast in me kept pushing for me to finish him. To end this once and for all.

But the human girl inside hesitated. The idea of taking a life, no matter how repulsive and terrible that life may be, was abhorrent. I couldn't do it. I remembered the resolve I made after Eklos revealed more of his past.

In that moment, that inner beast and slave girl warred in my mind, a battle of wills, both strong, both resilient.

Eklos noticed my hesitation.

A malevolent smile twisted his snout, and he blew a flurry of noxious smoke into my face that coated my throat. Coughing and sputtering, I retreated several steps, trying to get clean air into my lungs, my flames winking out.

Eklos was on his feet in a nimble maneuver, stalking toward me like a predator about to kill his prey.

Tarrin was on him in an instant, clawing and swiping at him, blood streaming down his own face. Eklos deflected, spewing a leash of smoke that encompassed the Prince's neck, tightening by the second.

"No!" I screamed. "Let him go!"

The smoke wielder's only response was a smile that made my heart stand still.

In that moment I knew. Eklos would kill Tarrin and my father, saving me for last. He would watch me lose everything.

I could not let it happen.

The beast in me would not let it happen.

Giving myself over to it completely, I let out a blood curdling roar that set the mountain trembling.

Everyone in the room froze.

But I did not notice.

For I was beast.

I was dragon.

I was wrath.

Ignoring all of Eldrin and Tarrin's warnings about magic, I jumped into that pit of magic in my gut and began drawing on it, letting it fill my limbs, my mind, my heart. I drew on its strength and it drew on my fury.

Tarrin was on the ground now, clawing at the collar of smoke around his neck.

My eyes fixed on Eklos.

Flame encased my body and lightning danced between my fingers. Tilting my head to one side, like a predatory animal, I took a step closer.

When I was filled to the brim with power, raw and writhing, I let out a fierce growl and launched myself at him. Fire and lightning exploded from my mouth and claws, daggers of magic shooting straight for Eklos.

He threw up a shield of smoke, but it could not compare to the strength of my magic. It ripped right through him, slamming into his chest and stomach, embedding themselves beneath his scales. A cry of pain burst from his mouth.

Thick blood seeped from his wounds, but somehow, he was still standing.

Eklos staggered backward until he reached the wall, leaning against it to keep himself upright. His breathing was shallow, wet and wheezing, as if there was blood seeping into his lungs.

He met my burning stare and the beast inside me smiled, wicked and cruel.

Fire and lightning crackled between my fingers, itching to be released. Raising my hands to send a death blow careening into Eklos, Eldrin suddenly appeared in front of me.

"Kaida."

The beast thrashed, fighting against my human name, unwilling to release control of my mind.

I didn't know where he had come from or why he was stopping me.

"Move." The beast in me ground out between clenched teeth.

My father remained where he stood, hands upraised to stop

me. Behind my father, Eklos struggled to his feet, leaning heavily on the stone walls as he moved backward, leaving bloody smears in his wake. He stopped in front of a large fissure in the wall where two peaks of the ceiling converged. Time stood still as I watched him move, as if everything else in the room froze but the two of us. Our eyes met. With a bone-chilling growl, Eklos stomped his foot into the ground, and swung his spiked tail, slamming it directly into the crevice.

For a moment there was only silence.

No one moved.

Then, as if from far away, a quiet rumble began prickling through the air.

The ground started to quake, imperceptible at first, but it quickly grew in strength.

The crack in the wall splintered wide, shooting up toward the ceiling.

As soon as the widened fissure collided with the peaked roof, time sped up, chaos breaking out like a plague.

The stone floor splintered in every direction, shaking so violently it was difficult to stay upright. Large stones and rocks rained from the ceiling, one barely missing my head, another crashing right into Eklos. He collapsed to his knees, dazed. Embers from the hearth scattered around the floor in front of it, filling the air with an ashy dust.

"Kaida, the whole mountain is coming down. We have to leave!" Eldrin shouted over the din of the earthquake, though he was inches from my face.

"No," my inner beast responded. Eklos had to die. The beast in me would not let him leave the mountain alive, even if it meant forfeiting my own life. I made to step around him toward Eklos.

"Don't be foolish!" Eldrin made to grab for my arm, but I skittered backward out of his reach. Flames encompassed my body again, keeping him effectively away.

"Don't be like him," he said, as if he knew exactly what my internal thoughts were, how badly my two halves were warring. I turned back to Eklos but ice poured through my veins and my flames winked out.

Tarrin appeared at my side, head still bleeding, but conscious. He gripped my arm tight, and I began to thrash, trying to escape.

"Kaida, it's me." His voice was calm, patient, his eyes pleading.

A roar bellowed from my mouth, the beast inside fighting to stay in control.

"Kaida." My name was a whisper, a gentle song on his lips, calling to that human girl, beckoning her to come back.

Like blowing out a candle, the wrath and hatred that had been fueling my magic blew out, leaving nothing but exhaustion behind. I swayed on my feet and Tarrin wrapped an arm around me.

Out of the corner of my eye I saw Eldrin smash a table against the back of Eklos's dazed head, sending him sprawling across the floor.

The ground buckled, and we all struggled to stay on our feet.

"He's as good as dead staying here anyway. We will meet the same fate if we do not leave." Tarrin's voice seared through the chaos, snapping through the last of the fog the beast had created in my mind.

Boulders cascaded from the ceiling. As one fell close to us, I offered a nod and Eldrin was instantly at our side.

Gripping each of our arms, he held my stare.

"Hold on."

CHAPTER FIFTY
KAIDA

ABSOLUTE DARKNESS WRAPPED around me like a blanket, air disappearing. I gasped for a breath but there was nothing. Blackness squeezed, harder and harder against my body. There was nothing but a deafening silence in this empty in-between place, my ears roaring against the lack of noise. I could not see Tarrin or my father, and I could barely make out the tight grip each had on my arms.

As quickly as it had descended, the darkness receded, the sudden light blinding. Air rushed into my lungs and I felt as if I were floating as the crushing blackness vanished.

The three of us were sprawled on our backs in the dirt, sunlight streaming through the canopy of trees above us. I squinted against the brightness, my thoughts fighting to catch up to what had happened. Though the sun was warm, the air was chilly, penetrating beneath my scales.

I could feel the ground trembling. We were still close to Belharnt.

"Where are we?" I rasped, trying to catch my breath to ease the aching that had settled into my lungs.

Eldrin was sitting up now, surveying the surrounding forest.

"A mile east of Belharnt. That is as far as I could manage with the two of you."

My mind spun, refusing to focus.

"What happened? How did we get out of the mountain?"

Eldrin was silent for a heartbeat, concentration etching lines into his face despite the scales that covered it. Tarrin scooted closer, pulling me into his side, his heat seeping into me and I pressed into him, my limbs like ice.

"I have the ability to travel great distances in an instant, jumping from one location to another with only a thought, traveling in the world between time and distance," Eldrin said, exhaustion in his voice. "It has been centuries since I have carried others with me. I was not even sure if I would be able to do it, but it was the only way to get us all out of there in time."

As if in answer, the trembling in the ground worsened, a strong breeze blowing through the trees smelling of ash and stone. A distant roar echoed through the skies, sending birds scattering into the air, and then cut off the moment the ground stilled.

The world seemed to pause, silence settling over the earth.

"Belharnt is gone," Tarrin whispered, and I winced at how loud it seemed.

Looking back to the west, the mountain that had housed Belharnt, one of the smallest in the vicinity, had collapsed, dust still rising in its wake.

"And Eklos?" I dared, my voice shaking.

"Hopefully dead," the Prince said, brows furrowed.

Eldrin remained quiet, uncertainty in his eyes.

Nausea churned in my stomach and I pushed away from Tarrin just in time to vomit in the bushes. Sweat gleamed on my scales and I found myself wishing for my familiar human body, to curl under a blanket and go to sleep for days.

"We need to get moving, get farther away from here." Concern flashed in Eldrin's eyes. "My magic is depleted, and walking will not be fast enough. We need to fly." He turned to me, questioning.

I had never flown a long distance before. My heart pounded at the thought. "Where do we go? Back to the palace?"

"No, we cannot go back there."

"But my father—" Tarrin started.

"We cannot go back there," Eldrin snapped. "We cannot go anywhere near Vernista. The Council will be watching, waiting for us, and the Remnant has far too strong a presence for us to escape their notice. If Eklos somehow does survive, that is the first place he will go. We need to find a safe place to rest and recoup."

"But—"

"We will go back when the time is right." Eldrin's voice was stern, leaving no room for negotiation.

"There is a stream nearby. We will go there first and get water and then we will take to the skies. Fly south toward Myrewell."

Tarrin's eyebrows rose, and I could tell he wanted to object, but he said nothing.

Eldrin began walking, trying to stay quiet, but there was a constant snapping and cracking of sticks and roots beneath his feet. He disappeared behind a cluster of trees. I made to follow him but Tarrin grabbed my arm, holding me in place. Turning back to him, he shifted into human form. I followed his lead, ignoring the fact that shifting was now as easy as breathing. He wrapped me in his arms, holding me tight.

I welcomed the comforting warmth spreading through me, the scent of night air and blue cypress tickling my nose, reminding me of home.

"I'm so sorry, Kaida," he whispered, his voice thick with tears. Pulling back, he held my face in his hands. Silver lined his eyes. "I never should have let them take you."

"Tarrin..." The words died in my mouth, unable to find the right ones to say.

Thank you. I did not trust my voice enough to say the words out loud. Brushing away the hair from my face, he rubbed the tears off my cheeks.

I will always come for you.

He touched his lips gently to mine, wrapping his arms around my waist. The kiss was soft and tentative, his hands light on my waist, as if he were scared that I was an illusion about to burst. His fingers dug into my sides, pulling me impossibly closer when a whistle sounded through the trees.

Eldrin was telling us to hurry.

I swallowed, looking up at Tarrin for reassurance. He stepped up beside me, taking my hand in his. It was warm and steady, my lifeline in that moment.

"We are in this together." A smile curved his lips.

Whatever this is. I responded through the bond.

Despite the fear still holding my heart, my lips twitched, and I found myself smiling back.

There was a lot that I still didn't know.

I didn't know where we were going, nor did I know what the future held.

I didn't even know if Eklos was dead or alive.

But despite all that, I had true hope for the first time in my life.

Tarrin's grip tightened around mine as we simultaneously shifted back into dragon form.

Whatever was to come, whatever we had to face, we would do it together.

That was the promise shining in his eyes.

With a smile still on my lips, we stepped farther into the forest, hand in hand, an unknown future ahead of us.

But we had each other.

And for now, that was enough.

Epilogue

The air was stifling, the dust circulating in the air stealing the oxygen from my lungs. Blood seeped into my eye, even more dripping out of my nostrils and into my mouth. There was an enormous weight crushing my leg, and a long stone shard protruding from my side. A dull ache pounded in my left hand. I barely managed to lift it, finding it hanging at a wrong angle from my wrist. Every breath was agony, a rattling wheeze barely making it past my lips. There was something wrong with my lungs, too.

Despite the pain I was in, a brittle laugh choked its way up my throat.

I was still alive.

A mountain fell on top of me.

My laugh grew stronger, louder, despite the roar of pain associated with it.

Even a mountain could not best me.

Rocks and debris continued to fall from the ceiling every so often, filling my mind with white noise.

My cousin and his pathetic daughter may have gotten away, but the battle was not lost. They didn't win. It was only just beginning.

"Eklos?" a voice called in the distance. The sound of rocks being kicked and shoved around met my ears. "Master Eklos?" Closer this time.

I coughed, drawing up more blood into my mouth. Moments later, a pair of red eyes pierced through the smoke and dust. I bared my teeth in a pained smile, blood spilling down my lips.

"Roldan."

The brown dragon spread his snout in that irritating smile I loathed and began pushing the crushing boulder off my leg.

"They got away," he said, his voice grating on my patience.

"As evidenced by the *mountain on top of me!*" I roared in response, causing Roldan to cringe away, covering his head with his arms. *Stupid dragon.*

When my words stopped echoing amongst the stones, Roldan got back to work moving the boulder, eliciting another roar from me as it shifted off my leg. The bone was utterly shattered. Wrath swirled in my gut, the promise of revenge the only thing keeping me from blacking out from the pain.

"One thing did go right, sir," Roldan spoke up, his voice trembling. *Good, he should be afraid.* "The King is deep in the dungeons, like you wanted."

My lips spread into a grin, momentarily pausing every ache and throb in my body. At the time, it had been a lie when I was goading the prince, but now it was just another part of the plan to check off.

"Excellent."

Roldan carefully wrapped his arm around my uninjured one, trying to help me to my feet. Several minutes of growling, yelling, and cursing later, I was on my good leg, Roldan supporting my weight on the other side.

"What are your orders, Master Eklos?"

Eldrin and the slave girl may have bested me this time, but they could only run so far. I knew my cousin's pride would not allow him to leave Elysia. He would be back.

Just like all the times over the previous thousand years, he would return to me.

And I would be ready for him.

Next time there would be no escaping, no way out.

The shifters would die. They had no idea what was coming for them.

A smile of wicked delight spread across my snout at the thought of Eldrin crushed beneath my feet. At the thought of the shifter race finally being extinct in Elysia.

A cold laugh pierced its way out of my chest as I met Roldan's fearful gaze.

"Prepare the army."

ACKNOWLEDGMENTS

Wow, this has been a long time coming. About 10 years to be exact. I still remember writing the very first chapter to this book back in creative writing class my senior year of high school. With some writing prompt, that I cannot remember for the life of me, Kaida and Tarrin were born, and with them an entire world that somehow came out of my brain. I often stare at this book, and I literally can't believe that I wrote the darn thing. But I did it, and I hope it shows whoever reads this book that it's never too late to go after your dream. Just pick it up and run with it. It can be terrifying and overwhelming, but it's also beautiful and exciting. I promise, it's so, so worth it.

To my husband, Cody—thank you for your endless support and believing that I would be successful at this from the very start. Thanks for listening to me stress and worry about this and freak out about whether I was doing it right, and still loving me (LOL). And thanks for putting up with a messy house while I finished this. Love you honey bunches of oats.

To my brother, Zach—you are one of the biggest reasons this book is now in the hands of readers. If it weren't for you, I don't think I would have ever finished this. Your constant encouragement was just what I needed, as well as how you pushed me to keep going even when I wanted to give up. You never doubted me, and I love that you're my biggest fan. I'll never get tired of geeking out with you about our love for dragons. Thanks for everything, bud. Love you lots.

To Bethany—who gave me the right kick in the butt to pick this story back up in the first place. I went almost eight years without touching this book. You read three (very bad) chapters that I wrote as a teenager, and to my astonishment, you didn't laugh at me. You told me to finish it. If you hadn't pushed me and infected me with your excitement and enthusiasm, this would probably still be sitting in the depths of my computer memory, untouched and unfinished. Thanks for being my book dragon friend.

To Rebecca Bergren, Jordon Harrison, Jamie Reeves-Chong, Cait Honig, and Bergy—thank you for reading the scary drafts of my book. Your words of encouragement, your constructive criticism, and your enthusiasm every step of the way has meant more to me than words could ever say.

To Andrea Hurst and Lucia Ferrara—thank you for editing my book and encouraging me along the way. This never would have been possible without both of you.

To my 2011 Creative Writing class—you all are THE BOMB! (Does anyone say that anymore?) I can still remember a lot of your reactions when we had a critique circle over the first chapter of this book, which was then called The Lone Dragon (it's come a long way since then). I couldn't believe how much you all liked the chapter I had written, let alone that you and Mrs. Decker thought I should keep going and try to publish it. Ten years later and I'm finally doing it. You guys were the catalyst, the thing I needed to discover how much I loved writing, and how much Kaida and Tarrin's story needed to be told. Thank you all!

Thanks be to God—for His never-ending faithfulness, provision, and peace throughout this entire process. He gave me the gift of writing, and a passion for it, and I am forever grateful. I couldn't have done any of this without Him.

And to my readers—I am beyond honored that you chose to pick up this book and give it a chance. All I've ever wanted was to write stories that provide an escape from reality for a while. Stories that have light and hope in what often feels like a dark world. Books are keepers of magic that can transport us out of anything we're facing and into something amazing. I hope when you pick up this book, you feel uplifted and have a big old grin on your face. Thank you for reading Kaida and Tarrin's story. It means the absolute world.

ABOUT THE AUTHOR

Emily Schneider grew up in Minnesota where she spent most of her life studying music and singing, which ironically has nothing to do with writing fantasy novels. While music had always been a passion, Emily could never get away from her love of reading and writing books full of dragons, Fae, monsters, magic, and romance. When she is not writing about dragons and magic, you can find Emily chasing around her two dogs, Pixel and Frodo, playing Mario Kart with her husband, or watching *The Lord of the Rings* for the one-hundred-and-eleventh time. Emily is the debut author of *Scales of Ash & Smoke.*

emilyschneiderwrites.com

Printed in the USA
CPSIA information can be obtained
at www.ICGtesting.com
LVHW102340130823
754933LV00005B/625

9 781737 495703